F   D263s   1971   APR 6 '72
DAVIS
SIX BLACK HORSES

                               FP   6.95

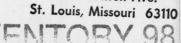

SIX BLACK HORSES

Six Black Horses

NOLAN DAVIS

G. P. Putnam's Sons

New York

To Mason,
who cared
To Sister,
who taught
To Carol,
who loved

SIX BLACK HORSES

1

The shadow of the mortuary stretched over the street, cooling the noon. Then Lawrence Xavier Jordan passed under the shadow in the summer of his seventeenth and most troubled year. He trudged past precise shrubs and climbed the limestone steps to the mortuary. That was his destination.

The door opened before he touched it.

Jordan coiled in anticipation. He had seen no one in the doorway. He glimpsed darkness and beyond the darkness a bleak ensemble of furniture: a long low couch, an empty coffee table, silent chairs. And the sculpted corner of a serene gray object, unmistakably a casket. His?

Suddenly a little man Jordan had seen before stepped from behind the open door.

"Afternoon." The man laughed. "I scare ya?"

"No, sir," Jordan lied. "Mister Lovingood in?"

"Uh-huh. Doin' a little work in the back. Be up front soon. You the Jordan boy, ain't you? Come right in, Mister Jordan. Ole Lovin'good told me to take good care of you. I'm Brother Bates. Major T. Bates. The em*balm*er."

They shook hands, Afro fashion. This man Bates had icy hands.

One of those hands gestured toward a door along the dark corridor. "This is our reception room," Bates said.

The room simmered in silence. Cool air—and a little light—slanted into it through tiered jalousie windows. "We have air conditioning," Bates said. "But we turn it on only when we have a funeral. Lowers the overhead, you know."

"Yes, sir."

Bates smiled at Jordan, and it was a warm smile, not chilly like the hands. There was an aura of benevolence about Major

9

Bates—and Lawrence Jordan relied heavily on auras. He could read the auras, the personal vibrations, of people. Lawrence Jordan decided that he could like Major Bates.

Bates had light-brown skin and a tawny mustache that twitched when he talked. Bates had immense bags under his eyes, and with his satchellike jowls, he reminded Jordan of a sleepy St. Bernard. The man was informal, hardly what Jordan had expected to encounter when he climbed the steps of the mortuary. The embalmer had removed his suit coat; his bright-tan shirt was open at the neck; he had loosened the Windsor knot of his blue-and-tan-striped tie.

But still Bates presented an impeccable appearance: His knob-toed shoes were burnished onyx mirrors.

"Make yourself at home, Mister Jordan," Bates said. "I'll be back directly. Got to help Brother Lovin'good. Got a case—a body—in the house." And Bates winked at Jordan.

Bates was a long time gone. Jordan heard water running somewhere down the corridor.

At first Jordan sat stiffly in the front window of the mortuary, watching traffic pass through the shadow beyond the jalousies. But slowly he relaxed. He sniffed the frigid air and found a kind of perfume in it. He sauntered away from the window and stretched out on the sofa. Lawrence Jordan was a tall young man, and he needed to stretch his legs. He found some magazines on a small table next to the sofa and flipped through them. *Time, Newsweek, Good Housekeeping.* Beneath these, Jordon found a more unusual magazine: *Casket and Sunnyside.* He coiled again, sensing what was inside the book before he opened it: photographs of caskets and hearses and gloomy surgical devices. Still he had to look, spellbound. Finally he slipped the book back under the others.

Jordan's eyes flitted uneasily over the reception room, hesitant to halt on any single object. He shouldn't have stared at those open coffins in the magazine. His eyes settled on the desk opposite the sofa. Jordan sought reassurance in the desk; the desk was just a piece of furniture. Mahogany. Why would it be different because it was in a mortuary? Ordinary moving men had carried it in through the front door. Major Bates probably sat at that desk, an informal, cheerful St. Bernard. With hands folded, hands that were not warm to the touch.

There was a potted palm in one corner of the room. It, too, smelled of perfume.

Where was Bates? Down the corridor, the water ran in gusts. Lawrence Jordan sat listening to the water. At first he did not connect it with the pictures in the magazine or the potted palm. When he did, he sprang from the sofa. In his mind's eye, Jordan saw Bates somewhere down the corridor bending over a marble slab, calmly running cold water over the naked remains of a tortured young man. Jordan's imagination hovered over the face of the body on the slab: It was his own.

Jordan paced back and forth in the reception room, wiping his mouth with a slender hand. He was sweating, but his lips were dry. He was trembling now from the chill. He had to think of other things. It was as if he were already dead, detached and looking down at himself. Yet still alive. His consciousness halved itself, split, just as his life had split from Lennie Valentine's. Jordan curled a finger between his teeth. He and Lennie were a kind. Up to a point—and that point was now. He and Lennie had found themselves on different paths, not by choice but by . . . what?

If Lennie were here now, if he saw what I'm getting into, Jordan thought, he'd probably laugh—or pretend to. Lennie was that way, cynical. Lennie had to be cynical to preserve his own sanity.

What would Lennie think of the way Jordan was dressed? Jordan was ashamed of the shiny blue gabardine suit he wore, his only suit. And his Sunday shoes, his only shoes. The dirt-slick sleeves of the suit could not be made to hide the cuffs of his shirt; Lawrence Jordan was growing. All the way to the mortuary Jordan had tugged at the suit sleeves, trying to hide the fraying cuffs of the shirt. The fraying made the shirt look dingier than it was. He kept looking behind him, Lawrence X. Jordan did, en route to the mortuary. He almost expected Lennie Valentine to spring from behind a bush or tree and grab him by the throat. He was afraid, really fearful, that somehow it would be Valentine who met him at the door. Lennie would be standing in the entrance of the funeral home with Southwall Lovingood and some others, and Lennie would look into Jordan's being with those piercing eyes of his and say, "Hey, man. We been waitin'. Your casket is ready."

11

But Lennie was in reform school.

Jordan would make it up to Lennie, what he had done to Lennie. He swore on that. But right now Jordan had his own head to save and face this undertaker, Southwall Lovingood. What did Lovingood want with Jordan?

It wasn't just the suit or the shirt or Lennie. It was Jordan's situation, his mother, his whole damn life. *Clare,* that whore. Clarisse Walker Jordan, his worst castrating enemy, personally had shined his shoes after he'd spent an hour waxing them to come to Lovingood. Clare hated his shoes; Lennie liked them. Clare called them "pimp's shoes" in that depressing idiom of hers: "Lord, son a' mine runnin' the streets in pointy shoes. Ain't nothin' but *pimp's* shoes. . . ."

The shoes were another way of Clare's getting at him. Why was his mother so anxious to please this Southwall Lovingood by shining shoes?

Surely Lovingood looked upon Jordan as some kind of luckless urchin. That's why Lovingood offered to help Jordan. Well, he was an urchin in a way. But Lovingood, fat ugly pig, would come in soon and see Jordan's clothes and be more ashamed than Jordan. And Jordan would feel it. This would make Jordan want to cry and lash out and hurt people and let them see what it was like to be scorned and patronized. That's why you coiled and went in the streets and carried a knife. Fuck it; Lawrence Jordan would show them all.

Here he was scrubbed by Clare and a cheap bar of soap until his neck hurt, waiting for some undertaker to patronize him. Jordan's scalp had cried out for mercy when Clare attacked it with her main instrument of torture, a cheap stiff nylon brush.

Clare had to humiliate him with words besides. "All right," she told him. "Now don't go down to the funeral home actin' like you know every damn thing 'cause you don't. And don't let me hear you being late. Not ten minutes. You goin' to *work,* boy, not some damn street dance!"

Then Clare sat on the side of the bed and slurped more of the acrid gold liquid in her cracked jelly glass and fixed Jordan with a bleary eye:

"Act like you got some sense even if you don't, big-ass-seventeen-year-old-boy-layin'-up-runnin'-the-streets-drivin'-your-mother-to-drink!

12

"These folks ain't got time to fool with you like I have, fool
that I *must* be. They're doin' you a favor; they don't have to do
nothin', nothin'. They're tryin' to help you, boy, 'n' the least
you can do is *act* intelligent 'n' say 'Yes, sir' and 'No, sir' and
'*Mi*ster Lovingood.' Been me, boy, I'da let your black ass rot in
jail. Shit. You probably won't be down there at the funeral
home a week. I tried to *tell* Southwall that. Still, it'll be good
for you to be there just a week 'n' see what's goin' on. 'Cause
you gonna end up there one way or another, right there on one
of those *back* room slabs at Lovingood's you don't straighten
up, you hear me? You hear?"

That was his mother.

Major Bates didn't sit at the desk when he returned. He
flopped on the sofa and draped a leg over the armrest. The embalmer loosened his tie farther and beckoned to Jordan to sit
beside him.

"Ever been in a funeral home before?" Bates asked.

"Yeah . . . yes, sir."

Bates said nothing else. He waited like a St. Bernard for Jordan to continue the conversation.

"I've seen you before," Jordan continued.

"Yeah? When?"

"When my grandma died. Mrs. Walker. In 1948."

Bates swung his leg from the armrest, folded his hands, and
leaned forward on the couch. "Lessee," Bates muttered. "Ole
lady Walker, huh? Not ole lady Walker used to walk with a
cane 'n' had a boy named Junebug?"

"No, sir. Miss Evangeline Walker, lived in Kansas."

"Hmmmmmm. . . ."

"A Seventh-day Adventist lady."

"Nineteen 'n' forty-eight, huh?"

"Yes, sir."

"Nope. Don't ring a bell. Nineteen forty-eight I wuz workin'
over at the Williams Brothers Funeral Home, had a lotta cases
that year. Williams used to be the biggest undertaker's in town
till Southwall Lovingood come up. Williams used to have 'em
goin' 'n' comin', pa'tner, goin' 'n' comin'. Ole Lovin'good wuz
with Fannie Fears then, same time I's at Williams. I threw in
with Southwall when he left Fannie. Forty years I been in Fu-

13

neral Service. Started with Ragnelle's down in Oklahoma when I wuz sixteen. Used to sleep right back there with 'em, pa'tner, right back there with the dead. . . ."

"Yes, sir."

"How long you knowed Lovin'good?"

"Three years. I know his daughter."

"Miss Herece? Cute child, pretty thing. Gonna be a lady someday."

"Yes, sir."

"Reckon she 'n' that boy gonna have it all someday. You know Wayne, too, don't ya?"

"No, sir. But I know who he is."

"Well, I'll tell you, Mister Jordan. Just 'tween you 'n' me, that boy's gonna be the death of ole Southwall yet. Oh, yeah. Now don't tell him I said that. . . ."

Just then a door slammed down the hall. Bates snapped to his feet, arranging his tie. "Southwall," he said. "Hear him comin'? Weighs three hundred 'n' thirty pounds, you know. But that don't stop Southwall. Ole Lovin'good takes 'em all, takes 'em all."

It was a private joke, and Bates chuckled to himself. He was still chuckling when Southwall Lovingood lumbered into the room.

The great dark man made the room small. Lovingood's shadow fell across the room, obscuring the desk, zigzagging on the jalousies. Lovingood's eyes were bloodshot, and where the eyes weren't red, they were yellow, an ancient longtime yellow like old newspapers. Lovingood wore a wrinkled black-and-white seersucker jacket and a pair of the largest black trousers Jordan had ever seen, fastened with a belt, the fat end of which Lovingood had neglected to tuck through the loop.

"Hey!" Southwall Lovingood roared.

"Hey!" Bates responded.

"Did we set him up, Bro' Bates, or did we set him upppppp?"

"Baby, we set his soul on fire." Bates laughed. "Cooked him to fine, brown perfection."

They stumbled about the room laughing, bumping into Jordan, throwing the chairs around. Then they slapped palms, soul brother style. They made funny signs in the air and embraced in a way Jordan had seen Frenchmen do in the movies. They mumbled words Jordan couldn't understand, an incanta-

14

tion. Lovingood embracing Bates was like a bear embracing a dog. Lovingood nearly lifted the smaller man off the floor.

Lovingood's red eyes rolled around to Lawrence Jordan, who had taken refuge in a corner. "Son," Southwall roared, "when you get a little older, get couple more years on you, wanna get you in the Masons, hear? Undertaker's got to be in the lodge. Right, Bates?"

Lovingood's voice was sonorous.

The big man seemed to be out of breath. He took Bates to one side. Jordan overheard part of the whispered conversation: "Bates, Brother Bates. I think this new case is almost in the bagggg. . . ."

Lovingood was perspiring. Rivers ran down his dusky forehead. The pigment of Lovingood's immense chest showed ebony through the big man's sweat-drenched shirt. Bates went to the desk and busied himself with a telephone book. Lovingood ambled to the door. He walked like a bear, throwing first the left leg, then the right, bringing his feet boomingly in front of him, his great shoulders and bruin midsection swaying from side to side as he waddled. Lovingood beckoned Jordan casually with one hand, not looking at the boy. "Come, we'll go in my office," Lovingood said. Jordan followed him out of the room.

As they entered this new room across the corridor, Lovingood batted a wall switch, and the dark corridor lit up, coated with unseen light. The corridor was powdery blue. "We don't turn on all the lights until we have a funeral," Lovingood said. "Lowers the overhead, you know."

There were two desks in Southwall's sparsely furnished office. Over one of the desks hung Major Bates' up-to-date embalmer's license. Lovingood collapsed behind the other desk, a larger one. Over Lovingood's head Jordan saw a picture of twelve tuxedoed young men and a white-gowned girl. Southwall's embalming school class. In the center of the otherwise pale group was a heavyset dark man with slicked-down hair. Southwall Lovingood. Portrait of the mortician as a young man. There was also a picture of older fatter men, all black, in fuzzy fezzes. In the center of this group sat Southwall, grinning. The picture said: "William Willis Lodge #27, Prince Hall Masons, 1955."

Lovingood's worn swivel chair groaned as its owner collapsed into it. Lovingood reared so far back in the chair that Jordan thought it would collapse too. Suddenly Lovingood's purple lips parted, revealing the whitest set of teeth Jordan had seen. Lovingood braced himself with his arms, swiveling around in the chair and back again.

Jordan's heart skipped when Lovingood extended his hand. "Young Master Jor*dannn!* Good to see you, good to see you among us." The man's voice was two octaves higher than it should have been. It came up eerie out of a man that size. It was the voice of an archangel with a music all its own.

"How's your mother?" Lovingood asked. "How's my Clar-eese-ah? How's Clar-eese-ah doinnng?"

Lovingood's straightforward manner and cheerful voice (it was almost joyous) made Jordan smile involuntarily. Lovingood exuded an aura of supreme sincerity. "Mother's fine, sir," Jordan said quietly.

"Well, Master Jor*dannn,*" said Lovingood with the glimmer of a twinkle in his dead eyes. "Well, young Mister Jordannn, fine young Mister Jordan, handsome young man. Brother Lawrence Xavier Jor*dannnnnnn!* We hope you'll like it here. Funeral Service, you know, Funeral *Ser*vice, is one of the highest callings a young man can turn to today, Mister Law-rence, Mister Jor-dannn. We know you'll be happy here among us."

Jordan felt good all over. He might have to revise his estimate of this man Lovingood. Jordan felt his tensions dissipating, his fear subsiding.

Suddenly the three hundred and thirty pounds of Southwall Lovingood bolted upright in the chair. With a lurching squeak.

"But, Mister Jordannn," the archangel whispered, "had a little trouble, a few problems at home. That so? Little trouble on the hearth?"

"Uh . . . yes, sir."

"Mother says you aren't mind-ing, aren't listen-ing, aren't do-ing. . . ."

"Uh . . ."

"Little trouble at home, huh?"

"Yes, sir. A lot of trouble."

"Know something?"

"Sir?"

"This will *cease,* Brother Jordannn!"

"But, Mister—"

"Fiiine young Mister Jordannn, good young Mister Jordannn."

16

"Well, you see—"

"Now, now, Mister Jordan. Don't let it worry you, Brother Jordannn. Don't let it get you down. I understand. Clare's havin' little trouble of her own, too, hummmmmm?"—this last whispered.

"Yes, sir."

"We'll make everything all right, won't we, son? You and me?"

Jordan sighed and fell back into his chair. There was no arguing with Southwall Lovingood, whose singsong voice belied fierce, burning eyes.

Lawrence Jordan got a tour of the Lovingood Mortuary conducted by the proprietor himself. Jordan followed the undertaker down the corridor into a perfumed place of dark—the room he'd seen from the doorway. As they advanced, Jordan became afraid. "Come on, son," Lovingood said in the dark. There was reassurance in that voice.

Southwall found a light. The immenseness of the room rolled back with the light. "This is the viewing room," Southwall said with an exuberance that made Jordan shudder.

Jordan resolved to be brave. He didn't want Lovingood to know that he had been scared, that he was afraid of everything —even life itself. Yet he sensed Lovingood knew these things. Jordan scanned the room, fearing that any second now he would spot the outline of the unmistakable rectangle. But it had been removed.

"When we have a funeral," Lovingood was explaining, "we usually have a wake the night before. We put 'em out here for viewing. The family is seated here." Lovingood pointed to the furniture, a modern arrangement with the couch flanked by four curved chairs. The coffee table was in the center of the ensemble, facing the corridor. The chairs—cool to the touch— flanked the couch, but only one could be seen from the corridor.

Jordan was standing beside a smooth gray structure. It was modern, simple, a stand of some kind. Jordan bent, saw that it basically was rectangular with its sides curving inward at the center, then out again in the fashion of an hourglass. Two floor lamps stood at either end. Jordan sensed what it was, but he asked anyway.

"A catafalque," Lovingood said, "for casket display."

There was another catafalque on the other side of the room. When someone entered the corridor, they would not see the caskets or the catafalques, Lovingood explained. But when they came into the room, sat on the divan or the chairs, they saw. They viewed the last remains in comfort.

A series of doors lined the south wall of the room. Lovingood lumbered to some double doors and, grasping the gold knobs of both, flung them open with a puff. The brightness of outdoors flooded in, relieving the room of its too-sweet coolness. "We bring the family in this way," Lovingood said. "And sometimes the friends, too. We have an in-house service, something in the chapel."

The chapel doors were on the east wall. There was a book on a mahogany stand by the chapel. The register. Jordan's fingers felt the gilt edges of the book.

Jordan liked the chapel. It too had jalousie windows, and they were open. There was the silence and sanctity of a church here. Complementing the pale-yellow walls of the chapel were six blond pews. At the front of the chapel room, set off in a little recess, was a stand of shimmery gray velvet. It was on wheels. Southwall Lovingood called it a "church truck." He said it was another kind of catafalque, a rolling casket stand. "We fold it up and take it with us to the cemetery."

Lovingood waddled down the aisle, leaning on the pews. He pulled a drawstring behind gray velvet curtains flanking the front pew. The curtains parted, revealing a door. "This leads to the display room," Southwall said.

There were pink caskets and gray caskets and copper caskets in the display room. Some of the receptacles were metal, some fuzzy, some plastic. Pointing to a brown metal model, Lovingood announced, "This one is the most expensive in stock." He smoothed the silk in the head section of the box. "One thousand five hundred dollars. Solid bronze. Hermetic sealer. Beautyrest mattress. Comfortable as a feather bed." Southwall waddled lovingly among the boxes, fingering this one and that, changing the positions of some, smoothing the linings of others. Along the wall, he had stacked some coffins atop each other. There seemed to be no order, no alignment, to these. But there was. "We like the finest couches to be seen first," Lovingood explained, tilting his head the better to view a profile of the

18

fifteen-hundred-dollar bronze sealer across the room. "You know the type of box can make or break a funeral, son. Make or break it. Oh, yes! Cloth-covered boxes—like these stacked up here—don't make it, Brother Jordan, just don't make it. 'Course, if that's positively all a family can afford, that's all they get. But we don't recommend it. That's why we keep them stacked up out of the line of display. Cloth falls apart on you in a few months, Mister Jordannn, mildews on you, gets green as money on you. Hate to see one of 'em disinterred. . . ."

They walked out another door into the big foyer of furniture and catafalques. "This is the bathroom," Lovingood noted of the next door. "Grief doesn't preclude the bodily functions, you know."

The last door, next to the catafalque Jordan first saw, was marked "Private" in gold letters. Lovingood did not open it. "That is the preparation room," Lovingood whispered though there was no one in the room but the two of them. "Fully equipped, the latest of everything. A pleasure to work in."

The words "preparation room" jarred Jordan. What else could it be but the room Clare so often had told him about? Jordan imagined what was in the Room. He took a deep breath and tried to smile. "Can I see it?" he asked weakly.

"Oh, yeah." Lovingood laughed. "Oh, yeah." Lovingood's great frame shook, and his red eyes rolled with the shaking. Southwall had to steady himself on the doorknob. For the first time since he'd known Lovingood, Jordan noticed then that he had a small patch of mustache under his nose. The mustache— like Hitler's—was the same color as Southwall's skin.

"Oh, you'll see it," Lovingood laughed. "If you stay with us, you'll see it all right. But not as much as you'd like to."

And Lovingood sighed. He whipped a dingy handkerchief from his back pocket and wiped tears from his eyes. Still heaving, Lovingood put a hand on Lawrence Jordan's shoulder. Jordan liked the feel of Lovingood's hand on him.

"You'll see that room," Lovingood went on. "But not today. You have to work up to that. Don't you think so, young Brother Jordannn?"

"Yes, sir. I guess so."

They exited, leaving the foyer in new darkness.

19

2

While her son toured the mortuary, Clarisse Walker Jordan drained half a pint of Old Crow and reflected on her thirty-seven years of misery. Clare elevated herself on two grimy pillows and toasted the gray walls of her boudoir. Cheers. Sons of *bitches!*

Clare was still very attractive. Although scarcely five feet three, Jordan's mother was more than endowed with her share of body. And the extra weight she had gained only enhanced her. Clare drew her knees up in the bed and gathered the wrinkled sheets around her; she was naked. The hipsters called women with Clare's endowments "stallions." In the profligate stable of stallions in Kansas City, little Clare stood out like a stout palomino pony. Clare was aware of her beauty and worked hard to preserve it. She spent hours at her dressing table, admiring the tan goddess staring back at her from the oval glass. Clare gloried in what her almond eyes took in: The face of the goddess was rich caramel. Her hair was long and black and blowy. Midnight shimmering on a caramel shore. That was the black of Clare's hair and the color of her countenance.

But now Clare thought of other things. Her life was all the more miserable because she had more than beauty. Clare Jordan had background, intelligence, potential and, most important, ambition. All her life Clare had wanted to be somebody, and at first she seemed destined to achieve that status. But several key misfortunes befell her.

The first was when and where she was born. Clare's earliest memories were of wearing overalls and pigtails in Oskaloosa, Kansas, scaling fenceposts by a dusty road. Her mother's but-

20

tered biscuits steaming on a china platter, mingling scents with chicken coops and feathers. Saffron sunrise; sunset scarlet. Old folks telling tales at night. Crickets in the cornfield and children seen, not heard. Clare was happiest then. Later, exiled to Kansas City's ghetto by the Great Depression, Clare forgot the hope of her ancestors and became a gloomy, morbid child. Like her African and Indian forebears, Clare loved stories. But all her tales had tragic endings. She dwelt on death.

Clare's beloved grandmother, a high-cheeked Osage woman, died of heartbreak in the exile. She was embalmed in her bedroom by Fannie Fears, a woman undertaker whom Clare assisted and came to know. Fannie liked Clarisse's fortitude and advised her to consider embalming as a trade. Lovingly combing her grandma's salt-and-raven tresses, Clare smiled to herself and said she might. Then they casketed the clay-gray body and had its funeral in the parlor.

But for her family, Clare undoubtedly would have ended up an undertaker. And she considered that her natural calling.

Clare's father, Jimmy Walker, was content within himself and accepted life. James Walker's father had been a slavery man. He killed his master, outran hounds, and joined the Union Army. In the late 1800's, Hut Walker arrived in the Indian Territory to homestead a farm. Hut got on well with Indians. His eyes were burning on the future. What he founded would be his children's and his children's children's. In the cabin by the firelight, Hut Walker puffed his corncob and, fondling a time-worn Bible with his black hands, read aloud his vision of the future: " '. . . when Ethiopia shall stretch forth her wings and rule the world.' "

Instead, Ethiopia was brought low and transplanted from Hut's land. In Kansas City, the only work James and Evangeline Walker found was menial. The old folks called it janitorial service, the kind of work that Jimmy Walker did. He scrubbed the walls and tended furnace in three Southside apartments and kept his family in the basement of one of them. Clare lived in janitorial service until she was eleven.

But the elder Walkers were persistent. Evangeline soon hired herself out as maid to a wealthy family and walked to work to save carfare. Jimmy Walker went to night school and eventually became an expert typewriter repairman. He got a civil service job—a plum then for black men—and the family bought a home.

The old house on Brooklyn Avenue had gables and wrought-iron gates and was well suited to Clare's temperament. She spent many hours brooding under its eaves. She hated the world for teaching her parents to say "Yes, sir" and "No, ma'am" for their daily bread. Clare swore it would be different in her lifetime. She would learn from this woman Fannie Fears and be a power on this earth.

Clare was an only child, and her parents lavished all they could on her. They gave her money, piano lessons, summer camp. Her parlor was the scene of endless birthday, graduation, and seasons' parties. And Clare, a charming little hostess, became popular among the "respectable" families of the ghetto—including the Lovingoods, a clan of friendly Southerners who lived not far away. Clare and the youngest Lovingood boy (curiously named *South*wall) became good friends and organized their games around their common ambitions to be undertakers:

"You s'posed to be dead, *Clare*."

"Not with your hand up my dress, I'm not!"

Giggles.

But Clare had found a purpose. In school, she excelled in her studies: Latin, English, drama (capitally important in Funeral Service), history. At home, she entertained and brooded. Southwall Lovingood met Fannie Fears through Clare Jordan and went to work at the funeral home while he was still a teen-ager. Clare's mother was appalled at the thought of her daughter working at all, let alone in a mortuary. Clare concentrated on her studies and marked her time. When she was a senior and about to be the first of her family to graduate from high school, she approached her father for the money to attend embalming college. Her father (damn him!) told her no. That was Clare's second big misfortune, that she wasn't born a man. Despite its comforts, her upbringing had been fairly strict. When her father, the son of Hut, said no, no it was. Besides, James Walker argued, Clare would get married soon. He just had that feeling. And he needed his money to purchase another farm in Kansas so her sons would have a legacy. Couldn't Clare see that was what he had to do?

Clare, too, was persistent. All right, it wouldn't be easy, but she would get what she wanted. She would take a job and earn her own tuition money. Clare, Southwall and others used to gather at Strickland's Drugstore one block north of the Walker home for sodas. Clare was complaining to Strickland one Saturday morning about her situation, and Strickland made her an offer. Clare accepted. She became a waitress at Strickland's, and that led to her third and worst misfortune. She met Francis Xavier Jordan there.

Frank Jordan made women love him. It wasn't the way he looked at them or what he said. Frank rarely paid attention to women because he didn't have to. All Frank Jordan had to do was be, and that made women weak.

Clare was weak. She noticed Jordan the first day she got there. He was new, too, the assistant manager of the place. Frank Jordan swept the floors and made the hamburgers; he cleaned the blinds and worked the soda fountain. Behind the counter he was lithe, a soda-making cat. Frank said very little, but whenever he looked at Clare, she hungered. Frank's glance was casual in his green-gray eyes. He was a light-skinned man, but his hair was coarse and manly. He towered over Clare. He was a little shy.

Francis Jordan was a struggling musician, and when he wasn't at work at Strickland's, he played trumpet at clubs on Twelfth Street. Sometimes his only payment was a round of drinks. Francis Jordan played the blues. The music depressed Clare. Clare's mother (then a devout African Methodist Episcopal) called it devil's music. Clare doubted that, but there was something in Frank's sound that frightened her.

Frank took Clare out down on Twelfth Street, and the night was very good. Clare's man sat in with old friends, and they spoke of Kansas City heavyweights: Turner, Basie, Canada Lee. The drinks were mostly highballs, but Clare had something fancy, something light. She couldn't resist Frank Jordan's suggestion that they go to a cheap hotel, especially since Frank had turned down a lot of women to stay with Clare.

In the hotel, Clare let her hair down with Frank Jordan. She gave it to him, and he was very good to her, the best thing she'd ever had. This tall man explored her little body, and Clare reciprocated. Frank gave Clare his whole attention, and Clare was hooked. That was her opium, Frank Jordan of the casual eyes.

23

In the nights that followed down on Twelfth Street, Frank relaxed with Clare. She listened lightly, nodding and caressing his pretty neck. Clare had comfort in her hands. Clare didn't care about Frank's past, what he'd done before. Frank had fled Louisiana after beating up a man who had called him "boy." He beat that man up awfully bad, Frank said. Clare hugged Frank Jordan and told him her grandfather was a man like him.

Evangeline Walker pressed her daughter to break up with Frank Jordan; the relationship was getting scandalous. Everybody who frequented the drugstore knew it. Wineheads down on Vine Street knew it. Little children knew it. Clare didn't care. She just knew she had to have Frank Jordan, and that was that. It was a thing that *had* to be.

Lawrence Xavier Jordan was growing in his mother's womb. Like his father, Lawrence Jordan had to be. Out of love comes life.

While the child was still *about* to be, Frank Jordan married Clare. She had told him about the baby, and Frank Jordan shrugged and said he'd marry her. The Walkers gave their daughter a glittering wedding, and Clare's girlfriends really envied her. They needn't have.

Clare was determined to make a home for them. But Frank Jordan didn't want a home, not yet. He had to make it. Frank had to play that trumpet. A year after their marriage, the Jordans were living in a cold-water kitchenette over a credit furniture store, and Frank Jordan left his wife listening to the suddenly screaming sound of a water faucet dripping. Frank walked out into the rain, cradling his trumpet inside his trench coat and headed for Chicago. He was going to make it there. He'd send home money.

Francis Xavier Jordan played his last gig in Chicago. And he was making it. Clare got lots of money to buy the bourbon she had learned to need. She'd saved herself for her husband by drinking loneliness away. A month before Pearl Harbor she got a telegram from Frank Jordan saying he'd be home by Christmas. He'd be home for good.

Frank never made it. Somebody shot him dead in a hotel in Chicago. Some cocksucker blew his handsome head off—and killed the woman, too. *The woman, too.*

24

After she endured that terrible winter—the pity of friends who went home and whispered, the inquest in that dirty city, the funeral conducted by Fannie Fears, the convalescence with her parents—Clare composed herself. Then she made a resolution: From that time forward, there was nothing a black-assed man could do for her but kiss her bloody motherfuckin' tail! (Clare could cuss.)

The spirit was willing, but the flesh went on. Like every woman, Clare needed satisfaction; no one could replace her murdered Frank. Clare left her son with the elder Walkers and went to work in a California war plant. In San Diego she slept with a series of horny sailors, searching for the one who could make her whole.

After the war she returned to Kansas City, determined to rise above misfortune. All Clare found was work as a domestic. Ironically, her once-domestic parents now returned to Kansas, where Jimmy Walker bought another farm and died a happy man. Clare sent her boy to Oskaloosa to grow up with her mother's corn.

Clare worked and saved her money. There was still a fire within her that would not let her rest easy. She swore that in spite of her lowly status, in spite of her lack of education and connections—in spite of everything—she would someday somehow be somebody. She would marshal all her assets and rise again. When her mother died, Clare discovered she had one special weapon which she had overlooked. Its name was Lawrence X. Jordan.

Lynford Valentine was scrubbing in the shower at the Jackson County Boys Industrial School when Turk surprised him. Even Lennie had to hand it to the Turk: The timing and the terror of the attack were brilliant, *pretty*. Lennie couldn't have made a better hit himself. And Lennie specialized in hits.

Lennie didn't know it was coming because he had soap in his eyes. He couldn't hear it; he was singing. Of course, the Turk anticipated all that. Turk must have ordered someone to flag him at just the right moment.

Lennie usually had a sixth sense that kept him out of danger. Why had it failed him? Maybe Lennie didn't want to see it. He had his ego to maintain. He was the leader; he couldn't show panic, fear. Yet all day there were signs. When they were rousted out of bed that morning, Lennie had an intuition; it would be no ordinary day. He felt a nervous tension unlike any he had felt since the Turk arrived to join him. Lennie's whole day had been unusual. In the mess hall, no one had sat beside him. In woodshop, no one had looked him in the eyes. In the fields one-sided conversation:

"Hey, man, why so quiet?"

Silence.

"Hey, nigga! What's goin' on?"

A shrug, a shuffle.

"Why's everybody quiet?"

"Ain't nothin' to say, I guess."

Just lowered woolly heads and guarded eyes. Not even humming. Only Turk was smiling. Then Lennie tagged it: *Turk. He's turned them all against me. Nigga wants to try my chin.*

But Lennie had no evidence, no warnings. No whispered conversations in the dorm. No scowls. No rumors. It was eerie.

Down in the fields, Lennie weeded the tomatoes and planned his strategy. He would forget about the others and go for Turk. Some time in a quiet moment when it was least expected. Maybe dinner. Turk often sat across from Lennie to show how bold he was. Lennie would jump the Turk when Turk's mouth was full of food. Of course, the overseers would grab Lennie after he had dusted Turk; they'd beat him with a halter until his back was raw. And the others would have to watch, and some of them would throw up. But Lennie would have stopped the Turk, destroyed his *coup d'état.*

At dinner, Turk sat out of reach with others. He never looked at Lennie. Conversation, laughter, everywhere. Mostly talk of what the guys would do when they got out. The future. That was good: When a man looks to his future, he is careful of his present.

Lennie was included in several conversations. The Turk made sure of that. Nobody challenged Lennie or gave him any sign. And that relaxed him. Even that night's beans and stewed tomatoes were as good as reform school fare could be. Upstairs, Lennie breathed easier as he watched the dorm master lock up their clothes. He got his towel and washrag and descended to the basement showers' concrete stalls. He'd relax and enjoy the evening and get the Turk in bed. Lennie decided he would strike hard, swift, and accurate and destroy the Turk forever. He'd make Turk give him some boody. He found those things distasteful, but he'd have to get used to such necessary matters, affirm his ruthlessness. Besides, he needed some, he'd been in the joint for three months. He'd beat Turk into submission and make the others watch while Turk gave in to him. He'd ravage Turk, and that would be the end of it. Without his manhood, Turk would be no challenge. He'd be too busy fighting off the others. *Sweet* Turk. Sweet bitch, kiss him.

Now Lennie's own manhood was in danger. He'd underestimated the Turk completely.

The Turk smashed Lennie in the neck and kicked him in the groin. He kneed him in the face as he went down. Automatically, from years of practice, Lennie curled into a ball as Turk started stomping. Turk had his brogues on; he'd hid them from the lockup. Lennie thought Turk would kill him.

Lennie no longer felt the blows. He merely heard them landing and acknowledged their rhythm as he would the raps of someone knocking on a door. It seemed to be happening in slow motion. Then the kicking stopped.

Lennie lay there hurting. The smell of blood was in his nose. He tried his arm and couldn't move it. That was when he panicked.

"Get up, nigga!" Turk commanded.

Lennie begged for mercy.

"Get up now!"

"Please, Turk—"

"Don't 'please' me, man."

"Oh, God!"

"God can't help you, nigga. Your black ass is mine."

The Turk was big and woolly. His muscles rippled as he fondled Lennie's behind. "I oughta fuck you, Valentine, sweet nigga—"

Lennie waited for the end.

"But I'm a give you a break. Save your ass for later. Understand?"

That was Turk's mistake. As far as Lennie was concerned, that change of mind was fatal. Damage already had been done. Turk's days were numbered.

27

Turk stood Lennie up against the stall. All the others—the whole reformatory—gathered. They looked ashamed and scared of Turk.

"Who's the boss, lil nigga?" Turk asked Lennie. "Who's the boss?"

Lennie slumped against the wall. "You are, Turk."

"You just got too ram*bunct*uous."

"Yeah."

"Kicked everybody around."

"Yeah, Turk."

"I coulda had your boody."

Lennie stiffened. The others watched his lips for confirmation. Their eyes glistened in the semidarkness.

"Coulda had your ass!"

"Yeah, Turk."

"I can't hear ya!"

"YEAH, TURK, YEAH, TURK, YEAH, TURK, YEAH, MOTHAFUCKA! . . ."

Lennie fainted saying that.

The Turk and Lynford Valentine had been fighting since they were kids. They grew up in the housing project together, Lennie and the Turk. When they were children, the big boys made them fight. Sometimes the Turk won; sometimes Lennie.

Lennie was very physical. He had a certain athletic prowess that in different circumstances would have made him a football or hockey star. He loved anything physical: a dance, a race, a fight. It was very important to Lennie not to give up. He practiced toughness in everything he did. He had to because he had no one to back him up. Lennie's older brother was a sissy. Lennie was short and brown-skinned. His brother was dark and husky. Whenever Lennie needed protection, Albert Valentine just shrugged and told his little brother, "Stay out of trouble, man." Lennie had watched some of the tough guys tease Albert. Albert just walked away. Lennie's mother babied them, and Lennie was her favorite. He looked like her, the boxy chin, the high forehead. Their father was a construction worker, thick and burly like his eldest son. Lennie was sure his father didn't like him. When he was small, Lennie's father tried to box with him. Lennie was afraid. His father told him he was just like Albert.

The Valentines were from Arkansas. They had a good life there. When they moved to Kansas City, things got rougher. Lennie's father started drinking, and his mother ran the streets. Albert stayed in his room on weekends, reading science fiction comic books and later bigger books.

Lennie roamed the project. His fights with Turk became a standing thing, and that made Lennie tough. The Turk was always springing something new. He could run and jump like Lennie and didn't like to give. They fought at home, at school, and at the movies. In some ways, Lennie liked the Turk.

There were big girls in the projects who let boys in their homes. Lennie accepted an invitation and learned the facts of life. He got many invitations. Lennie thought of girls like he did everything else, objects to be conquered. Lennie recognized that matter could be controlled by force of will. He thought of life as a jungle to be negotiated and men as objects to be controlled. He preferred to control matter with matter. He made up strategies involving force—his own against another's.

Lennie Valentine hated school and liked the movies. He liked pictures like *Little Caesar*. Lennie was not affected by what he read until he found a children's series on great generals: Alexander, Caesar, Genghis Khan, Napoleon Bonaparte. Lennie read the series over and over and dreamed of being a general. He practiced on the girls; he was Napoleon, and they were resisting provinces. He planned his strategy and struck. "Hard, swift, and accurate" became Lennie's Law.

Lennie was practicing for something and even he didn't know what it was. He knew he had to prove something to his father. But he had something else inside him that wanted itself felt. It was not ambition or lust, but *force*. Lennie lashed out automatically at the world he knew, the trap he lived in. It was important to him somehow not to give in to anything.

He gave in to Turk to save his life. But why had he given in to Lawrence Jordan?

Herece Beatrice Lovingood slumped in a comfortable overstuffed chair, reading *The Adequate Woman*. She should have been doing homework. If the nuns knew what she was reading! Ah, well, Herece would confess it tomorrow before she went to communion. Herece sighed and contorted nervously in her chair. In the kitchen, her mother was fixing dinner and humming a religious song. Herece was happy for her mother: Psyche had been humming ever since she'd married Southwall Lovingood.

Herece was an ebony Aphrodite. But her neck was Nefertiti's. She had a willowy, graceful way. When Herece was deep in thought, her delicate hands lay in her long lap and her back curved elegantly upward to the fine wisps of hair on her dark neck. She projected an image of mystic, tragic grace.

Tragedy had touched Herece when she was twelve. Her parents were divorced; that was Herece's tragedy. Her father was Catholic, but her mother wasn't. Before Herece was born, the couple agreed to raise their children in the faith. Herece was the only child. She remembered her home as a model of tranquillity. Her father was quiet-spoken and observant; her mother talked a lot. All three loved music: Herece took dancing; Psyche had taken voice. When the family broke up (over nothing it seemed to Herece), Psyche's daughter turned to the church. And her mother encouraged her, too. Herece took some solace in reading *The Lives of the Saints* and using priests as father figures. Nothing could depress Herece forever; she was a creative, spontaneous girl. Often Herece went south to go north or walked a different way to school. She didn't care where she was going until she got there.

Herece entrusted her well-being to her deities, and that left her free from worry.

What interested Herece? The usual matters: clothes, her beauty, friendships, phonograph records, books. And lately a home and family—something she'd been without once in her life. Although Southwall Lovingood provided and Psyche and Herece enjoyed, Herece wanted more than that. Southwall was rarely home. Usually, he was attending to that strange business of his. Herece didn't like to dwell on that. For a time, Herece had had a brother, Wayne, a frivolous sort, but friendly. Wayne took Herece to movies and even accompanied her to church. Then Wayne was off to school, and they'd never really talked.

A marriage, Herece felt, could be something creative, something blessed by God. It could be perfect. That was Herece's consuming interest—perfection. She searched for that. That's why she was reading *The Adequate Woman*. Did she want to have an affair? Her father had been very touchy about Herece's playing with boys when she was little, and her mother agreed with him. Psyche never told Herece about copulation. So Herece learned the hard way; though her body was still a virgin's, her mind was not.

Lately Herece had been confused. She was sixteen, growing up, and feeling the pressure of temptation. Confession did no good. She had been tempted only three times in her life, once when she was thirteen, once at fourteen, and once with Wayne. She overcame two of these temptations. The third was not so easy. That was when Herece met Lawrence Jordan.

Jordan was Herece's ideal—intelligent and handsome, sensitive and strong. He ignored Herece at first, as if he didn't see her. He was different from other boys. Was it his eyes? His touch? He was *sexy*. There was much in Jordan that frightened her, a dark side, a devilish power that bound Herece to him. She liked to be frightened. She hadn't seen him since her mother married Southwall; she heard he was running the streets with a thug named Valentine. But she sensed that Jordan had to do that, had to alter something in his life. He was too independent to let his environment control him. That was what she sensed. Now he was altering life again. He was back on the periphery of life, working at her stepfather's funeral home.

Herece went back to *The Adequate Woman*. She knew her purpose now. She wanted to be adequate for Lawrence Xavier Jordan.

3

Lawrence Xavier Jordan was a force of nature. He exuded a psychic energy that made people glad they knew him. Lawrence Jordan glowed. If he walked into an amphitheater, his aura filled the room. Jordan's presence centered in his eyes and hands. His eyes were fawn's, very large and soft and slightly slanted; they had neat folds where they flanked his flaring nose. They cast a look of crystal innocence, Jordan's soft brown windows on the world. Often Jordan's eyes were veiled, as when he would look down as though in thought. Then he was merely sensual, a pretty calf with silk eyelashes. But when Jordan looked straight at his beholder, his eyes were full of knowledge; the look was always casual, gentle, calm. Lawrence Jordan looked casually at the world, and the world looked back with respect.

Jordan had to touch things. Of all his senses, his touch was most acute. He remembered many things by the texture they transmitted to his tan and tapered fingers. Jordan liked to seize heavy things and move them around, rearranging them to suit his fancy. He had an unconscious habit of trying the impossible as he talked. He would seize the edge of an armchair or press against a wall in the midst of speaking and flex his arm; when the object didn't move, he looked surprised. When there was nothing else in reach, Jordan caressed a person's shoulder, balled up his own coarse hair or slapped his thigh. His voice was mild and quiet, but his hands were loud. He clenched his fists, threw out his skinny fingers, sculpted images, clapped his hands. Few people ever forgot it when he touched them.

He inherited all the peculiarities of his parents. Like his father, he made women weak; like his mother, he searched for love. His look was casual; his moves were deliberate. Even-

32

tually, Lawrence X. Jordan grew to a height of five feet nine. When he jabbed a delicate finger and unveiled his knowing eyes, Apollonian Jordan could get anything he wanted. But he didn't know that. For each of his strengths, nature had given him a weakness. Counterbalancing his sensuality was a blemish: Jordan was born with a huge gap in his front teeth. This kept him from smiling and gave him a grim-mouthed look. Jordan thought himself an oddity, a calf-eyed clown.

Against his psychic power, life set a crippling environment and something worse—an abnormal fear of death.

When he was still a baby, Jordan found a dead rat in his grandma's barn. He touched the creature's tail and liked the feel. Jordan dragged the carcass outside and played with it, twirling it around. Some worms got on his hands. Jordan didn't mind them, but his grandmother ran out and grabbed him. She was screaming. He seized the horror in her body and absorbed it. He applied it to everything he knew and multiplied it. He created a cringing fear. Clare intensified it, and this gave her power over him.

Jordan remembered little about his grandmother's death except that Clare came out to Kansas when Evangeline got sick and one day Clare pulled a sheet over his grandmother's quiet face. An ambulance came to the Walker farm, and Clare said Evangeline had passed away. A few days after the ambulance went away, Clare took Jordan for a ride to see Evangeline Walker. She said they would see his grandmother with other people who had passed away. Jordan thought that meant the people went to Missouri because that's where Clare said Evangeline Walker was taken.

They rode in a large black car. It was dark and raining. Jordan sat in the middle of the back seat, close to his mother. He watched the twinkle of streetlights refract through rain-run windows on the limousine. The man driving the car wore a dark coat and hat. He said nothing.

His grandmother was under a little tent, white and filmy like fine gauze or cobwebs. Another man came and lifted the veil so they could see his grandmother. Jordan remembered the man's funny mustache and tawny skin. That man was Major Bates.

Evangeline wore a stiff white organdy formal. She was in a silky bed. Jordan spoke to her gently: "Hello, Grandma."

She did not respond. She was hollow like the man in the dark

33

suit in the bed across the room. Clare said the beds were caskets. Jordan studied what had been his grandmother. There was no snoring, the bosom was not heaving. In the glove on the breast, the hand did not move; the face was mud. The movement and talking that had been his grandmother were gone. There was nothing but a dark doll in white organdy propped up on silk pillows.

Clare was crying softly. Jordan ran his fingers over the casket. It was furry. He looked at the remains inside again. He heard a stillness. It twinkled in the room.

Major Bates left the room after lifting the veil. He came back while Jordan was hearing the twinkling. Bates tugged at the veil.

"No, Major," Clare said. "Leave it up."

Clare's eyes were red. She watched Bates go back in the other room; then she bent and kissed the body. Jordan turned away. Clare stepped back and sighed. "Guess she's better off than the rest of us," Clare said. She wasn't talking to Jordan. She wasn't talking to anybody. Clare just stared down at her mother.

Finally, Jordan said, "Can we go now, Mother?"

"She doesn't quite look herself, does she?" Clare asked. "She's so thin. She suffered. . . ."

Instinctively, Jordan pulled back.

Clare seized his hand. "We all suffer. . . ."

She pulled him back to the casket and frowned at him. "Be still," she said. He was. He respected the Presence in the box. He had heard it twinkling.

"Kiss her," Clare commanded.

"Ma'am?"

"Kiss her, kiss the dead."

"I'm scared to, Mother."

"Why? You kissed her in life, didn't you? Kiss her now!"

"But I'm scared, the worms. . . ."

"What worms?"

"In dead things. I've seen 'em."

"Hush, Lawrence. Kiss her! That's your *grand*mother."

"I don't want to, Mother. Please. . . ."

"Hush, boy. Kiss her, kiss her head."

"Mother, please. . . ."

"Lawrence. I'm not going out that door until you do it. Just do what I tell you to. Shit, boy; you're scared of your own

34

shadow. She would want you to do this. Go on, bend down, do it, and be quick!"

Jordan stood on tiptoe. He gripped the edge of the casket very tightly and put his face down into the stillness. As his lips touched the icy thing on the pillow, he knew he would look down into many caskets. And he knew he had to beware of Clare.

When Lawrence Jordan had finished, he spoke to Clare in a voice chillier than the chill he felt in the kissing. "It's cold," he said. "Grandma's awful cold."

Silence twinkled all around them.

Lawrence Jordan hated his mother. He didn't always. When he was a baby, Clare was a good thing to him. She came to take him to the movies; he liked his mother's beauty and her voice.

Now the beauty was one reason he hated her. Clare used it. She tested her own charm, flirting with men half her age. Jordan remembered a young truck driver Clare dated. The man was skinny and shifty-eyed; he reminded Jordan of a weasel. The man was constantly pawing Clare in front of Jordan. Clare didn't seem to care. One summer night when he was twelve, Jordan ran in from playing under the streetlight, anxious to tell his mother something. He burst into the apartment. He thought Clare was out until he heard the porch swing creaking. Jordan peered through the screen door and saw the weasel man humping on his mother.

He hated the sound of her voice now, too. Actually, the form of Clare's voice was pleasant enough. But as time passed and things got worse, Jordan came to hate every syllable Clare uttered. She cursed incessantly: "Boy, get those *damn* dishes done right now!" "Lawrence, I'm so tired. *Shit,* slavin' for these *damn* rich folks every *goddamn* day. Sometimes I think I'd rather sell my *bloody ass* than work a *fuckin'* job!" She talked like that at home; she talked like that in public. Jordan was ashamed to have her meet his schoolmates. When he was out with her, he avoided speaking to boys and girls he knew because he didn't want Clare to embarrass him. Still, Clare found a way: "Lawrence! Don't you know that little boy there? Well, say some-*fucking*-thing!"

She nagged him constantly. Sometimes the nagging appeared to have no reason: "Boy, you'll never amount to nothin', you know that? Not a goddamn thing. Shit!" Clare did this to him

35

whenever he did something unsatisfactory to her. What was unsatisfactory to Clare could be something as basic as the strokes he used to scrub the floor: "Give me that goddamn rag, Lawrence! Boy, don't you know anything? Don't even know how to wash a fuckin' floor." And Clare would scrub it *her* way.

She seemed to be trying to mold Jordan in a certain way. What Jordan wanted, what he liked, didn't matter. "You don't know shit; I have to teach you" was Clare's excuse. She used the excuse to dictate how he would dress, how he would act, even what he would study in school.

Why did she always call him "boy"?

Jordan didn't know what made his mother like that. Once he asked his grandmother about Clare. "Land o' Goshen," Evangeline Walker said, throwing up mahogany hands. "I just cain't say, I just cain't. Why your mother was brilliant in school, Lawrence. Brillllllllllliant. She was the first one in our family to get a high school education 'n' we were s' proud of her, your Granddaddy Walker 'n' me. We'd worked s' hard, the both of us.

"We had high, high hopes that Clarisse would go on 'n' be a teacher—though she was interested in funeral parlor work at that time—but she never did; she just never did. Nobody knows why, child."

His grandmother supposed it may have been because of his grandfather's untimely death. "They was real close, Jimmy Walker 'n' his daughter," Evangeline Walker said. "She took it kinda hard. . . ."

Or it may have been what Jordan's own father did to Clare. "Your daddy was a smart man 'n' nice-lookin'," Grandma Walker said, "but he just had tarnation in him."

When Jordan was ten, Clare brought him back to Missouri to live with her—after Grandma Walker died.

Kansas City, Missouri, fascinated Jordan. They lived on the east side of the great metropolis, the largest city Jordan had ever seen. There were limestone buildings in Kansas City twenty-five stories tall. There were endless boulevards like the Paseo with green parks running right down the center of them.

The city rose up from the muddy bend of the Kaw and Missouri rivers on a series of bluffs commanding ever higher the yellow flat of Kansas. It marked the end of the plains and stock-yards and to Jordan the end of his childhood. Kansas City, Missouri, was alleys and stoplights and the blur of dressed-up people scurrying past oblivious mannequins in Emory, Bird, Thayer's downtown windows. It was orange and green night glowing atop the Power & Light Building and a cacophony of factory sirens at noonday. It was corrugated, rusty fenced junk-yards along Eighteenth Street and bright-pink adobe stores be-neath the red tile roofs of the Country Club Plaza. It was peo-ple with Southern twangs and Northern r's and cowboys riding horses in the American Royal Parade. It was concrete streets, Katz Drugstores, Liberty Memorial and Swope Park. It was crowded pages and tiered headlines in the Kansas City *Star*. It was weedy hills under high bridges sloping down to the run-ning railroad tracks. It was pool halls and barbershops, cafés and dentists' offices on Twenty-seventh Street around the cor-ner from Clare's apartment. It was the Green Duck Inn three blocks away, where there was fighting over women on Saturday night.

Kansas City, Missouri, was not a Kansas place.

And the people weren't as friendly as Kansas people. Muscu-lar boys with gold teeth and white caps hung around the schools, taking money from the kids. Grown-ups passed you on the streets without a "Howdy" or a "Mornin'." People kept their doors shut tight at night—even in summertime.

Jordan had trouble making friends at school. His classmates looked upon him as "country" and made fun of the way he talked. Slowly (and with Clare's constant prodding), Jordan stopped saying "I reckon" and "I 'spect." He began to walk like the other boys and girls; he began to speak their idiom. He even learned to dance.

But he kept mostly to himself. As a defense against his new environment, Lawrence Jordan daydreamed of the day he would return to Kansas and live in his grandmother's house. He thought of himself as someone special, one of the few to whom it was given to lead a happy life. He was glad he had spent his childhood with his grandmother baking cookies and making a fuss over his nose colds. He felt fortunate to have grown up with chickens, to have seen a real cow and, more im-portant, real corn and to have attended school with kids who

37

weren't a single color. These were his blessings, and he would go back to the simple life as soon as he was able. Meantime, he would stay with Clare and remember everything he observed so he would appreciate the old life better.

Evangeline Walker had converted to Adventism. She smothered Jordan in it. She read storybooks and showed him pictures of the Resurrection; she told him about his guardian angel. Jordan was a lonely boy who needed playmates. So he invented some. He discovered a liking for the smell of lead and crayon at Sabbath school and started drawing. His first playmates were angels, which he drew. He pretended the pictures were real.

Evangeline's associates, Adventist ladies, liked his pictures. They said Lawrence Jordan would someday be a preacher. Jordan drew more elaborate angels and finally devils. The devils were no threat to him. He moved them about as he desired.

In real life, he contended with the devils of daily living; in his heart, he soared with angels. Sometimes the two worlds ran together. Unconsciously, Lawrence Jordan wanted them to merge.

Clare destroyed his dreams before he passed under the shadow. First, she sold their home in Kansas to support them while she was out of work. Next, she challenged his ambitions. Finally, she drove him into the streets.

Clare was the antithesis of all he held sacred. Jordan's hatred hardened when she came out against his art. When he was fourteen, Jordan announced that he wanted to become an artist. Clare's reaction was predictable.

"What? Paintin' pictures 'n' things? Shit, you'll starve. Ain't nothin' out there for an *art*ist, boy, 'specially a black one. Better you get yourself a *trade*. Layin' bricks or somethin'. An artist, hell. Be somethin' rea*lis*tic. In this world, nigga needs a hussle. Ain't nothin' respectable you can do 'cept be a preacher or an *un*dertaker!"

Jordan disregarded her advice, tried to shut her out. Clare just didn't understand. The only reason black men weren't artists was that they didn't believe they *could* be artists. Because their mothers, instead of being in their corner, nagged at them to be preachers. Or hustlers.

Herece Phillips brought out the devil in Lawrence Jordan.

Clare tried to suppress Herece—and that meant suppressing Jordan's art. The two were tied together.

Herece lived in the apartment under them, and Herece's mother, Psyche, was dating Southwall Lovingood. Like Clare, Psyche did domestic work and was gone from home most of the time. The children were left to their own devices, and they discovered each other one day on the landing. Herece fell under Jordan's spell when she looked in his eyes. They stood staring at each other, and the next thing Herece knew, he had kissed her. Jordan turned and walked away. No words had passed between them.

Later Herece spoke to Jordan.

"Who are you?"

"My name is Lawrence Jordan."

"What do you want from me?"

"Dunno."

"You're kind of weird."

Jordan veiled his eyes like Harry Belafonte.

They spent a lot of time together, held hands. Finally, she confided in Lawrence Jordan. She felt she should tell him what happened to her when she was thirteen. She had a girlfriend who went in basements with boys. The girl was always telling Herece how good it felt to let a boy get on you. One day in a park, Herece and her girlfriend met three boys who suggested they go with them to the basement of the girls' apartment. Herece was frightened, but she went anyway to show that she was "regular." The boys said they just wanted to kiss, but in the basement, Herece's girlfriend pulled up her dress and let the boys fondle her organ. She lay down on an old couch with one of the boys and gave him some. Herece said she was going to tell, and her girlfriend told her to stop acting like a kid. Herece tried to run, but the other boys grabbed her and threw her down. One of them got on top of her.

"I couldn't get him off of me," Herece told Jordan. "His pants were open and everything. I wouldn't pull my panties down like they wanted me to. This one boy named Willie hit me in the face, but I still wouldn't do it, so he said, 'Okay, we'll do it dry.' And he started moving around on me. Then the other boy said, 'Hurry up, Willie, I wants me some, too!' The other boy put his in my mouth and made me suck it. It was hor-

39

rible. I never played with that girl again, and pretty soon we moved away from that neighborhood. Oh, Lawrence, I'm so ashamed."

Jordan was very understanding. He felt sorry for Herece. He had heard of things like that in Kansas, but in Missouri he heard about them every day. He daydreamed of taking Herece to live with him in Kansas and being an artist and Herece posing for him. Then he got an idea. Why not let Herece pose now? He began to think about it.

He first saw Southwall Lovingood with Psyche Phillips. He remembered Lovingood only as a fat dark man with red eyes. He assumed it was because Lovingood drank whiskey. Once when Jordan visited Herece's apartment, Lovingood was there and told Psyche about knowing Clare.

"Went to school with her," the big man said, " 'fore old Miz Walker moved back to Kansas."

Jordan didn't pay much attention to what Lovingood was saying; he'd heard it all before. Clare and Southwall were friends since childhood.

Herece whispered, "Mister Lovingood comes over here every Friday. I think he likes my mother. They might get married."

Jordan smirked.

"No, they really *might*. He gave her a ring. He's a nice man but—"

"What?"

"You know what he does, don't you? For a living, I mean."

"Don't think about it. Cross that bridge when you come to it."

"We met him when my father left. His wife died, and he has a boy named Wayne, a funny, quiet boy. . . ."

Herece went to Catholic school and got home earlier than Jordan. So he knew she was there the day he was ready to execute his plan. First he washed the dishes. Then he went down into the yard, where he knew Herece would be waiting.

He found her sitting on the brick wall by the alley. Herece didn't see him come down. His eyes darted quickly over the contours of her body. Yes, he thought, this is what I want. She was deep in thought, hunched over, encased in absentminded loveliness. Purposely, he made sounds as he hurried to the wall.

40

Herece's dark eyes settled on him. He studied her pug nose and long limbs. Perfect.

"Hey," he said.

Herece's eyes turned slowly and looked at the ground beside him. She stood up, her arms drooping, waiting for him to say more. Why did she act in this manner? No matter, Lawrence Jordan—the artist in Lawrence Jordan—knew what he wanted, what must be done.

He sat on the wall next to Herece, discussing school, his drawing, beauty in general and Herece's in particular. "I love you," he said, turning on all the power of his eyes. Herece averted her eyes and said nothing.

"I want you to pose for me," he said, "in your birthday suit."

Herece giggled. What ever made Jordan think she would do a thing like that?

"Because I love you," he said.

"That don't mean a thing."

"And because I don't want to repeat what you told me. You know, about down in the basement with those boys."

"Lawrence Jordan, I didn't think you were like that."

"I mean I wouldn't tell it voluntarily. But you know how it is. There's a lot of tough cats hanging around, right down on Twenty-seventh Street. They're always looking for girls that do that. They come right up to you and ask you if you know anybody. If you lie, they beat it out of you."

"You're not my boyfriend anymore."

"I might tell them about what you did. They would come up here and hang around."

"I'm going in the house."

"They'd say filthy things. They curse a lot. Your mother would find out. Everybody would find out. All over town, anywhere you went, boys *and* girls—even girls, great big ones—would say, 'Hey, Herece. Suck me off today.' "

Herece broke down in tears. Gently, tenderly, and full of emotions he had never experienced before, Jordan led her off to his apartment.

In the apartment, Herece said, "Suppose your mother caught us?"

"Look, I'm just sketching you."

"She wouldn't know that."

"She won't come in till seven. We got plenty of time."

"You won't tell those people, will you?"

"Wouldn't think of it."

"Okay."

Jordan's legs felt wobbly. He couldn't believe what was happening before him. He heard Herece's skirt unzip, saw the tight band of her silk slip hugging her dark waist. He pretended to concentrate on his sketch pad. The skirt plopped on the floor. The band of the slip popped. Herece eased onto the bed beside Jordan, tucking her legs under her, turning her head toward the wall, away from his gaze.

"There," she said, almost inaudibly.

"There what? Take off the rest of it."

She did it slowly, lying on the bed. Jordan felt faint. Was this real? What had got into him? What happened to his dreams of Kansas and getting away from the city and its temptations and its sorrows? He knew he could not sketch. He touched the inside of her thigh. He touched it lightly.

"Here," he said in as professional a voice as possible. "Put this leg here."

His hand did not retract.

"What are you doing, Lawrence?"

"I'm just getting the feel of it. The shape. So I can put it down on paper just exactly like it is. You understand?"

Herece understood. Clare did not. Clare came early and found them in her bedroom. When Psyche Phillips came home that evening, Clare dragged Jordan down and told Psyche the whole story—as Clare saw it. Mostly it was true, but Jordan denied it—for Herece's sake. Their mothers whipped them soundly, Lawrence Jordan and Herece, right there in Psyche's apartment. They forbade them to see each other.

"Honestly, Clarisse," Psyche said, "I do need a man around the house."

What Lawrence Jordan needed, his mother informed him, was a change of environment. Children around these apartments were just too *fast,* just didn't appreciate the finer things of life. All they knew how to do was sneak around and lay up in their mothers' beds when their mothers weren't around. Here was this poor woman Psyche downstairs working *hard,* scrubbing floors and taking care of rich folks' children to send Herece to school, to feed and clothe the girl, and what does the thankless little heifer do? Lays up in Clare's own bed, not a stitch on, teaching Jordan filthiness and trash. That's why Jordan was so mannish. These children were leading him astray. But they wouldn't do it any longer, not to Clare Walker's boy. No, ma'am. Not as long as there was a breath in Clare's body and she could raise an arm to provide. No, ma'am. Obviously, what Lawrence needed was to get away from all this, go where the air was fresh and the sky was blue and learn about the other things in life. Manners, neatness, decent conversation. That little *heifer* Herece! What Lawrence needed to do, young man, was keep his eyes open and his mouth shut for a change and observe what things were like in polite so-ci-ety. Soak up a healthy atmosphere. Find out what culture and breeding are. Study at niceness and ci-vil-ity. Ponder mo-ral-ity. Analyze what's done among the gentry. Mind his elders. Be seen and not heard. Get with fiiiiiine, upstanding citizenry. In short, see how the white folks lived!

"Accordingly, boy," Clare decided one bright springtime day, "you'll go to live with me on the job when school is out. You'll get away from all these little heifers layin' in your mother's bed."

As Clare spoke, a picture flashed in Jordan's mind of his mother with the weasel man humping between her legs. But Jordan said nothing. At least Clare worked out in Kansas; he would see home again soon.

In Kansas, Jordan met Mister and Mrs. Goldman and their children, Ruth, Anna, and Milford. The man and the woman and Ruth were very polite but made no conversation with him. Ruth was an awkward-looking girl of seventeen or eighteen, and Jordan sensed that she was trying to be grown-up. She regarded Lawrence Jordan as if he were some Martian, newly landed. Jordan ignored her. He kept his mouth closed tightly to hide the space between his teeth.

Anna and Milford Goldman were friendlier. Anna was about Jordan's age, wore blue jeans, and continually flicked a curve of curly brown hair from her eyes. "Hi," she pumping Jordan's hand vigorously. "Clarisse's told us so much about you I feel I already know you. Do you play tennis? Well, you will before

43

the summer's over. We can play next door. We don't have a court—"

"That's enough, Anna," said Mrs. Goldman, a tall, thin woman with piercing cold-blue eyes and jet-black hair. "Give Lawrence a chance to know us." Jordan was thankful to her for that.

"Ah, yes," said Mrs. Goldman, reaching behind her. "This is . . . this is Mike. Say hello, Mike. Miiiiiike!"

A little boy came from behind her, stood on one leg, and pouted.

"Milford Goldman!" his mother growled.

"Howdyado?" the boy croaked, breaking into a grotesque little grimace that made Lawrence Jordan grin in spite of his discomforture at being inspected by these strange people.

"He's only called Mike," Anna Goldman put in, "his name is really Milford."

"Oh."

Jordan noticed that Mike was cross-eyed. There was an awkward moment of silence as Jordan stood before his white-aproned mother and the new people. Did they like him? Casually, Mike Goldman regarded Jordan from head to toe. Then Mike happily broke the silence: "Would you like to see my turtle?"

As the boys ran out of the room, Jordan heard the girls laughing and Mrs. Goldman telling Clare: "Don't worry, dear. Something tells me Master Lawrence won't have any trouble adapting to this household."

And he didn't.

What excited Jordan most about the experience was living in the Goldman house. The Goldman mansion stretched on the land like a magnificent brick lion. It lay down a winding gravel road behind the stately elms and broad bushes. Only hints of the bricks could be seen from the street.

The house was enormous. It boasted servants' quarters in the basement and on the first floor, where Clare had her room. There were several bathrooms; the children shared one, Clare had her own, the chauffeur had one in the garage, the Goldmans had one with a walk-in closet, and near the front door there was a powder room. The living room of the house was larger than Clare's entire three-room apartment.

44

Often when Mike and the girls were gone with their mother to the club and Clare was busy preparing the evening dinner, Jordan walked the rooms of the Goldman house, his memory photographing every detail. He daydreamed of having a house even larger than the Goldmans with a front lawn as large as a park. And a maid who looked not like Clare but Herece. Indeed, she would *be* Herece. Clare, of course, would live with him, but if she got out of hand, Jordan would order her to go to her room much as Clare ordered Mike Goldman to if he knocked over her dishes in the cavernous kitchen. Jordan dreamed of being a famous artist with commissions from around the world and driving up in his little sports car to a house like the Goldmans' and a maid like Herece.

And Mrs. Goldman encouraged him in that vision. "Honestly, you're a very unusual person," she told Jordan. "There's no reason why you can't do anything you want."

Clare tried to crush his renascent ambitions, but Mrs. Goldman would not be dissuaded. "Now, Clarisse," Mrs. Goldman cautioned. "Really, this boy's got talent. That drawing he did of Anna is better than the painting of her we have in the living room and paid five hundred dollars for. I don't believe you should discourage him the way you do. Why, I encourage my Milford to try anything his little heart desires, though I'm afraid Mike doesn't have *half* the talent Master Lawrence has."

"Yes, ma'am, but—"

"Now, Clarisse. I know what you're going to say. But it isn't true that poverty or an undesirable environment means a man is foredoomed to unskilled labor. Believe me, I know. It hasn't been so easy for my people, either. Believe me, we know what it is to suffer, Clarisse, we know what it is. . . ."

Anna Goldman held a special fascination for Jordan, and he found that she, too, could not master the directness of his gaze. Anna was a tomboy, and Jordan tried to relate to her as that. But one day she surprised him. Jordan was watching TV in the wood-paneled Goldman romper room when Anna came down clad only in panties and the soiled boy's dress shirt that with her dungarees was her trademark. Her panties were thin, and Jordan could see pink hips beneath. Anna strode nonchalantly to the couch where Jordan was sitting and plopped next to him. Flicking back loose curls with one hand, she looked at

45

Jordan. "What are you gaping at?" she asked. "I'm sure you've seen girls' underpants before, haven't you?"

Anna dealt out a deck of cards and positioned herself cross-legged on the couch. "I'm sure you'll enjoy this game," she said, grinning at Jordan. "And don't be so nervous. Mother, as usual, is at the club. Mike and Ruth have gone to the store with your mother. So there's just the two of us, you see?"

Yes, Clare decided, this summer at the Goldmans' was precisely what Jordan needed. Why, look at him: He was acting completely different. He rarely even mentioned that what's-her-name anymore, that Herece. He just needed to be away from that place for a while. Besides, Clare announced, Herece didn't live at the apartments anymore; Psyche Phillips had married Southwall Lovingood, and Herece had gone with Psyche and Southwall and his son.

Jordan's exposure to the wholesome Goldman children and the decent atmosphere of the Goldman house would make everything all right. Clare didn't mind Jordan playing with Anna. Indeed, she wished he had played with her more than he had. Why couldn't all little girls be as sweet and as well behaved as Anna Goldman?

"Well, I thought you'd like it here," Clare said. "But I had no idea they'd take to you so well. I just brought you here, you know, to observe. Mrs. Goldman is nice, but she doesn't know what she's talking about when she talks about artists. After all, *she's* rich."

Mrs. Goldman wasn't that well-off. As the summer ended, she tearfully told Clare Jordan that the Goldmans had to make an economy move. Ruth was starting Stanford in the fall, and the Goldmans wanted her to have a nice allowance to go with her tuition. Clare was laid off indefinitely.

The loss of her job depressed Clare. She moped around the apartment for two straight weeks, staying mostly in her room, consuming endless glasses of cheap liquor. She screamed at her son over imaginary things: "Where you been now? Out screwin' some funky little whore, that's where you been!" She wore the same dirty gown and a faded housecoat which she

46

didn't bother to button. Her room stank of bourbon. And other things.

Several men came to the apartment during this period. They went into the bedroom with Clare. Jordan knew one of the men, a young gambler. The gambler, a well-known hustler, didn't notice Jordan when he came in. Jordan was on the balcony, making a sketch. As the hustler left, however, he saw Jordan and came out on the porch. "Hey, man," the hustler said, "that *your* mother? I'm sorry, man."

The gambler never returned.

But others came—Jordan tired of the groans and sighs he heard coming from Clare's room. He wanted to knock Clare's door down, surprise her and whatever man she was sleeping with, grind their faces to pieces. Couldn't the woman see what she was doing to him?

Jordan began running the streets. He drifted from street corners to parks to housing projects. There were lots of boys with mothers like his in the projects. But he found little in common with them until he met Lynford Valentine.

Lennie lived in the biggest of all the projects. Jordan was walking down a project street when he passed a thin boy with a toothpick in his mouth. The boy was leaning against a telephone pole. There was an aura of energy in that boy.

"Hi," Jordan said.

Lennie Valentine rolled the toothpick around his white teeth and took hold of Jordan's collar. "Hey, man, you know who I am?"

"Uh-uh," Jordan said, knocking Lennie's hand away.

"I'm the project bad cat."

"Oh."

"What do you think? Think I should beat your ass?"

Jordan studied the boy. He was Jordan's height, but thinner. He didn't look very tough. And he wasn't dressed like a thug. Jordan figured he could take him.

"I wouldn't try that," Jordan said, staring Lennie down.

"Why not?"

" 'Cause I'd have to fight back."

Lennie leaned back against the pole, rolling the toothpick. "Well, in that case. . . ." Suddenly he leaped at Jordan, his fist moving to strike.

47

Jordan kicked Lennie Valentine in the crotch. Lennie crumpled and rolled on the ground, moaning. Jordan knelt next to him, afraid he had fatally injured the boy. "You all right?" Jordan asked. The quickness with which Jordan had responded surprised even him.

"Yeah," Lennie decided. "Why'd you have to do that, man? I was just foolin' around."

"Didn't look like that to me," Jordan said, helping Lennie up.

Lennie groaned. "You got guts, man. You got heart. I like that. What's your name?"

"Lawrence. Lawrence Jordan."

"Okay, Jordan. Valentine's my name. Lennie Valentine. And I'm still the project bad cat. Can you dig it?"

"I can dig it," Jordan said.

They became fast friends. Lennie would come by Jordan's house or Jordan would go to the project, and they would roam the city, staying mostly on the East Side or, as Lennie called it, their own turf. Lennie never invited Jordan inside his apartment. He said he was ashamed of the roaches—and his mother. Jordan saw Lennie's mother a few times, walking through the project. She was a light woman, wore excessive makeup, and had dancing eyes. Sometimes she walked past her son and Jordan without speaking. Lennie didn't discuss his mother, but other boys in the project told Jordan Mrs. Valentine was on "horse." Heroin.

Lennie suggested they called themselves the Devil and the Deacon. Lennie adopted the former name for himself, noting that while Jordan with his burning eyes *suggested* a demon, Jordan was much too "diplomatic" in his approach to people. Too quiet and reserved. Like a deacon.

They became known on the streets by those names. The East Side was in the middle of a teen-age gang war, and Jordan and Lennie drifted into a group called the Avengers. Fighting together, they held their own but established no special reputation as warlords. Mostly, they shoplifted, chased girls and stayed out late. But they were on call when the Turk or other leaders of the gang needed them.

Jordan hung back in gang fights; Lennie enjoyed them. Once

Jordan watched as Lennie and Turk and others stomped a tamale wagon man to death. Jordan was horrified, but to show his heart, he emptied the man's pockets after the work was done. He also took the man's shoes. The others forgot about Jordan's refusal to join the killing, but they remembered that Jordan stole a dead man's shoes. "Deacon, you somethin' else!" they said.

Lennie Valentine was caught walking Turk's girlfriend through the park. He and Jordan were drummed out of the gang and warned to stay off the streets. They ignored the warning but carried their knives at all times in case the Turk's Avengers should appear.

One night, Lennie startled Jordan. "I know how I can be King of Kansas City," Lennie said.

"How?"

"You know how Turk and all them dudes hang out at the pool hall?"

"Yeah. So what?"

"So I make me this bomb, see, 'n' one day we go whistlin' by the pool hall with it, just mindin' our own business, you understand. Then—zap!—I run down, plant the package, and we get in the wind. Doommmmmmm! No more Turk, no more Monk, no more Billy or any of them niggas. 'N' I'm the King of Kansas City."

"Shit, you'd be king of the gas chamber."

"Naw, man. I let the word out easy like, let it be known that the Syndicate did it. 'N' I'm the Syndicate, see? Me 'n' you—you're my right-hand man, my main man. We lay low for a while, maybe go see my aunt in Bonner Springs. When it blows over, we make it on back and take over. Nobody'd fuck with us then. We could get anything we want."

"It's a lousy idea, Lennie," Jordan said.

Jordan pulled his jacket collar up around his neck. He put his hands deep in his pockets and plodded slowly down the street behind Lennie Valentine. Lennie was whistling. Jordan felt cold vibrations in Valentine.

Three weeks later Lawrence Jordan was sitting in an enormous wood-paneled room; his long and wiry legs sprawled under a wide oval table. His head fell toward the table until it

49

rested on his breast. Beyond the breast, Jordan's delicate fingers pressed against the table. His fingers blended perfectly with the brown of the table. At that moment, Jordan wished his fingers *were* the table. Then they would stop pressing, stop striving.

Everywhere in the room, Jordan saw the specter of Lennie Valentine. Lennie would materialize on a wall, in a chair, his eyes shooting accusation. "You turned us in, man, you turned us in," Lennie said over and over. "You called the goddamn cops. . . ."

But Jordan had had no choice. It was becoming unbearable. Clare had got her job back, but her attitude toward him did not improve. Instead, it worsened; she locked him out of the house. He had to do what he did. He had no place else to go.

He was afraid Lennie would find out. With Lennie locked up, Jordan would be safe. But what if they sent Jordan to the same place?

Jordan recalled the night he ended it for the two of them. Lennie must have thought Jordan really meant to rob the store. There was a look of horror in Lennie's eyes when he heard the sirens. Lennie almost got away; but Jordan pretended to stumble, and Lennie stopped to help him.

Fortunately, Lennie was too shaken to ask the police how they knew to come to the store.

In the paneled room, Jordan raised his head. He studied the hands across the table from him: black hands. He studied the hands next to him: tan hands, delicate and tapered like his own. These were Clare's. At one curve of the table, he saw thin pink hands barely moving above the zot, zot, zot of the stenotype. And next to the zotting hands were the pale manicured hands of the Man.

Jordan's gaze returned to the black hands. They were the hands of Southwall Lovingood.

Lovingood nodded cordially at Jordan. The Man was revolving in his chair, chewing a pencil.

How huge Lovingood's hands were. What was *he* doing there? Jordan jumped. Surely Lovingood wasn't there on that certain business. No. It couldn't be that: They were only charged with attempted robbery. Clare must have needed a ride, and Lovingood gave it to her. That must be it.

50

Clare's hands brought forth a frilly handkerchief. They dabbed it around her eyes. Jordan was glad to see Clare crying. Now she knew what she had done to him, to his pride and to his hopes.

The Man's right hand tapped the pencil against the table. The Man grunted, then swiveled in his modernistic chair—too modernistic for a judge—and fixed a blue eye on Jordan.

"What's your name, boy?"

"Lawrence," said Jordan.

"Deacon?"

Jordan did not look at the Man. He kept his eyes on the table. "That's a nickname," Jordan replied.

"You haven't been living up to it, have you?"

"I don't know. I think so."

The Man frowned. "You know, son," he said, "I'd just as soon ship you out to the farm with your friend Valentine. You know that, boy? Here, look at me."

Jordan gave the judge his most disdainful look.

"I'm all for sending you there and throwing away the key, but—"

Southwall Lovingood winked at Jordan.

"But . . . Mister Lovingood here has offered to help straighten you out. That right, Mister Lovingood? Fine. Now what was it you wanted to say on the boy's behalf, sir? Just speak right up, Mister Lovingood."

Lovingood rose and leaned across the table on his fists. He resembled a bear pushing down on a log.

"Well, sir . . . I mean, Your Honor . . . Lovingood's is a fine old company, a fine institution, well established and *known* in the community, if you know what I mean—"

"Yes, you seem to have a lot of respect among your people. Go on."

"*Well* known. And we want to, we're anxious to, give young Mister Jordannn here, fiiiine young Mister Jordannn, a chance to . . . get himself together. It's been hard, Your Honor, really hard, for the mother alone to raise this intelligent but sensitive young man. We—those of us at Lovingood's—want to help now, Your Honor. We want to offer young Mister Jordan a position with our firm. We'll pay him thirty dollars a week. . . ."

51

And the big fat man went on to plead Jordan's case like a lawyer. It made even Jordan blush. He was getting attention from Clare, beating the rap, and getting offers of money besides. Thirty dollars a week!

But in a funeral home?

4

On his way through the foyer, Southwall Lovingood roared over the hum of the vacuum cleaner: "Let's move that couch now, Brother Jordannn; let's get under that couch, son. Don't want nothin' to crawl out and bite the ladies on their legs during a wake."

Jordan liked the way Lovingood always made a joke with you when you did something wrong. Not that Jordan got told anything too much; he learned fast. He'd been at Lovingood's two months now, working three days a week. Really, it was easy working for Lovingood. You did your work, and he left you alone. He had a way of making you feel important. He didn't come checking behind you. Mostly, Lovingood wasn't even there—or "in the house," as Major Bates put it in his strange parlance. Lovingood moved around town constantly in one of the three limousines they kept in the garage. Jordan didn't know where they kept the hearse. Whenever there was a funeral, they brought the hearse in from somewhere. Maybe they kept the hearse at Lovingood's house.

When Southwall was at his establishment, there was warmth and cheer in the house. Jordan liked the way Lovingood had of paying his staff. It wasn't anything set. It could be on Monday or Wednesday or Friday. The pattern was always the same: Lovingood never called you in; he would be passing through en route to the Room or out to the car. He never said the word "money" or hinted that he would pay you. He would waddle up and stand over you like a friendly bear. He always smelled sweet, very sweet. You smelled him before he got there. He wouldn't say it was payday. Sometimes Lovingood fooled you and didn't give you anything. When he did pay you, the approach was oblique: "Well, Brother Jordannn!" Lovingood would observe, rocking on his heels. "How's everybody treatin' you around here? Okay? Fiiine, fiiiine. Uh-huh, uh-huh. Fine, fine, glad to hear it. Okay, fiiiine young Brother Jordannn, all right. Well, you go ahead and knock off. Bates and I got to handle a little body, a little case. See you in two days, okay?" Then as you walked away, Lovingood would remember: "Oh, yeah, son. Here's a little somethin' for you. Get yourself a little somethin'."

And Lovingood would slip a wad of bills in your hand, all ones. It was never the same amount—twenty or twenty-five, sometimes thirty. Last week, when they had buried someone in a seven-hundred-dollar plastic sealer, it had been fifty dollars. The sealer had a replica of the Last Supper on its viewing side.

As Lovingood gave Jordan his cleaning instructions, Jordan perked up. He thought Lovingood just might pay him. But Southwall lumbered on by, passing into the room marked "Private," and closing the door tightly behind him. Once when Jordan started to follow him in there, Lovingood whirled and grabbed Jordan by the shoulders, nearly lifting Jordan off the carpet. "Don't worry about cleanin' *this* room, young Brother Jordannn," Southwall said. "Just take care of everything out front here."

The Room was constantly on Jordan's mind. Once when Major Bates went hurrying in there, Jordan was dusting a catafalque opposite the door. Jordan caught a glimpse of a stainless-steel table through the door. There was a sheet on the table, but Jordan didn't have time to see if there was a body under the sheet. Bates slammed the door before Jordan saw too much.

When was he going to get inside the Room? At first Jordan was thankful that Lovingood didn't require him to go in there. But Bates and Lovingood spent a great deal of time in the Room. Often, Jordan heard them laughing. Once they took lunch in. When Psyche Lovingood came to see her husband, she went in and out without even a change in physical expression. So it couldn't be *that* scary in there. Most of the time they had the water running. Jordan wondered if it was really water or a pump of some kind. Bates frequently talked to Lovingood about the old days as they went hurrying in, Bates remembering the days back in Oklahoma when they used six brown horses for children, six black horses for adults and six white horses for old folks. Once Jordan heard Lovingood call from the Room: "Bates! Where'd you put that goddamn aspirator?" and Bates yelled something back about "under the sink." Jordan wondered what an aspirator was. And he wondered how Bates and Lovingood worked on the bodies. He couldn't keep himself from wondering.

Today Bates was in the reception room poring over papers again. Bates had the radio on, and all the way back in the foyer Jordan could hear rhythm jumping from the local soul station. It was different working at Lovingood's from what Jordan had imagined it would be. He never dreamed that they played radioes in places like this. It wasn't as grim as outsiders thought. Actually, Jordan thought, I'm beginning to like it here. I won't let Clare know this of course; Mother would try to ruin it for me.

Jordan liked the way Lovingood called him Mister and Brother, and he liked earning his own money for a change, especially for such easy work. It wasn't at all grim working in a funeral home. And from what Jordan could see, Bates and Lovingood hardly were suffering from overwork. Yet undertakers made a lot of money, more than anyone else. That's what Clare said. And she seemed to be knowledgeable about what undertakers did. "If you have to get a trade," Clare said, "you can't go wrong in the funeral business. People *sure* got to die. . . ."

Jordan shut off the vacuum cleaner and went into the display room to dust the caskets. Now he knew the names of the boxes. If it was a box where you could see the whole body from head to feet, it was called a full couch; the entire top was one piece and you had to use both hands to raise it. If it was one where you could see only half the body, the top half, it was a half couch. The half couch was the most popular model. Lovingood's had only one full couch on display. In the half couch, Lovingood explained to Jordan, you didn't bother to put the shoes on the body. Nobody could tell the difference anyway. And the deceased wouldn't need them. Sometimes the men had on pants, and sometimes they didn't. Women were always fully clothed and had stockings on. Some caskets came with an

L-shaped key that locked them and made them airtight. These were sealers. Lovingood said sealers were required for communicable diseases, but a lot of people bought them anyway because they would lock. For some reason, they thought a locked box would keep the inevitable decay away from the Loved One.

The boxes ranged in price from seventy-five dollars for a hinged-lid, cloth-covered coffin with satin lining to fifteen hundred for the silk-lined bronze sealer with genuine Beautyrest mattress.

Jordan laid his dustrag on the closed half of the bronze casket. This box had a queer smell to it—metal mixed with perfumed paint. How cold it felt! Jordan's long fingers ran down the silk lid of the sealer. He worked the lid; it made no sound. The coffin lay upon a wine-colored church truck. Jordan pushed the truck. It squeaked.

Close up like this, a casket wasn't frightening at all. It was just metal and cloth and a mattress. It was an encapsulized bed, an odd-shaped couch that could be in any furniture display room. It needed a presence to set it apart from other furnishings. Alone and separated from what it was meant to hold, a casket was just a bed. For each person, a casket was made. For each person, a final couch. Was it comfortable? Jordan pumped the boxspring mattress with his fist. It felt accommodating: He wanted to climb in the box and try it out. He tried to tell himself that this desire was only because he was conscientious about his work. If he was going to be helping out at Lovingood's, then he might as well know. He felt for a mechanism to open the bottom half of the box. But he found none. How comfortable? Could a dead man tell?

Jordan's mind raced inward, backward, to the time when he had been in the room with the huge dolls who looked like his grandmother and other grown-ups sleeping before going to a party. He couldn't tell if they could sense him in their surroundings; Jordan had sensed that they were no longer there. They had faded into a larger reality, gone back to the wellspring of life that is connected with rocks and mountains and deep water. But if they could feel! Jordan wondered what it would be like to lie in a casket and hear organ music and the soft sound of feet passing your bier. As they came past to look down on you and pity you, you couldn't move or open your eyes. But you could feel. What was it to lie still and cool and have them close the lid over your discolored face? Would the lid creak then, make a sound that would linger with you in your casket inside your skull for eternity? Long after they had taken you away in the hump-backed hearse and thrown moist earth over you and your shining bronze bed had moldered?

It occurred to Jordan that the people who made this device of hinges and lids and silk pillows might consider themselves craftsmen, even artists. They might take pride in their work. After all, their work is exhibited, however briefly, to the public. And those who view it never forget it. How could anyone be proud of producing a receptacle to hold a disgusting thing in the ground with tumblebugs and moles and all manner of creeping, sunless things? Yet in a way it was fitting: Why not make art that no one can see after it's installed in its earthen gallery? People didn't appreciate art anyway. Certainly Clare didn't. What a joke it would be on Clare and everybody else like her if Jordan became a great sculptor of coffins, if some of the most beautiful forms in the world were carved and mounted on these earth boxes and they begged Jordan to give up making them and put his work in stone and metal and put it in art galleries and museums instead. But he wouldn't. Oh, no; he would laugh at them, a long, eerie laugh, and would tell them, "Only the dead and those who are beyond them can appreciate my work."

Through the wall, Jordan heard water running. Lovingood was in the Room again, doing whatever it was he did to them back there before dressing them for the party. Lovingood was at whatever it was that kept men like him practicing a science older than Babylon. Lovingood called it a case. Jordan wondered what it must be like to be a case, to be on the table with Lovingood leaning over you, doing surgery on you.

The Room opened only to those who had the secret. That's what Clare told Jordan. "The undertakers guard that secret with their lives," Clare had said in some long ago. "It's the secret of embalming, and they tell me it's so horrible that most people wouldn't want to know anyway."

What did they do in embalming? Pump fluid? Jordan knew they did that because Clare said so. And when she talked about things like *that,* Clare had an uncanny way of speaking with authority. But did they strap the bodies on the table? Clare said they did. Did they take your clothes off? Clare said they did. Jordan felt a rising within him at this last thought. Did they work with women in there naked and big-breasted? Were the women still warm? Clare said they pumped fluid into you with needles, and the fluid was poison. You had to wear rubber gloves. The fluid was so powerful that if you spilled it on you, you would die. It would harden any part of you it touched. Fumes from the fluid gradually weakened your body until it killed you. Meanwhile, you became the living dead. Before the fluid killed you, it made an alcoholic of you. Clare said all undertakers drank; that was the price they paid for being undertakers, she said. One other price undertakers had to pay: They remembered the faces of every body they worked on. When an undertaker died, Clare told her son, each dead face was remembered. "All those faces pass before their eyes before they die."

The water in the Room stopped running. Jordan could hear Southwall Lovingood moving around, hear what sounded like wheels. A table turning? Was Lovingood wheeling the body around? Jordan hungered to see what was happening. He knew he would be afraid. He wanted to be afraid. But there was something that frightened Jordan even more: He knew he had to participate, had to touch bodies and caskets and death. He was drawn to the Room by a force stronger than any other in his life so far.

Had Lovingood ever killed anybody in the Room? Clare knew an undertaker who did. The man committed suicide after it happened. "You remember Althea, Otis' mother?" Clare asked Jordan once, out of nowhere. "Well, Althea had a sister once before you were even thought of. Great big girl. Ate a lot of sweets. Diabetes. Well, this girl—Charlotte was her name, Charlotte Jefferson—this girl died. At least they thought she was dead. Over at General Hospital she went into a coma after insulin shock, and a couple of days later she stopped breathing. They couldn't find a heartbeat, so they called the undertakers. They tell me she had catalepsy, where you don't appear to be alive but you really are. If they hold a mirror to your nose, it doesn't get moist. But you're still breathing. Only very, verrry slowly. Like sleeping a deep, deep sleep, they tell me.

"Anyway, child, they took Charlotte down to Tatum's on

Eighteenth Street—all the colored funeral parlors used to be down there back then—and put her on one of those back room tables. Took three full-grown men to lift her. They didn't work on her right away. They let 'em cool nowadays, but in those days they had to get them right away because embalming wasn't as advanced as it is now. But this fella was busy on somebody else. And funny thing, he told me he *thought* he heard somebody groaning, real quietlike, a soft moan. But he didn't see anything—or anybody. He thought it was his imagination. You know these undertakers—after they've been in it for a while, they start hearin' all kinda things, honey. Anyway he thought it was his imagination, and he turned around and kept on working. Pretty soon, he got to this girl Charlotte. *Pretty* girl. Pretty hair. Big, heavy, light-skinned girl. He took the clothes off and washed her down with a hose and put that needle to her. And this scared me, Lawrence, really scared me. He said when he hit her with that needle, she let out a scream that you could hear a block away. She started to get up from that table with the needle in her, leaned up on one elbow, then fell back down. She kept screaming, 'Oh, God, help me. I'm not dead.' But she was very dead then. It was too late. I remembered that child well, honey, used to play with her every day down on Brooklyn Avenue. Her daddy used to have a big Hupmobile; always kidded her about that. Shit, this undertaker fella quit the business behind Charlotte's death. Few months later he was dead. Killed himself. But I saw him before he died, and he told me, 'Clare, I killed Charlotte, killed her just as much as if I'd taken a gun to her head. . . .' "

It was a slow summer. Bates said, "Don't understand it, Southwall. Statistics say we should be havin' pretty good flow right now. Not good as fall, maybe, but good still. Better'n this. Man, we should be comin' 'n' goin' at least once a week."

And Bates sat staring at his uplifted hand, waiting for it to get hard. Bates said he could tell when they had a body coming because his hand got hard.

Besides sweeping and vacuuming and dusting, Jordan had been asssigned to answer the telephone and check on the ambulance. It was slow: Jordan hadn't taken a call yet. Oh, he had

59

taken a message or two, but never a *call* for a pickup. "Well, you'll get it pretty soon, son," Southwall hummed, rocking in his worn-out chair. "Yeah. You'll get it. Bound to, son. Just keep listenin'." And Southwall slipped Jordan his pay (only five dollars this time) and reminded:

"Now just keep calm and don't panic. If we're here and have the radio on or if we're laughin' and talkin' and clownin', just shush us. Don't hesitate to do that. Remember now: no background noises, no noises in the back. That's very important, very im-por-tant, Brother Jordannn. It gives a bad image to Funeral Service, a baaad image, if somebody's grievin' and you got soul music playin'. So just shush us. Now when they call, they're apt to be in shock or deeply bereaved, understandably, by the loss of their loved one or friend. So don't say, 'Good morning' or 'How are you?' Just say, 'Lovingood's.' Just 'Lovingood's.' Right, son? And wait a minute. Give 'em time to collect their wits. If you still get no response, then ask 'em, 'May I help you?' and identify yourself as 'Mister Jordannn.' Speak in a cheerful tone—not too cheerful now—but firm and even. You don't have to show sorrow or offer your condolences to the survivors. They'll have enough of that. The main thing, the maaiiin thing, Mister Jordannn, is to kinda let 'em know that Lovingood's is in charge now. Yeah, *Lovin*good's is in charge. Yeah! If you know what I mean. And you can be soulful about it. Let 'em know Lovingood's in charge, got the bull by the horns, and everything's gonna be all right. By the way you talk. Now get the name and age of the case, uh, deceased. Talk slow 'n' easy, now, and get them to talk the same. Be sure and get the name right, get them to spell the last name and put it on your pad here, and make them repeat the age twice. If they don't know the age, which many of 'em don't, or they can't remember it, ask 'em: 'Adult or minor?' If it's a kid, *about* how old is he? Now this is very important, all very important, Brother Jordannn, fiiine young man Mister Jordannn. We must know the age. Looks bad, Mister Jordan, looks bad for Funeral Service in general and Lovingood's in particular if we go runnin' in with a bassinet for a thirteen-year-old or a stretcher for a baby, you understand? Now I know that sounds a little harsh, but it's one of the things we in mortuary science face, Mister Jordannn.

You'll come to understand all this directly. We do a lot of things, young Mister Jordan, that the public don't always understand. But we sort of keep 'em to ourselves. No sense tellin' folks about it, gettin' 'em all shook up for nothing. So you don't have to tell your mother, don't have to worry your fine young mother, about how we answer the phones, okay?

"Now another thing, Master Jordannn: Find out fast where the case is to be found. Get that address down straight and whether it's *East* Thirty-ninth or *West* Thirty-fourth, is it business or residence? Get the deceased's home address and phone number and the caller's name and numbers for our records. This way, if we get there and somebody—Sister Fears or young Brother Will-iams or one of them—has already made the pick-up, we can get over to the home and talk to the family and pin responsibility for the call on somebody, a family friend or maybe even the boyfriend when Mamma called 'bout Poppa. Understand? Means a lot to our profession to keep these things straight. Now I'm not sayin' our fellow morticians steal cases out from under us, you understand, but mistakes can be made and too often are, young Mister Jordannn. So get those numbers.

"And get the rest of that information I told you about: name of the doctor, was he present at death, just the brief circumstances of death. Trauma or natural? Got to handle each case differently, you know. Soon as you've got all the info, call us. If I'm in back, use the house phone; don't go bargin' in there. If ole Bates and I both are out, call us at home or call the answerin' service—you've got the number right there—call us and relay it, all of it. While you're waiting for us, go out and check the wagon. Now will you remember the sheets, please? Clean sheets on every call. The first call is important, and the impression we make on that first call is what keeps the business comin' in."

Jordan wasn't minding the office as he should have been when his first call came.

He was in the chapel, pacing around the catafalque, listening to his feet scruffing the soft rug. He was getting as bad as Bates when business was slow: He walked back and forth around the bier, staring at the curving sides of the stand. He was nearly breathless when he reached the phone. "Hello?"—Lovingood wouldn't have liked that—"uh, Lovingood's!"

Silence.

"May I help you? This . . . Mister Jordan."

He felt a sense of command when he said that. *Mister* Jordan. Why not? He was coming into his own. He would be eighteen soon. Maybe people should start calling him Mister; he was going places most people never are privileged to go. He would become known as a man in the community long before he was a famous artist in the world. The sense of command increased as Jordan heard the first sobs on the other end of the line. It was female, adult, someone he didn't know, and somehow Jordan felt a strength he didn't know he had in having an adult depending on him for something she couldn't handle. He had known it was a *call* as soon as he heard the silence.

"Mister Howard is dead," the woman sobbed. "He just died, and the doctor is here. The doctor asked me to tell you that."

"Yes, ma'am," Jordan said. "Now what is the full name of the deceased? What's his full name? . . ."

Lovingood was well pleased. "Yes, sir, Mis-tah Jorrr-dannn!" he bellowed, cuffing Jordan affectionately on the shoulder. "You did just right, just the right thing, everything. Name, address, next of kin, yes, sir. And everything we need right there in the ambulance."

And Bates, lingering in the door of the off-limits Room with his gray felt hat in his hand, said, "Come on, Lovingood. Let's git t' gittin'. Sister Fears'll be there already time you get outta door."

"All right, old man," Lovingood said. And to Jordan: "You know how to drive a car? Well, you gonna start learnin', start to learn. Take lessons from Mister Bates here. In the family car, hear? Now you got a birthday next month, your mother tells me? All right, next month then, you gonna start drivin' in a coupla funerals. . . ."

"Thank you, Mister—"

" 'N' know something else?"

"No, sir."

"Little while longer, just little more longer, son, little more good work like you did today and we might just let you kinda *assist* back there, help out in the preparation room."

62

"Goddog!"

The black panels of the ambulance flashed past the office window as Jordan helped himself to the cushions of Lovingood's own chair. It was a high chair, and Jordan sat very high indeed.

5

The mortuary became the anchor of Lawrence X. Jordan's life. It was the only certainty that fate thus far had granted him, and Jordan reached for it eagerly. Besides, the mortuary—its presence, its aura, its ritual—lay at the end of everything and therefore was more permanent than anything. Life was an illusion; the reality was death. Life spent itself in a moment of eternity; death went on forever. As Clare put it: "Honey, people *sure* 'nuff got to die." Southwall would have added that they also just as surely had to be buried.

For most people, the mortuary was the end of life; for Lawrence X. Jordan, it was the beginning.

During his first six months at Lovingood's, Jordan began to evolve into a man. His evolution was decided by his circumstance, and Jordan put his manhood together in that context. He discovered that he could smile again—especially since he had earned the money to purchase the gold filling that now occupied the space between his front teeth. Jordan flashed his new smile incessantly. It was classy, it was elegant, something that added flair to the business of Funeral Service.

Jordan took a new interest in his hair. At home, Clare often found herself applying her makeup standing before the tiny bathroom mirror because Jordan had commandeered her dressing table for endless brushings of his sandy top. Jordan kept his hair evenly cropped now: For some reason it looked better matted and even all around like the thick rich carpet at Lovingood's.

At school, Jordan found new relevance in his studies, particularly English and history. His interest in English stemmed from his duty as a funeral scribe at Lovingood's. Among other chores, Jordan was charged with writing Lovingood's funeral notices each Thursday. First he scribbled the notices at the mortuary. Then he delivered them personally to the *Afro-Citizen News.* "A man in mortuary science is often called upon to produce notices, brochures and eulogies—and even to do a little public speaking," Southwall Lovingood had informed him. And Jordan had got the message. Southwall also hinted that the time was coming when Lovingood's would need radio spots written for a weekly program of inspirational music. Jordan began learning his English. He had little interest in grammar and composition, but he wanted to please his employer. He began writing the notices by copying those in the back section of the *Afro-Citizen.* But he quickly noticed that the items were poorly written and grammatically unsound. After he pointed this out to Lovingood, the undertaker nodded understandingly and gave Jordan freedom to write the notices as he saw fit. Jordan would sit at Major Bates' desk across from Lovingood when he wrote the notices. First, he would write down all the facts he could gather about the deceased and the upcoming funeral. Then, carefully, he would compose the notices, putting each one on separate sheets of manila paper. At the top of each page he wrote "Funeral Notice/Lovingood Mortuary, Inc." Later he began to type the notices on Bates' battered Remington. He used two fingers and pounded the keys very hard. Lovingood told Jordan that if he kept his typing up, someday he'd be better than Bates, who couldn't type with ten fingers. Usually, there were four or five notices a week. One week there were seven, and Jordan felt a surge of pride at being employed by such a prosperous institution as Lovingood's. And he was pleased to note that the editor of the *Afro-Citizen,* a snotty woman, addressed him as *Mister* Jordan that week.

When school had reconvened, Jordan could envision it only as seven hours of irrelevant diversion from his work at Lovingood's. His emotions about school were mixed, however, because he was quite anxious to see what new girls would be attending Central that year. But he saw his classes as nothing more than the pastimes of a world he didn't understand, a world of which he was never meant to be a part. He took one look at the sentence diagrams and verb inflections in his English text and complained to Lovingood that he'd just as soon drop English if that were all right. It was then that Lovingood explained the importance of English to Funeral Service. After that, Jordan had his head in his English books even at the mortuary. He was surprised to see how well he did in school without half trying. Now he had a reason. As long as he kept in mind that he needed his studies in his work at Lovingood's, Jordan breezed through school. He was even considering taking Spanish in case Lovingood's had any Mexican burials. He imagined himself taking a first call from someone on the West Side and consoling the bereaved in subdued but rapid-fire Spanish.

History was another matter. Actually Southwall's admonition about English was enough to make Jordan at least mildly interested in reading his history book. Besides, he was interested in people and everything they did. Especially as it affected Funeral Service or death. Thus the section on Egypt and the pyramids got Jordan's full attention. He went to the public library and dug up Herodotus' old account of the process of Egyptian embalming ("First an Ethiopian stone is used to gain access to the vital cavity . . ."). Jordan read the account over and over until he had it memorized. He had thought the ancient embalming process was totally unknown. That's what Clare told him. "It has remained a mystery down through the centuries," she said, "and to this day it is considered far, far superior to any other process used." Now Jordan knew the only unknown was the gauze of their mummies. Someday, Jordan's mind fancied, Lawrence Xavier Jordan, wealthy mortician with his own laboratory and enough money and time to experiment at night, might rediscover the ancient process and revive it. With fame and profit soon following. The history teacher told why people should study history: "Those who haven't learned the lessons of history are doomed to repeat them." If just the study of Egypt had fired his imagination, Jordan reasoned, then he could benefit more from Greece and Rome and France. Jordan learned his history.

Lovingood gave him fifty dollars for his birthday. Jordan bought a second suit with the money and that reminded him of Lovingood's definition of the best-paid type of mortician, the funeral director: "A funeral director is an undertaker with *two*

66

pairs of pants." After Jordan promised her he wouldn't buy a pair of pointed shoes, Clare gave him the money to get some new ones. He compromised by purchasing a straight pair of lace dress shoes that only hinted toward a point. Clare was not over-joyed at his selection, but she let it pass with a mere "Humphhh."

Actually, Clare was pleased by Jordan's changing. But she resolved not to let him know that. She wanted him to continue developing just as he was. If she was too enthusiastic about Jordan's new attitudes, Clare reasoned, he'd question them.

Jordan noticed certain changes in Clare, too. She had become less antagonistic toward him, asking him how he was doing in school, at the mortuary; she even inquired frequently about his health. Jordan suspected her actions, but he didn't have time to analyze them. He did sense that she remained opposed to his wanting to be an artist.

Although he was excelling in English and history, Jordan had gone down slightly in art. He was bored with the class, really. It was a repeat of the previous year, and Jordan was anx-ious to look into some new approaches to mirroring the world. At the moment, he had no time to pursue art outside class and no real desire to. But he wondered whether Clare's new atti-tude toward him was prompted more by his slippage in art than his rise in history. Not that Clare encouraged him too much in any studies. "History's all right," she said. "Used to be good in it myself. But you can't eat history, Lawrence. English neither. Better take yourself some trade like bricklayin' or bookkeepin' —something that'll feed you. You're going on eighteen, child, and I ain't gonna be feedin' you forever." When Jordan tried to explain that he needed English for his work at the mortuary, as well as to satisfy college entrance requirements, Clare said, "College, hell. Can't even afford a pot to piss in, let alone college."

Along with increased academic prowess, Jordan also experi-enced a personality crisis. He couldn't understand it, but he knew it was linked with his new interest in clothes and brushing his hair. It was an awful state. Sometimes he felt he could swal-low the whole world, he had so much energy. Other times he was extremely depressed (especially if the weather was cloudy),

67

and he despaired of ever getting away from Clare or ever learning anything else about the funeral business. Or anything. Frequently these moods were tied to his relationships with girls.

Jordan was driving now, wheeling one of Lovingood's sleek leased limousines on mortuary errands after school. Sometimes he would see a girl he knew, stop, pick her up, and take her where she was going. Inevitably she would ask him where he got the car, and he would answer that it belonged to his boss. He did not tell what company he worked for, and the girls rarely asked. When they did, Jordan merely replied, "Oh, it's just a real big operation. We make lots of money." He began to have fantasies about driving some girl very fast out Twenty-seventh Street to Blue Valley Park and parking the car out there where the road dipped down and there were shady trees and the day was blue and the sun turning orange as it fell behind the city. He and the girl would get in the back seat of the car and pull down the slatted blinds and. . . . SHAZAM!

One thing confused Jordan about this daydream: He couldn't have this fantasy unless he first imagined that he was coming from a funeral in a car and the car was a hearse. Jordan fluctuated between this thought and visions of totally obliterating his consciousness. He was developing a philosophy about destiny now. Destiny was when things in life were fixed, *locked up* in a way beyond just the physical, so that the things that happened to you were going to happen whether you willed them to happen or not. It didn't really matter if you were conscious; just your functioning, breathing body needed to be there. If it was your destiny to be outstanding—to be an upcoming young mortician in this case—then you just went through your destiny. The only thing you personally could do was prepare yourself to accept it.

Jordan became obsessed with the idea of dying a good death. And what was a good death? It was dying without cringing, without begging and bawling at the inevitable. It was meeting the thing that would take you (it could be a disease or a sudden smashup into thick concrete) and gliding into it easily, naturally, instead of registering and clinging to life. It was those who were conscious of themselves who died the worst deaths, the ignominious deaths. The few who, like Jordan, realized the value of wiping out the Self died well and with honor. Lawrence Jordan feared death more than anything; he embraced it in order to forestall it.

Jordan worried that he was really *too* conscious. He caught himself thinking of pleasures like the girl-and-the-hearse-in-the-park-thing. How selfish! How clinging-to-life! He would lapse into this fantasy at the strangest times, walking to school, vacuuming the rugs at Lovingood's, in the bathroom. And his body would undergo an unwanted, an uncontrollable change when his mind flew away like that. It was a change of breathing and of pulse. It was sweating; it was animal. It was the change of sexual desire. When it came, Jordan's organ would swell up and hurt until he thought it was going to break off. Sometimes he didn't even know it had swelled; he was too engrossed in the fantasy. But it was frustrating. There was a point of imagination beyond which he could not go. And he was too afraid, too conscious, in real life to approach the real girls about it when they were in the real car. He let them pass by, not knowing what was in his mind.

When Jordan reached the limit of imagination, he would become aware of his body and its hunger. And he would strike out with his fist, a measured blow, at the weak part of his organ. That would stop it. He was ashamed for hitting himself like that. He could injure himself irreparably doing that, destroy his manhood one day, so he had to measure the blow. Sometimes he could overcome the hunger by relieving himself, sometimes by thinking about something else, something pleasant like the peace and serenity of a funeral home. He preferred to do the latter; each time he masturbated seemed to him one day off his life. Besides, there was something weak about imaginary sex; Jordan liked his real. He must abandon himself, abandon fantasy. He would protect himself against all the little deaths people inflict upon you on the way to the big and final one. Yes, that was his job. To be beyond this life, to be insensitive to it, to be distant.

Jordan fluctuated between riding girls in Lovingood's car and plunging into his work. Southwall was surprised when Jordan offered to work at the funeral home Saturdays and even Sundays when there was a service. Southwall told Jordan that it wouldn't make any difference in his pay, but Jordan didn't care. Jordan was inconsistent in his weekend work, however.

One time he would arrive at Lovingood's early on a Saturday morning, dust, sweep and vacuum, humming and whistling. He would work through until four in the afternoon, often without lunch. Other times he would choose to go to the movies on Sunday night even though Lovingood was having a late-evening service and could have used the help. Lovingood never complained. He said he was glad to see Jordan take the interest he did in the business.

Lovingood encouraged Jordan at every opportunity. Besides his employer, Jordan had two other informative sources: the weekly *Afro-Citizen News* and the other undertakers of the city.

Jordan did little else at Lovingood's on Friday apart from reading the *Afro-Citizen*. As soon as he arrived, after greeting Lovingood and Bates, Jordan went to the foyer, where he would find the latest copy of the *Afro-Citizen* on the coffee table. He sat on the divan in the foyer or occasionally on the back steps of the establishment, reading the funeral news.

The *Afro-Citizen* was typical of community newspapers of the era. Poorly laid out, poorly edited, almost pathetically narrow in its range of interest: crime, gossip and "society news." Indeed, one of the best-read sections was "Police Blotter," a dingbatted column which brought the reader briefly up on who on Twenty-seventh Street had shot whom and who on East Forty-second Street had divorced whom for the week. Another well-read column was "Ponchita Perez's Social Whirl," which featured a boxed caricature of winking Ponchita above a three-column spread of gray type that stretched all the way to the bottom of the page. Jordan didn't know who Ponchita was, but Clare had told him: "She sure ain't no society lady, I'll tell you that. I know Ponchita Platt—Platt's her real name, you know. Known her for years. Her husband too. An *old* man. They caught Ponchita years ago, back in forty-five, in the back seat of a car with a Marine. Right out in front of her own house. Social whirl, shit."

The funeral page was little better than Ponchita's column. But Lawrence Jordan read it faithfully. For him, it was a running account of which mortuaries were challenging Lovingood's that week. Jordan read it like a racing form.

All the black undertakers had notices in the *Afro-Citizen*. The others were listed in the daily Kansas City *Star*. Jordan had read about the nonblack institutions: P. G. Newbody's Sons, Applebaum & O'Reilly, Teuffel Mortuary, Orbach's. And Valentino Brothers—supposedly an outlet for the Mafia. All these except P. G. Newbody's remained mysteries to Jordan. Newbody's, with its four "funeral chapels" in Kansas and Missouri, was a regional institution. Its Number One Chapel, a rambling, pink tile-and-stucco rectangle enclosing a landscaped Spanish-styled courtyard, was one of the wonders of the world. People took their children to Newbody's on Sundays just to see the courtyard. Jordan swore that someday he would have a house as splendid and as important as Newbody's.

Through the *Afro-Citizen,* Jordan came to know the names of the Lovingood competitors long before he met them. There were the big companies: Williams Brothers, Fannie L. G. Fears. From the way Lovingood talked about these larger companies, it was obvious that he considered "Sister" Fears the real threat, followed closely by the Williamses, Robert and Billy. Southwall wasn't worried about the medium-sized firms: E. E. Brashears and another institution with the impressive legalistic-sounding name of LaCour, Fortune & Wingate. In the lower echelon of the trade were C. E. Lewis, McGinnis, and Tatum's. The Lewis Funeral Home was nearly defunct. Lovingood told Jordan that old man Charles Lewis in his time had been the biggest and the best back when Fannie Fears was still struggling to make ends meet. But Fannie Fears and a newcomer, Robert Williams, Sr., overtook the ailing Chuck Lewis. The old man died, leaving his business to his widow, who kept up merely the appearance of an establishment. Adele Lewis lived upstairs over her funeral home and opened for business every day. But she went months without a funeral, sitting in her time-worn chapel reliving the old days when Chuck Lewis was the first black undertaker in the city to come out with Packard rolling stock.

The Tatum Funeral Home was sadder than Lewis'. "Ole man Tatum don't get nothin' but city business, charity cases," Bates had informed Lawrence Jordan. "Hell, he's scared of the dead. *Scared,* can you believe that? Scared of his own shadow. Shaky; drinks. He has them ole wineheads doin' his work. Brings 'em in off the streets, buys 'em a bottle of something— anything—gets 'em drunk, 'n' tells 'em how to do it."

Lovingood's was the only funeral home that reserved a space

permanently in the *Afro-Citizen News*. And Lovingood's was the only funeral home proud enough to show itself off in the paper. Each week, the Lovingood notices appeared beneath a line drawing of the long modern building with its name emblazoned just above it. When Fannie Fears or the Williams Brothers had four bodies, Lovingood managed to advertise five. Even when the other funeral homes had no notices (during the low-mortality spring thaw), Lovingood had at least two. There weren't always that many in the house. But Lovingood always had notices, Jordan quickly learned, because he would run the names of upcoming cases if he got a call before press time—or rerun last week's names if he didn't. It was a smart way to keep an impression before the public.

Across the river in Kansas, there were the three other ghetto mortuaries: Hatcher's, Mrs. G. W. James', and Aretha Vinson Funeral Home. Hatcher was the leader in Kansas and often did as well as Mrs. Fears or Lovingood's. The other Kansas houses did moderately well, with Aretha Vinson trailing slightly. Kansas, of course, was not as competitive: The city was smaller; the people were friendlier—in a sense more innocent. Countrified. Jordan had seen Hatcher's and Mrs. G. W. James', and they reflected Kansas—Hatcher's was an attempt at modernity, some landscaping but small and undistinguished; Mrs. James operated out of a converted clapboard church with a garish purple neon over her front door.

Now Jordan was a part, albeit minuscule, of this funeral world. He was already putting his mark on the funeral page. He took pride in drafting Lovingood's notices so they read more smoothly. The language in one of the Williams Brothers' notices was precisely what Jordan avoided:

> Mrs. Lula Mae Leonard. Passed away last Friday at home, attended by loved ones. A native of Jackson, Miss. Funeral services, May 23 Wednesday the chapel at Williams, with interment in her native state. Sadly missed by Billy, a son, Sue, daughter, and Jeffers P. McSpoon, a dear friend.

Instead, Jordan lead off with the last name of the deceased, which he decreed should be set in boldface, the other names and relevant information in decending order of importance:

MAYS, FREDERIC L., aged 39. Services at 1 P.M. Friday, May 25 in the chapel. Mr. Mays died May 21 after an illness. He was a lifelong resident of the city, a carpenter, a Prince Hall Mason and attended Trinity Baptist Church. Surviving are a son, Thomas; two daughters, Mrs. T. B. Torrell and Miss Sandra Mays; and one grandson.

Jordan always arranged the notices in alphabetical order before delivering them to the *Afro-Citizen*. Soon after Jordan was assigned to write his funeral notices, Lovingood began to get compliments from readers and grateful customers.

It was also in the pages of the *Afro-Citizen News* that Jordan learned of the appointment of one Southwall Lovingood, Mortician, to the presidency of the Twin Cities Funeral Directors Association.

6

Lovingood approached his new position energetically. Often, late into the evening, Southwall read mysterious documents at his desk while a body waited in the preparation room. To the undertaker, a corpse was merely business; a body stretched on a table was equivalent to a car that needed fixing. He would get to it when he could.

Lawrence Jordan's involvement in the business of undertaking increased with Lovingood's election to head of the Funeral Directors Association. First Jordan became entrenched in the mortuary. Now he became enmeshed in the wider world of mortuary science. Many afternoons Lovingood paid visits to his peers. He took Jordan with him. Lovingood would plop in the back seat of one of his limousines, and Jordan chauffeured. When they arrived at one of the mortuaries, Jordan raced to open the rear door for his employer. Southwall always reached for his own door, but Jordan got there first. "That's all right now, Brother Jordannn," Lovingood protested, "I got it, got the door." But Jordan continued to accommodate the undertaker. He sensed that Lovingood secretly was pleased by the attention. And if there was one thing Jordan wanted to do, it was please Southwall Lovingood.

Jordan waited in the big car most of the time, listening to the radio and daydreaming of girls. Occasionally, Lovingood remembered Jordan and said, "Ever seen the inside of Williams Brothers, son? Come on!" And Jordan would wait in the reception rooms or foyers, studying the immobile occupants of endless myriad caskets while Southwall conducted his business in other rooms. The bigger places had receptionists or associate directors on duty, and Jordan often asked them questions about their establishments. In this way, he became familiar with most of the firms he'd already been tracking in the *Afro-Citizen.*

Each funeral home possessed a personality. An aura emanating from the carpets and drapes and walls, the placement or caskets, the position of offices and chapels.

And cars or *rolling* stock were part of this spirit. You can tell an undertaker, Jordan was instructed, by the cars he drives—especially the hearse. McGinnis, for example, pushed a fleet of late-model Cadillacs. They were standard models, shorter than the classic Sedan DeVille—the only funeral coach, really, for the discerning undertaker. McGinnis' hearse had little chrome and humpy roof which made it little more than a meat wagon. In its time, it was a sleek van. But now it was merely respectable. The hearse was older than the company's family cars. And the Gothic "McGinnis" sign in the window of the casket compartment was out of kilter with the car. McGinnis parked his cars in the weed-grown lot behind the converted apartment building which served as his headquarters. A man who neglected his rolling stock neglected his embalming. And his name.

People, leaden-eyed and sullen, lived on the floors above McGinnis' Funeral Home, a family of ten. The little children upstairs seemed to have worn their ragged overalls and dresses since birth. Often they wore no underwear.

You walked right into McGinnis' preparation room through the peeling back door of the place. Jordan knew the back door was peeling because he opened the rusty screen door. The door swung uneasily on its one good hinge.

It was obvious that McGinnis cared little about the façade of his funerarium. The place was located in an especially undesirable neighborhood. A block away lurked a storefront series of urine-smelling bars and dusty pawnshops.

The front of McGinnis' was a row of venetian blinds and streaky windows. The sidewalk was littered with trash, and the iron railing leading up to the dusty front door was rusted. The door commanded a square hallway. Through it was an open archway which revealed ranks of folding wooden chairs. This was the McGinnis chapel, a depressing, bleak-walled affair illuminated by dim opaque glass lamps. At the end of this narrow room stood a moldering church truck, trimmed in faded purple. The walls, the room, the rug—all were dank. To the right of the entrance, running parallel to the chapel, was a door marked "Office." Inside was McGinnis' metal desk. Beside the desk was a curved-back wicker chair where the "client" sat. McGinnis' office was filled with memos, notes, old licenses, photographs of mortuary college classes and relatives and McGinnis' ornate diploma.

This was all there was to the McGinnis establishment. An office, a chapel, a preparation room. It reeked of heavy perfume and exploitation and death. And Lawrence Jordan loved it.

He knew McGinnis' business averaged two bodies a week. Excluding the cost of extra help (McGinnis worked alone except on pickups and funerals), overhead and advertising, McGinnis easily cleared ten thousand dollars yearly. Of course, Jordan wouldn't want to be in that position. Ten thousand was nothing in the funeral business. But at first, when you're just starting, it wouldn't be so bad. In his mind's eye, Jordan saw himself fresh out of mortuary school hanging his diploma and class picture on the gray walls of the McGinnis premises. Actually, there was much to be said for a small, dank place. You could save money on the upkeep. If you had a family, they could live upstairs over the place until you'd saved a fortune. And the people in the neighborhood wouldn't bother you, that was for sure. They wanted no part of funeral parlors. "Good morning, Mister Jordan," they would say, the winos and runny-stocking ladies, as you sauntered across a weeded lot to the office.

"Yes," Southwall Lovingood confirmed. "It's best to start in a little place, build your clientele, then move on. Don't you think so, Mister Jordannn?"

Jordan found himself nodding, being thankful for the free advice. The next minute he was wringing the car's steering wheel as if to choke it. He had to discipline himself. Why was he thankful to Lovingood for advice on how to set up business? The funeral coach rolled on.

LaCour, Fortune & Wingate fascinated Jordan. That institution was headquartered in a lattice-windowed limestone building on the corner of Nineteenth and Vine. Across from a liquor store and half a block from the concrete canyon of the railroad tracks, LaCour, Fortune & Wingate did not partake of its surroundings. What Jordan especially appreciated about this firm were the barred windows and battlements of its solid old edifice. Lovingood informed Jordan that LaCour's had its preparation room on the second floor overlooking the street. Jordan's imagination flashed on again: He saw the gowned proprietors of the establishment gathered around a marble slab before the upstairs window, conferring in hushed voices before performing all manner of precise surgery in the gray afternoon of a rainy day. Jordan envisioned himself among them. A little motto echoed in his mind: "An institute of applied artists using only the finest implements with surgeonlike skill."

"What's wrong, son?"

"Nothing, Mister Lovingood. Just daydreaming, I guess."

"Nothin' wrong with that, son."

"No, sir."

A wrought-iron gate, consistent with the trim of the windows, clanked open, giving access to the double mahogany doors of the company. From sidewalk to reception room, LaCour, Fortune & Wingate, Funeral Directors, exuded an aura of history, reliability, perpetuity. The aura emanated from the discreet, gold-on-black name plate on the double doors to the comfortable but not familiar French Provincial foyer. Jordan was never permitted past the reception room of LaCour *et al.* When he accompanied Lovingood there, he was directed to a small chair by the window by black-shawled Mrs. LaCour. Through the window, Jordan admired the black Chrysler Imperials of the firm.

The cars were parked precisely in quiet dignity. In imitation, Jordan aligned his feet on the wine-colored carpet of the cool reception room.

Madame LaCour was a handsome woman. Stoic, gray-eyed, graying, pale. Indeed, LaCour, Fortune & Wingate appeared to be an establishment of light-skinned people. Jordan believed he had seen all three of the principals at one time or another. But he couldn't tell which was Wingate, which was Fortune. He assumed that the tall, pipe-smoking man in the black sweater who greeted Lovingood most of the time was LaCour. The tall man was very fair with curly hair graying discreetly at the sides. He had a look of youth about him despite his obvious seniority.

77

His face was an adolescent's, though lined at mouth and eyes. LaCour did not smile, nor did he ever acknowledge Jordan. He greeted Southwall merely with a nod of the head.

The two other men were also fair, though not as fair as the nodder. They smiled at times, said hello, and seemed to follow the graying man. One of them had tousled straight black hair and was pudgy. He possessed a discreet mustache. The other man's hair was slightly coarse, well greased and parted into twin mounds of waves. He seemed the jolliest of the three, if that meant anything in their business. Jordan was tempted to ask Lovingood or the chilly Madame LaCour who was who. But somehow that didn't seem appropriate, discreet. If I ever went into the business, Jordan thought, I would carry myself like the house of LaCour. . . .

"Daydreamin' again, son?"

"Sir?"

Tatum's on the West Side was a storefront. Lewis Funeral Home, on Undertakers Row a few blocks from Williams Brothers, was old but tidy and quite spacious.

Gouty Mrs. Lewis received only a single visit from Lovingood since she wasn't really active in the business. Yet she kept her chapel immaculate (she was painfully dusting when they arrived). The two-story Lewis establishment was mostly chapel. A pitiful, theatrical arrangement of painted and plywood on the far wall encompassed the casket stand representing canopy and valance. The stand was empty. It seemed to ache with emptiness.

Williams Brothers was an augmented, three-story mansion of overstuffed chairs and fringe lamps boasting two kitchenettes for out-of-town mourners with no place to stay. Williams Brothers wasn't as modern as Lovingood's or as elegant as LaCour's. But it compensated for this in comfort and roominess. Apart from Southwall, mustachioed, chubby Billy and Bob Williams and their families were by far the friendliest of the undertakers, and their establishment was as much social hall as funeral home. A gaggle of cousins, aunts, uncles and friends seemed always to be present. At Williams', Jordan relaxed his guard and became a human being. It was all bright and cheery, the Williams Funeral Home. Powder and pastel. Jordan was unable to discover a touch of black anywhere on the grounds—including the funeral cars. They were powder blue with cream interiors.

Jordan liked the Williamses and loathed their style. Give him black, black, black. *Six black horses.*

Even worse than the Williamses', however, was the colorful flamboyance of Fannie L. Fears. Mrs. Fears' hillside redoubt was a new single-story structure, windowless. The Fears establishment was Japanese-decored and painted shocking pink. Pagoda-like roofing and sliding doors gave it an alien, sinister look in a neighborhood of two-story wood-frame houses. The Fears Funeral Home was on the corner of a steep street overlooking Undertakers Row. The length of the building ran parallel to the hill. It was L-shaped, and its entrance faced the white porch of a tiny frame house—Fannie's home next door.

In front of the entranceway stood a long pink marker, marble—not unlike a gravestone. In silver script, the marker proclaimed: "Fears." That was all it said.

There was no mistaking Fannie Fears' favorite color. In and out of the pink garages facing the entranceway, Jordan saw an array of polished pink Cadillacs, fat and heavy with chrome.

"That's ole Fannie for you." Lovingood chuckled. "She's kinda wild, son, but she does a heavy trade, a booming business. Does good work, too. Don't laugh, Brother Jordan. Don't laugh. Fannie'll fool you, son, fool you in a minute. Always remember that."

7

Fannie Fears didn't look or act the way Jordan thought she would. The first time Jordan met her, he took Southwall by on business. "Come on in, come in meet Sister Fannie Fears." Southwall chuckled, pulling Jordan playfully through a sliding door. A dark white-haired man greeted them and informed them that "Fannie" would be in in ten minutes. She was working on a case.

"Ever seen anything like this, son?" Southwall asked, leading Jordan along the pink carpet through various rooms. "All these walls slide, every one of 'em." Lovingood touched a pink wall as if to move it. "Sister Fannie can make anything, any kind of room she wants to, small chapel, slumber, family room. Fine idea, fiiine idea, son. Ain't that somethin'?"

The day of Jordan's initial visit, the walls were arranged in a series of four large slumber rooms leading to a chapel. The chapel was set up for a funeral, with movable pews. Organ music oozed from the walls. Soft white illumination came from hidden recesses. The carpet was deep and soft. Looking in on the sleepers in the various makeshift rooms, Jordan got the impulse to go in and lie down. The inner walls of the units gave each room variety. The outer sides of the walls were pink, giving a unity to the chapel. Here and there the pink was broken by surprisingly tasteful silk screens depicting subtle landscapes. In all, the arrangement gave the place an illusion of being larger than it was. Along the wall were a series of three permanent offices and a passageway behind the chapel.

The old man, Lovingood explained, was a licensed funeral director and embalmer who had been with Fannie more than twenty years. "Did a lot of drinkin' and gamblin' in his time, but he's settled down. Ole Brother Thomas!" and Lovingood laughed to himself until he had to wipe his eyes with the grimy handkerchief he dug from one of his cavernous pockets.

Fannie Lartarska Gorham, so Lovingood's story went, came out of nowhere; nobody knew where she came from, and few knew who she really was. She was a pretty girl. And a girl was all she was when she started waiting on bars in a nightclub on Twelfth Street a long, long time ago. It was at the bar that she met and fell in love with Harlan Fears, a young embalmer who had a reputation with both the ladies and the dice. Fears was a handsome man from somewhere in the East. He wore a black felt fedora and carried a cane. He was an undertaker's undertaker. He took 'em all, handled anything that came along. He used to get so drunk he couldn't stand up, but he still took care of business, and when the Chuck Lewis Funeral Home was on top, Harlan Fears sometimes did two and three a night. Harlan was the best in the business, and as long as he was alive, Fannie didn't have to lift a finger. She had three babies by him. Eventually, however, burning the candles at both ends caught up with Brother Harlan Thaddeus Fears; yes, it did. It almost caught up with him earlier.

There was a man, who's still alive and living in a great big house in total seclusion, Lovingood confided, who was a bigtime gambler, really big-time, back in those good times. Mob connections. An enforcer and collector. Nobody else on the streets dared cross him until Harlan Fears came along. Fears knew no fear, none at all, and before long Fears was going openly with the gambler's wife. One time in July, a hot night, Harlan Fears was leaving C. E. Lewis' by the back way when half a dozen shots rang out. They got him in the stomach. But Harlan lived to tell about it. It took him a long time to get well, but he left the gambler's wife alone. Harlan started drinking heavily after that, about the same time Fannie started limping. No one knows why she started limping. She just did. Her husband curtailed most of his activities and did most of his drinking in the Room at Lewis'. But he loved a good crap game, really loved it, and in a way, it was craps that finally killed him.

It happened in December—one of the bleakest, coldest Decembers Kansas City ever had—cars could hardly get home, the snow was so deep. In those days, all the big undertakers used to get together every now and then for a little game. Some of the most respectable names. Everyone brought a bottle. They even came from Kansas to get in those games. This one year (it was almost Christmas), C. E. Lewis got a frozen case. At least they thought it was frozen. An old winehead who got drunk and passed out in the alley. They found him covered with snow. Harlan Fears personally made the pickup. Harlan put the man on the cooling board down in the basement at Lewis' to let him thaw out and went upstairs to rejoin a game in progress.

They used to stay up all night in those days. Money changed hands in incredible sums. Many a man went broke in those games, but Harlan always held his own. Well, this night they played long and hard, and Harlan was winning. He completely forgot about the case upstairs. But alcohol won't freeze, you know, and after about three hours, that old wino woke up and found himself on the cooling board at Lewis'. He didn't know why he was there; he just knew he had to get out of there. He groped around and finally found the door. Harlan was down on his knees facing the door when that old man came through, red-eyed and soggy as if he had just come from the beyond. Harlan happened to look up just as the man came through the door, and Harlan was so scared he couldn't even cry out. He just gestured toward the door.

The other undertakers took one look at the newcomer and nearly tore the doors down.

Legend has it that Kansas City never saw such a collection of Packards and Hudsons racing down Eighteenth Street before or since. They all got away, though, except Harlan. C. E. Lewis found him the next day, still clutching the dice in his hand, dead as a stone. He had had a heart attack right on the spot.

Fannie Lartarska Gorham Fears was left without a penny. Most people didn't have insurance in those days. And Harlan left a lot of gambling debts. Fannie turned the children over to relatives and took off for Chicago. She worked her way through mortuary school by stripteasing in some pretty notorious speakeasies. It took her two years to get through school because those were hard times and because she sent most of the money back to her children, two girls and a boy. While she was in Chicago, she met the old man who was her employee, and together they came back and opened the Fannie L. Fears Funerals establishment on Undertakers Row along Eighteenth Street just a few blocks from C. E. Lewis, where Harlan had died. Fannie never talked about her husband. And she outlived most of his friends. She was a hard-driving woman; in less than ten years she was rivaling C. E. Lewis. And a few years later she was on top. Nobody knows why; but she had it in for Lewis after Harlan died, and in a way, she pushed old man Lewis into his grave. Wherever Chuck Lewis turned, Fannie had got there first. She was very adept at talking a person out of a body even after he had decided to send it elsewhere. Lewis' business declined before his eyes, and before long he was dead. Some say he died of a broken heart; he lived for his business.

A lot of the old folks said Fannie Fears was the devil herself, a casket snatcher and a grave robber, but she was always nice to Southwall and Clare, who went to school with her oldest daughter. Fannie Fears was always glad to see the kids and give them a word of encouragement. In those days, black was her favorite color. When Southwall was sixteen, he went to work for Fannie Fears as a driver and funeral attendant, and she gave him his first job when he got out of school. Lovingood worked for her eight years until he and a silent partner started the Lovingood Mortuary Incorporated.

Southwall Lovingood remembered Fannie Fears as being as fearless as her husband before her. In the early days when she was first getting started, Fannie didn't have enough money to afford a limousine or ambulance. She drove an old Plymouth, and when she got a call, she'd roll the body up in a blanket, throw it over her shoulder, and walk out of the ill-fated house. Then Fannie Fears would sit the body upright in the front seat, get in next to it, and speed away holding it up with one hand. She handled a body just like a man, and she never "lost" a case.

In later years, Fannie Fears cut her long hair, took to enjoying a frequent cigar, piled on jewelry and makeup to hide her advancing age and developed bizarre tastes that to Lovingood's mind were not always in the best keeping of Funeral Service. But she stood up with the best of them and trained some of the best of them, and that's why you didn't laugh at her pink hearses and limousines.

Jordan expected the legendary funeral woman to be short

and stocky, plastered with makeup, and, for some reason, to have a phony French accent. When the real Fannie entered (to Jordan it seemed rather that she *appeared* in) the hallway by the chapel, he revised his estimation.

One met Fannie L. G. Fears from the bottom up. Fannie made no sound when she walked since she was usually barefoot. The feet were lined with veins, but there were few other signs of age. She wore a high-collared blue-on-blue silk brocade dress slit up the side. It was the most elegant dress Jordan had ever seen. The slits revealed lithe, shapely, luscious legs. Fannie was well proportioned, no doubt of that. Her curves were pleasing, and her bust was attractive without being overpresent. She was the kind of woman a young man worked up to. Fannie Fears was tallish with braided, dark, dyed hair. What impressed Jordan most about her, however, were the intense, bright eyes in her gaunt face. The gauntness and thinness of her face, her burning eyes and the wideness of her mouth gave Fannie the look of a disciplined animal—a horse.

She spoke first to Jordan: "Come here, baby. What's your name?" Her voice was alto, honey-toned.

"This is young Bro' Jordannnn," Southwall cut in.

"Well, I declare!" Fannie shouted. "Sure is a pretty child."

"This is Clare's child, Fannie, Clarisse Walker."

"Do tell?" Fannie arched an eyebrow. She winked at Jordan. "Knew your mother when she was just a pup. Well, boy, you come back 'n' see me, hear? You come on back, hear?" The eyes were bright and dancing. What they said made Jordan blush, and he was thankful that the eyes had lingered on him only for a moment, then flashed to Lovingood. That woman could devour a full-grown man.

She said to Lovingood, "What's on your mind, darlin'?" and they went in the back to talk. Jordan waited in an office, entertaining himself by reading a back issue of *Mid-Continent Mortician*. Fannie and Lovingood were in the back a long time. Jordan heard them laughing and joking in loud voices. Southwall smelled of alcohol when he got back. "Come on, son," he said, "got to catch Brother Williams before he gets out on the streets. Won't see him till Tuesday otherwise." It was an in joke. Fannie shrieked.

84

Jordan stood by a sliding door to let Lovingood pass, then started out it himself. Suddenly Fannie Fears reached out and grasped his elbow. Her grip was like pliers. "Southwall?" she called out. "Southwall! What you got this boy doin'? Got him workin' funerals?"

"Well, yeah. Reception 'n' drivin'. No services yet."

"Well, honey?"

"Huh?"

"You get this child on services, hear? Let him work a couple. Put him up front where he can be seen. Hear?" And eyeing Jordan: "This boy's good-lookin'. If you know what I mean."

And for a moment, her grip tightened, and Jordan felt her cool breath on his cheek. "You come back and see me, hear, son? Southwall! I like this boy, hear? Put him up there. This boy's gonna do something someday."

"It's strange, son . . ." Southwall Lovingood mused back at the office. "Really strange. Fannie don't take to just anybody, never did. Man, she never took to anybody like that since she took to me. Thought you had a fine appearance, a fine look. Yes, sir, a look. Come to think of it, you might not look bad at a funeral. . . ."

A few days later, Lovingood informed Jordan he was upgrading him to funeral assistant. "Still want you to work reception," said Lovingood. "Drive the family car, too. Soon's you get 'em signed in now, you come on in the chapel. I think ole Sister Fears's right, son. Think you gonna be a real asset to Funeral Service, a real asset." Lovingood cuffed the young man. "Brother Jor-dannnnn!" And waddled off.

Lawrence Xavier Jordan stood at the head. It gave him a feeling of importance to stand there, rocking invisibly on his heels. He had some meaning in life. It was like giving a party every week. Here he was, Lawrence Jordan, neat as a mannequin in his blue serge suit. Trousers continental cut. Hair close-cropped, gold tooth polished. He was growing strong and tall, and he was not a bad-looking young man. A little thin, perhaps, and a little unsure (a pro could see it). But he was getting there. Suave and urbane. Sympathetic. He tried to imagine what he must look like to the audiences, that ever-changing list of guests who came to be entertained at the Party. Because entertaining was what it was.

On his second funeral out, Jordan met Sister Carrie Samuels. It was she who gave him the insight that funerals were entertaining.

Jordan was in his appointed place, staring stoically ahead as the audience filed past the casket to view the last remains. The choir was humming softly. The family mourning tearfully. Lovingood at his post at the end of the aisle, directing the mourners. Major Bates at the feet, nodding to the line. Sister Carrie Samuels, stooped and wrinkled, was in the line. "Oh, oh, oh," Carrie Samuels bellowed. "Oh, my, oh, my." The line stopped. Carrie Samuels stood over the body, almost leering, looking down with a strange little smile. "Oh, *Je*-Zus, *Je*-Zus Lord. He's with You now. With You in Paradise." Her skeletal fingers trembled over the veil at the head of the box.

Bates nodded to Jordan, indicating that this one had to go. Get her moving. Now. "Yes, ma'am, yes, ma'am," Jordan said, firmly removing Miss Samuels' grip on the coffin. "Yes, ma'am. He's resting now in the—he's resting now. It's all right."

Carrie Samuels relaxed completely in Jordan's arms. He began turning her away from the casket. Her body turned with his, effortlessly. Momentarily, he stiffened. She was wearing a little white cap. Her eyes were yellowed. Her breath stank of salmon croquette or tuna fish. The eyes ran over Jordan's face like the fingers had flitted over the veil. "Oh, you done such a fine job on him, Brother Livingood," she whispered to Jordan, resisting. "Fiiine job." And turning back to the box: "Looks just like he's sleeping. Sleeping. He was tired, and he went on to sleep. . . ."

He finally got Miss Carrie Samuels down the aisle. A few days later she was back again. Then two weeks later. She was the queen of the vulturesses, the hangers-on—and there were plenty of them. One or two at every funeral. Always they were little old ladies, usually attired in the white dress and cap of the Pentecostal church mother. Lingering head shakers. They were not long for this world, and in the demise of others they found solace. Their trademark was the inevitable comment "Looks like she just sleepin', honey, just fallen on asleep!" Vicariously, they participated in their own deaths. Impatient for the grave, they accompanied others there—at least to the edge. And they longed to go over the precipice themselves. Is there a premonition of death, a kind of sixth sense that informs us of impending surcease so that we may prepare? A death-wish mechanism that, tripped, eases us into the change? Such thoughts frightened Jordan. He had to be stoic. He stood at the head. He had to control himself: If the undertaker cries, is there balm in Gilead?

The vulturesses usually got in a couple of funerals before it was their turn to be guest of honor. Sister Carrie Samuels, however, seemed to live on in perpetuity. She made every funeral she could, and she always leaned on Jordan—not on Bates or Lovingood. Southwall found this preference amusing. "Well, Brother Jordan"—he chuckled one day—"looks like you got your first customer, son, the first one. Sister Samuels ain't gonna die until you're ready for her. Mark my words now." Jordan tried to tell himself that he felt sorry for Carrie Samuels. But he didn't. The truth was more unnerving: He identified with her.

The fawnlike eyes of Lawrence Xavier Jordan took in everything in Funeral Service, and he filed away his impressions for future reference. Southwall Lovingood told Bates that Jordan learned faster than anyone he'd ever known.

Accordingly, Lovingood intensified his indoctrination of Lawrence Jordan. Jordan was instructed to extend certain of his observations of the vulturesses to the entire funeral ensemble. This was the key to controlling the service and therefore profits. The key word was "control." "First, there's your own self-control," Southwall Lovingood pontificated. "This lets 'em know that Lovingood's is in charge, gives it some kind of meaning, something for folks to relate to. The most important reason for Funeral Service—next to hygiene—is creating a memory picture that the loved ones can take away with them. This picture remains in the unconscious and is often called to mind, son, years later in time of trial or tribulation. How the funeral director acts, what he says, the way he says it, are all part of this picture. A funeral must have order, an order of unfolding. Listen, Brother Jordannn: It's like a rose. You seen pictures of how a flower grows—first it's all bunched up like this 'n' next the tips of the petals push through like this? 'N' then it's a full-

87

grown rose? Well, son, a service is like that. It *unfolds*. The control of all factors of Funeral Service—your reception, your music, your eulogy, the appearance of your case and coffin, your manner (firm but calm, now!)—the control of all these things is how you make that rose unfold. . . ."

Yes, Funeral Service was mighty interesting.

Indeed, it had its moments of pure ecstasy. Jordan's most memorable moment in these early years came during a service at Ebenezer Baptist Church. When Brother Willis T. Pate, Private First Class, United States Marine Corps, passed away in a tragic auto accident in San Diego, Southwall Lovingood was retained to put the boy away. In style. Young Pate had been with Ebenezer since before he was born—as Southwall put it. His mother sang in the choir. His father was a deacon. An older sister taught Sunday school. Young Pate himself was close to the pastor, Reverend Carlee Slide. Wanted to be a minister himself. A fine family. Fiiine family. And they had a little money.

It was Jordan's biggest funeral so far. He had never seen so many flowers. They filled up the chapel and overflowed into the vestibule. Southwall bought a new suit (which on him looked as rumpled as the old one) especially for the occasion. There was a wake, which Jordan didn't attend, and a service in the four-hundred-seat sanctuary of Ebenezer. The fifty-voice Ebenezer Wings of Love choir sang, sans the grieving Mrs. Pate. A perspiring Reverend Slide delivered the eulogy—and a lengthy sermon on the evils of drinking besides. Southwall had brought in a housewife who sometimes acted as "hostess" on big funerals, a fourth driver, and a motorcycle escort.

Jordan became immersed in the splendor.

With the closed casket of Pfc. Pate at his feet and the choir singing behind him, Reverend Slide, a very black man with snow-white hair, stretched out his arms:

"Whatsoever Gawd giveth, Gawd also taketh away. For a while, just a little while, he gave us Brother Willis T. Pate, gave him to us to love and cherish—oh, yeah!—and to share. Now he's taken young Brother Willis back. No, not taken—*called*. Called him home. And I say to the family today, I say to this fiiiiine, fine family today: Let your soul be comforted. Let your sooooooooul be comforted! Comfort this fine family

88

today, Lord. Ease their sorrows. Hear us, Jezus! Hear us, Gawd! Young Brother Pate's just gone on to Bright Glory!"

Amen, Amen, Amen. Amen, Amen.

Part of Jordan's job was to administer the smelling salts to anyone who passed out. With Reverend Slide orating and the ceiling fans of Ebenezer failing, Jordan kept busy. It was a long funeral and a long viewing line. Handkerchief in hand, Southwall Lovingood mopped his brow and kept the line moving. The heat was telling on Lovingood, who had to loosen his tie and open his coat. Lovingood's shirt was soaked with perspiration, and the imprints of his huge breasts showed through. Major Bates remained cool. But Jordan could see that the long standing was taking its toll on Bates as well.

Jordan was nodding encouragement to Bates halfway through the viewing when it happened. What looked like a commotion broke out in the pews. It was a fighter; Jordan had seen this several times now. Someone so overcome with grief he flailed about with hands and feet, striking those around them. For the safety of the others, such a person had to be revived with salts immediately. Or removed. Mourners returning to their seats crowded the aisle opposite Lovingood, and the part-time "hostess" was no match for them. She looked at Jordan with distress. Gently nudging his way through the crowd, Jordan pushed toward the source of the trouble: a stout young woman dressed entirely in black, eyes shut tightly, fists flailing the back of an elderly man in the pew in front. Asking one of the younger men to assist him, Jordan tried to hold the woman and put the salts under her nose. But she struck Jordan on the forehead, mussing his hair.

"Take the legs," Jordan ordered his assistant. "Move outside!" The speed with which he made the decision surprised Jordan. Over the heads of the mourners, he could see Southwall nodding approval.

They placed the woman on the back seat of a limousine parked behind the waiting hearse. The woman sprawled on the seat, moaning. Her skirt was short. Her thighs were plump. Jordan thanked the man for his help and got in the car beside her. He reached for his stick of smelling salt. The woman caught him off guard; he had one hand in his suit coat pocket and the other braced against the seat. The woman suddenly jerked upright, flung her wide-brimmed black hat into the recess of the back window and locked both ample arms around Lawrence Jordan's neck. She kissed Lawrence Jordan, probing his mouth with her tongue. And he let her. He really dug that.

Major Bates sent someone out to get Jordan back on funeral duty.

The woman was Thessalonica Wingate, twenty-two, daughter of the third member of LaCour and Company. A luscious plum. Pint-sized, well padded, and very hot. Thessalonica was shaped like Clare and had the same long, wavy hair. She had seen Jordan from a distance and liked something about him; she guessed it was his style. She had just come home from college and needed a steady friend. Would Jordan be it?

Jordan invited Thessalonica Wingate out for a Sunday's drive. She met him after church at Lovingood's, and they rode very fast across town in Lovingood's best funeral coach. They sat on the grass of the cliffs by the river; they shared a malt together at a drive-in. They slipped into the reception room at LaCour, Fortune & Wingate and kissed warmly. Thess put Jordan's hand under her dress, but Jordan felt uncomfortable in enemy territory. Nervously, he asked her if she would like to see the chapel at Lovingood's. She said she would. Most definitely.

Lovingood's was darkened. Thess Wingate said she didn't need the light. They sat in the front pew in the chapel, looking at the church truck, exploring each other with trembling hands. They professed the usual undying emotions, and Jordan told Thess Wingate how he chanced to be working in the funeral business.

The sun was setting. They began telling each other secrets which grew more intimate as shadows lengthened across the room.

"I don't know what's wrong with me," Jordan whispered, fingering Thess' vulva. "I have this *thing*."

"What thing, baby?"

"I dunno. . . . a crazy thing."

He jumped. She was touching his organ. Her eyes were glazed. She whispered, "Tell me."

"Well, I've been wanting to . . . kind of . . . *do it* in the limousine. And in the mortuary."

A long, long silence. Then Thess laughed, tossing back her hair: "I've wanted to screw on a church truck. And inside a casket."

She got up and rubbed the velvet church truck. Jordan put his arms around her waist and mouthed her neck.

"Get on it," he commanded.

It was good; he liked it. He liked it in the silk-lined casket, too. He *really* liked it in that casket.

8

"It's just where we treat the body for purposes of preservation and dress it and casket it," Southwall Lovingood hummed. He was eating a sandwich.

"But can I see it?" Jordan begged.

"Not much to see, son, not a lot to see. Just some tools and things, the tools of our trade, you know."

"Please?"

"Got a case in there now."

"Is it ready?"

"No, not quite. It's still . . . firming up."

"Is it covered up?"

"Well, yes."

"Please?"

They went into the Room, passing through a narrow hallway. Jordan saw two smocks, a rubber apron and a pair of latex gloves hanging on pegs in the hallway. Beneath the apron was a pair of rubber boots.

The Room was frigid. On a metal table with rounded ends lay a still form under a peaked sheet. Lovingood moved to the table and lifted the sheet. Under it was the waxen head of an elderly man with the stiff and flattened look of the dead. The head was propped upon a rubber block. The face was very dark but caked with a milky substance, a hideous contrast. Jordan felt weightless. Lovingood reached out and resmeared the white on the corpse's temple, all the while still eating his sandwich. "Cold cream," the undertaker said, sensing Jordan's alarm. Jordan tried to appear unimpressed.

"Cold cream prevents excessive dehydration," Lovingood said.

Jordan walked religiously. If he made sounds when he walked or even breathed too loudly, he was afraid it might upset the atmosphere of the place.

It was a large, well-ventilated room with a green-tiled floor. Jordan heard the whir of an invisible fan. In one way it was a pleasant place to be, away from the hot air of summer. Lovingood's thick hand pointed to a porcelain table abutting a small sink. The table was tilted slightly downward from the sink. "This is the preparation table," Lovingood said. This larger slab was parallel to the aluminum table with the case on it. You walked between the tables to get to the door. Where the metal table was was another entrance, this one with double doors. Jordan knew immediately what that was for. Parked in front of that door was a strapped cot on rollers. It seemed to be expecting someone at any moment.

Lovingood walked around the porcelain table by pressing down on it with both hands and throwing his great weight around to one side. Jordan had the impression that this was Lovingood's usual method of getting from the table to the white metal cabinets facing it. Lovingood flung open one cabinet. Inside were neat rows of bottles and jars. Jordan read the lables of the bottles: Frigid, Champion, Bondall-embalming fluids. And there were bottles of cavity fluid ("A stronger concentration for tougher places," Lovingood explained), firming fluid, water conditioners. In a series of small jars were dusting powders of various shades, cold creams, skin bleaches and makeup. In other boxes were bottles and ordinary materials: detergents and disinfectants. Also at the bottom: a hairbrush. Lovingood opened another cabinet, twin to the first. Here on porcelain tiers were laid out the instruments of the Surgery itself: shiny needles and long rubber tubes, forceps and scissors, scalpels and hemostats, hypodermics and syringes. In the bottom of this cabinet was an untidy pile of braces and blocks, one of the latter corresponding to the head block Jordan had seen under the corpse.

"How do you do the embalming?" Jordan asked.

"We raise the arteries and veins," Lovingood replied, wiping mayonnaise from his fingers with a rag. "We pump the fluid in through the arteries, and it pushes the blood out through the veins into the sink.

"The fluid, most of it, remains in the vascular system, soaking the tissues, preserving the body. Sorta cooks it."

Lovingood showed Jordan the pump and the gravity apparatus, which were kept in a small closet. The pump consisted of a large glass vat resting on a square of metal containing several dials and a pressure gauge. The gravity setup was merely a tall pole mounted on a squat tripod.

"How do you raise an artery?" Jordan asked.

"Well now," Lovingood said, rolling the pump back into the closet. "You have to make an incision and—But maybe I'll confuse you, young Brother Jor-dannn, telling you too much at one time. Takes time, tiiime, son, to learn what it's all about. Not as simple as you may think. Undertaker's got to be like a doctor in some ways. Got to know a lot, son, before you can work in a room like this."

"Is embalming a secret process?"

"Wouldn't say that, son. It's not *widely* known, but those who're *called* go to school and learn it."

"Could I learn it?"

"Oh, you will, son, you will, Brother Jordannn!" And he cuffed Jordan halfway across the room—nearly on top of the sheeted case.

Afterward Jordan was admitted to the Room. Indeed, he began to work in the preparation room, as well as the offices and chapel and display room. He now had free run of the entire funeral home. He was barred from the prep room during "operations," of course, but as soon as the embalming was done, he was admitted to help ready the body for showing. For the summer, Jordan was working at Lovingood's full time, and in addition to his reception, chapel and chauffeuring duties, he was assigned to help with the manicuring, dressing and casketing of the cases.

All the cases Jordan was allowed to work on, however, were "naturals." Trauma—distortion and mutilation—was forbidden. Southwall said he owed it to Clare not to expose Jordan to something that might upset him. He raised this argument when Jordan came to him, begging to see the charred body of a man whose wife had doused him with coal oil and flipped a match at him. Jordan begged Lovingood just to let him see the case before it was sealed in a closed coffin. Lovingood looked deeply at Jordan, his heart obviously at odds with his mind. He tramped off into the preparation room and came back, shaking his head. "No; much as I'd like to," Lovingood said. "Better leave things the way they are. He's pretty messed up. And you're a long way from case-hardened."

Jordan swore quietly. It couldn't be that bad.

Lovingood liked to get together with Bates and reminisce over the old days on Friday evenings. Often Jordan was allowed to sit in. It was during one of these sessions that the coroner brought in a woman who had dropped dead while trying to board a public bus that afternoon. Sleepy Major Bates answered the buzzer. Bates came running back into the office wide awake and out of breath. "Southwall, Southwall," he panted. "You better look at *this*." Lovingood rolled from his chair, and Jordan started to follow him; but Lovingood signaled the boy to remain still. The big man lumbered off after Bates, and Jordan heard Bates blurt the word "dropsy" in the hall.

Lovingood floundered back to his office, sweating. "Better go on home, Brother Jordannn," he said. His eyes were redder than usual. He fumbled in the drawer of his desk. Bates came in. "Go on home, Brother Jor-dannn!" Lovingood snapped.

Jordan begged to stay. "I think I'm ready," Jordan said. Lovingood glowered at him.

"Let the boy come on," Bates broke in. "Let's just get in there."

Lovingood reached in the drawer. "Here," he told Jordan gruffly. "Finish it." He handed Jordan what was left of a fifth of bourbon, Early Times. "Kill it all."

Jordan was high, and the Room was good and warm and benevolent. Down through his stupor Jordan saw a gray head on the cot by the door. Lovingood motioned for him to take hold and he did, nearly stumbling. They moved her to the porcelain table. Bates adjusted the slab, and Lovingood cut the clothes away with a pair of scissors.

Jordan sobered instantly. He backed away from the slab, his mind refusing to deal with the reality it took in. He tried to think of other things: sunshine, pretty girls, ice-cream cones.

Lovingood began rolling the head of the corpse between his

huge hands to relieve rigor mortis. "Don't touch her, son," the mortician warned over his shoulder, unaware that Jordan had no such intention. "Those swollen legs could go on us at any moment."

Lovingood's broad back hunched over the body. He was analyzing it, seeking an approach; then he made a decision. "Bates, elevate those legs," he ordered. And to Jordan: "Boy, hand me a knife and stand back."

Jordan froze. He stared at the scalpels in the supply cabinet but couldn't make himself move toward them. Bates saw what was happening and got one of the instruments. He plopped the knife in Southwall's hand.

Jordan turned his face, but his ears took in what his eyes avoided.

Bates, himself grimacing, cautioned Lovingood: "Get the boy outta here. He's seen enough for one day."

The undertaker, pouring sweat, looked up from the corpse. He had a look of bother on his face, nothing more. "Yeah," he said. "Better go on home now, Brother Jordannn, get along now. Be sure and wash up before you go. See you tomorrow."

Jordan didn't wash. He stumbled out through the foyer, confused, drained, raw. He was halfway home before he realized that he had taken the first step toward being case-hardened.

9

Southwall Lovingood was a friendly, compassionate child. Clare remembered that he always had a kind word for everyone. Southwall lived on East Twenty-sixth around the corner from Clare; she couldn't remember when she met him; they played together as little children. Southwall was happy-go-lucky; she remembered that. The other kids made fun of him. They thought he wasn't bright. And Southwall did have an odd air about him, a way of going around smiling to himself when nothing was funny. And a certain far-off look owing to an eye disorder that gave him the appearance of looking through everyone. Also, he was not fast to anger. Many a person took advantage of Southwall Lovingood for years at a time before Southwall lost his temper. This gave him the appearance of being naïve and even stupid. Yet Southwall Lovingood went on his way. He even seemed to get happier and happier. He began smiling, and he'd probably die laughing. It was hard to understand. The parents, real elderly people, were inordinately strict. Clare remembered Southwall's father beating the boy so long and hard that Clare was moved to tears. Southwall rarely went to the moving pictures and even less frequently attended a party or school social event. "He stayed off to himself a lot; he was not a *big* child. Stocky, yes. But he always did like to eat." That was one thing about old man Lovingood—whatever else his faults, he couldn't stand to see a child go hungry, and as a result, little Southwall never wanted for bread. The parents literally gorged the child with food. And he grew and grew until he was playing tackle on the Lincoln High team and going with a big honey-colored girl named Maybelle Hanley. That was his first wife, Clare said. Tragic: she died years ago, right after the baby. Natal complications. In those days, Clare's best friend was Fannie Fears' oldest daughter, and Clare used to go out of her way to walk the girl home every day. Clare was fascinated with the stories Fannie told about the funeral business. Southwall walked with Clare and the Fears girl one day to Mrs. Fears'. The Fearses had their old place in those days, down on the Row. The oldest girl used to help her mother at the shop. Southwall didn't know any of the Fears children then, and Clare couldn't understand why he walked with them that day. Maybe he didn't either. But after that, it became a regular habit. He walked with them once or twice a week. One thing: However many times he walked with them, he always walked down there on Fridays. Invariably. Fannie Fears was always nice to them, very nice. She had a kind word for everyone, even Southwall, and whenever she was around, Fannie Fears always found time to talk to the young people about their plans and their futures. Fannie had a way about her. Clare thought she was just about the most sophisticated lady in town in those days. "Just had a way about her."

Anyway, Clare didn't remember Southwall ever saying five words to Fannie at a time, and the next thing she knew, Southwall was working down at Fears every day after school. Quit the football team. Got a car. Didn't walk the girls anymore, but he was glad to give them a ride. Southwall was getting bigger. He must have weighed almost two hundred in those days.

For some reason, Clare expected Southwall to become more somber after he started with Mrs. Fears. Why'd she think that? If anything, Southwall became even more happy-go-lucky. A lot of times on Saturdays, Clare would be going down the street and who'd drive up alongside her but Southwall asking in that shrill voice of his, "Where ya headin', Little Bit?" Clare'd jump in, and he'd take her wherever she wanted to go. Never talked about his work. Southwall Lovingood was a swell fellow, swell. Maybe not the most cultured, but sure a friendly, happy soul. In a way, he was well suited for his chosen profession. After all, an undertaker was supposed to bring comfort to the bereaved, wasn't he?

Southwall graduated a year before she did, and Clare didn't see him except occasionally at Mrs. Fears'. Hardworking boy, did a lot of heavy work. Kept that place immaculate. When

Clare graduated—carrying Lawrence—she was embarrassed and unhappy. A lot of her friends turned against her. Southwall Lovingood came to her graduation, and afterward he took Clare and her mother out to the biggest dinner Clare had ever seen. A fancy place. And Southwall achieved the impossible: He cheered Clare up, cheerfully predicted that Francis Jordan would marry her before the year was out. Which he did, that snake. Clare would always remember what Southwall said that night, right in front of her mother: "If he don't want you, I'll marry you, Little Bit. But I'll wager that he does." Soon after, Southwall went up to Chicago to study funeral science. Clare heard he'd had a terrible argument with his father over that, and for years they hardly spoke; but old man Lovingood finally died being just as proud of his son as a father could be. In those last years they had been quite close, and Southwall hardly missed a day running over to see his father, who was confined to a wheelchair. Southwall really put his father away in style. Clare didn't even see Southwall when he got back from school. He was home only a few months—just long enough to marry Maybelle Hanley—and he was in Europe. The Army claimed him.

Major Bates remembered that Southwall had a distinguished military career: "Really distinguished. Southwall served in the Quartermaster Corps. Burial detail. They were just diggin' holes and pushing 'em all in with caterpillar tractors, there were so many of 'em. Southwall handled mass burial details, as well as the embalmin' of high-rankin' officers. He did such a fine job that he was given a special decoration after the war. The Congressional Medal or somethin' close to it."

The most striking features about Southwall were his immense size and his light voice. Jordan's memories of Southwall seemed to be shaping around these two facets: In his mind's eye Jordan could see Southwall as a giant hulk of a man with rounded shoulders, shaking with laughter, puffing up stairs, skirting a casket. Southwall's appetite was voracious. He was fond of greasy foods and often brought in a soiled bag of neckbones or chitterlings and greens, which he consumed in great quantities in his office or even in the preparation room.

Lovingood's consumption was large when it came to other appetites too. Since the time that she lived in the Jordans'

99

apartment building, Psyche Lovingood had been called upon to have three more children, and Jordan heard she was expecting number four. Southwall was known to have a taste for bourbon, good or bad, and Jordan frequently was asked to search out a favorite haunt to find the obese undertaker and bring him back to duty. The doctor had warned Southwall several times about both his drinking and eating habits. Too much of a strain on the heart. Southwall, however, good-naturedly thanked the doctor and came immediately back to the funeral home with a carry-out order of pig's feet and pinto beans, polishing off the meal with a swig of Early Times. Jordan wondered if Southwall's eternally bloodshot eyes were the result of long drinking—or lack of sleep. Lovingood had no real hours; he seemed to work around the clock. He could doze anywhere, and doze was all he did, except on Sundays, when he slept all day. Jordan remembered dropping Southwall off at home early one Sunday morning after an emergency call. "Come on in, Brother Jordannn," Lovingood puffed, dropping into an easy chair. Southwall folded his hands over his bloated tummy and sighed. Jordan hadn't sat down yet when he heard the snoring. Sheepishly, the boy tiptoed out to the car. Psyche Lovingood told Jordan the next morning that Southwall had slept for ten hours straight.

Southwall's size wasn't a hindrance in his business. When Jordan first met him—long before he came to work for Southwall—he had the mistaken notion of the fat man barely getting around in the funeral home; grotesque, out-of-place, physically unsuited for his profession. Now Jordan knew better. One day, Jordan was forcing gloves on the rigid fingers of a female case that must have had a dead weight of a hundred and forty pounds. Southwall waddled over, the corners of his white smock dangling behind his bulbous thighs. "Come on, son," Southwall said, "help me lift her into the box." Jordan moved toward his allotted place at the legs. Meanwhile, however, Southwall got the top of the cadaver into his great arms and began to lift it. He was huffing and puffing. But no more than usual. Stooping slightly, Lovingood began rounding the slab toward the adjacent casket. He was intent in his work. "Easy now, easy now, son," Southwall was saying to Jordan, a signal to the boy to turn slowly with the legs. But Jordan wasn't lifting the legs. He wasn't lifting anything. He was too awed. Southwall had lifted the body by himself and now, with only a grip on the torso, was single-handedly maneuvering it into the silk-lined box. Southwall never knew that Jordan hadn't helped him lift the body. And Jordan was too frightened to tell him.

A few days after that, Jordan first dreamed about Southwall Lovingood. This same dream—or variations on it—was to repeat itself many times: Jordan and Southwall were sitting in the reception office saying nothing, just watching each other. There was no overt hostility between them. The day before, they had buried a case—the last one left in the world. Everybody else had died, and Jordan and Lovingood had survived them all. Now they were waiting each other out. Jordan felt secure in his youth. He could afford to wait. Why was Southwall waiting? He was old and fat and sick, and he should have been able to see that it was Jordan's show from here on. It was very difficult for just the two of them to handle yesterday's case. Not only did they have to prepare the body. They also had to conduct the funeral service, read the eulogy and mourn for it. Then they had to drive out to the cemetery with it and dig the grave. It took them hours to find a suitable site; every available corner and crevice had been used up. Now they seemed to wait for eternity. Neither said anything, but both knew what the other was thinking. This would prove which one was the greatest undertaker in the world. The greatest was he who buried the last man, his fellow. At one point, Jordan would be having doubts about himself: Perhaps Southwall was the greatest after all. Maybe he knew something Jordan didn't? Had there been an epidemic? Perhaps Jordan had the disease, and Southwall was immune to it; perhaps Jordan's number was next. They waited. Jordan felt tired, very tired. Then, just as Jordan's head began to fall forward, Southwall's huge body rolled over and thudded to the floor. Southwall was dead. Jordan had waited him out. The rest happened so quickly, but there was Jordan with a saw and hammer and nails, splicing two coffins together. A crude job, but it had to be done. Ingeniously, he got the big man's body into the joined boxes. He wheeled it into the chapel and went around to play the organ. Opposite the organ window, there was a gaping hole in the wall. At that point, the dream ended.

Jordan told Southwall one day: "Brother Lovingood, man, when you go—if you ever do go—they're gonna have to put you in a special box and cut a hole in the wall to get you to the hearse." Lovingood just chuckled, shaking with fat, and said he 'spected they would.

Southwall enjoyed mixing facial makeup, and some of Jordan's fondest memories of his employer were of the big bearlike apparition, his eyes red as blood, his face so black it was nearly blue like a fine mass of tan clay accidentally baked too long, haphazardly besmocked, humming a little tune to the ever-present radio, delicately mixing powder in a hammy hand. It contrasted so with his size, Southwall's infinite care in mixing the facial appliqué. And he dusted it on with so much tenderness, so much patience that Jordan was moved to notice that Southwall had a number of feminine traits about him, not the least of which was his incredibly high-pitched voice.

Whenever he got excited, Southwall's voice shot up two octaves. Sometimes he really sounded as if he were singing. The voice contrasted with the size and appearance even more than did the size with the mixing of face powder. But Southwall was also eloquent, and somehow the voice was right for the eloquence to come through.

Southwall was a comforter, a caresser. He had a penchant for saying just the right thing at the right time to the preachers and churchgoers and hangers-on who were the major players on his stage and the most important characters in his world. Indeed, Major Bates often told Lovingood that Lovingood could have been a preacher if he had heard the call. One of the hangers-on at Lovingood's was a woman Jordan knew only by the name of Sister Lottie. Small, stooped-over and wizened, Sister Lottie was a toothless old acquaintance of Lovingood who never failed to come in to the office the day after a funeral, plunk a passel of homegrown mustard greens on Southwall's desk or compliment the mortician on what a "fine" job he'd done on dear Brother So-and-so. Southwall took it all in stride. Indeed, Jordan believed Southwall actually looked forward to the comings and goings of Sister Lottie. When Lottie's light step was heard on the doorway, Southwall was already halfway out into the hall, greeting the old woman: "Hey, hey, Sister Lot-tie! Hey, girl!" And Lovingood would take the old bag of bones in his huge arms, literally lift her off the carpet and squeeze her so hard that Major Bates would wince. For some minutes, Southwall would stand wide-legged in the hall, hugging Lottie to him, greens and all, rocking her in his ample bosom, cooing to her in his best soprano. Like a little satiated bird back in the nest at last, Lottie would relax in Lovingood's grip, her eyelids would flutter then close over yellow eyes, and she would appear to be asleep, enclosed on three sides by the mass of the city's leading undertaker, and Southwall's strange voice cooed: "Aw, Lottie, Lottie, Lot-tie. . . ." Involuntarily, Jordan himself would begin to rock, and more than once, he found himself wishing Southwall would take him in his arms and coo like that.

Lovingood would talk to the bodies. Jordan had heard him conversing quietly with so many cases that it wasn't even novel anymore. "Yeah, Brother Wil-yams," he'd hear Southwall breathing behind him in the prep room, "gonna fix you up real nice now." Or in the chapel, Southwall limping to the occupant of a quiet casket, observing: "Well, Sister Mac-Roy, gonna read some words over you tomorrow." And he would brush her hair.

Lovingood was truly concerned with the comfort of his charges, and it was this empathy, this rapport with the unapproachable, that kept Jordan from hating Southwall the day the undertaker told him what they did to Francis Jordan.

They were working on a body, and Jordan recalled that Clare said his father was buried by Fannie Fears. "Oh, yeah, oh, yeah," Lovingood mused, resting his rubber-gloved hands on the case's thigh. "Very traumatic case, your father. Someone shot the head off, demolished the back of the skull. It was almost Christmas as I recollect. Shipped him from Chicago. They'd done piecework on the skull up there. But they just left ole Frank in pieces. I did the best job I could, you know. Removed the whole head from the body. But I never got it back together right."

Clare got angry with her son that night because Jordan wouldn't touch the dinner she prepared.

"Ole Southwall"—Major Bates chuckled—"will take 'em all. Just give him a syringe and a bottle of formalin, son, and he'll take 'em *all*. Blind, crippled 'n' crazy. Natural, trauma, decomposition."

Southwall never bragged; he left that to Bates. If any generalization could be made about Southwall Lovingood, it was that he was a study in contrasts—the voice and the size, the concern and the callousness, the success and the simple tastes. Jordan figured that Lovingood's income must have been far above that of most people in the community. Yet the man wore the same blue suit most of the time. The suit was slick with age. And as far as Jordan knew, Lovingood had only one pair of shoes—a wrinkly pair of knob-toed kangaroos with a hole in the sole of the right shoe. The shoes were so old they were worn down in the arches. In some ways, Jordan was ashamed of Southwall at funerals; his employer's attire often contrasted in quality with even Jordan's clothes. And those of Bates, an immaculate man. Jordan wondered if Southwall knew the meaning of the word "impeccable."

The first day Jordan went home with Lovingood, he expected to find a mansion containing a well-appointed living room with a huge mirror over the fireplace and tapestried divans so expensive and delicate they were kept under plastic covers when not in use. Instead, Jordan found a ramshackle bungalow on a corner in a neighborhood he would be ashamed to live in. There was nothing striking about the house: It had no yard to speak of, just a patch of weeds and well-worn dirt. On the porch were several children, including the little Lovingood offspring. Southwall's kids were easily identified—short, matted hair, the same burnt-cork skin, the fey smiles and yellow eyes. And they were fat and ugly. There were two infants there, and one, obviously a Lovingood, had an undershirt but no bottoms. All the children were covered with dust (Clare used to spank Jordan for getting like that) and very noisy. They hardly interrupted their play for Lovingood, who happily stepped in and among them on his way through the peeling door which was standing ajar, admitting all and any flies. To Lovingood, the children also were Sister and Brother, and the big man greeted them just as if he were talking to his most mature customers: "Hey, Sister Jo-Anne, how you doin'? How's the family?" The children seemed to like Lovingood and accept his being there on the porch. Nor, for that matter, did they seem impressed by the swank limousine he pulled up in. One thing: They were all well fed.

The living-room furniture looked as if Lovingood had picked it up at a secondhand sale, which he had. The stuffing was emerging from numerous punctures in the divan, and Lovingood's easy chair was positively grimy. About the only things elegant in the house were the huge icebox (brand-new) and Psyche Lovingood's new dress, which she wore with bare feet. Without a doubt, Lovingood had taste in fabrics—even if he didn't apply it to himself. Mrs. Lovingood always dressed well, and it was a joke with Major Bates how Southwall fussed over the draperies for the chapel when they first got the funeral home. Southwall tooled around town in gleaming black limousines, but when he was off and Psyche wasn't using it, he usually drove his rusty old Plymouth. Lovingood would pull into a service station with his old blue car creaking and banging and order the best oil and gas in the place. Southwall was also very particular about the hats he wore, and he was known to have as many as five custom-made Stetsons, all of gray felt with navy blue sweatbands. Southwall's hats were tools in his work. At funerals, Jordan always could tell at what stage they were by watching the way Southwall handled his hat: When he sat it down, neatly on the organ (or on a windowsill if they were in church), Jordan knew the funeral was about to begin; if Southwall picked up the hat and twirled it idly on his left finger, Jordan knew the viewing was about to begin; if Southwall grabbed the hat in his right hand, holding it so hard it crushed the brim, holding it down by his legs, Jordan knew the service was at end, the casket would be closed and the pallbearers called to duty.

And Southwall's taste in funeral coaches was admirable. Although Jordan personally would have chosen cars of a different style—perhaps larger and more dashing—he admired Lovingood's fleet of leatherette-topped Cadillacs. And he remembered Southwall telling him: "Son, your rolling stock—your family cars, your hearse—are the best advertisements for your business. They always should be black. There is no other color." Southwall leased the cars from a downtown firm and every year got new ones. In the casket window, the metal frame holding the firm's name was collapsible, and Lovingood would crawl in, take out a set of Italic Chrome letters saying "Valentino" or Gothic ones saying "Teuffel" and replace them with a modernistic tag saying "Lovingood's." This last tag was perfect for the size of the window, and when it was in place, it made Jordan proud to be associated with the firm. It bothered him, however, that Lovingood leased the cars. If rolling stock was indeed your best advertisement, then best to have distinctive, custom-made cars that said *you* all over.

Jordan envied Southwall Lovingood. In all, Lovingood seemed a man who had found himself. And what is more beautiful? Lovingood undeniably was happy in his work. Even at funerals, Lovingood smiled, although it was not a joyful kind of smiling. Rather a *reassuring* kind. And people needed that. It amazed Jordan that Lovingood never expressed ambitions beyond his frequent references to improving Funeral Service. Southwall never talked about expanding his own business or branching out into other things. He seemed only to live for today and was content with his past performances.

Major Tecumpseh Bates, on the other hand, was entirely different. Where Lovingood was so fitted for his work, Major Bates seemed to be a man who gloried only in the appearances of things. He talked about them too much to be immersed in them. Jordan thought of Bates, with his pomaded hair, his penchant for drinks and women, as an old-style dandy. Bates was forever asking Lovingood for money: "I'm in a bit of a jam, Bro' Lovin'good. Met this new gal, you know. Can you give me a little somethin' till Friday?"

Lovingood always would comply, but not without a lecture: "Aw, Bates, you know you ain't got no gal, man. You gamblin' again." But to Jordan once, Southwall observed: "Now don't make fun of ole man Bates. I know he seems pretty wild, son, pretty wild, but Bates's got a little money. Yeah, little mon-ey. He's just tight, that's all."

Bates was a morbid man. At first Jordan wasn't positive, but he sensed that Bates dwelled on death and things deathly as a way of convincing himself that he wasn't afraid of it. Bates often returned to the story of Ellis Tatum, the old West Side mortician who bought men wine to do his bidding. And at the end of the Tatum story, Bates invariably added, "A man scared of his own shadow. Scared of the dead. Ain't that somethin'?"

Now to let him tell it, Major Tecumpseh Bates certainly wasn't afraid of any dead folks. "No, been settin' 'em up for goin' on forty years. Grew up with 'em, boy," Bates said. "Right down there in Oklahoma, worked right with the famous Rangelle, started when I was twelve. Ole Rangelle and his wife took me in, son. Didn't have nowhere to go, they went 'n' took me in. My daddy was part Cherokee Indian, Bro' Jordan, and my mother was a Creole woman. But they died or somethin'. Don't know much about 'em. Anyways, ole man Rangelle took me in when I was a pup, 'n' I used to drive the *meat wagon,* as we called it in those days. Had horses then. For children we used to hitch up six brown horses. For a-dults, we used six black ones, and for old 'uns, we'd put in six white horses. Ole Rangelle was one of the best. One of the first to do cavity embalmin' down there.

"No, sir; I sure wasn't afraid a no dead. Ole dad Rangelle sent me to school in Cincinnati (you didn't need no college in those days), and when he and the Missus died, I went to work for a man down in Tyler, Texas, and they were hard times. Didn't make much but room 'n' board. Well, I tell you why I couldn't be afraid now: I lived right there in the Tyler funeral home, slept with 'em. I mean, right back there with 'em. Sometimes at night, I'd wake up, and there they'd be moanin' and groanin' just like they'd come back to life. Air 'scapin' from their lungs and such, you know. Well, sir, I'd just turn right on over and go on back to sleep; that's how scared I was. Slept right in there with 'em."

Bates had a shipment to Kansas City one summer, and he came up from Texas and ran into a lady named Fannie Fears, who was handling on this end. Fannie showed him the town, the best he'd ever seen for good times ("They got some pretty hefty mammas here, Brother . . .") and he stayed on. Worked Williams' and later Fannie's, and that's where he met Southwall Lovingood. Funny thing: It was soon after coming with Lovingood that Bates discovered his peculiar talent. This was the way his hand stiffened just before Lovingood got a case. After Bates broke up a conversation between Jordan and Lovingood with "Southwall! We gonna get one! We gonna get one, man. I know it, I can tell it," Jordan was apprehensive until Southwall winked at him as a sign that Bates was harmless.

Jordan didn't believe that theatrical bit about the hand, although to date it seemed to have worked more times than it failed. Jordan rationalized it as probably just an illusion. With a big funeral home like Lovingood's, it was easy to predict business was coming.

Jordan was fond of Bates. He began to like the lying old man the rainy day they were sitting in the dark in the inner office waiting for business. Bates was slumped down in the big cloth-covered easy chair, hands folded, rubbing the tips of his long fingers incessantly together, his yellow mustache twitching. Suddenly, Bates sprang from the chair and bellowed at Jordan, "Could you embalm your own mother?"

Jordan mused a minute, then said, "I don't know. Could you?"

Bates had a far-off look. "Son," he said importantly, "I'd take my ole lady back there and set her soul on fire!" Jordan laughed so hard his sides ached.

Whenever he got a chance, Bates would regale Jordan with stories of the old days, stories of Rangelle and Harlan Fears and Charles Lewis and the greats of yesteryear. Bates, with straight face, also was fond of telling ghost stories. It was after recounting such a story that Bates almost lost his wits one summer night. Bates had just told Jordan a chilling tale about a white dove which appears on your windowsill just before someone in your family dies.

At that time, a cosmetologist who lived next door to Lovingood's was on call, and she used to come over at night when she had several cases to do. She was a thin, wiry woman, kind of handsome, very quiet. Jordan and Bates were closing up the office, and Bates asked Jordan to wait by the back entrance while he checked the preparation room to make sure everything was orderly. Jordan stood with his finger on the light switch, morbidly engrossed in the story. Bates came backing from the prep room and turned out the light there, leaving them with one dim hall light. Bates looked tired, and Jordan let him pass in front before turning out the last light. It was summer, but a wind had risen and swept across the barren parking lot of Lovingood's. Jordan heard a fence clink and figured it must be the hairdresser coming over to do some work. Bates did not hear the fence. He turned around to lock the door, and the cosmetologist came walking across the parking lot. She wore house slippers and made no sound. As she came into view, her long flimsy housecoat billowing powder white in the wind, Bates, who claimed to have slept with the deadest of the dead, turned, took one look at the billowing gown in the full moon and started shrieking, "Oh, Jezus, Jezus, heeellllppp! Oh, Jezus, don't let 'em get me. Annnh!"

They had to calm Bates down. "You scared me, Sister," Bates admitted, trying to catch his breath, stroking his mustache with a trembling finger.

The woman looked down at him. "You all right, Mister Bates? You sure got a fright. You didn't ever do nothin' to those bodies, did you, Bates?"

Jordan tried to laugh. But it wasn't at all funny. Major Bates asked them not to mention a word to Southwall Lovingood.

10

Lord, keep so busy
Workin' for the Master,
Keep so busy
Workin' for my Master,
Ain't got time to die.

Southwall Lovingood and Lawrence X. Jordan busied themselves in the preparation room, stopping only to share a moment of song. Afterward, Lovingood lumbered to the cabinet
and removed a pair of scissors and a dusty woman's traveling
case. Jordan rolled the embalming slab away from the sink.

On the table, under a sheet, was the new case, an obese yellow woman who had a heart attack. Jordan folded the sheet
back over the feet of the corpse. The right foot wasn't straight;
it listed to the right. Why did that happen with every case?
They came in that way, and they went out that way. Of course,
it didn't matter. The legs were hidden under the lid of the casket couch. But Jordan nevertheless was curious. Why was the
left leg always straight and neat while the right was twisted and
the knee flexed ten or twenty degrees? Jordan had seen this
disparity so often over the past two years that he now believed
it to be a law: To enter death's door, your right knee must be
bent, your eyes staring, your mouth gaped.

Jordan looked at the head of the new case. Its eyes and lips
were tightly sewn. Before it was wheeled into the chapel, Lovingood would hide the stitches with sealing wax and makeup.

Jordan had pulled the sheet too far down; the woman's pubic
hairs showed, and Lovingood didn't like that. Blushing, Jordan
adjusted the sheet and began clipping the fingernails.

Lovingood had face powder, nail polish, eye shadow, cold

cream and shaving equipment in the traveling case. He opened
the case and brushed old powder from the mirror in the lid as if
someone were still going to look in that mirror. He lifted out a
small brush and a woman's compact. Blowing audibly on the
brush, he spewed fine brown particles onto the floor. Then he
began his delicate work, mixing various powders in the palm of
his hand until he had just the right shade for the light-tan
woman on the slab. He patted the forehead of the corpse, leaning over the ashen face as he began dusting on the powder and
cooing: "Now then, Sister Sally! Got to get you read-yyy." As he
made up the body, Southwall sang:

> Spend alla my time
> Praisin' my Jesus,
> Alla my time
> Praisin' my Lord.
> If I don't praise Him,
> Rocks're gonna cry out:
> "Glory 'n' honor
> "Glory 'n' honor!"
> Ain't got time to die.

Jordan got clear polish from the traveling case and brushed
it on the fingernails. He put daubs of polish on the flesh below
the cuticles, too. This, he reasoned, gave the skin the appearance of vitality.

"That's right, Brother Jordan," Southwall Lovingood cooed.
"Get Sister Sal-ly to-gether, get her together now. Got to make a
pretty picture for the survivors, son, got to get a pretty picture
together. Lord, ole Sally sure was hefty!" And he grunted:
"Mmm-mmphh!"

Lovingood hummed on, dusting the face, then curling eyelashes until Jordan put down his polish, moved back from the
table and cleared his throat.

"Mister Lovingood," he said.

"Yeah, son? What's wrong, son? Sally got you down, son?"
Lovingood didn't turn around. He was brushing the lashes.

"No, sir. Uh, well, I—"

"Go on, son, don't be *scared*. What's on your mind, young
Mis-tah Jor-dannn?"

And Jordan told him that he wanted to leave the funeral

home. Here he was about to graduate from high school, and he planned to go to college and study art. He'd get a job somewhere, maybe in a museum or something, and work full time at his art. It wasn't that he didn't like the funeral home or didn't appreciate all that Mister Lovingood had done for him. But he had to get out on his own now, try something new, something different.

. Jordan had been thinking about it, he said, and he was really interested in sculpture. He hadn't done much—only some clay modeling at school—but he was pretty sure that was what he wanted to do. He had been drawing all the time, and in his junior year he began to paint in watercolor. A few months ago he had done some oil. Drawing and painting were all right, but somehow they were too limited. What Jordan wanted to do was something big, something that would involve the viewer totally. Sculpture. Roundness. Painting was too "flat." With a sculpture, you involved the viewer more, made him move around more—not just move his eyes. You affected him. You created more than he could take away in his head. Besides, there was something Jordan liked about the feel of the cool clay. It was his; he could do anything he wanted to with it. It was kind of like being God bending over the beginnings of Adam.

"Really serious 'bout this art, huh?" Lovingood asked.

. Jordan blushed. "Yes, sir, I am. But I liked the funeral business, I really did. Even thought about going into it at one time."

"Did, huh? Mmmm-mmmm. Too bad. You're made for mortuary science, you know. A born undertaker if I ever saw one."

Lovingood put down the curling brush, unstrapped his rubber apron, and washed his hands. He took his suit coat from a nail and motioned to Jordan, who was still holding the polish brush. "Come on, son," Lovingood said, his voice deeper and serious. "Let's go on in my office. Sally can wait. She ain't goin' nowhere."

"I mean I always think about the backs of things," Jordan said in the office. "Not just the front of things. Or the sides. You can get depth in painting, but it's illusory. Not three-dimensional. Not like in sculpture—"

"Mortuary work is sculpture, too," Lovingood interjected. "No, it really is, Brother Jordan. It's all built around sculpture, all built around it . . . uh, son. What you really want to do is put out something big, something that's gonna make the viewer sit up and take notice, isn't that right? Something that the viewer will want to come back to, to study some more, right?"

"Yes, sir. Exactly."

"Well, a well-prepped case is like that son. It's art. We even call it a memory picture. But it's more than just a picture, son. It's something real, something you can touch, something you can walk around, turn around, *feel* around. It's clay; that's all the body is, all it is, son. And you can mold it and change it and twist it to suit your purpose. There's a lot of study that goes into producing a good mortician, son, and it's really one of the world's oldest professions. It has a lot to do with the kind of art you're talking about. Why, what's-his-name . . . uh, Michelangelo or Leonardo—one of them—kept pieces of bodies, anatomical specimens, right there in his studio to model by. Leonardo. That's who it was. Leonardo da Vinci. Tell me Leonardo even embalmed his own specimens. One of the world's earliest embalmers, Leonardo was. Devised his own method of injection. Think about that, Brother Lawrence Jordan, think on that: If you could embalm, you could have your own specimens to model by. . . ."

"Yes, sir, but—"

"There's nothing . . . no better preparation . . . for sculpturing than the study of anatomy. And you get a lot of anatomy in mortuary school."

"Yes, sir, but I want to be an artist."

"Nothing wrong with that, son. But a man's got to eat, too." Jordan sighed.

"Why can't you do both, Brother Jordan? Sculpture and embalming. No, not embalming. *Dermasurgery*. Ever heard of that? A dermasurgeon makes lots of money. And he's a sculptor. He models the faces of the dead; he makes beautiful what before was ugly. There's no higher calling. The dermatologist works in clay, and he actually sculpts the eyes and ears and noses that trauma has taken away. Restorative art. Takes a lot of study and a lot of talent to be a dermasurgeon, a good dermasurgeon. I know only one. And as a matter of fact, he sculpts, too. Down in Texas. He's had several one-man shows down there. He just does his sculpture until the county calls him in on a case."

The thought of patching disfigured corpses nauseated Jordan. Was that art? He remembered the case they had in last summer. Two brothers out in Leeds had been left to mind their father's store. One brother was always good; he never got into trouble. The other was mischievous, irresponsible. The father kept a shotgun under the counter. He told the boys not to touch it. He put the good boy in charge and went into town. No sooner was the father down the road than the bad brother got the gun. He pointed it at the good brother, and the good brother told him to put it down. "Aw, it ain't loaded, man," the other brother said. But the good brother said it was. "I watched Daddy load it just the other night. Been some prowlers." The boy with the gun scoffed. "All right then, nigga, it's loaded and I'm goin' blow your head off." And he pulled the trigger. Lovingood got the case.

Jordan remembered Bates and another man bringing it in through the back way in a bog. Lovingood told Jordan to take off the rest of that day. "Got a serious case here," he said. "Havta work all night on this one." When Jordan came in the next day, he went into the Room and looked at it. Lovingood had done the best he could, but it was horrible. In the end, they had a closed casket funeral. Jordan heard the family closed down the store and the remaining brother lost his mind.

Dermasurgery wasn't for Jordan.

Clare was enraged about Jordan's decision to leave Lovingood's.

"Shit," she said, "that man's done everything he could for you, treated you like his own son when your own daddy wouldn't piss on you. What you better be doin' is holdin' on to what you've got. Southwall give you a chance when nobody else would, child. Took you off the streets. Art, my ass! Hell, art never paid no bills. Sound like your daddy, talkin' 'bout art. That's all he ever talked about: his music, his style, his art. You see what it got him. He wasn't even a man, let some woman get him murdered. Shit."

They argued. That's what was wrong with the old folks

today, Jordan told her. Never believing all things were possible. Anything the mind of man could conceive was possible! Hold on to what you've got? Hell, he didn't have anything. What did he have to lose? Security is the suburbs of hell.

"Honey, there's some cold people out there in that cold world," Clare told him. "You just don't know. Folks'll stop at nothin' to keep you down. Go on, get on out. Do what you want to; you goin' do it anyway. Just watch out, hear? Watch out."

She began to cry. Jordan thought she looked at him with eyes full of hatred, but he wasn't sure. He hated to see her that way, hated it.

"Okay. . . ."

"Here I worked 'n' scrimped 'n' scuffled, really scuffled, to bring you up and keep body 'n' soul together—"

"Aw, Mother. . . ."

" 'N' what thanks do I get? You run out on me, that's what you do. It's just *like* a nigga man, run out on his wife 'n' children, run out on his mamma, all the people that try to help him. Shit! That's all the thanks I get. Go on; you can rot in hell for all I care. I've got *mine*. Hell, runnin' around with a woman twice your age, old enough to be your mother—"

"Mother, Thess isn't twice my age. She's only—"

"She's still a grown woman, ain't she? Go on, run out to her. See what she'll do for you. Any grown-ass woman that'll lay up with children ought to be shot. I don't care if her daddy is an undertaker. 'N' a fine one too. . . ."

Jordan got his coat. As he opened the door, he heard Clare sputtering behind him. "Just go on, hear? Son of mine, goin' walk out on me. I'll show you. I'll show you, Mister Smartypants. You *will* do right, you just wait 'n' see!"

Jordan slammed the door as hard as he could, staggered down the steps and collapsed on the landing into a wretched ball.

The seniors had been given time off to purchase their school rings, yearbook photos and graduation gowns. Jordan caught a bus and got his gown. Then he got a few photos taken. But he rejected the school ring. It cost too much anyway. Besides, he looked forward to the day when he would wear two rings of his

115

own design. He would wear the rings on his little fingers. They would bear symbols of the sun and the moon and the stars and be made of sterling silver. In his mind's eye, Jordan could see himself, tall and handsome and artistic, talking to a customer with his rings flashing and his gold tooth shining. He didn't want an old school ring on one of his hands ruining the effect which he saw in his mind. Why the sun and moon and stars? That represented the entire universe and Jordan saw that as his artistic province, the entire perimeter of existence. He was going to get out of the narrow world of the funeral business and into the universe. The funeral business was good experience, however; someday perhaps he would make use of some things he learned as subject matter for his art.

On the bus going back to Lovingood's, Jordan thought about Thessalonica Wingate. She had become too possessive lately, made enormous demands on him. At first, just after they made love in the Lovingood chapel, he saw her once or twice a week and then they didn't always do it, although she always wanted to. As he got older, she made more and more demands on him. He found himself slipping away at night, at noon, to keep her happy. It really wasn't fun anymore, just drudgery. Didn't she realize he wasn't yet a man? What was wrong with her anyway? It struck Jordan: Perhaps she was a nymphomaniac. Thess Wingate was a nympho, and she was doing it to him as well as ten other guys. He couldn't face that; he didn't know what he would do without Thess. In a way, she was like a big sister or a mother. She seemed to worship Jordan. She gave him advice and when he got feeling insecure or lost—as he often had over the past couple of years—Thess was there to comfort him and guide him. "You can do anything you want to do, Lawrence," she would say, and the way she looked into his eyes made him believe her. No, Thess was hardly a nympho. Even now, there were many times when they only talked or said nothing, just being together. But Thess Wingate did have an enormous appetite, that was undeniable. She had long ago lost her first attraction for Jordan, her curvaceous beauty. There were many younger girls around who surpassed her in this department. And Jordan longed for some of these girls. But he always hung back: It was all he could do to satisfy Thess Wingate. She acted as if she owned him. She did whatever she wanted to with him,

and Jordan actually was ashamed of some of the things she
made him do for her. Really, that was why he refrained from
going after some of the younger girls: Thess Wingate made him
feel old and dirty and used. And he wasn't sure a younger girl
could make him feel like Thess did. Anyway, how could they
understand his fondness for making out in hearses and funeral
homes? A picture of Thess Wingate, naked and impatient on
her back on the slab of her father's preparation room, flashed
into Jordan's head. He twisted from sight in his seat on the bus.

As he entered the chapel door, Jordan heard the voice of
Southwall Lovingood, calling him into the office. Lovingood
was in high spirits and offered Jordan a drink—something he
had never done before unless they had a hard case. "Sit down,
my boy, sit down, Brother Jor-dannn!" the old man sang. Jordan sucked in his cheeks and was seated. He glanced up at the
photograph of Lovingood and his lodge brothers behind the
mortician's chair. Something in the picture made him suddenly
afraid of Lovingood.

"Son, I been thinkin' on what we talked about the other
night," Lovingood said. "Thinkin' 'bout that art and all. . . ."

"Did my mother call you?"

"Well, as a matter of fact, she did. But I'd been meanin' to
talk a little more about that, anyway, son. Didn't want it to end
on the note it did, you know, didn't want you to leave us
thinkin' we didn't appreciate all the fine work you put out for
us here."

"What did she say?"

"Oh, not much. Just about your maybe being a little hasty in
your decisions, that's all."

Oh, no, Jordan thought, she had to bother him with that.
Why wouldn't she leave him alone?

"Now, Brother Jordan," Lovingood said, "don't be down on
Clarisse, now. She's had a hard time, you know. Havin' to raise
you single-handed, workin' that domestic job 'n' all. Ain't easy
on a woman, you know, ain't e-zee. She didn't have too much to
say. Actually, she cried a lot. 'N' I can understand that. Got
children of my own, you know. Thought it best if I went on
over and cheered Clare up. That's a fiiine young mother you
got, Brother Jordan, 'n' I just want you to know that."

117

"Thank you."

" 'Sides, Clare 'n' I ain't got together in a month a Sundays. I was really glad to have that chance to see her. It'd been a long time, long time, Mis-tah Lawrence X. Jordan, since we, ah, talked."

Jordan nodded earnestly. Lovingood was working up to a pant. Jordan noticed that the old man's red eyes flickered nervously in the dim office light. A painful look came over Lovingood's face. His brow wrinkled, and Jordan saw that he was sweating. That's how Southwall Lovingood was: He worked hard at everything he did.

"Brother Jordan? Oh, Brother Jordannn! I still think you'd make a fine undertaker, fiiine young mortician, Brother Lawrence X. Jordan. It's gonna be a real loss to mortuary science if you leave us. A real loss. But, Mis-tah Jor-dannnnn?"

Jordan jumped. "Yes, sir?"

"I don't think you're gonna leave us. Now, now. That's just my opinion. Anything can happen, anything. But I just got a feelin', son, 'n' my feelin's, when they feel like this feelin' feels, my feelin's are ofttimes correct. Anyway, I just wanted you to know how much we think of you here. Now, relax, Brother Jordan; you're among friends here. Want some more . . . painkiller? Fine, fine. Now listen. I got something to tell you. I had planned to keep this a secret till you graduated from school there, but events are forcin' me to speed things up a bit, son. Know somethin'?"

"No, sir."

"Brother Jordan, we think you're so well suited to mortuary science, so decent and deserving and so full of potential—whether you think so or not—that we've been plannin' to give you a little more help than we have, a little more encouragement. Now we've been in this business a long time, and in this business you learn to understand people or you're dead. I mean you don't last long. 'N' one thing we know: If a young man, a fiiine young man like you, Mister Jordan, if a fine young man's got his mind made up, there's no changin' it with love or money. That right?"

"I guess so."

"Right. 'N' you are a fine young man, sir. That's all right, all right now, just keep your seat a minute longer, can you do that?

Now let me just get this out, son. As I say, we been in this field for some little time now, 'n' we've seen 'em all, Fannie Fears on back. 'N' know what, son? I've never seen a young man so well suited to the mortuary callin' before in my life. Never. There's not a one that comes close to you in intelligence, courage and just pure abil-ity. Now I'm not puttin' you on, son, wouldn't do that, Mister Jordan. The time has come to face this thing 'n' talk frankly about it.

"Now I realize that you have your own life to live. Lord knows, life is too short and too sweet to waste it on things that are not meant for us. But I have to agree with your mother on this, have to go along with Clare. Your mother's a smart woman, you know that? Now we know you're smart. And you'll have to admit, Mister Jordan, that you may be just a little hasty in your decision. Right? And you have to think about your mother, son. After all, Clare ain't gettin' any younger. 'N' I know you love your mother, I know you do. Look here: Wouldn't it be nice if someday you could get Clare out of all that drudgery and see your mother right, I mean really right, outta sight, in a fine home with a fine car and lots of things people work all their lives for? Wouldn't that be fine?

"Now you've been here two years, son. That's a short time in this business. You haven't seen what it can do for you yet. But you have seen how most of 'em come in—feet first. 'N' without a dime past the insurance money. 'N' the cost of mortuary serv-ice today is so high—the overhead is just killin' us—that time the insurance is used up payin' for the last rites, there's nothin' left for the survivors. 'N' this is particularly true of *our* people. Now you know that.

"So it sure is nice to be on the receivin' end, if you know what I mean. Sure is nice, son. 'N' only a fortunate few can enter.

"Now let me come to the point. I'm willin' to compromise, Mister Jordan, 'n' I don't often do that. Now look, didn't I give you a chance? Didn't I show you some things? Didn't I stand by you? All right, all right. Now I'm not askin' for gratitude; I'm not askin' for that. All the gratitude in the world won't set one table a bones 'n' beans. What I'm askin' is this: We gave you a chance. Now will you give Lovingood a chance?"

"Well, sir. . . ."

"Just hold still a minute, son. Now, Mister Jordan, we think so much of you and we believe so much in your eventual good judgment, sir, that we're willin' to put our money where our mouth is. I mean *money,* son. Greenback dollar bills. Now I want you to pursue your interest in art, in sculpture, I want you to do that. I'm even willing to invest money in that. As a matter of fact, after I talked with your sweet mother, son, your sweet, sweet mother, I went down to the bank and opened up an account in your name. Here's the passbook. That ought to get you through junior college. I mean I'd like to see you all the way through a four-year institution, son, but I have my own family to think about and there's the business. . . . "

"Oh, no, Mister Lovingood, I can't accept—"

"You ain't accepting nothin'. Nothin'. Just put that in your pocket, son, 'n' listen. Just put it in your pocket for now. All right. This is a business proposition just like anything else. The deal is this: You take that money 'n' go on to jaycee over here 'n' take art. Take anything you like. But just to cover all bases, take a little chemistry 'n' biology, too. Now I don't care if you take just one course in chemistry and one course in biology. But take 'em. Take 'em now; take 'em later. 'Cause you're gonna need 'em when you go off to mortuary science school, my school."

"But I don't want to go to mortuary science school."

"Son, I'm doin' this for your own good. 'N' you haven't heard my full proposition yet. I'll pay your way through college there 'n' pay your way through Gresham, too, *on the condition* that after all this education is through, you, Mister Jordan, will then decide what you want to do. After your schoolin', you're on your own. No strings attached. Look at it this way: If you try it and don't like it, you lose nothing. Now isn't that fair?"

"I . . . guess so."

"Of course it's fair. Most folks'll only go so far with you, Mister Jordan. Lovingood'll go with you to the grave."

"But—"

"Naw, naw. Now don't be hasty, son. Go on home, think it over. Think hard about it. Take another look at that passbook. When you get out of City College here, we'll give you another account, a bigger one. That'll get you through Gresham. They've got some fine elective courses at Gresham, too, you

know. Art and music, lots of things. 'N', Brother Jor-
dannnnnn?"

"Yes, sir?"

"Goin' give you a little raise, too, 'round here. Been meanin'
to do that. Starts as soon as you graduate, this summer. Go on;
see you later."

Jordan stayed away from Lovingood's for three days. He
didn't go home. He stayed with Thessalonica Wingate. She told
him he was God. "No," he said. "I'm Lawrence Jordan." On
the third day he went out to lunch with Lennie Valentine.
They ordered thick steaks, the thickest Jordan ever ate. Lennie
had just got out of jail. He had been arrested on a purse-
snatching charge. Jordan felt sorry for Lennie. Here Jordan
was, having all the luck, and Lennie wasn't having any.

"Don't you worry," Jordan told Lynford Valentine. "If I
make it, you will too. I promise."

"Sure," Lennie said. "I'll remember that."

After lunch, Jordan went back to Lovingood. Jordan's
clothes were wrinkled, and he looked as if he hadn't slept for
days. He hadn't. He marched in through the front door, nodded to Major Bates, who had come to answer the door, and
marched straight into the chapel. Lovingood was in the chapel,
sitting in a front pew, his head bowed, keeping watch over Sister Sally, now nicely encased in her half couch, waiting for burial. Jordan slipped into a pew behind the bulk of Southwall
Lovingood.

"I'll take that offer," he whispered over the pew.

11

Herece B. Lovingood set foot in her stepfather's establishment only twice during Jordan's apprenticeship. The first time she came in saddle shoes and purple scarf to the wake of a boy named Phillip Lafollette. The second time—the very next day—she left Phil Lafollette's grave and came in high heels and black mantilla to see Lawrence Xavier Jordan.

It rained the night of Lafollette's wake. The chapel was icy. Lovingood told Jordan to check the thermostats, and Lovingood left to bring the family down. Jordan got the heat going and sat in the office window, watching the night mourn for Phillip Lafollette, wondering why he, and not the boy in the chapel, had been spared. Jordan had never worked on anyone he knew before. Now here was Phil Lafollette encased like all the rest. Jordan never dreamed it would happen like this. He was glad now he hadn't envied Phil, as did so many others. He nearly did. But Phil lived down the street from him, and when they were little, they played. Actually, they didn't *play!* They sat on Phil's terrace and talked about Christianity and Catholicism and Judaism. Jordan told Phil he was a Jew. Why? "I'm Catholic," Phil Lafollette said. He said it with assurance and quietness and dignity, with command. Jordan learned about Judaism from the Goldmans. He learned a little. To Phil Lafollette, it was a lot. "You're very smart." Phil Lafollette laughed. "But I know you're not a Jew." "Oh, yes, I am," Jordan had replied, trying to sound assured and comfortable like Phil Lafollette. Phil's mother, a pale woman with green eyes, thought Jordan was dirty. She never said it, but Jordan felt it. The Lafollettes had a large, comfortable living room with a fireplace and two sofas. Once when Jordan came inside, Mrs.

122

Lafollette complained to Phil that Jordan tracked mud on the carpet. The Lafollettes had everything: a dishwasher, carpets, television, patio with wrought-iron furniture. When he was small, Jordan thought they must be as rich as the Goldmans, though he couldn't say why. He'd supposed in those days it was because they were light-skinned. Phil's father wasn't light. He did have wavy hair and a brushy mustache, and Jordan thought he looked and talked like Clark Gable. He was very nice to Jordan and protected him from Mrs. Lafollette, and when Jordan told him he didn't have a father anymore, Mister Lafollette hugged Jordan for a long time and hugged Phillip, too. Phil's father was one reason Jordan could have envied. But he didn't, by the grace of God.

Like his older brother and sisters, Phil was curly-haired and fair-faced. Jordan thought Phil looked like a calf. In one way or another, the whole family did. With Phil, it was the eyes and the mouth. But girls liked Phil's looks. They couldn't stay away from him. Even when they were very small, grown women used to remark about Phil's "cuteness." If Jordan had any real reason to envy Phil Lafollette, this was it. For a while one day, Jordan did envy Phil. Jordan had played hooky with Lennie Valentine, and they were walking down the street laughing and singing, and they passed a group of Catholic girls and a boy. The Catholic kids got out early. As they passed, Lennie whistled at the pretty uniformed girls and tried to flirt with them. The boy just laughed. It was Phil. Jordan saw Herece with them and spoke. She acted as if she hardly knew Jordan. She was too busy vying with the other girls for Lafollette's attention. Later she told Jordan Phil was her boyfriend, but he knew better. Phil was shy. He told Jordan he was afraid of girls because they acted funny around him. And if there was one girl he especially didn't like, Phil said, it was that Herece. Jordan believed this, but the day he saw Herece with Lafollette, he hated Phillip for a while.

Chimes sounded. Bates, who was manning the reception room, answered the door. It was a group of Phil's classmates— girls. Jordan heard them talking excitedly in the hallway. That was something about these Catholics: One minute they were happy. Then tragedy struck. They stopped and mourned. Then they were laughing and talking again. They didn't shout and scream and tear their hair out like Baptists. Now, in the hall-way, Jordan could hear the girls grow silent. He heard the word "rosary." Bates came in with an armful of wet coats and went out to escort the girls to the chapel.

Jordan stared out the window again. Phil Lafollette never had been an athletic boy. He avoided contact games. Jordan remembered wrestling with him once. Phil gave up easily when Jordan got him in a chokehold. Then Jordan saw that he was crying. He apologized. But Phil replied, "That's all right. I suppose I'm not much competition." Jordan didn't know Phil had a heart defect. Maybe that developed later. After he got out of trouble and started working at Lovingood's Jordan saw little of Phil Lafollette. It struck him: Always in the back of his mind, he had thought of Phil Lafollette remaining forever young and delicate and calflike, walking eternally to his mother's home followed by a gaggle of girls. He had left Phil like that, and somehow he had always expected to find him that way. Now Phil was dead. He had grown into a stooped stalk. The body came in ashen and twisted and with a look of terror on its face. Jordan had assisted on it and turned his head away and tried to be a man.

Presently, Bates hurried back to the office, whispering, "Southwall's girl is in there. Sure is grown into a pretty thing."

Indeed she had. Jordan needed diversion, something to take his mind off Phil Lafollette. He slipped into the family alcove next to the chapel. Across the casket, he saw Herece Lovingood fingering beads. She faced Jordan but could not see him because tonight the chapel was lit only by candles and the alcove was in shadows. Jordan had requested the candles, one at each end of the church truck in tall holders. He thought Phillip La-follette would appreciate that.

Fire flecked Herece's face, giving her a mystic beauty. Jordan's blood pressure pounded. In the flames, her eyes flickered and shone like a fawn's. She looked down at the body, then up to heaven. Her rosary dangled on the coffin pillow. With one dark hand, she brushed away wisps of hair, set loose from her wrap.

Jordan had done a good job on the hair. He fluffed it on the forehead, just the way Phillip wore it. He took great pains to see that Lovingood built the face up to mooncalf proportions.

One girl touched Phillip Lafollette's hand. Another wept audibly. Herece looked down. A tear rolled from her cheek onto Phillip Lafollette's pillow. But under the quilted lid of his casket, Phil's face was indifferent and immobile. Herece tightened her scarf, wrapped the beads tightly around her hand, and went out. One by one, each of the girls retreated until only one remained. She was not very pretty; but she was serene and stately, and Jordan knew that if Phil had loved anyone, she was the one. She placed her rosary on his coffin and backed out. From the shadows, Jordan heard her join Herece and the other girls. They weren't laughing, but they had cheered up.

On Friday, Jordan was taking inventory in the display room when Bates sauntered in. "Yes, sir," Bates whistled, running his finger over a cloth-covered case. "That Miz Herece sure 'nuff grown into a pretty thing." And he watched Jordan out of the corner of one eye. Jordan shrugged: "Mmmm." He tried to appear engrossed in a pink plastic vault. Bates fluffed up the silk inside the cloth box. "You know, Brother Jordan, wouldn't be a-tall surprised if you 'n' Miz Lovin'good got to know each other, m' boy. Sure 'nuff got to be now. She never been down here before, you know. 'N' her daddy tells me she asks 'bout you all the time."

Jordan perked up.

"Real regular, I hear. 'Daddy, what is Law-rence doing? Daddy, how much money does he make? Is he a real undertaker? Isn't he scared of all those dead folks?' Yeah!"

The proprietor of Lovingood's Incorporated waddled in, fedora in hand, out of breath as usual. "Let's get on over to th' church now," he huffed. "Got to take young Brother Phil-lip farther on up the road."

The church was on the same boulevard as Lovingood's. It was a huge, vaulted cathedral that echoed footsteps on the stone floor. It smelled like incense. Jordan wheeled the coffin to the nave while Bates and Lovingood set up the registry and brought the flowers down to the alter. The casket thudded as Jordan pushed it off the truck onto a marble catafalque. The thud reverberated through the pews and pillars.

Lovingood checked the coffin. "Got to be more careful, son," he said. "Call me or ole Bates here to give you a hand on things like this." The big man opened the lid of the coffin and let out the throws. The body inside was skewed, its hair tousled. Lovingood smoothed out the hair with his hand. Grasping the body by both shoulders, he worked it back to the center of the couch and tucked in the silks around it. Phillip Lafollette's body wore a gray suit and tie, matching the cloth casket. Lovingood straightened the tie. Jordan glanced at the head inside the box. It hardly looked like a boy now. It looked more like a calf-faced old man, lost in meditation. Lovingood pushed it down deeper in the casket. That was the last time Jordan looked at Phillip Lafollette.

Jordan admired the black vestments of the priest and the dignity of the service. And he admired the way the Lafollettes took it. He stood between the pillars of an arcade, near the altar. The family sat across from him, and the deceased's brother recognized him; but Jordan got no sign from either Mister or Mrs. Lafollette, Senior. Only the mother cried, and she only dryly. She wore a black veil which she kept lifted during the mass. Dark-suited Peter Lafollette, now in college, sat on the other side of his mother, looking morose and out of place. Next to Peter, lined up according to age, the Lafollette girls sat with downcast eyes.

Jordan searched for Herece but did not see her. Perhaps she hadn't come. Oh, well, it was best. He had to forget her. She wouldn't want to see *him*—not after what he had done to her back at the apartments. Had she told Lovingood?

Outside the church the procession lined up in the street. Peter Lafollette and other pallbearers were bringing the remains to the street. Rain spattered brightly on the hearse. Jordan breathed in the moist air. But it did no good. For once he didn't look forward to the ride to the cemetery. He felt afraid. Lovingood came out smiling and climbed into the hearse. "I don't feel like goin' to the cemetery," he told Lovingood. "I don't feel well."

"Better come on," Bates interrupted. "Miz Herece goin' be there."

Lovingood rolled a red eye at Bates, and Bates retreated laughingly into the first family car. "Son, I got nobody to drive that second car, 'n' it's too late to call someone else in," Lovingood said, leaning out the window of the hearse. "Don't let this get you down, son; don't let it get you. Goin' bury a whole lotta your friends 'fore it's over. The good die young."

At the cemetery, Jordan stayed in the car. Down the road he saw them gathered under a tent. He did not see Herece.

The other relatives decided to go home with friends. Jordan took his limousine back to Lovingood's and went in the reception room and lay down on the couch.

While her father was taking the dead boy's parents home, Herece Lovingood caught a ride to the funeral home. She got out in the driveway of Lovingood's and paused before the gray building. Then she climbed the steps and rang the chimes.

Lawrence Jordan appeared.

"Hello," she said.

"Hello."

"May I come in?"

"Why not? It's your—Sure."

Jordan had his suit coat off. He stopped in the Room and put it back on. He had to be formal with her. He had to pretend they had never met before, had never been friends because she might get angry and tell Lovingood on him. Jordan had too much riding on her goodwill to mess up now. The boss' daughter! Wasn't that a drag? A picture flashed in Jordan's mind of the young Herece back at the apartments pulling up her dress. No; he had to forget.

He took her into the foyer. There was a body in a casket there. Herece looked at it and shuddered. She got close to Jordan. He walked her to the divan.

"I never came here until last night," she said. "I mean I was scared to. Aren't you scared?"

"No."

"Really? I mean I think even Daddy—I call him Daddy now —I think even Daddy is scared sometimes."

"No, he's not. He's the greatest undertaker in the world."

"You really like him, don't you?"

"Yes."

"I knew that boy that died, you know. I used to go with him. He was always sickly. He missed school a lot. They said he got overexcited. . . ."

"I know."

"Yes, I guess you would."

"You waiting for your father?"

"Not really. I came to see you."

"Me? Why? I—"

"You never came over or anything. I always wanted to see you. I didn't forget."

"Forget what?"

"What we did. You know. When your mother came in and caught us."

"Oh, *that*. Look, that was so long ago. I'd forgotten about it. I'm . . . sorry."

"It's okay. I didn't tell anyone about it. I guess you thought I did, didn't you?"

"I didn't know."

Herece walked to the chapel, dangling her purse behind her. She stood looking at the door with her back to Jordan for a long time, then whirled around, grinning.

"Lawrence," she said, "I want you to show me around."

"Your father will be in pretty soon. He'd better do that. Besides, I think he'd want to."

"I want *you* to show me around."

"Well, I'd like to. But Mister Lovingood might not like that."

She squinted her fawn eyes and let out a peevish snigger.

"If you don't show me around right now, Lawrence Jordan, I'll tell him what you did, I really will."

"Is this blackmail? Is that what it is?"

"You blackmailed *me*, didn't you?"

Jordan showed her everything except the preparation room. "That's where they fix them up, isn't it?" she asked. "I don't want to go in there." They went back to the reception room, and he was seriously considering showing her the garage and kissing her out there when Bates and Lovingood drove in in the hearse and family car. Jordan jumped up and ran to get the door. They came in through the foyer, Lovingood first. "Break out th' bourbon, Bates," Lovingood cried, tossing his hat onto the divan. "Just shipped another one off to Stiff City." He put a hand on Jordan's shoulder and was about to speak again when he saw Herece standing in the hallway. "How long you been here?" he asked, looking at her and then at Jordan.

"Not very long, Daddy."

Lovingood grunted. He hugged Jordan to him. "Thought you were sick, son."

"Oh, he is, Daddy," protested Herece Lovingood. "And I had to come in here unexpectedly like this and ask him to show me around. Mister Jordan was so kind and respectful, you ought to give him a raise."

And she and Lovingood walked away toward his office, having a mock argument about how much money undertakers did and didn't make. Bates loosened the cap from a pint of bourbon he had in a paper bag, pushed the bag down around the bottle neck and took a long swig. He winked at Jordan and handed him the bottle. "Don't you say anything now, Mister Bates," Jordan said. "I mean I was in here sacked out, and I heard the door, and there she is."

Bates collapsed on the divan and tipped his hat over his eyes. "I'm not gonna say anything!" he announced.

"Brother Jor-dannnnnn?"

Lovingood was calling him from the inner office. Jordan gulped. "See you later, old man," he said, cuffing Bates' hat onto the floor. Jordan hurried to Lovingood's office. Outside the door, he checked his tie to make sure it was straight.

Herece was sitting in her stepfather's chair, her legs comfortably crossed on the desk. Lovingood sat in his easy chair, his tie loosened and his coat unbuttoned. "Come on in, Brother Jor-dan," he motioned. He mopped his brow with a big handkerchief.

Jordan did not sit. "Yes, sir?"

"Sit down, Brother Jor-dan. Sit down, son. Rest your weary bones. Take a breather."

Jordan sat erect, facing Lovingood. He did not look at Herece, who was twisting in her chair.

"Well, Brother Jor-dan," Lovingood said, folding his hands across his belly. "Goin' off t' college next fall, goin' on t' higher education."

"Yes, sir."

"City College, isn't it? Yeah. Gonna take a little art, take a little hist'ry, maybe little English. 'N' a little biology and chemistry, too. Right? Fine, fine." He mopped his brow at Herece.

"Wants to be an artist, Brother Jordan does. Wants to be a sculp-tor."

"Well—"

"But wants to go on to mortuary science school, too. Maybe be an undertaker, too!"

"That's swell," said Herece, making a face.

Suddenly Lovingood threw his handkerchef on the floor and looked straight at Jordan. "But you know somethin', Brother Jor-dannn? Got to stay in them books, got to burn that midnight oil. Yeah. Got to stay away from them lil girrrls, them little chicks. Yeah. Them lil girls'll get you, son, give you a hard way to go. Whole lotta lil pretty girrrls out there'ta City College, whole lotta lil girrrls."

"Oh, Daddy—"

"Hush, Herece. See she's talkin', protestin'. Heck, she gonna be out there in the fall herself, right, Herece? Now 'Rece is pretty lil girrl herself, don't know that, though. Goin' be right out there at City College with th' rest of 'em, Mistah Jordannn, right out there. Now that's a big temptation."

"Look, Mister Lovingood—"

"Big tempta-shun. But you know somethin'? I'd rather see two children like yourselves gettin' together 'n' hittin' them books, studyin' harrrrd, Mister Jordan, workin' harrrrrd, do you hear me? Now you 'n' Herece've known each other since childhood, right? Grew up together. Goin' off to school together. Comin' 'round the funeral home together. Right? Now I know both of you; I know your strengths 'n' I know your weaknesses. 'N', Brother Jordan, I know you study, I know you work hard. Goin' be a man soon, a natural man. 'N', 'Rece—I know you don't hit them books any too hard, don't fight them pages enough now, don't get into it.

"So, Jordan, here's what I want you to do out there at City College: Kinda keep an eye on ole Herece here for me, watch out for her, keep them lil boys off her. Now I know that's askin' a lot, but I wouldn't be askin' it if I didn't think you could handle it, son. Understan' what I mean?"

"Yes, sir, I understand," Jordan smirked, turning to the girl in the corner, who was taking her feet off the desk. "But Miss Herece might not . . . she might not go for that, sir."

"That's right!" Herece shrieked, jumping to her feet.

"Shut up, girl!" Lovingood said, not looking at Herece. "Miz Herece ain't in charge here, not yet. She'd do well to mind her elders in the meantime. Now. Mister Jordann, I just want you to kinda watch out for 'Rece, take care of her, 'n' don't let nobody bother her. Is that clear? 'Rece, I want you to do the same: Watch out for Brother Jor-dan here, keep him in those books 'n' watch out for *my* interest, hear. Now I don't mind if you kids go out to a movie or something sometime together or go to a dance. But I want you to stay together. Now listen to me both of you: Neither one of you had a daddy when I came along, neither one of you. Now I admit maybe I've been too wrapped up in my business, off in my work 'n' all, 'n' haven't had enough time to spend with you, any of you—Herece, you or your stepbrother. Or you, Jordan. But I'm doin' the best I can. Now you may think I'm bein' harsh about this 'n' casehardened. But maybe I know some things both of you don't. An undertaker's life is a good one, but it's a hard one, too. Many are called, 'n' few are chosen, children, and an undertaker has no friends but those in his family 'n' those in his profession. Remember that. Outside folks just don't understand. It's not easy for an undertakin' man to be *liked* in the community. Socially I mean. And that goes for his daughter and his son. So in a way, we have no choice but to stick together."

Lovingood picked up his handkerchief and mopped his brow again. "Go on, children. I've said enough," he said. "Jordan, get the car, 'n' take Herece on home, son. Then come on back, 'n' pick up your wages, 'n' have a little taste with Bates 'n' me."

They skipped joyously out to the family car. It had stopped raining. Before they got in, Jordan tore off the mantilla and pressed Herece up against the car. He stole a deep, soulful kiss, opened the door for her and roared off into the world. Phillip Lafollette was in his grave, Southwall Lovingood in his cup, and sunshine in the heavens. It was the best of all possible worlds.

12

Jordan had graduated from high school with honors in art—
a surprise. On top of that, he got another surprise when Southwall Lovingood showed up at the graduation commencement
with his wife, Psyche. Afterward Clare took a picture of Southwall and Psyche standing with a capped and gowned Jordan on
the steps. Southwall pumped Jordan's hand and, as he walked
away, slipped something into Jordan's hand in his usual manner. "Just a little somethin' for doin' such a fine job at school
and at the funeral home," Lovingood said. Jordan had been expecting a "little somethin'," but when he looked, he found a
crisp new hundred-dollar bill.

Jordan used the money to put down on a car, a black 1951
Buick Sedan with air holes in the fenders. Jordan had the car
repainted and the seats recovered in black leather. He hung
purple curtains in the back windows. He bought new white
wall tires. He polished the car and had the motor tuned. It was
an ancient straight-eight motor. When it was finished, he drove
it to Herece's house and asked her what she thought of it.
"It's sharp," Herece said. "But it looks like a hearse."
"Of course," Psyche Lovingood said.
During the summer he took Herece to the drive-in twice.
Each time they climbed into the back seat and drew the curtains.
Surprisingly, Clare was delighted with Jordan's purchase. For
one thing, he could drive her to the grocery now, and she could
go farther out to some good stores. The stores in the neighborhood were expensive, and Clare said the food wasn't of good
quality. "We pay more for groceries than the Goldmans," she

said. In addition, she just liked the car. But then she would: Clare liked anything fancy, especially if it had an air of mystery about it. "Very smart," she said, and she climbed in the back seat and clowned with Jordan and said, "Home, Jeeves," and "Left at the next corner, Chillingsworth." They had a good time. Jordan took Clare out on the Kansas Turnpike and opened the car up full throttle. It did only sixty-five. But that was enough for Clare. "Lawrence, slow down," she shrieked. "Slow down. We'll all be down there at Lovingood's if you don't. At least we have a car suited for the occasion."

Business was slow that summer. Lovingood had workmen remodel the chapel. Jordan liked the old chapel better. Now, when Jordan took Lovingood out on his rounds, he often took him in his Buick. Lovingood would ride in the back, opening and closing the curtains. "Feel right at home," he quipped. Often, at midnight, Jordan made long, solitary journeys into the countryside. One night he picked up a prostitute. They went to a motel north of the city and Jordan had to lie about his age. The woman did not respond to his caresses. She charged him too much money, but he paid. Back at home, he threw up in the bathroom.

Why did women make him feel dirty? That was the first woman he'd had since Thess Wingate. He didn't dare touch Herece—not in that way. He had petted and felt around with Herece, but he never went all the way. He picked up the prostitute because he felt frustrated by Herece. Not that Herece wouldn't have let him, but he remembered Southwall's admonition: "Kinda look out for her."

He had broken up with Thess Wingate the night of the senior prom. At first, Jordan was determined not to go. But Clare derided him. "What kind of man are you? All work 'n' no play. . . . You better have *some* fun while you can, boy, 'cause when you get out there 'n' really start breakin' your back, you gonna look back on these days 'n' wish they were here again." Breaking his back? What did she think he had been doing? Finally, he relented. He would go. And he would take Thess Wingate to the prom. Clare chuckled. "Been many a year since that hussy saw th' inside of a high school. Damn whore; old enough to be your grandmother. . . ."

Jordan was embarrassed by Thess Wingate's conduct at the

dance. He had bad feelings about it even before they got to
school. He had taken special pains to pick out a tuxedo which
afforded the best lines and texture and cut commensurate with
his height and build and skin tone. He spent prodigally on a
corsage. Then when he drove the limousine to Thess Wingate's
house, she came out in a stunning blue satin gown which extended all the way down to the tops of her white pumps. But
when she modeled for him and removed her evening coat, Jordan saw that the back of the dress plunged much too far. He
could almost see Thess' rump. That was the first sign. The second was that she insisted on disappearing every fifteen minutes
into the girls' bathroom to smoke. She spoke down to some
other girls, Jordan's classmates, when they whispered about her
rather revealing ballgown, and she cursed one of the girls sin-
fully. And she seemed to dance more dances with the handsome
gym teacher than she did with Jordan, wriggling her behind os-
tentatiously and laughing in a very loud voice.

In the end, Jordan insisted that they go. "Go where?" she
asked him in front of the gym teacher.

"I don't know. Your place, maybe out to Cliff Drive. . . ."

"Cliff Drive? Is that the only place you know?"

He took her off to one side. "Thess, you're sure acting funny
tonight. What's wrong?"

"Nothing!" she rasped. Jordan's classmates shook their heads.
"Shit! I shoulda known better than to come to a goddamned
high school prom! It doesn't show me shit. Take me home. Cliff
Drive! Hell, I thought we'd go dancing after this, someplace
nice, really put on the dog."

When he let her out of the car, she said, "Don't bother to
come in."

"I mean I'm not really that excited about you, either," Jordan said. "Especially after the way you acted tonight."

"I've never been terribly excited about you, either," she said,
admiring the way her pumps complemented her dress. "You're
just a child. Not only that: You couldn't satisfy me in a thousand years. You don't know the first thing about making love.
But I've met a man, I mean a *man,* who does. Ohh, he's got a
thing that long, honey!"

"Who's that?"

"Never mind who. He's almost a licensed embalmer and a good one, too."

Jordan walked around the limousine. He opened the door and put one foot into the car. "You make me feel dirty," he said. "You always did. You been screwin' everyone in town anyway."

"If you say anything to Jerry about it, I'll fix it so you'll never work another job in this town, Lovingood or no Lovingood," Thess shouted. "You black bastard."

Jordan drove off. He was glad it was over.

Thess Wingate was going with T. Jerome Montague, a new undertaker in town. Montague, a tall, thin, brown-skinned man with a pencil mustache and slick hair, was the best friend of Wayne Lovingood. They had gone to Gresham together the year before and came back to Kansas City together. Wayne had written his father about Jerry Montague and asked the old man to give Monty a chance. But Lovingood replied that he had no openings, with Wayne coming to join the firm and Jordan already there. T. Jerome Montague came anyway with tailored suits and manicured hands and went to work for LaCour, Fortune & Wingate, where he met Thess. Jordan chuckled. Thess probably had cornered Monty right there on one of her father's second-floor embalming tables.

He didn't know Monty very well. They had met briefly when Jordan took Lovingood to LaCour's late one weekend. Lovingood had been called in to help with a difficult case, and Jordan sat downstairs in the LaCour foyer, reading magazines. T. Jerome Montague, tall, bronze, impeccable, walked up and said, "Are you the boy who works with Wayne's old man? Hiya doing?" Monty extended his hand, and they shook. Jordan looked straight into Monty's eyes, and Montague turned his eyes away. Jordan immediately disliked him; there was something sinister and oleate about the man. They talked about the mortuary business, and Montague told Jordan about the Gresham College of Mortuary Science in Chicago.

Jordan was surprised to hear that Gresham students were required to take classes in microbiology and something called toxicology, and he became a little apprehensive about whether he could even make it through the school. Chemistry and microbiology *and* toxicology! It was going to be harder than he imagined. "I want to be an artist," Jordan said.

"I *am* an artist," replied Montague, brushing imaginary lint from the sleeve of his Hart Schaffner & Marx suit.

A month later Montague passed his state board examination impressively, was awarded his license, and was listed in the *Afro-Citizen News* as LaCour, Fortune & Wingate's "resident embalmer."

Wayne Lovingood was another case. All Wayne cared about, according to his father, was spending the hard-earned profits of Lovingood Incorporated in wild weekends with T. Jerome Montague. "Brother Wayne's gonna be the death of me yet," Lovingood complained to Major Bates. "That boy's lazier than a twelve-toed sloth. And twice as greedy. . . ."

Wayne rarely came into the funeral home. Like Montague, Wayne was a smart dresser, although Jordan observed that the younger Lovingood's taste was less refined than Montague's. While Montague dressed subtly and distinctly, Wayne Lovingood was gauche. The first time Jordan saw Wayne after the latter's return from Gresham, Wayne came in the back way wearing a brown suit with black shoes and a black leather cap. The suit was tasteful enough, but the shoes and cap were totally out of place. And young Lovingood had not shaved or, it seemed to Jordan, even washed his face that morning. The only acknowledgment Wayne conceded to Jordan's existence was a quick "Hi," and Jordan knew from that moment they wouldn't get along. Wayne went into his father's office, and the elder Lovingood could be heard remonstrating in an especially shrill voice about his offspring's prodigal ways.

Dark, high-voiced, intense, Wayne Lovingood was a thin, pimple-faced caricature of Southwall Lovingood. But he had none of the old man's industry or charm or competence. Wayne Lovingood didn't start working at his father's immediately after graduation. Indeed, he didn't do any work for two years.

It was particularly hot that summer, and Jordan relieved himself many nights drinking lemonade in the cool of Herece's porch swing, listening to the crickets. Other times he sped away in his makeshift hearse to the Kansas Turnpike, racing to Wichita or Topeka or Bonner Springs, making the night flow cool around him. In the fall, he matriculated into junior college, and despite his expressed ambitions, he daydreamed in life drawing class about marrying Herece and rising to the summit in a world of catafalques and vacuum pumps while Wayne Lovingood dissipated his life away, singing drinking songs in the unemployment line with T. Jerome Montague.

13

Although it granted minor degrees in what it termed art, City College was a long way from being another Pratt Institute. Lawrence Jordan was about to graduate, and all he had to show for two years at the school were a few generalized courses in art history, graphics, studio drawing and painting and two semesters of "individual work" in which he attempted some mediocre castings in imitation bronze.

He was having second thoughts about sculpture. First of all, he hadn't realized how expensive the process really was. Second, he had expected to learn much more about sculpting than he did. The attitude of the teachers at City seemed to be that sculpture was just another hobby or craft, and indeed, the same faculty that taught crafts was assigned to work with those few misdirected students like Jordan who worked in clay and metal and paper. And the other students weren't really sculptors at all. Without exception, they worked with blowtorches and flux and did things with wires and pipes. The flux turned rainbow colors at the joints of abstract right angles and ellipses. No, they weren't sculptors; they were welders. And working without torch or visor, Lawrence Jordan was an alien, an anachronism still dwelling in the Stone Age of representational dimensional realism.

He had tried to help Herece in her studies. And while Southwall Lovingood seemed to approve of the courses she was taking, Jordan felt they were all wrong, dead-ended. Herece insisted on pursuing "liberal" studies, which to Jordan meant random courses. He believed that everyone, undertakers' daughters included, should specialize, major, in some unified body of knowledge. Perhaps that was Clare in him: You had to have a trade. Maybe not Clare's strict interpretation of the word, but some profession, something you *professed* to be able to do. In the end, Jordan couldn't profess to be a sculptor or even an artist. But art was the only discipline at City which really interested him, and he clung to it. He knew he needed more practice, more theory, but at least he had taken the first steps. In a few years, perhaps he would realize his goal.

All Herece Lovingood seemed to care about was getting married. Not that Jordan was against this. But he still had a whole year to do in embalming school. He still had to satisfy her father, and then everything would work out. The years at City had come and gone as if they were a dream. A few classes, the smell of burning leaves, two snows. Endless funerals at Southwall Lovingood's. Taking Clare to the grocery on Saturdays. Transmission trouble. And now here he was, one month from being a man. His dates with Herece slacked up in winter, grew steady again in spring. More and more she talked of children; she visited married friends. Her grip on his hand was tighter. She began to speak seriously of "the family," meaning its business and its inclusion of Jordan. They looked at rings. But Jordan began to think: Herece was charming, attractive, easy. But as an artist-undertaker, he needed not only charm but intellect, not only attractiveness but understanding of what he was trying to do and what he wanted to do. Art would be secondary, of course, until he had found himself. But it would be there, and it would detract from business and responsibility and even love. He needed understanding, and he wasn't sure Herece could give him that. Of course, he wasn't above a marriage of convenience. He remembered Southwall's words about the undertaker's plight.

Jordan had become much more relaxed in the business. Clare was wrong: You didn't remember the faces. They came and they went, and after a while they all were the same. Gaping mouth, twisted right leg. You washed them down and positioned their arms and rolled them to the slumber room. When the casket was lifted from the church truck, you forgot who they were. Even the caskets you couldn't remember. After a while they all looked alike—rather *felt* alike. It was a feeling, a coolness in your fingertips, casket and people. That was the only permanence in life.

He had begun to look forward to embalming school. It couldn't be that difficult. Bates had done it, and Bates surely was no Einstein. Bates was even afraid of the dead. That was one thing Jordan wasn't. He had been, but he had forced himself to change. He wanted to find out how much. At school, he would know. Major Bates said you worked on lots of cases there, actually embalming them, altering them. Jordan had been admitted to the prep room long enough now that it had lost its mystery. The only mystery that remained was what Bates and Lovingood did to them when they were in there alone. Another thing that fascinated Jordan was the money you could make. His salary at Lovingood's had grown, but it wasn't enough. Clare got too much of it. He needed real money now. He wanted to impress Clare. He wanted to buy paintings and clothes. And girls. He thought about the money so hard he considered postponing his entrance into embalming school until fall so he could take some business courses at City during the summer.

In chemistry and biology, he had done well after all. He hadn't copped A's in the subjects, but Lovingood was satisfied enough to see Jordan making an above-average effort to prepare himself. By this time it had occurred to Jordan that you didn't need that much chemistry and biology to study embalming—if you needed them at all. Otherwise, Bates wouldn't have made it. But Jordan said nothing to Lovingood about this. Instead, he listened when the big man talked about the prerequisites to mortuary science.

Of course, Jordan's impressive work in chemistry and biology was calculated. He thought it best to secure his standing with Lovingood. He made certain Lovingood saw him with his head in the biology or chemistry books. He asked the right questions. And Lovingood related everything to mortuary science. When Jordan started chemistry, for example, he asked Lovingood to clarify what the subject really was all about. And the undertaker, pleased that he was consulted, replied, "Why, it ain't nothin', son, but knowin' how things are put together and how they come apart." And Lovingood went on to explain that temperature, pressure and compatibility made every substance the way it was. "Change one, or change any two, or change all three," Southwall averred, " 'n' you got somethin' new. Either it tastes different, feels different or acts different.

"It's all a matter of association and commutation—or organization and putrefaction, if you will."

Jordan did so well in science and impressed Southwall Lovingood so much that he nearly took analytical chemistry his second year. But Herece begged him to take music appreciation so they could be together. Deciding that Lovingood was sufficiently impressed, Jordan took music. Besides, he rationalized to himself, a knowledge of what was good in music was a necessary concomitant of the funeral director's art. The class did him little good: He learned nothing about sacred music, *gospel,* and he could never distinguish the difference between Beethoven and Bach, symphony and sonata.

His work in art had been tolerable, and he knew it. Fortunately, the department was of the persuasion that he had potential somewhere deep within him, "I wouldn't be discouraged," his adviser told him. "You've got an eye for form, and all you need is concentration on values, edges, and perspective."

But Jordan was discouraged from the start. In high school, it had been easier. They weren't as demanding, and most of the students took the classes as electives anyway. At City, they were nearly all artistic. So many of the students around him had better backgrounds, had grown up in environments where terms like "foreshortening" and "chiaroscuro" were household words. And some of them—far more than he cared to acknowledge— had greater talent. His sketches and canvases came up flat, and he longed to do something with depth in it and around it and over it. But the adviser said, "Remember, excellence in three dimensions is improbable, perhaps impossible, without discipline in two." So Jordan struggled along, doing little and finally no work away from the studios at school. And his indifferent grades showed it. Besides, while the others were studying at home, he was at Lovingood's, and that was no place for canvases and palette knives.

Clare was laid off by the Goldmans after seven years of service. "I'm terribly sorry, Clarisse," sniffed the graying Mrs. Goldman, "but with all the children off at the university, we've found we cannot afford you." Jordan could picture Anna and Ruth and Mike, striding to class at their respective schools, Harvard and Vassar and Stanford, not a care in the world, their cars and apartments and club privileges paid for by his mother's misfortune. Why did she have to be who she was anyway, forever depending on others, always in need? He cursed her wretched life. Clare, however, received a tidy little bonus, and that plus Jordan's earnings kept them going.

For a month Clare sat in the house, crying and drinking bourbon. Southwall Lovingood paid her a visit but came back complaining that he couldn't get her even to walk around the block. "She seems to think she's failed in life," Southwall said. Psyche Lovingood had greater success with Clare. Jordan figured that Lovingood must have told his wife about what happened because Clare told him Psyche called when he went home. That was the first time Clare smiled since she got laid off. She still wouldn't leave the house, but after that she looked forward to Mrs. Lovingood's calling each afternoon. Finally, Psyche came by in person and, telling Jordan by phone not to worry, succeeded in getting Clare to go downtown with her. In no time, Clare's spirits soared. Psyche invited her to a meeting of Les Dames, the prominent social club composed of dentists' and undertakers' wives. Through one of the women she met there, Clare eventually found work as a receptionist for a group of doctors and dentists sharing a common building. She earned more money than she ever had before.

Jordan was not surprised when she told him she was dating one of the dentists at the building. One night Jordan found the oily little man pawing his mother in the living room. He slammed the door in their faces and went back to the funeral home. He did not turn on the lights. For a long time, he sat in Lovingood's office in the dark. He sat in Lovingood's chair.

Wayne Lovingood, the prodigal son, finally condescended to join the family business. Jordan looked forward to the time when they would be business associates, if not friends. But he hardly saw Wayne. Like any apprentice mortician, Wayne was expected to work as an assistant embalmer under a licensed mortician. Southwall got his son to join the firm only after Southwall's doctor assured Wayne his father was seriously ill and needed to get away from it all. Lovingood asked Bates to take charge while he rested at home. But from the time the elder Lovingood left, Wayne never entered the preparation room. When Bates referred to him as an apprentice, young Lovingood called himself a "funeral director" and reminded both Jordan and Bates that it was only a matter of time until he was master of the house. Wayne announced that he would come in only when there was a service to conduct.

Southwall Lovingood was home two weeks, the only vacation Jordan ever remembered him taking. Lovingood couldn't wait to get back to work—partly because he could no more stay away from funerals than stop breathing and mostly because he was troubled by the scandalous conduct of his son. Wayne got into trouble almost as soon as he arrived.

Lovingood got in an elderly female case. The woman had been a lifelong member of the New Jerusalem Spiritualist Church of God in Christ and had risen to the revered post of church mother, which meant that she had a reserved seat in the front pew, wore a white bun cap and played a tambourine, and was always the first to shout "Amen" and "Fix it on up" when the Right Reverend Richard Daniel Rideout said something soulful. Naturally, the church went all out to give the old lady a mighty sendoff. Church folks always put on good shows. Lovingood himself embalmed the old woman, then went home to rest. Bates handled the arrangements. Wayne Lovingood insisted that he be allowed to direct the service in order to get acquainted with his father's affairs. After discussing the request with Lovingood by phone, Bates granted the request. With two notable exceptions, Wayne's handling of the service was correct.

The first exception was that on the day of the service, he insisted on going strictly by the mortuary school textbook and checked all equipment and work before the funeral. The corpse, he complained, was not adequately sealed against leakage. Bates called Southwall Lovingood, but the old man did not answer. So Bates spent a whole hour and a half respraying and repatching the body, with the result that the corpse lost much of its lifelike appearance.

Next, Wayne decided that the funeral coaches needed washing, although Bates assured him all they needed was dusting and that it was the responsibility of the leasing agency to wash them anyway. Wayne was adamant. He made the mistake of sending the cars to a common car wash for a quick waxing, which, of course, ruined the hearse's leatherette top.

Wayne's real difficulties, however, came when he tangled with Sharoline Mobley, a garish, gabby hairdresser who used too much makeup on herself and on the dead and who had a penchant for wide-brimmed hats. Southwall used Sharoline on all big outside jobs, and it was her custom to come in just before a service to touch up a body after it had been moved to the church.

Sharoline worked on the New Jerusalem church mother, and she arrived at the funeral home late in the morning, just as Wayne and Jordan were putting the body in the hearse for transfer to the church. Sharoline Mobley had on a turquoise chapeau adorned with enough red quills to make a feather duster. The sides of the hat were so wide it looked as if she had wings on her head. Sharoline had a comely-looking girl of fifteen or sixteen in tow. Wayne and Jordan greeted them, and Sharoline spoke; but the girl said nothing. The girl was very plainly dressed and wore pigtails and smirked constantly. She didn't seem to know where she was. Jordan noticed immediately that her head was slightly misshapen, and he guessed her plight. But Wayne Lovingood didn't. He pressed the girl to say something, and she smirked at the hearse. "Won't do any good to talk to *her*," Sharoline Mobley admitted. "She's my niece, but she's as retarded as a rubber duck, honey."

They rolled on to New Jerusalem, Jordan and Wayne with the body, Sharoline and her niece following in their car. At the church, Jordan opened the casket and propped up the torso of the body on blocks in the casket. The old lady's hands clutched her church mother's cap. Bates put it there. Sharoline put a little bib on the body and began combing the hair. Wayne Lovingood climbed into the pulpit and proceeded to deliver a mock sermon: "Dearly beloved. . . ." The girl with pigtails sat in a pew in the back of the church, conspiring with some distant comedy in the stained-glass windows.

The phone rang three times in the pastor's study. Then it rang again. It was Bates. He said he had just picked up a new

144

case, a man shot in front of a tavern and would be late. Would Jordan and Wayne pick up the flowers? "You do it," Wayne Lovingood commanded. "There aren't that many. Most of 'em are already here."

"I need some things from my shop," Sharoline Mobley said. "Could you— Oh, never mind, I'd better get them myself. Mister Lovingood, could you keep an eye on my niece? I've got to go 'round the corner."

Sitting now on the edge of the pulpit, his eyes fixed in an oblique gaze as removed and as shiny as the retarded girl's, Wayne Lovingood agreed. He said he wanted to get a "feel of the place" while they were gone.

It was a sweaty day. The flowers at the mortuary were already wilting, and Jordan noticed that they lost their funeral odor once they were brought out into the steaming air. En route to New Jerusalem, he stopped for a Coke. His watch told him to race the rest of the way. He propped open the church doors posthaste and rushed an armload of wilting flowers into the sanctuary. Loud voices in the church made him set the flowers down. It was Sharoline Mobley and Wayne Lovingood.

"You, you . . . imbecile!" Sharoline Mobley shouted at Wayne. "Just wait till your daddy hears about this shit!"

"Aw, Miz Mobley, I didn't do nothin'," Wayne protested.

"You call that nothing?" shrieked Sharoline, pointing to the pulpit.

Behind the lectern, between the gilded thrones of the elders, the retarded girl stumbled in a daze like someone who had been blinded. Her smile was gone. Her underpants were down around her ankles.

Sharoline backed Wayne Lovingood against the casket, and as he put out his hands to fend her off, Sharoline grabbed a pair of scissors from a box on the lid.

Lawrence Jordan prevented her from disemboweling Wayne right there in the church.

Two days after the funeral, Southwall Lovingood came back. "Just thought I'd see how things went the other day," he huffed. "Any trouble, Mis-tah Majorrr?" He flopped into his chair and added as an afterthought to Bates that he'd better start looking around for another cosmetologist to take the place of Sister Sharoline Anne Mobley, who apparently had been hitting the bottle a little too much.

"Don't say?" said Bates.

Wayne Lovingood didn't come back for a week. When he did, he was very rude to Lawrence Jordan. Jordan was in the foyer, studying for finals, when Wayne tramped in, swinging a set of keys. Jordan tried to look nonchalant. There was no case in the house, and Bates had gone to visit a lady friend on the pretext of scouting for another hairdresser who wasn't feared of the dead.

Wayne Lovingood pointed a key at Jordan.

"That all you do, sit around and read books?" he wanted to know.

"No."

"Well, that's all I ever see you doing."

"I do other things."

"Like what?"

"Keep people off my back."

"Who? Me?"

"Naw. I said *people*."

"I'm 'n kick your ass."

"Try it, chickenshit child molester!"

That was the first time Wayne Lovingood looked directly into Jordan's eyes, and what he saw made him back down. It was a sudden, abrupt backing down, and it caught Jordan by surprise. Jordan was angry enough to kill, and he knew it wasn't all because he hated Wayne Lovingood. Some of it was because he envied him, his position, his father, his friendship with Jerome Montague. And his being left alone with the retarded girl. Come on, baby, Jordan thought as Wayne stared at him, just you and me, just you and me. But Wayne's eyes blanked. He made a self-righteous kind of face. Again, he seemed to be staring between Jordan's eyes. It was the same kind of look Southwall Lovingood got when he was working on a case. Wayne looked at Jordan's forehead for some seconds, then turned and slouched away. Jordan watched him go out the side way, then went into the empty preparation room and got a scalpel. He put the scalpel between the cushions, and behind the book he wondered what Wayne thought of Jordan's going with his sister. Then he resumed his reading in the foyer. Now if *he* had been left with that retarded girl. . . .

"Psyche says Southwall's got a liver ailment," announced Clarisse Walker Jordan. "And he won't listen to the doctor."

Jordan's jaws flexed. It didn't seem possible: Southwall, the undertaker's undertaker, the battler of syphilis and cancer and dropsy, the man to whom sickness and decay were no mysteries, the man who had turned death inside out, Southwall had an ailment. Jordan's mouth got dry. He felt something rising within him, and he knew it was fear, the mortician's worst enemy. He fought it off.

"He'll be all right," he said in his calmest voice.

"Oh, I don't know. Psyche said it may be serious. Southwall won't tell her anything. Did he say anything to you?"

"No."

"Psyche says he just insists on going to work and he just comes home exhausted."

"That's the way he is," Jordan said. "He's completely dedicated. But that's why I say he'll be all right. He works like that all the time. *That* won't hurt him. What'll hurt him is if they succeed in keeping him at home, keeping him from his work. That could kill him. Remember, he's the undertaker. And the undertaker must be strong when everyone else is weak."

"Boy, you sound more and more like one yourself every day," said Clare. "But I guess you're right. Somehow he survives. I remember one time when Southwall was real little and they thought he was going to die. He caught the infantile paralysis and couldn't even walk. One night they called the preacher, he sunk so low. But he pulled through somehow. That's when he got real happy. A year later you'd never know he was the same child."

The doctor told Southwall to stop eating so much. And more important, to stop drinking. For a time, Southwall abstained. Instead of consuming enormous helpings of chitterlings and cornbread and cracklings, beans and slaw, he brought sandwiches from home. Instead of bourbon, he drank vermouth, which he kept in the bathroom. He sweat constantly, more than ever. He looked as if he had pounds of Vaseline all over his face. Light ran down his forehead in ragged streams. His voice got hoarse. His eyes turned yellow, and liquid poured from them constantly as if he was crying. He used three, four handkerchiefs an hour.

Business was slow, and Southwall just sat in his office, calling home. Most of the time he slept. One night Bates had to take him home. He was asleep again as soon as they got him in the car. Even Wayne, who came around to collect his pay for the New Jerusalem job, expressed concern for his father's health. Herece told Jordan she was afraid.

Then they got a case. Bates had been sitting up with the nodding Southwall for days, telling Southwall that his hand was stiff. Southwall grunted and went back to sleep.

"Hey, old man," Bates said, nudging the sleeping giant. "Man died over in the north end. We got a case."

"ZZZZZZZ. Huh? Huh? Case? Where? Who?"

Lovingood was wide-awake. He grabbed his hat from the doorknob. "Brother Jor-dannnnnnn! Get th' cot, son. Bates, wheel out the wagon!"

It was like old times again. Lovingood was like a man possessed. He insisted on making the pickup himself, collecting the vitals himself, setting up the case himself, making the arrangements himself. He was in the preparation room all night. The next day Jordan saw that Southwall's eyes were red again. And the old man cuffed Jordan affectionately as in the old days. "Go 'head, Brother Jordannn."

"Yes, sir. Yes, *sir!*"

"Where's that good-for-nothin' son a mine?" Southwall roared. "Bates, find him and tell him to get his buns on over here. Gonna make a embalmer outta that boy yet!"

On Friday they celebrated with bourbon and bones and beans. Jack Daniels. Lovingood had his share.

"Now, *South*wall. . . ."

"Hush, Bates. Never knowed a undertakin' man yet didn't drink, did you? Heck, man, I'm gonna bury you and th' doctor 'fore it's over. Yeah."

It became a standing order that Southwall was always out when the doctor called.

One evening, as Wayne, now pressed into service as the apprentice embalmer he was supposed to be, came out scowling, Lovingood called Jordan into the office. Jordan heard his heavy breathing. It had become like music to him. Lovingood had his coat off, mopping his brow. He spoke in light, cheerful tones. "Sit down, Mister Jordannn. This won't take long, m' boy."

Then for an hour, Lovingood rolled this way and that in his broken-down chair, mopping the dark reaches of his forehead, reliving the days of the greats: C. E. Lewis, Bill "Goose" Tatum, Harlan Fears, Cesare Valentino, who buried more people than he was called to. And he spoke of the Gresham College of Mortuary Science.

"It was a great thing to graduate from Gresham in those days," Lovingood recalled. He pointed proudly to the fading photo of stern-faced young men above his desk. In the front row a tuxedoed, mustachioed young Southwall Lovingood, his coarse hair pomaded down with Dixie Peach.

"For a long time, you know, funeral parlors were our people's greatest asset. Every undertaker was a Mason then, and that was how a lot of us, I mean a whole lot of us, got on the freedom road. If you know what I mean. Many a hunted man came North in a cloth-covered full couch, Brother Jordan, 'n' they weren't *dead* either. Anyway, the funeral parlor also offered fine opportunity, fiiine opportunity, for an enterprisin' young man like me, Mister Jordan, like you, Mister Jordan. Wasn't no art then. 'N' no bankin'. A young man cast about 'n' saw he could be a sweeper or a digger or a driver. That was it. Otherwise, he could be a preacher or an undertaker 'n' there was enough preachers, always will be.

"Anyway, ole Sister Fannie told me about what was then called the Gresham School of Restorative and Embalming Arts, the country's finest, 'n' I decided right then I was going to go. Had to, boy, had to. 'N' I worked hard at Gresham. It wasn't easy, but I made it through.

" 'Course my service interrupted things, set things back a little, Mister Brother Jor-dannn, and I was afraid I'd forget half the things they'd taught me at Gresham in the inter'm. But I was wrong, thank you, Jesus, thank you, Lord. The curriculum at Gresham is much harder now, much stiffer—no pun intended—but it wasn't a bed a roses then, son. They taught me well. Well, soon as those ole quartermaster people found out that I'd had a little education, havin' been to Gresham 'n' all, they put my talents to work. Before it was over, I used everything I knew of anatomy and embalming in the service of our country 'n' I'm not braggin', but my mortuary detail work in the trenches there and the front lines of Europe was some of the best, son, some of the best. I'm still proud of it to this day. In some ways, it was better'n some of the stuff I do right now. The battlefield was great preparation, great preparation, for civilian work, 'n' I'm proud to say I trained a lot of young men as my assistants who later went into Funeral Service when they got out, comforting countless others all over this troubled land.

"I mean it was invaluable experience. You came up against every kind of trauma known to man and then some. If you could stomach that, you were really cold-hearted and case-hardened. I mean we cleaned up those concentration camps, too. But that's enough of that, Mister Jordan.

"When I got back to the states, old Fannie Fears offered me a hundred dollars cold cash if I'd go down there to th' capital and ace my state board exam in mortuary science. It was called embalming then, just embalming. I was afraid I had been doin' things my own way, the Army way, too long, son, and might not even pass the board. So I wrote to Dr. Sam Houston Eason at Gresham, my old prof who's now the president of that great institution, 'n' he sent me all the latest literature on preservation and figuration.

"Well, it turned out that the military, as usual, was years ahead of civilians at that time, and I saw I knew more about the technical side of undertakin' work than most civilian embalmers. So I concentrated on the administrative side, son, 'n' I studied night 'n' day, night 'n' day. I studied right there in Fannie's back room on some of those cases. More important, she let me look at her books, showed me how they were kept. 'N' she let me sit in on some of the arrangement conferences so's I'd get a firsthand knowledge of merchandising and sales. I studied the building codes, and I read up on my mortuary law.

"But when the time came for me to go down, I was still so nervous 'n' unsure that ole man Thomas, Fannie's director, drove me down 'n' pumped me full of Early Times all night 'n' half the morning so I'd have it easy on the test. In the end, I collected that hundred dollars. When I took my oral, I answered every question loud 'n' clear, 'n' one of the examiners said, 'Heck, this man oughta be sittin' up here with us. He knows more than we do.'

"Boy, you shoulda seen ole Sister Fannie when Thomas and I came back hootin' 'n' snortin' 'n' passin' the booze around. 'I knew you would do it,' she said soon's she saw me. She reached right down between her titties and brought out a brand-new hundred-dollar bill right there on the spot. 'N' I shouldn't be tellin' you this, son, but that wasn't all she gave me that night, she got so happy. 'Nen the next day, she says to me: 'Southwall, you ain't nothin' but an undertakin' man!' 'N' I wuz, son, I wuz."

Jordan was to get a thousand dollars if he aced *his* test. "Gonna be harder for you than for me," Lovingood decided. "They cover more of everything now: six-point injection, cosmetic fluids. 'N' when ole Fannie give me a hundred, well, that was worth then what it takes a thousand for today."

In the meantime, Jordan was to be granted five thousand dollars—an incredible figure to him then—to complete his studies. Three thousand of these dollars he was to get in two installments, six months apart. This was to go for room, board and clothing during his year at school, with perhaps a little left over for a cheap movie or, as Lovingood chuckled, sowing a wild oat or two. The remaining two thousand would remain in Southwall's possession. Southwall would parcel it out every quarter to the school. It would go for books and tuition, laboratory and student fees and such "incidentals" as rubber gloves and surgical smocks. "You use a lot of incidentals at Greshammm," Southwall said.

Jordan's grades were to be sent directly to Lovingood. Jordan was to maintain at least a C average, and it was implicit, although Southwall didn't say so, that if he failed, his stay at Gresham would come to a screeching halt.

14

The next day Lovingood had Jordan dial a long-distance number, and Jordan knew it was Gresham before he called. A woman answered, and Lovingood took the phone. After not a moment's pause, Lovingood's eyes got wide, and his lips rolled back on his grinning teeth. "Dr. Easonnnnnnnn!" Southwall cried, and was exceedingly happy.

Jordan retreated, closing the door tightly.

Two days later a telegram arrived impressively from Gresham by urgent delivery. It was directed to Master Lawrence Xavier Jordan, Esq., and signed by Dr. Samuel H. Eason, president. It informed Jordan that on the basis of Southwall Lovingood's priceless recommendation, Gresham had waived its usual application procedures and would be pleased to admit Jordan in either the summer quarter or the winter quarter. For the record, however, the requisite papers and the college catalogue were arriving separately by airmail special.

Southwall mailed an entrance fee of fifty dollars to Gresham and told Jordan he had advanced it to him from his trust fund.

Jordan read his catalogue over and over. He carried it with him everywhere. He read it at home; he read it at Herece's house; he read it at work. He carried it with him when he graduated from City College. He asked Lovingood and Bates and even Wayne Lovingood questions about the school, its history, its graduates, its offerings.

"Damn, Brother Jordan," observed Major Bates, "if you look at that pamphlet any longer, you'll know it by heart."

From the catalogue (he resented Bates' calling it a "pamphlet"), Jordan learned that the Gresham School of Restorative and Embalming Arts was founded in 1913 by Dr. C. L.

Gresham, an itinerant undertaker who had distinguished himself in the flash floods of 1898, or, as the catalogue put it, "Being the only practitioner of modern funeral methods on the scene, Dr. Gresham was able to render rewarding service with confidence, compassion, sanitation, efficiency and dispatch."

Major Bates elaborated on Clyde Leland Gresham's achievements. Getting wind of the tragedy, Bates said, Clyde Gresham hightailed it downstate with the newfangled portable pressure equipment and twenty pine boxes, quickly assembled a crew of meat wagon drivers, and rendered most of his service with quicklime and gunnysacks, reserving his more detailed and compassionate attention for the rich and well-to-do. The townspeople, faced with the possibility of widespread death from typhoid and other infections, were only too glad to let Clyde Gresham work his dismal wonders. Clyde's service was indeed rewarding: With his earnings, which it took him two years to collect, Gresham moved to the big city and opened up a funeral parlor that was the showplace of its time. He became one of the first to use the new Bisga embalming fluid, the first to use motorized funeral coaches, the first to offer pre-need burial plans. Within a decade, he was doing so well and Funeral Service was expanding so rapidly that he felt obliged to share his knowledge with others of his calling.

The Gresham School opened in a storefront across from the city morgue with two faculty and three students. Tuition was fifty dollars, and the curriculum consisted of three months' lectures and practice in "preservation and figuration" after which the student was awarded a scroll adorned with Egyptian pyramids and sacred symbols which proclaimed him a "certified embalmer." The scroll was signed by Dr. C. L. Gresham, president, and one Samuel Houston Eason, dean of students and professor of restorative arts.

At the school, Gresham taught the "preservation" aspects of the trade while Eason, former mule team driver and Gresham's second-in-command in the flash floods, concentrated on "figuration." One of the original students, Percy Goodwin Newbody ('13), went on to found the great dynasty in Jordan's own hometown which boasted four thriving chapels on both sides of the Kaw River. The second member of the class saw distinguished service in World War I, married well, and went on to become one of the nation's largest supplier of burial gowns and baby bottles. The third, unfortunately, died of arsenic poisoning a year after he graduated. Lack of proper *asepsis*.

In 1929, with nineteen students, the school changed its name to Gresham College of Mortuary Science and to new quarters in the suburbs, a three-story ivy-covered stone edifice with a very cool cellar. The great Dr. Gresham gave up the ghost in 1948, and Sam Houston Eason, now himself a "Doctor," succeeded the Founder as president and director of public relations. With Gresham, Eason had fought long and hard for state licensing of embalmers and requirements of mortuary school certificates. In 1950, the school was authorized by the state to grant associate degrees in mortuary science to those students who had completed a year or more of college before entering Gresham. The others received Gresham's "equally as coveted" Funeral Service Education Diploma certifying that they had been graduated as funeral director-embalmers.

Today the school, a nonprofit institution, averaged one hundred students a year, most of whom came from established mortuary families. Tuition and fees were two thousand dollars. In addition to "salaries comparable to those at other colleges and universities," Wayne Lovingood explained, Gresham faculty members, now numbering a round dozen, supplemented their incomes by publishing embalming textbooks and histories, doing "basic" research, and serving as consultants to and directors of assorted trade publications, fluid and equipment companies, memorial parks, ambulance companies, funeral homes, and insurance companies. "The best thing about mortuary science," Wayne Lovingood asserted, "is money."

From the start, Clyde Gresham had emphasized *practice*. The catalogue was replete with references to it. "An embalmer learns to embalm by embalming," Southwall Lovingood remembered the Founder saying. To give his understudies practical experience, Gresham at first took them once a week across the street to the city morgue. There, thanks to Gresham's excellent public relations with those in municipal service, the tyro undertakers were allowed to cut and sew and hack on those unfortunate citizens Gresham fondly referred to as "the indigent dead of our fair city."

When the school moved to its new quarters, the Founder

found a way to continue providing "clinical materials" for his needy bunch. With the assistance of friends at City Hall, he set up a licensed, noncommercial mortuary in the cool cellar of the school, and the new Ivy Chapel contracted with the city to dispose of the poor and homeless "in a dignified and discreet manner." What the inmates at Gresham did with the cadavers between the first call and the grave was nobody's business but their own. A compassionate man, Gresham was always careful to ensure that any morgue attendant on duty during a pickup by his students received a little token of appreciation. "Usually a vial of liquid refreshments," Southwall Lovingood recalled fondly. Lovingood said Clyde Gresham might have withheld his tokens had he known that the morgue attendants referred to his institution rather irreverently as Frankenstein University.

At any rate, Ivy Chapel was the pride of Gresham College, and every student who ever trod the unusual campus served his time in the basement mortuary. "Real-life setting is provided throughout the Gresham experience," the catalogue declared. What Gresham had done was integrate all phases of the funeral parlor operation into the curriculum. Thus on a rotating basis for each case, pairs of students were assigned as ambulance drivers, embalmers, funeral director and assistant, survivors, mourners, musicians and sextons. When the city morgue called with another case of indigence, the student "survivors" placed a mock phone call to the student "directors" to make the final arrangements. And so on, right down to the simulated chapel service. "Often the services in Ivy Chapel are so reverent and so realistic," the catalogue proclaimed, "student mourners are moved to actual tears."

Jordan could see himself sitting in the Gresham pews now, emoting as the spirit moved him.

Ivy Chapel was complete with reposing rooms, arrangements office, preparation room, chapel, merchandizing room and "anatomical storage vault for temporary repose of backed-up cases." In the merchandising room, "caskets, vaults, burial garments and wreaths of every color and description may be viewed."

Jordan studied the photographs and captions of the Gresham chambers, imagining himself trodding the sacred carpets, rubber gloves in hand, becoming privy to the rites and arts of Mortuaria. He saw himself among his colleagues in the east wing of the great amphitheater pictured on page 18, taking notes on incision procedure, and standing before a circulatory chart in the physiological sciences lab on page 24, knowingly pointing out the carotids and femorals with a long stick. How great it was going to be: Pathology I.

And Accounting II. That summer he took *three* courses in business administration at City, wrote Gresham, and told them he was coming in the fall and informed Clare that he would buy her a castle after he had learned how to render "rewarding service with confidence, compassion, sanitation, efficiency and dispatch."

15

Jordan wasn't the only Greshamite living near the school.
But the others, scions of wealthy funeral families, lived there
out of a need for adventure, something to remember years later
at Mu Sigma conventions. Jordan lived there because he had to.
It was easy for the Gresham counselors to dispense with Jordan's housing problem; Jordan had no money. "Now it isn't
much," Dean Thomas Ickle had said, "but there's a perfectly
adequate rooming house a few blocks away that might suit your
pocketbook. It's run by this marvelous old colored
woman. . . ."

So Jordan had moved out of the downtown YMCA, which
was too expensive for him, into the gargoyled and rotting Fifty-
fifth Avenue Arms, or, as the few other poor Gresham students
called it, The House of the Seven Gargoyles. In the grimy halls,
the old gaslight fixtures were still jutting from the walls like
disembodied arms with clenched fists. In the dingy rooms, the
brass-posted beds waited gloomily for the exhausted and the
bored and the sick.

Sam Eason, however, himself resident of a three-acre estate
along Chicago's North Shore, gave Jordan some consolation
when he told him, "Now don't feel badly cause you're over at
the Seven, Mister Jordan. You've joined some select company,
including yours truly and the great Southwall Lovingood himself, though it was a little more elegant in our day."

Jordan had met Eason during orientation week and liked
him ever since. One day Eason stopped Jordan in the halls between anatomy and hygiene classes and whispered, "Hear you're
quite a restorative artist. My specialty, you know. After Christ-

mas, we'll drop in and see how you're coming." Eason kept his word.

Southwall Lovingood indeed had once roomed at the Seven Gargoyles. He confirmed it in a letter to Jordan which congratulated Jordan on his fine grades at Gresham. Mrs. Simpson, the brown-toothed old landlady, said she remembered Lovingood well. "The devil hisself," she growled. Jordan thought her memory must be failing. That seemed an odd thing to say about Southwall Lovingood.

Gresham College was considerably smaller than Jordan had anticipated. The catalogue cover, with its distortion of perspective and scale, had suggested the grandeur of a Taj Mahal. Really, it was quite squat, an aging two-story edifice half a block long but very shallow in depth. The ivy on the neo-Gothic façade had seen better days, as had the school. Inside, plaster crumbled from the walls, shaken by the frequent arrival and departure of the ambulance in the basement. On the corner by Gresham, the young toughs taunted Jordan: "Hey, Brother, you goin' to Frankenstein U, huh, baby? I hear they do it to dead women in there."

Jordan's first quarter had been roughest of all; the wind cut through coats like a scalpel. Most days, all Jordan had to eat were Mrs. Simpson's stale beans and rye bread. Board, such as it was, was included in the rent, which was incredible and left him with no money to go to a café. He ate with two other roomers, reclusive elderly people who gave Mrs. Simpson their entire Social Security checks.

It was a pleasure to go to school or have weekend duty. Most of the Gresham students were men, although Jordan noticed two or three women in every class and women's bathrooms in the halls. Nearly all the students came from well-to-do mortuary families—what undertaker wasn't well-to-do?—some of them going back three and even four generations. The wealthiest Gresham student that year was reputed to be Sean O'Flarrety IV, whose grandfather established a chain of mortuaries in three New England states. Freckle-faced Sean, short, stubby and squinting, lived on the lakeshore and belonged to an exclusive tennis club. His father sent him money every week and Sean paid others, chiefly Lawrence Jordan, to stand his weekend duty.

Often Jordan found himself standing three, four watches a weekend. This, added to his pay, gave him just enough to eat lunch and dinner out during the week and have something brought to him on watch Saturdays and Sundays. He went to the movies out of what he had scrimped. He kept the money in his pocket: If he hid it under his pillow or in some book back at the Seven, Mrs. Simpson was certain to find it. Jordan knew she searched his room, looking for back rent. He despised the wrinkled-up old hag. With her ashy skin she looked like a case ripe for Ivy Chapel, which was probably where she would end up. It was rumored on campus that the only reason she took in Gresham students all those years was in hope that the school would give her free burial.

Jordan was saving to go home for Christmas. But the weather got so bad and Mrs. Simpson so demanding that by November he was obliged to buy clothes and pay some rent. Christmas found him still in the big city with Mrs. Simpson and the elderly pensioners. Mrs. Simpson was too cheap to buy even a tree, but they did share half a pint of bourbon on Christmas and hog's headcheese and black-eyed peas, which Mrs. Simpson, a Kentuckian, said were "black eyed-ed beans. Never seen no peas look like that."

Jordan didn't dare ask Southwall Lovingood for money to come home; Lovingood already had done too much. And he didn't want to ask Clare, who bitched at him afterward for not coming.

His room was cold and dim and littered with slugs of wax, textbooks and plaster of paris molds. On a tattered ocher card-table Mrs. Simpson had dragged up from the basement and sold him for seventy-five cents, Jordan modeled ears and eyes and noses for different facial contours under a bald light bulb hanging obscenely from a converted gas fixture in the ceiling. Jordan didn't even have a bookcase or desk, although Sam Eason lent him a radio later. On the floor, Jordan kept the books on which his fortunes depended: *Scientific Embalming*, the basic text by C. L. Gresham and S. H. Eason; *Embalming Principles and Procedures* by Pliny A. Stubbs, licensed embalmer; *Introduction to Pathology: An Illustrated Text* by Doctors T. E. Gordon and D. F. Grant; *Bacteremia* by Joabim Cisneros, PhD; *History of Funeral Practice*, copyrighted

159

by the American Morticians Association; *The Psychology of Grief: A Text with Adapted Readings* by C. L. Gresham; *Vascular Anatomy and Anatomical Guides* by a pair of physicians; *Chemistry of Arterial Fluids, Preservation Demand,* and *Dilution Water,* booklets put out by Gresham College; Eason's famous *Art of Restoration*; another restorative art work called *Dermatine Figuration* by a lesser Gresham staffer; and *Modern Funeral Direction* and *Accounts and Balances,* two books Jordan had yet to get into. Old copies of *Mortuary Management* and *Casket and Sunnyside* were crammed under the bed. Jordan had lifted the magazines from the school library.

Sometimes Jordan stayed awake all night, reading his books and working in wax. Often he caught himself modeling tiny animals or people instead of facial features. Once just before Christmas, he modeled the face of one of the prostitutes he'd seen on the street.

Gresham College smelled of death. It emanated from the basement of the school in the storage vaults and wafted through Ivy Chapel up through the air vents. It floated permanently in the Clyde L. Gresham Memorial Amphitheater—where they watched professors apply the latest techniques in cosmetic embalming and motorized aspiration—and in the halls and classrooms. The smell got into your clothes and in your skin and in your soul. Jordan smelled it everywhere, on others, in the coats of the professors, even those who were nonembalmers. In the preparation rooms, Jordan washed diligently with alcohol and antiseptic soap, pungent roses, but he could not erase the scent. Even the receptionist in the front hall had it.

Herece's letters were infrequent, brief, unsatisfying. Jordan needed somebody. In the window across from his, he saw the shades pulled, heard springs creaking. In the streets, whores beckoned, young girls. Two months after he came to Gresham, he lay on his bed, on top of the covers, and masturbated toward the window where the prostitutes lived. Then his room smelled like Clorox. He tried to read, study, blot out his shame. But the smell got in the pages of the books, mingled with the death scent. He stole two jars of antiseptic soap from school, washed his whole body in it, then masturbated again.

During that desolate Christmas hiatus he met Ebenezer Minifee. He was headed for the student library to keep from thinking about Herece and home and the Clorox smell his body made. As he plodded toward the library in the cool building, he spotted Eb in the student lounge, dozing.

Eb was a midyear student. "I've never been away from home at Christmas before," Eb said as they sipped stale coffee in the lounge. "Thought it would be interesting to get here early to get the feel of the place. Guess I'm the only one that did that."

"Yeah," Jordan observed. "It's pretty damn lonely around here now."

Eb was staying with relatives near the lake. He was bored there, and Jordan got him to keep him company on watch, though Eb was not allowed to go out on calls or into the Ivy Chapel morgue. When school reconvened, Eb moved in with Jordan and they shared the rent. With Eb for company, Jordan had a pleasanter time during his second and third quarters. It was mostly practice. Jordan handled all kinds of cases and even managed to cry real tears in the simulated services of subterranean Ivy Chapel.

Gresham College was Jordan's only entertainment. Otherwise what was there? Before he had arrived, the college had sent him brochures touting Chicago's yacht harbor, its night life, its art galleries and concert halls, its Museum of Science and Industry. Jordan had looked forward to sampling some of the culture-by-the-lake. Not nights in the rooming house with one naked light bulb hanging bloomily from the leaky ceiling. Gargoyles laughing at him from the ledges. Jordan and Eb Minifee lying on their beds, holding endless light discussions to keep from thinking. Eb's hot plate in the corner. The landlady's rotten teeth, demanding rent.

Ebenezer Minifee was a quiet, likable fellow, short, slender, dark, an undertaker's son from some small town in North Carolina. They all were undertaker's sons, the Greshamites. In one way or another.

Eb lent Jordan money that Jordan knew he couldn't repay. Eb's family was wealthy. He could have been living in Lake Towers or La Salle Park instead of on the rotting South Side; but he didn't know better, and Jordan wouldn't tell him because he was too glad to have Ebenezer's company. Together,

161

they made forays into the street to buy groceries and cook them on the hot plate rather than go downstairs to Mrs. Simpson's putrid dinners. Together they reviewed the anatomy of arteries and veins. Jordan, unable to visualize the anatomical guides, would pretend to cut on Eb, a stand-in corpse. "Man, I'm glad this ain't for real." Eb laughed.

When Eb had night duty at Gresham, Jordan lay alone in the room, yanking stuffing from the divan, listening to the radio. He sure would like to patronize the prostitutes next door, but prostitutes cost money, more money nowadays than when Southwall Lovingood was there. Why didn't Southwall write?

On the nights when Eb was gone, Jordan would review his lessons. Involuntarily, maddeningly, he tossed and turned, tried to think about other things, his future, Lovingood, Herece. But he couldn't still the fears.

It was warm. Soon the vapors from the lake would make it muggy. Down in the alley, worms in open garbage; strewn waste contaminating dogs and little children. *God, the worms.* Jordan would sit upright on the divan, adjusting the radio volume, mopping his brow.

Got to get the worms out. Kerosene or DDT the only solutions. Disinfect the respiratory tract, prevent leakage, purge and invasion of insect larvae. *Larvae.* Jordan's mind flew back home, five hundred miles away. He had been fourteen or fifteen when he noticed them, the worms. His flesh crawled. Clare had given him wrapped garbage to take down to the can. It was a sunken can; you had to step on a lever to lift the lid. He knew something was wrong when he saw the lid popping up and down. At first he thought it was rats, something familiar. But it was the worms. *Damn you,* Clare said. *Scared of your own shadow. They're just worms, maggots. Haven't you seen maggots before? Get back down there 'n empty that damn garbage, boy. Go on!*

The sack wouldn't sink, so Jordan got a stick and mashed it down, mashed *them* down. He lit a fire in the trash and burned the stick to a black point.

When the garbage men came, they didn't even notice what was writhing in the can. The garbage men were used to it. Something was in the can. Courage? Manliness? Jordan couldn't imagine then that he would ever be a man, ever be hardened against filth and rot and decay and the feasting of slimy things.

Jordan was afraid to sleep the nights Eb Minifee was on duty. To distract his mind, he would raise the curtain just an inch and look across the night to the prostitutes' room. Once Jordan saw one girl in bed with someone. That made him forget the worms.

Sooner or later, he would fall off to sleep and have the Dream. It had begun in his first quarter at Gresham and was always the same. The Dream.

In the Dream, square-jawed Clare was coming up the walk in fine clothes and a hat with bright feathers. The building was the rooming house, with only one story, all painted up. There was a neon sign up over the porch, and Jordan couldn't read the sign; but he knew his name was on it. The windows of the house were closed, and heavy draperies hid what was inside. Jordan was both observer and actor in the Dream; he was inside and outside his body. He could see himself coming into the porch in his apron to greet Clare, and he could see Clare's face all at once. She looked peaceful, as though there were nothing wrong and nothing about to be wrong, though Jordan felt there was and that she knew it.

"Did you get the insurance?"

"Yes, I got it. I want to see your new place."

"Not today, Mother. Got the case in there."

"That's good. How long did it take? Can I see it?"

"No—it's a special case."

"I just want to look at it."

"Mother, it's a mess."

"Where are you going?"

"In there. Got to check it. Got embalming powder all over it. Hardening compound."

Clare stepped back from him in the Dream, but as she did, she had a dead rabbit in her right hand, carried it by the legs. Her suit turned beige and hat black with a long iridescent crow's feather in it. She was angry about his not letting her in, he could feel it. But instead of arguing, she merely stepped back with a funny smile on her face. Jordan knew something was going to happen.

163

It was so close in the house, stuffy and hot. Only a shallow room with stained-glass windows and his desk and a big door behind the desk. Jordan went through the door. Then he was back outside, crouching behind the desk. He saw himself back out of the door, shielding his eyes. He was sweating and crying. His self ran to the porch, looking back at the door.

"What's the matter?"

"Mother, I can't go through with it."

"It's almost time for the service. And I've got the insurance. I won't give it back."

"Please."

"I'm going in there and see. I'll handle it myself."

"No! You mustn't. . . . They're in there, them, it's crawling with them. I can't do it. I'm going to quit."

"Boy, get back in there! You've come too far to turn back now. Scared, scared of your own shadow. And I got the money. Five hundred dollars. Our big chance. Get out of the way; I'm going in there myself."

Just then Southwall Lovingood and Fannie Fears came by in a car together and said they were out looking for cases to disinfect and did Jordan know any? Clare looked intimidated, but Jordan brushed his mother aside and, composing himself, told Lovingood: "As a matter of fact, I've got one now." And the beads of sweat on his forehead were gone. Lovingood and Fannie Fears floated in like ghosts. He saw himself standing there now young and handsome and without fear, in a crisp new tuxedo, his hair wavy and slicked down like Lovingood's in the class picture.

Jordan told Clare: "I'm going back inside with them. Want to come?" But Clare was afraid. Her face showed it, and Jordan was relieved. She was very much afraid: He had that over her forever, and Clare would never bother him again. He stood there grinning on the porch. Then Southwall Lovingood called to him from the preparation room: "You comin', Brother Jordannn?"

164

16

Formula: one point five gallons' embalming fluid for every fifty pounds of body weight. Formula: one step deeper into Funeral Service for every unit of fear.

Lawrence Xavier Jordan indulged his fear by studying vascular anatomy, the chemistry of arterial solutions, injection and drainage techniques, cavity embalming and cosmetic restoration. He packed the orifices of dead bodies with cotton soaked in astringents. He washed them down with hoses and spatulated plaster of paris over missing sections of their skulls.

The embalmer, Jordan learned was a preserver, a fixer, a *memorializer.* Incessantly he battled the terrible agents of decomposition and disease—the invisible saprophytes and micrococci of the human respiratory and intestinal tracts liberated by their host's demise. Girded for the hunt in apron, rubber gloves and vinegar-soaked surgical mask, the embalmer pursued saprophytes through chilly labyrinths and narrow tributaries of the River Styx: the cooling veins and arteries of the dead.

Bending over a body like an impatient lover, the embalmer anxiously parted the lips of his surgical incision, fondled arteries and veins. Deep into the purple arteries he thrust the embalming needle, deadly phallus sperming fire: germicides and tissue fixers, wetting agents and anticoagulants, odor suppressants, dyes. Formaldehyde, mercuric chloride, borax, lanolin, citrate of sodium, sorbitol. Oil of cloves and lavender and ponceau.

Pulsed by contractions deep within the injection apparatus (the testes of embalming), the embalming fluid spewed through death's domain: up to the aorta of the heart and down again into every branch and subbranch of the system, chasing micrococci. The fluid diffused lovingly through the walls of the arterioles and capillaries into the tender tissues, toughening them, fixing them, converting the soluble albumins into jelly, throttling the enzymes of the decomposing agents. The fluid followed paths of least resistance first, then later backed up into bypassed areas—collateral vessels' clotted passageways. It saturated the body, pushing the dying and dead blood ahead of it, out through the drain tube into a bucket or a sink.

When it was over and when he was convinced the body was preserved, the memorializer washed with alcohol or antiseptic soap. He sterilized his instruments and scrubbed down his preparation table. He incinerated the contents of his trash can to prevent disease from spreading.

Then he went out front to greet the public.

Jordan had one more quarter to do at Gresham. He was anxious to get back home, rejoin Lovingood, apply what he had learned. Someday he might even be a better embalmer than Lovingood.

He wanted to get back to art, too, with his new knowledge of anatomy. At junior college, they looked at the outside of people and deduced the anatomy within. At Gresham, they looked at the anatomy and deduced what should be without. Jordan reasoned that his understanding of both perspectives could only improve his art. That's what he planned to do: spend a few years with Lovingood, making money to support his sculpting. When he had enough to live on and had made himself a name in art, Jordan would take Herece away from the mortuary and they would live a happier life.

Anatomical knowledge was the secret of restorative art, and Jordan excelled in restoration. He learned to use the inner tissues and matching parts of a body to determine what was missing. Matching parts were best: the beauty of duality, bifurcation, the symmetry of face and arms and torso. Posterior maximus. Woman. Butterfly. If the embalmer had one side of a face, he could re-create the other side. And if the face was entirely missing? Then the embalmer went by the contours of the muscles and the skull. And by photographs. "The embalmer," Doctor Sam Houston Eason had informed the dermatology class, "is a creator of illusions. As such, he is obliged to bring out

166

some things and hide others." The embalmer made his re-creations through the use of wires, waxes, plasters, powders, spotlights and even broomsticks. (The heads of decapitated persons were replaced on their torsos with broomsticks—at least in the classic method described in Eason's *Art of Restoration*.)

Jordan was drawn to dermasurgery in spite of his distaste for what was ugly and disfigured. Or perhaps *because* of that distaste. He couldn't resist the opportunity to apply his sculpting and was never satisfied until he had transfigured what had been distorted. Lawrence Jordan excelled in the most fearsome aspect of the undertaker's trade just because he feared it most.

He had done so well in restoration that Doctor Eason himself, gaunt, white-haired and Southern-toned, had taken time to come in and show Jordan a few tricks. His muleskinner's background belied it, but Sam Eason had learned a lot about dermasurgery (Eason still called it "figuration") in his years at Gresham, and he passed much of it on to Jordan.

"Theoretically," Eason said, "it should be possible to reproduce a passable facsimile of an entire human body, although I've never heard of any mortician doing it." Jordan was fascinated with this idea. Re-creating a person from nothing! The next step was replication of life itself. Casketing the model and passing it off to the loved ones as the real thing. The embalmer had help: The survivors *wanted* to see it was the deceased anyway.

The so-called mortuary science phase of his education now was coming to a close, and Jordan tried to arrange with Eason to do "independent research," building up a case from only the skeleton. But Eason said Gresham lacked the facilities and equipment for that. "Besides," Eason told him, "the mortuary management phase is just as important, if not more so, as the mortuary science quarter, Mister Jordan. It is the management quarter that separates the mere embalmer from the funeral *director*."

Now in two weeks Jordan would be studying management: psychology, public speaking, accounting, funeral directing. Eason was right. The embalmer, after all, was in business to make money. Like a carpenter or chiropractor or, more precisely, the garbage man. To do that properly, he had to know how to manage his affairs—and his customers. The main reason for funeral practice was for living, not the dead. And embalming was easy enough, provided you had the stomach and knew the technique.

Jordan was sincerely interested in improving his embalming technique. But Gresham was very thorough, and already he felt confident to perform any routine operation in the prep room. And with time and practice, he would be able to handle even the most difficult and dangerous cases. Except—but he refused to think about that. Anyway, in the management quarter the morticians kept up with their embalming techniques by working every week on actual cases—the backup from the city morgue. In some ways, Jordan was looking forward to the management quarter. The students who went the full year enjoyed a kind of upperclassman status. They worked pretty much of their own and were allowed to miss classes without penalty. It was accepted that students who graduated in both embalming and funeral directing would go farther in their careers. And make more money.

Still, Jordan would miss restorative art—both because of his interest in the class and because he no longer would be working alongside Marcella Ransom.

17

Marcella Ransom was Lawrence Jordan's laboratory partner. Jordan had seen girls like her in his dreams, Creole aristocracy: long, straight hair, piercing eyes of green or gray, lithe limbs. There was an aura about them that Jordan associated with gypsies. Phil Lafollette's sisters had it. A mystic beauty, the best of several worlds. Apartness, aloofness. Inscrutable, enchanting, haunting.

Marcella Ransom had chestnut in her hair, hazel in her eyes, and flawless cream in her complexion. What fascinated Jordan most were her pierced ears. He'd always been charmed by pierced ears: echoes of gypsy barbarism, nights under spangled heavens. Marcella's little earrings, tiny gold *o*'s, danced in her lobes as she scurried about the restorative art laboratory. The earrings were an extension of that aura he perceived. The way they complemented the cool landscape of her neck, the way the fluorescent lights in the class burned crescents on them, the simple elegance of the earrings—all this made Jordan's blood athletic. He imagined himself doing a torrid Spanish tango with Marcella, among the sheeted corpses.

Before Ebenezer Minifee arrived, Marcella was the only other Gresham student who really noticed Jordan, who really cared about him. Yet something—Marcella's too perfect beauty, her sense of aristocracy—prevented them from being intimate. She was warm toward Jordan, and Jordan appreciated that. But she was a light-skinned woman, after all, and it had been Jordan's experience that light women were not particularly attracted to him. Marcella had none of Herece Lovingood's dusky invitingness.

He'd never expected Marcella to notice him. He noticed her

right away. He saw her talking to the other women in the class. There were more women in restorative art than in any of his other classes. At first, he thought Marcella was Italian, Spanish, but the flare of her tiny nose, the breadth of her lips indicated that hers was partially an Afro beauty. Still, he hardly expected her to speak to him. Light women acted funny sometimes, haughty. Some of them denied they were black. But this one had pierced ears and an easy manner, and that was a good sign.

When the professor in restorative art asked the students to pair off for laboratory work, Jordan had hung around in the back, hoping to spot some other lonely student who needed a partner. Marcella, diminutive and creamy, was up front, her back to him, communing with the shrouded lab specimens. The others began to pair off. Marcella stood among the bodies for a long time, lost in thought. Nobody came up to Jordan. The room was filled with buzzing. The teacher was about to tap Marcella's shoulder, instruct her to find a partner, when she turned abruptly from her reverie and walked straight back to Lawrence Jordan.

"I'm Marcella," she said, her eyes piercing his skull. "I hope you wouldn't mind being my partner."

What could he say?

In lab, her hands were delicate and soft. Jordan held them when she asked him to guide her in modeling. He got behind her and put his arms around her and guided her hands. There was subtle perfume in her hair. Soft wisps; her hair brushed his neck. The scent of death didn't cling to her. Her lab coats were always immaculate, crisp. She called him Mister Jordan out of respect. She didn't seem to notice or to mind the closeness with which they had to work. When Jordan was with her, he was oblivious of the others, of the teacher making his rounds among the tables, pointing out errors in technique.

Marcella was good with hair. She said she got it from her mother, who did all the cosmetology on her father's cases. Her father, Achilles Ransom, had started in undertaking as a boy of sixteen in Baton Rouge. In the early days, he moved north to the big city, the very city Gresham moved to, and founded a funeral home with a local man, Vertis Picou. Ransom and Picou were modestly successful in the city; but competition grew fierce, and Achilles Ransom, astute in business, had moved to a smaller city farther up the north shore to serve a growing minority population there. He and Picou were the only black undertakers within a radius of thirty miles. There they prospered. Marcella was born in Chicago not far from Gresham. But she grew up in the small town, Kewaunee, on the shore. When she was a little girl, Vertis Picou had a nervous breakdown and sold his share in the business and moved to California. Achilles Ransom, however, still kept the name of Picou in the business, a condition of the sale.

Often, Jordan and Marcella didn't talk. Jordan would do most of the wax work on a case while Marcella observed. Then she would apply the cosmetics and trim or dress the hair. He was amazed at her composure around even the most disfigured bodies. She appeared not to notice. There was something about Marcella that chilled Jordan. If she had been an ugly woman, he might have understood, but she was strikingly pretty, even beautiful. Yet here she was at Gresham, aproned and rubber-gloved like the rest of them, her nervous system absorbing trauma that most men would shrink from. Really, she had more stomach than Jordan, though he would never let her know that.

Marcella was mixing dusting powder at one end of the table. Jordan was checking the body between them for signs of embalming failure. There were none; someone had done a good job. The room reeked of formaldehyde. He was afraid to look up—Marcella might be watching him with that strange directness of hers, her eyes still and wide. They were the eyes of a big cat. She was humming.

"How'd you get started in this?" he heard himself ask.

"I've always been in it. Dad had a place right here once, you know."

"Yes. You told me."

"I mean I've always liked it." She stopped mixing. "Some of my most pleasant memories are of that place my father had down here. We lived upstairs. So I'm used to it. I dream about it all the time."

"I do, too."

She came toward Jordan. Her skin showed yellow through the latex gloves. She still had the spatula in her hands.

"One of my earliest memories," she said, "was playing with

171

my girlfriends downstairs in the caskets. We had a lot of fun, then. We used to put our doll babies in them and hold mock funerals. I would always play the part of my father."

"Mmmph."

Marcella came closer to Jordan. He dared to look at her. She was brushing unchained wisps of hair away from her face with her forearm. He wondered if she had ulnar and radial arteries in her wrist like other people. She looked at Jordan, her eyes bright and distant. Jordan felt her looking through him.

She nearly threw the spatula down. It clattered by the body. She gripped the side of the table; her knuckles whitened under the gloves by the pressure.

"I had a vision," she whispered, looking over Jordan's shoulder, as if at some specter in the air. "I came home from college, and I had a vision.

"I went to one of those convent schools in Michigan," she went on. "You know, nuns and novitiates and things. Very restricted. Prayers before every class, adoration in the chapel before lights out. It was stodgy. But I liked to read, so I majored in English. I read my way through school." She laughed, a sudden snigger, and her earrings twinkled. "Then I graduated and came home and sat around. Mother tried to get me married off."

"To whom?"

"A boy named Tommie Roddenberry. You know, Major, Weaver and Roddenberry, that one. Right here in Chicago."

"Why didn't you?"

"Well. I didn't. . . . I wasn't interested in marriage. Not then. I had to find myself. I started going down to the mortuary, asking my father all kinds of questions. One day he let me help him down there in the basement—our prep room's in the basement—and I liked it. It was so quiet and peaceful. Almost *reassuring*. But I wasn't sure. I mean at one time I thought seriously about being a nun, too. But that wasn't my cup of tea. I don't think I could be celibate, not all my life."

"What about the work?"

"Oh, yes. *That*. Well, I just had this vision. It was after I had been helping my father for some time. I felt pretty useless around the funeral home, really, and it began to get me down. Mostly, all I did was observe. And keep him company. So one day, after we'd had a funeral, and he was across town visiting this other undertaker, I felt useless, and I went to church and asked God to show me my vocation. And to give me some kind of sign."

Her words rung in Jordan's ears. "And?"

"And I had this vision. That night. It must have been very late. Mother and Daddy were gone. I was lying there tossing and turning, having a terrible time getting comfortable. Then"—she made signs in the air with her hands—"suddenly, I could see it. It was really vivid. I saw myself working on a case. Working by myself, doing all the work. I was an embalmer. Right then, I knew that was my vocation. I knew that was what I wanted to do for the rest of my life."

"That's quite a story."

"I know. But that's the way it happened. I told my father, and he advised me to come down here to Gresham, and here I am. I mean, a lot of these people are just here because their parents told them to do it or asked them. But I'm here because I feel it's my destiny, my vocation. I feel a calling." Then: "Don't you?"

He told her about himself, how Clare encouraged him in it, how Lovingood made a deal with him. But sculpture was his real love, Jordan added.

Marcella said, "I don't care. It still sounds to me like you've got a calling too. How else can you explain all your good fortune? You've had more luck than most people. How can you explain your work in here? No, listen: Any man who does the things you do in wax simply has to have been called, Mister Jordan. You think my story is weird. Look at yourself, your work. It's uncanny, it really is. There's something . . . super-natural . . . in the things you do. It's so real. Like you were in touch with the dead."

Jordan laughed nervously, self-consciously. In touch with the dead! He hoped not. "Let's finish up," he said, and turned back to the presence below them.

Clare was the only one who wrote regularly. Why wasn't he hearing from Lovingood? He knew Lovingood was pleased with his progress, especially in restorative art. Lovingood had said so in a brief note addressed to Jordan in care of the school.

But after that note, congratulating him on his excellent grades, and one other asking him to research the latest in jaundice fluids, Lovingood hadn't written any more. Major Bates wrote once, a cheerful unintelligible note. But Clare wrote regularly:

LAWRENCE,

Sunny days. People doing nothing but shooting and killing each other. Like animals. Southwall called the other day. He's under the weather again. Nothing serious, I gather. Psyche says he went right back to work. Well, not too much longer to go! I can't believe it. My little boy a full-fledged undertaker. And a job waiting! Keep the faith. I know it's hard work. Oh! Fell out with Eddie (dentist). "Les Dames" gave a social and saw Herece there with T. Jerome Montague and some other young man, nice-looking. There's a new undertaker's in town —Universal. Started by a young man who went to your school. Brown-skin fellow, a militant. That's all this town needs, another undertaker. Guess you'll have lots of competition (smiles). I'm looking for a house, two bedrooms. Saw Mrs. Goldman the other day, downtown. She says Mike sends his hello. Well, that's all for now. More later. Oh, yes, here are the clippings.

MOTHER

At first Clare had been curious—morbidly curious, he thought—about what they did at Gresham. Her letters were filled with questions about funeral procedures based on hearsay and superstition. Once she had asked him if it was true undertakers removed the vitals (she called them guts) before putting fluid in the body. And if they always put pennies—Charon's fee —on dead men's eyes to keep them shut. He had written back, answering her, but Clare said his explanations of the processes were too technical for her.

She sent him the funeral notices and other clippings from the *Afro-Citizen News* religiously. That's one thing he liked about Clare. She kept you informed, *over*informed really.

He perused the latest news: Lovingood had four cases, Fannie Fears four. Williams Brothers three. Isadore Michaels elected to the board of the Urban Betterment Committee, whatever that was. Thessalonica Wingate engaged to Mr. T. Jerome Montague, up-and-coming junior partner in the venerable old firm of LaCour, Wingate & *Montague*. Old man Fortune now in business with McGinnis: McGinnis and Fortune, Funeral Directors. Grand opening of the Universal Undertaking Company, a new kind of mortuary service: all funerals one hundred and forty-five dollars, no more, no less. Universal's director, Brother Abdullah Jamal. Lynford "Lennie" Valentine sought for questioning in a drugstore robbery. The Michael Lafollettes celebrating their silver wedding anniversary at St. Dunstan's. School bond election expected to fail because of conservative opposition, apathy among ghetto parents. Three murders. Art exhibit at the Plaza.

Herece at a party with somebody else? Well, she'd probably tell Jordan about it in her next letter. Whenever she wrote it. He could understand Lovingood's not writing; the business drained a man. But Herece? She wasn't working, had plenty of time during the day to write.

He told Marcella about Herece Lovingood, and in turn, Marcella mentioned that occasionally she still saw Tommie Roddenberry, who still lived with his parents. Tommie had a Ferrari and spent most of his spare time chasing girls. He was listed in his father's promotions as associate funeral director, but Marcella said Tommie had no real interest in the business. Like so many others, Tommie Roddenberry did it because it was the only work he knew.

Jordan had waited to open the letter from Herece. Mrs. Simpson gave it to him at lunchtime. Jordan opened it in restorative art class during lecture.

DEAR LAWRENCE,

I don't know how to tell you this, I know it will hurt you. Just when everything is going so well and you're about to graduate. I guess I'll just say it. I met this guy, a real nice boy, one of Jerry Montague's friends. I have been dating him. Last night, he asked me to marry him. I said I would.

Oh, Lawrence, I know you will understand. I've been in such turmoil ever since you left. Daddy's been sick, very sick, he asked us not to tell you. Wayne's been drinking and Mamma's been too worried about Daddy to help me.

That was unfair of me, I guess, not telling you about Ronald. That's his name. He sells insurance and last week he got a commendation from his boss. It was unfair of me not to

175

tell you, but I know you have been having such a hard time at embalming school and I didn't want to add to your sorrows. But I have sorrows of my own too, much greater. I haven't told them yet, but I will have to. Oh, Lawrence, I'm so much in love. Just hope you will understand. I wouldn't have made a good undertaker's wife anyway.

Love,

h

Marcella saw him downhearted after class. He steadied himself on the water fountain.

"Hi. What's wrong?"

He handed her the letter.

"Oh, I'm sorry . . . Lawrence. I'm really sorry."

There was real concern on her face. His eyes were misty; Jordan was afraid Marcella would see him cry. He had to get out of there, go back to the rooming house. No. Walk the streets. He had to digest it all somehow, rise over it. Marcella walked along beside him in silence. In the student lounge, some new arrivals were discussing the stages of somatic and cellular death, Icard's test, death certificates. He told Marcella he had to leave.

"Pull out of it, Lawrence Jordan," she said, her hand on his shoulder. "I mean it's not as if the whole world has come to an end. Think about your career, your future. You're brilliant, talented."

He tried to laugh. "I'm not sure I have a future now."

"You mean you don't think her father will—"

"No, it's not that. Mr. Lovingood is my friend, my best friend. It's just"—he was crying on the spot—"that . . . I . . . *trusted* her so much."

Marcella followed him out into the entranceway, clutching her textbooks to her bosom. "Listen," she said, "listen now! Go on; take that walk. But come back and meet me on the steps after class. Okay? Think you can make it that long?"

"Yeah. Sorry I put you through this, too."

She smiled.

Jordan had forgotten to find someone who would pay him to assume his duty over the weekend. Jordan could now make it without the extra money he made standing watches. Then why did he want to do it? Was it a way of getting back at them, the rich and the fortunate around him, young men with everything to live for with fathers who had thought enough of them to found self-perpetuating dynasties? Jordan couldn't compete with them outside school; he knew that. He couldn't live in the nice neighborhoods they did, couldn't have the fancy cars, the fine food they did. But he could get back at them. He could turn their smugness and their indifference to his own advantage by taking their money.

He saw Marcella standing at the bottom of the stone steps, and his heart quickened. Sun made chestnut of her hair.

"Hi. You all right?"

"Uh-huh. It's okay. I'll make it. See you Monday."

"Not till Monday?"

"Yeah. I got to find somebody that's got the duty so I can get some coins."

"Forget about coins," she said. "What you need right now is something to take your mind off that girl. Go out this weekend; do something; get busy. Have a wild time. Forget it all. Don't you ever go out?"

He was ashamed to admit it, especially to a light-skinned girl. "No; not often."

He took her books. She put both her arms around his free arm and in feigned struggle pulled him down the street, away from the human disgorgement of Gresham. Abruptly, when they had got down the street, she pulled away from him and looked up in his eyes with her concerned look. Then she took his arm again.

"I've got an idea," she said. "Why don't you and I do something, go out this weekend?"

"Thanks. Maybe some other time, some happier time."

"But this is when you really need it."

"I'd probably break out in tears again."

"I know! We could drive up to see my father. We've plenty of room."

"No."

"We could do something right here, maybe see a show, have dinner, take in the town."

"What about Tommie Roddenberry?"

"Oh, *him*. I haven't seen him in a month. I just went out

with him because he's a friend of the family's. He's really nothing to me."

"You're a pretty girl, Marcella. You can find better guys to go out with than me. I'm dull company."

"Let me be the judge of that."

"Don't have any money."

"I have some."

"No car."

"I have a car."

"Tommie Roddenberry—"

"Lawrence, for crying out loud!"

He threw up his hand. "Okay. It's your funeral. I mean—"

He scrubbed with antiseptic soap. Eb said, "Man, you must have a girl. Who is it? Marcella? Sure is a foxy thing."

Jordan couldn't get the scent out of his hands. Did Marcella notice it? Perhaps if he soaked them. . . .

They went to the Art Institute. Jordan wouldn't have any woman taking him out: art galleries were free. He borrowed money from Eb Minifee for dinner afterward. Something fancy: capon, sherry, one of the hotels.

Marcella said, "Nobody's ever taken me to an art gallery on a date before. You have taste."

"No." Jordan laughed. "It's just that it's free."

He was surprised at her interest in art. She fairly tugged him through the marbeled halls, calling his attention to things he had never seen before. He could see himself doing a sculpture for her, something in stone. And her appreciating it, commenting on it. He particularly liked Munch. "The Vampire." There was something erotic about this lithograph of a cypress-haired woman biting intimately, tenderly, into a man's neck. It excited Jordan. He imagined what Marcella would be like biting into him!

"Lawrence, do you come here often?"

"Only place I do come."

"Then we will come again."

When she took his hand, under the huge El Greco crucifixion, it felt right, natural. She was giving him the lead, and Jordan liked that. He liked the way she pursued him the day before, begging him to take her out. He had been the one who played hard to get. But there was still the chasm between them: her aura. Best to let it coast, nothing aggressive on his part. If he inclined toward her too strongly, if he wanted her, Marcella might disappear.

On the steps, she said, "Stay there a minute. Like that. I want to remember you like that, this day."

"Why?"

"Oh, I don't know. You're . . . *splendid.*"

"Me?"

"Yes. You're very *hand*some. I like your hair. And the way your clothes hang all loose on you. It gives you intensity, power. You're quite a man, Lawrence Xavier Jordan."

"I like the way you say it."

"What?"

"My name."

They did go back to the institute. And to the Museum of Science and Industry. And dancing. And to parks. And funeral homes. That spring he was enraptured with Marcella of the glittering ears, right up to the day Clare phoned him at school, breathless and anxious, to tell him that Southwall Lovingood was dead.

18

At the train station, Jordan called Clare. Then he went straight to Lovingood's. He had tried to reach Major Bates on the phone from school; the line was interminably busy. Across boulevard traffic, framed by moving taxi windows, the funeral home looked as it always did, cool, placid, ready for quiet business. Jordan paid the driver and hurried up the steps with a suitcase in his hand.

A thin dark man Jordan had never seen before came on tip-toe to the door. The man had on an outdated black suit and a dingy shirt with frayed collar reminiscent of the kind Lovingood himself wore. The man stank of perfume different from the perfume of embalming fluid, and Jordan saw powder dusted over the pocks of his cheeks. Over his shoulder, Jordan saw one of Lovingood's potted palms in the hall. It was good to be home.

"I *am* sorry," the man murmured musically, effeminately, "we're closed for the rest of the week. Mister Southwall Lovin-*goood* has passed away, you know, and they're having his funeral tomorrow."

"I know all that," Jordan snapped, setting his suitcase down. "I'm Lawrence Jordan."

The man looked confused. "Are you one of the . . . em*balm*-ers?"

"Yes. No. Is old man Bates in there?"

Diffidently: "Yes, sir . . ."

"Well, get him. Now."

Bates apologized profusely.

"It's all right," he told the perfumed man. "Brother Jordan

is a friend. This is the young man Southwall was putting through school."

The man's eyebrows fluttered, and his mouth formed a round, knowing "Ooooohhh."

Bates took Jordan's suitcase. "Who is that?" Jordan demanded, nodding at the retreating frayed collar.

"One of the relatives, a cousin. From down South."

"What's going on? Tried to reach you all day yesterday, but the lines were humming."

Bates' eyes were puffy, as if he hadn't slept for days. His mustache drooped, and his pomaded hair stood up in the front in crinkly stiff little *w*'s. Bates sat the suitcase by the potted palm and wiped his brow with a shirt sleeve. "They're doing the body right now, in the back," he said. "Montague's doing the main embalming, assisted by one of the Kansas undertakers. Williams Brothers conducting tomorrow, along with Sister Fears. But we're using our cars. Southwall would want that, am I right?"

"Mmmm."

The door to Lovingood's great office was locked. There was a wreath on the door.

"Come on in here," Bates said, motioning toward the reception room. "We can talk in there."

In the room, Jordan stood facing the window. A hearse went by.

"What happened?"

"Aww Brother Jordan, it was rugged, really rugged. I haven't left here since Tuesday night. Psyche, the family, they're taking it real hard. All 'cept that boy. I think *he's* glad it happened."

"Calm down, old man. How'd it happen?"

"He meant to write you, talked about you all the time. Real pleased, real pleased, with your work. Just want you to know that."

Lawrence nodded.

"Worked right up to th' end, Brother Jordan. Right *up* to th' end. See, we were doin' a case. Don't know where that boy was, up front or somewhere. Ole Southwall had just raised the vessels and was getting ready for the preliminary injection, you understood all that . . . now?"

181

"Yes, sir."

"Well, he had the forceps in his hand, I'll never forget it. I was over at th' cabinet, getting out some Gibraltar because it's fast-acting without too much dehydration. We'd already washed the body down with one one-thousandth bichloride of mercury soon's we got it in.

"Well, Southwall turned to get some cotton in the forceps, and all of a sudden he fell out. Just like that. Dropped the tongs 'n' everything. He hit his head on the waste can when he fell. Doom! It was the loudest thing you ever saw. I thought one of the chemicals had exploded or something.

"I ran up to Southwall soon's I got my wits together, and I realized what'd happened. Liver gone out on him, you know. Man, he had no business down here in that condition. Everybody tried to tell him. But you know Southwall. It got kind of bad right after Christmas. He wasn't eatin' so much, but he just swolled up real bad, *heavy*, fatter than he was, and for a time there I thought we'd lose him then. That's when they hospitalized him. But he was back down here hardly a week after he got out, had to get on with it. You know you never could keep Southwall away from a case. Plus I guess he was worried about that boy. Man, Wayne's no damn good. Montague's been doin' most of Wayne's work on the sly. Well, after that, we thought Southwall was all right. He's always had his ups and downs, you know. Doctor told him definitely to lay off any and *all* drinking, and Southwall, as usual, swore he had. But you know him: nip here, nip there. Always a celebration after comin' back from the cemetery.

"Well, there were signs, Brother Jordan. Signs. He started losin' weight then, too fast. Got down to two fifty: skin and bones for Southwall. And you know how kinda black 'n sweaty Southwall always was? Well, he got all ashen after that. Complexion like mud, a sure sign. Doctor said he was goin' to hospitalize him right then, but Southwall begged off till after we got this last case disposed of."

Jordan turned away from the window. He put his arm around Bates' shoulder, steadied himself. "Yeah, I know. I know just how he was. Helluva man, though."

"Oh, yeah," Bates concurred, perking up. "Helluva man. I

ever tell you 'bout th' time a man come in here talkin' 'bout he wanted to get an elephant embalmed 'n' Southwall not battin' an eyelash 'n' asking him if it'd be a shipping case or an in-home job?"

Jordan tried to laugh. "Naw, man."

Bates kicked at the desk leg. "He never regained consciousness, Brother Jordan. Took four men—Brother Wayne and I and two ambulance attendants—to lift him off the floor. They took him to St. Monica's, and he never regained consciousness, coma all the time. I couldn't sleep, the doctors done all they could, and I just stayed here all of Tuesday getting that case ready to show. The next morning Southwall succumbed, 'n' I told Miz Lovingood I thought it best if we suspended operations. We sent the other body over to Miz Fears, and she said it was probably the finest septicemia case work she'd ever seen Southwall do, 'n' I didn't have the heart to tell her that I did that corpse."

"What you gonna do now, Bates?"

"Aw, I don't know, Brother Jordan. Don't much care now. Goin' try to carry on, I guess. Glad your schoolin's almost over. Kinda lookin' forward to workin' with you, son."

They stood in silence for a while, Jordan remembering Southwall Lovingood, remembering how all the way back home he thought he heard Southwall's calling him in the long, shrill moan of the train: "Jorrrdannnnnnn, Bro' Jorrrdannnnnnn. . . ."

Then Bates took on a detached professional air. Walking toward the door, he said, "Man, they had to tie two prep tables together to support the body."

Knowing the old man had to talk it out that way, Jordan followed him. "No stuff?"

"Yeah, Brother, this is a real case. Damn. Used almost 'leven gallons a low formaldehyde kickapoo set it up."

Jordan remembered his prediction. "How they gonna handle it? I mean the display, the casketing?"

Bates understood immediately. He shook his head thoughtfully. Now they were in the hall. "Casket's in the ga-rage," Bates whispered. "Gonna wheel it on the ramp and put the body in it there. Then take it to the church. Never could get him out otherwise. Had to send all th' way to Chicago for that box, Brother. Seven by four 'n' a half!"

"I'll be damned!"

Psyche nodded to Jordan in the foyer. She sat there in an overcoat, clutching a scarf. She seemed to be praying. Wayne, in shirt sleeves and gray trousers, acknowledged Jordan's presence by looking up. But that was all. Herece, dangling a rosary, came up and embraced him. Around the room sat various members of Southwall Lovingood's family, Southwall's mother, unbelievably tiny and frail, the perfumed cousin, a corpulent uncle and aunt. Others, distant kin. Except for Psyche, they all were dark people. Except for Wayne, they all were poorly dressed. In the corner, by the display room Jordan saw a discarded shoe with a hole in the sole. Southwall's, momentarily forgotten.

Jordan paid his respects to Psyche Lovingood and shook hands with some of the survivors. Psyche told him they were going to have an old-fashioned dinner with collard greens and sweet potatoes, chitterlings and ham after they came back from the cemetery on the morrow. Jordan sat with Herece on the edge of her overstuffed chair for a long time. Behind the walls, he smelled the body scent and the embalming fluid's lavender. "I just wish I could do something," he told Herece.

Finally, Wayne Lovingood came over, thin, black, yellow-eyed. He had a vacant look on his face.

"Thanks for coming down," Wayne told Jordan, staring somewhere off Jordan's right shoulder. "Whyn't you go on home now? There's nothing you can do. There's nothing any of us can do."

Jordan stood up from the chair. "I know one thing I can do," he announced, eager to be away from the dismal gathering. "I can write the eulogy. Anybody done that already?"

Bates came over. Inside, the water was still running.

"No," Bates said. "Nobody's thought of that. Let me help you. Guess I knew him good's anybody, son."

Jordan's silky black tuxedo was too big for him. It kept bunching up behind his neck. He sat with his mother in the back seat of a Lovingood limousine. The curtains were open.

Clare, in a curvy mid-length black dress without frills, smoothed her skirt continually over her muscular legs. Major Bates was driving. The limousine floated silently down Brooklyn toward the heart of the city and New Jerusalem Spiritualist Church of God in Christ.

Actually, thought Jordan, it wouldn't have been a bad idea to casket the body in the prep room and tear the wall down getting it out. An ultimate tribute to the man. That was the least they could have done for Southwall Lovingood. The old man would have laughed at that—his timeless, melodic, earthshaking belly laugh. And Jordan's prediction would have come true. Jordan's imagination blinked on, and he could see himself as Lovingood's son, in Wayne's slender body, ordering workmen to tear down his father's walls. In ancient Egypt they buried the pharaoh's wife and servants with him in the tomb. That was style. Tearing some walls down in mourning for a great man was the very least you should do in modern times.

An armada of Cadillacs was parked outside the church, two of them tropical pink. Fannie Lartarska Gorham Fears. The city's embalmers, a grim elite. On the street, Jordan saw them greeting one another solemnly, fraternally, old friends. For the moment they had forgotten their quarrels, their petty jealousies. Just for today, they were united, the embalmers. Just for today, they were one family, come to bury a beloved brother. Jordan wondered if they would turn out the same way for him someday.

The limousine inched past the other cars. A crowd of people crossed the street in front of it, and Bates stopped the car. On the sidewalk, Jordan saw the young men of New Jerusalem, dark and fierce in their white church uniforms. The young men held back a crowd of spectators.

It was like Hollywood movie premieres Jordan had seen on television. The young New Jerusalemites were the ropes. And the crowd—tattered children, working-class men and women, some in their Sunday best—pressed against the ropes to get a glimpse of the rich and the famous and the fortunate.

New Jerusalem's double oaken doors opened and closed incessantly as the black elite of Kansas City came to pay respects to Southwall Lovingood. Between the rows of white suits flanking the double doors passed the Beautiful People Jordan had read about so often in the *Afro-Citizen News*: civic leader-businessman Isadore Michaels, graying slightly at the temples, pious, at the same time plain and well dressed in his trim tuxedo; socialite Thessalonica Wingate in midnight blue, flashing a new diamond; prominent mortician Robert McGinnis and his new partner T. T. Fortune, both in patent-leather shoes, followed by their socialite wives; *Afro-Citizen* columnist Ponchita Perez in wide-brimmed black hat with black ribbon, note pad and pencil in her hand for jotting down the impressive assemblage of Names gathered here today; bosomy Mrs. Sally Gibson Garrett, sister of the Right Reverend Richard Daniel Rideout, in furs; the first lady of funerals, Fannie Lartarska Gorham Fears, in black full-length overcoat with sable collar, black-on-black brocade Chinese collared sheath beneath; Clare's dentist, Eddie Lovelace, carrying a pointy umbrella. They were a collection of hats and stoles and shiny shoes, all going through the door.

Bates double-parked in front of the church entrance and came around to open the door for Clare. On the seat next to her, Clare had a plain black hat with veil. She put the hat on and adjusted the veil over her eyes. Bates opened the door smartly for her, and as he emerged, Jordan had a feeling of pleasure, of importance, of pride, that he too was one of the select people, a member of Lovingood's fraternity.

The faces of the New Jerusalem honor guard were impassive and ebony above the white collars. As he reached the sidewalk, Jordan was flanked by Thaddeus Hatcher, the Kansas mortician, making his way into the church. They greeted each other, and Jordan heard a woman spectator behind him whisper, "Who's the young pretty one?" He escorted Clare into the cavernous church and tried to look tall and prominent for the people. But he felt the tuxedo creeping up his neck.

The vestibule was stuffy with people. They greeted one another in whispers, patted one another's hands. Jordan saw many he knew. The embalmers: LaCour, Wingate, Montague, Williams, old man Tatum in a 1940-vintage tuxedo with wide lapels. From the other side of town had come Applebaum, Teuffel, one of the dark-eyed Valentino Brothers. From across the river Hatcher and dark-suited Aretha Vinson.

A bony hand took Lawrence Jordan's. It was Carrie Samuels,

the old vulturess. "Mmmm-mmmph, Brother Jordan!" Sister Samuels croaked into his face. "All growned up! Mmmm-mmmph. Sure was a fiiine thing Mister Lovin'good done for you. Too bad about him, isn't it? 'The Lord giveth and the Lord taketh away. . . . '"

Jordan was glad to see Carrie Samuels in her old flowered hat. Her presence made everything, the funeral, the spectacle, official. He introduced Mrs. Samuels to Clare so they could commiserate together.

A blue-suited usherette tiptoed through the gathering, tapping the men on the shoulder with a white-gloved hand. "Service is about to start," she said. She was dark and muscle-faced, like girls who came from big families that used to pick cotton.

New Jerusalem Spiritualist was like no other church Jordan knew. It had borrowed rituals and customs from every other denomination: statuary and candles from Catholicism, pretentious middle-classness from African Methodist Episcopalism, belief in total immersion from Baptism, obsequious proselytizing and pestering from Seventh-day Adventism and Jehovah's Witnessism. As they shuffled toward the sanctuary, Jordan stopped to light a candle in the bank of flames flanking the entrance. He noticed that church members made the sign of the cross—backward—before they entered the sanctuary. Jordan made likewise motions.

The sanctuary was brightly lit. To the left of the door, parallel to the long wall stretching back into the church, was Lovingood's casket, a full-couch bronze sealer, wider than any Jordan had seen. As he entered the door with Clare, Jordan could see only the hair and forehead of what had been Southwall Lovingood. The forehead was clayey, ashy black, like the hair. They were of one fabric. Tapered candles swayed at either end of the casket. Jordan pulled his mother closer to the huge box. In it, Southwall Lovingood was stretched out unnaturally, both hands at his sides. The flesh of Lovingood's jowls was muddy and compressed and the starched collar and bow tie done up too tightly. Lovingood looked like some great dusty hulk placed in the box by accident.

The tuxedo—tails—was perfect; however, it was strange to see Lovingood so formal. Yet it seemed right.

Jordan stood before the casket as the others filed by, filling out the church. The entire wall was banked with flowers of all descriptions, many of them from florists and funeral directors who advertised their names boldly on sashes slashed across the displays: "Williams Brothers Inc.," "Sincerest Sympathies. La-Cour, Wingate & Montague," "McKinney's Florists." There were flowers leaning against the accordion-legged church trucks, two of them, on which Lovingood's incredible casket lay. In the box, Southwall slept, oblivious to the pungent petals around him. It seemed incredible to Jordan that Lovingood would not at any minute lift himself up out of the box, let frog-like lids roll up over his red eyes, and sing out "Brother Jordannnn!" in greeting. Instead, he lay there, his stomach nearly bursting the buttons on the immaculate white shirt, the tails of the suit pressed under and around the body without so much as a wrinkle. In one way, Jordan noticed, Lovingood resembled a great dark Dracula laid out for honor in some elaborate and mystic cave. Clare daubbed her eyes.

And the inner sanctum of New Jerusalem *was* mystic. Up by the balcony, high on the wall above Southwall Lovingood and his sea of flowers, was a crudely painted mural of Christ rising through an orifice of clouds. The rays emanating from the head of Jesus were iridescent gold paint, like old Byzantine work. On the balustrade of the balcony stretched a series of ornate crosses, cluttered with phony jewels. On the opposite wall was a painting of Christ with staff and crook. It was lurid. The Saviour wore a blazing red tunic, and the folds of the garment were done all wrong, as were the nose and eyes. And the sheep. The paintings were cartoons, caricatures, rather than icons.

Jordan frowned up at the picture of red-robed Jesus. It was a standard scene; he had seen it in a Sunday school primer. Here were Southwall and Jesus. The Lamb of God and the walrus-backed undertaker. Which one was the Saviour? Jesus had done nothing for Jordan. Southwall had.

Jordan took Clare. They were ushered into the choicest pews on the ground floor of New Jerusalem immediately behind Psyche and her family. To Psyche's right sat Wayne Lovingood, looking as uncomfortable in his tux as his father did in his. To Psyche's left was Herece, flanked by an attentive, mustachioed young man who must have been the fiancé. Around Psyche and her children were the relatives and friends, business associates and competitors. Jordan was in the same row with Fannie Fears, Jerry Montague, Thess Wingate, Tatum, McGinnis, and others. Bates came in and took his place next to Jordan.

Across the aisle from them sat the church mothers and sisters, elderly women with tambourines and hair in buns under little white caps. Sister Samuels in her thin white maid's uniform took her place with the church mothers and began to rock back and forth, humming to herself. She saw Jordan, nodded, then went back to rocking.

Quickly the church filled to capacity, much faster than it did at Sunday night musicals. Jordan remembered the musicals well. New Jerusalem was famous all over town for its musicals. Every Sunday it was a different program. People of all ages, all religions came to enjoy it. They had some sissies who played in the band, and usually one of the queers sang a solo, too. New Jerusalem had more fairies in its congregation than any other church in town, and Jordan didn't know why. It was rumored that some of the most prominent doctors and lawyers in town were sissies and showed it when they sang in the choir at New Jerusalem—but that was just talk. The church's Light of the World choir was fabled for deep voices as well as falsetto.

It was also rumored that the Right Reverend Richard Daniel Rideout had feminine tendencies, but Jordan overlooked such talk as prompted by jealousy. Rideout and Lovingood were close, and Lovingood certainly was no weirdo. Under Rideout's guidance, New Jerusalem had prospered and attracted prominent citizens, many of those there today, and Ponchita Perez, a lifelong member, speculated in the *Afro-Citizen* that the church was now worth upwards of one and one-half million dollars. The Right Reverend Mr. Rideout ran the church's business affairs like the erstwhile real estate broker he was, and the church looked up to Rideout as Saviour Incarnate. It was rumored that Rideout had ten diamond rings, one for each finger and both thumbs.

Jordan twisted in his pew next to Clare, and Clare, rubbing the ends of her handkerchief together meditatively, said, "Keep still." Jordan stared up at the great pulpit. Flanking it in sweeping curves were the tiers where the Light of the World held sway. To one side was the band box where the sissies played. New Jerusalem believed thoroughly in the maxim "Make a joyful noise unto the Lord," and on Sunday nights the church rocked with all the abandon of a pop rock festival. The organist, a bony woman with a penchant for flowing robes, could turn some keyboard tricks that would make Jimmie Smith or Isaac Hayes blush. New Jerusalem had soul, no doubt about that. In the center of the modernistic, spacious stage stood the throne of Right Reverend Rideout and the microphone over which he delivered his fiery, rambling sermons. Rideout (in the parlance of the old preachers) "stood all over your toes" in a sermon. He pulled no punches, and he took down the mighty with the low. Bates told Jordan that once when Rideout preached a sermon on the evils of drinking, the preacher turned to Southwall Lovingood, present as always, and roared, "And I most especially mean you, Brother Lovingood!"

To either side of Rideout, the elders sat, twelve in all. The church smelled of flowers. One of the sisters—Carrie Samuels—rapped her tambourine on the back of a pew. Someone said, "Amen." The church was ready.

Suddenly the lights went out. The congregation stood. Jordan knew the routine; he had done it a hundred times at Sunday night musicals. Noisily, the congregation turned around in the pews and faced the back of the church. Jordan looked over at the candles burning at Lovingood's casket. In the box Lovingood was still, indifferent. Like a man who had stretched out on a bed and gone to sleep before the service started. The candles flickered on the flowers. Footfalls thudded in the pulpit.

They waited a full minute, their faces to the rear. Then the Reverend Rideout's doomsday baritone boomed out over the public address system, filling every corner of the church:

"Jezussss . . . is the Light . . . of the World!"

Horns blared, drums beat. The sisters beat on their tambourines. The lights came on, and the congregation turned to face the pulpit. The choir came marching in past the coffin.

There, in the center of the stage, stood the Right Reverend Richard Daniel Rideout, tall, white-haired, attired in a black silken robe that trailed behind his feet. The sleeves of the vestment shimmered down from Rideout's upraised arms like black angelic wings. Rideout's face raised up to heaven; his hands supplicated the ceiling for mercy on his people. To the pulsing of tambourines, the choir danced into the tiers, clapping and humming. Jordan recognized the song immediately. As they reached their seats, the choir exploded:

> Lord, keep so busy
> Workin' for the Master,
> Keep so busy
> Workin' for the Master,
> Keep so busy
> Workin' for my Master,
> Ain't got time to die. . . .

It was staccato, driving, joyful. The music flew out across the church, reverberated against the walls. Someone got happy and did a little dance in the aisles.

> If I don't praise Him,
> Rocks gonna cry out:
> "Glory 'n' honor,
> "Glory 'n' Honor!"
> Ain't got time to die.

They sang it over and over. Psyche Lovingood broke down in tears. Herece comforted her. Wayne was impassive. Across the aisle Carrie Samuels cried out: "The Lord taketh!" One of the elders, a bald, skeletal man with square spectacles, wiped his brow. A demonstration broke out in the balcony. The choir sang louder. Rideout stretched to heaven. The song was interminable; the church was on fire. If they could have accomplished it that day, New Jerusalemites would have raised the dead.

The choir never stopped. The volume went down, but Jordan heard a bosomy woman in the background pacing the singers on and on while the Right Reverend Richard Daniel Rideout's hands came down gradually from God to point straight at Southwall's widow.

"Psyche Lovingood!" Rideout shouted. "Weep not! Weep not, I say, Southwall ain't dead!"

"Amen."

"Southwall ain't deadddd!"

191

"Preach!"

"He ain't deaddddddd!"

"No!"

"He's only resting in the arms of Jeeeeezussssss!"

"Teach!"

"Do you hear me?"

"Yes, Lord."

Jordan studied the movements of the preacher intently. Already sweat was pouring down Rideout's brow, staining the robe.

"Whad'd I say?"

"Yeah!"

"I said he ain't deadddddddddddd! Ain't deadddddd! Ain't deaddddd!"

"Amen."

Rideout paused, moved back from the microphone. One of the elders leaped forth and wiped Rideout's brow. The choir volume rose up; they chanted until Rideout's hands came up again. He wore a single diamond.

"No, he ain't dead," the preacher said in a lower voice. "He's only resting in the arms of Jezus!"

Rideout smiled benignly, came to the edge of the pulpit, and bent over Psyche. "Psyche," he said, "Sister Psyche B., Psyche B. Lovingoodddd! Stand up, Psyche. Stand up for Jezus." Rideout motioned up to heaven with a black wing.

Shaking, crying, Psyche stood up. Rideout got a concerned look, bent over farther until he was almost looking straight at the woman. He started to speak, then stopped. Momentarily, the choir volume rose again.

"Your man ain't dead, Psyche," Rideout said suddenly with a tenderness approaching a lover. "He's up there now with Jezus." Pointing again up to heaven. "He's gone to Bright Glory." Motioning her to sit down. "He's gone home to God."

The choir sang and the tambourines clinged as Rideout went back to the microphone.

"The *Bi*-ble sez: 'Weep when they come into this world; make a joyful noise when they go out.' Am I right?"

"Fix it on up, Rev."

"Tell it like it is."

"Speak."

"Teach!"

"Sez: 'Make a joy-full noise!' "

"Teach!"

"*South*wall was a joy-ful man. . . ."

A woman screamed in the back of the church. Jordan thought he heard her saying, "Ride on, Rideout! Ride on, Richard!"

"In his field, he was without compeer."

"Amen."

"He knew death was coming. He was prepared to meet it. Knew he couldn't beat it."

"Teach!"

"We all got to go that way. Someday."

"Ride on, Richard."

"He wouldn't want to hear Psyche cry."

"No!"

"Wouldn't want to hear Sister Her-ece cry."

"No!"

"Wouldn't want to hear Rideout cry."

"Sho 'nuff."

"He's gone home to Bright Glo-ry."

"Amen."

"Make a joyful noise unto the Lord, let Jezus hear us today. This ain't First Baptist, this ain't Christ Episcopal. This is the New Jerusalem. This is a COGIC church! Make it sound like one. Make it sound like *New* Jerusalem. Let Jezus hear you. Let Psyche hear you. Let Southwall hear you! Go on!"

And the church wailed.

It was the greatest funeral Jordan had ever seen: majesty, pomp, color, Rideout bestriding the pulpit with his great out-stretched wings, the elders getting happy, the tambourines jingling, the church mothers prancing. And the tiny church woman with simple dignity, reading the eulogy from Jordan's carefully composed paper. "Southwall Lovingood," it began, "was the keeper of a seal. . . ."

Jordan had included it all, from the apprenticeship with Fannie Fears (at that point, Sister Fears broke down) through the war years to Lovingood's founding of the firm that bore his name. A lifelong resident of the city, befriender of fatherless boys. Lovingood's contributions to the community: the Lovingood Mortuary softball team, the Lovingood Memorial Pavilion at the YMCA, a lifelong member of the NAACP, his Masonic order.

The night before, the Masons had conducted private services for Brother Southwall. Only Masons attended, men Jordan had seen on the wall. Major Bates was among them. He told Jordan most of the ceremony was secret, but Bates told Jordan that Lovingood's body was positioned the way it was by the sanctuary entrance, head in the east, feet in the west.

The church woman also read an *Afro-Citizen* editorial entitled "A Self-Made Man." At this reading, even Reverend Rideout, mopping his brow on his throne, shed the tears he cautioned against.

"But his greatest contribution was the comfort that he gave to others in their time of need, the compassion with which he bore his awful office, the dedication with which he approached his calling, the infectious cheerfulness that characterized his. . . ."

Now Lovingood, master of the ancient art, was himself being serviced with a compassion, sanitation, efficiency, and dispatch that rivaled his own proud handiwork.

You must have that
Holy Ghostin' fire, that burning
Flame that
Keeps the Prayer Wheel turning,
That kind of
Religion you can't do without,
Makes you sigh,
Makes you cry,
Makes you shout! when it's real . . .

Keep your hand
Right in the winding chain
Until your soul
Gets anchored in my Jezus' name,
It makes you
Free from sin,
Don't you see?
Can't you see?

> Got to be
> Born again, oh, yes! Born again . . .

"All right."

"Amen."

"Ride on!"

The church was spent. With the Light of the World making their joyful noise in the background, Robert and William Williams, the mortuary brothers, closed the quilted lid over the dark head on the pillow. The last of the mourners trouped past as Richard Daniel Rideout, his composure regained, winged his way to the edge of the pulpit, his hands beckoning to the front rows: "If the pallbearers will rise. . . ."

Jordan rose with Bates and Tatum, LaCour, young Lovingood, and McGinnis. Fannie Fears also rose. Her veil completely obscured her face. Its edges brushed her black suede collar. The Williamses wheeled the brassy coffin around into position, and Fannie Fears took her place at the head of the casket. As the choir belted out one more stanza of "It makes you free from sin, don't you see?" the bearers and their terrible burden passed out the doors Robert Williams opened. Fannie marched before them to the sleek black and humpbacked hearse where Bill Williams threw open the back.

Somehow it wasn't right, someone else closing the lid on that great couch. Jordan had almost expected Southwall to reach up from his bed and do it himself.

Bob Williams had to help them get the casket onto the rollers of the hearse, one of Lovingood's own with his nameplate in the narrow window. Fannie Fears stood with her back to the struggle, looking across the street. Thomas, Fannie's old funeral director, got out of one of the pink Cadillacs and got her. She got in the lead pink car and waited veiled, in the back. Billy Williams stood on the sidewalk, watching pensively. He looked quite the prominent mortician in his elegant tuxedo. He was bareheaded. Some men from the church came out, broke through the white-suited honor guard, and asked Williams where to put the flowers. He directed them to the cut-down, chrome-trimmed vehicle just behind the hearse. The flower car had been lent to the Williamses by P. G. Newbody, the city's biggest undertaker, who sent regrets that he could not be present. P. G. sent one of his sons instead.

Jordan found Clare, and they got in their car. Jordan rode up front now with Bates while Clare shared the back with Sister Carrie Samuels, who persisted in asking Bates if Southwall didn't look *just* like he was sleeping. Bates nodded silently, his eyes fixed on the hearse.

The church spilled people into the street. They stood around talking, staring at the great procession preparing to roll. Some of them peeked in the hearse windows at the immense, flower-decked bronze loaf in there. Jordan could smell the flowers all the way across the street.

The hearse and the first family car, driven by the Williamses, started up. The flower car between them, driven by Tatum, nearly ran into the hearse. The cars pulled up to the corner and turned around in the wide street. As the hearse passed Jordan's car, Hyman Applebaum of the improbable firm of Applebaum & O'Reilly, ran into the street by Bates' window. Applebaum doffed his old gray hat and waved it as the ponderous remains in the bronze case rolled by. "Shalom, old friend," Applebaum said.

Bates pulled into the line behind the second family car carrying Southwall's Southern relatives. Behind him came Fannie Fears in her garish limousine. As they turned the corner onto Brooklyn, Jordan saw a line of black Cadillacs stretching endlessly two to three blocks past the church.

All along Brooklyn and all the way out Fifteenth Street to the cemetery, people stopped on the streets to gape at the impressive train slipping by.

No rain for Southwall. It was sunny and clear, and Jordan heard birds singing somewhere in the cemetery. It was the ancient, weed-strewn cemetery where his grandmother lay buried. Indeed, everyone he knew in the city was buried there. It was the only place they had. Their car made cracking sounds as they rolled on gravel toward a green tent set up near the road. They got within only a few hundred feet of the tent. A sea of people blocked their way. Some of the church folk had speeded on out to the cemetery and had waited for them there. Bates shook his head and went around to let the ladies out. Jordan got out and walked down by the tent. He pushed his way to the side of the tent. There the bronze vault gleamed smartly in the sun, suspended above a rectangular emptiness on taut cloth strips.

Jordan loosened his bow tie and got as close as he could to the bier. Flowers in all types of containers were being piled around the tent. There were so many flowers that Tatum let most of them remain in the flower car. Jordan should have been under the tent. But he felt better in the crowd. Carrie Samuels nudged up next to him and was about to speak, but Jordan motioned her to be silent. He held back tears, he who had such trouble emoting in the basement at Gresham.

The crowd parted to make way for the Reverend Richard Rideout, sun dancing in beads of water on his head. Accompanied by members of the choir and some of the elders of the New Jerusalem, Rideout came in measured steps through the grass, intoning the traditional verse: "Yea, though I walk through the valley. . . ."

Water, perfumed, splashed Jordan as Rideout passed by, flinging drops from a dumbbell-shaped vial. At the graveside, Rideout made signs over the casket, kissed it, and reminded the assembly over his hand-held microphone that dust they were and unto dust they would return. With that, Rideout flung the wings of his robe upward to the fluffy sky, sweating, water pouring on his collars. Two men in overalls cranked a machine. On the cloth strips, the cool metal wavered. The men strained. The coffin sagged. Then it sunk rapidly, once, twice, three times. Jerky motions. The flowers on the box shook off. Dirt tumbled down onto the sinking bronze. Under the tent, Psyche fell into young Wayne's arms. Fannie fell into her funeral director's. Clare was there, too. Jordan saw her turn her back. He could not see her face. He sensed that Clare was crying.

There was a moment of summer silence as the plunging coffin thudded Southwall Lovingood to his rest. Then Richard Daniel Rideout shook a hundred hands, and the choir broke out in jubilation.

197

19

Brother Abdullah Jamal was a funeral broker. He had no prep room, no chapel, not even a hearse. He contracted with private families to dispose of their dead, then used the facilities of others to do it. Jordan had first learned of this frowned-upon practice at Gresham. "The funeral broker," Sam Eason had lectured, "is a pariah among our fraternity. He scorns tradition and flies in the face of sanctity. He looks upon the deceased human body, which we consider hallowed as God's own temple, only as garbage to be thrown out as quickly as possible. For this reason, the principles of scientific embalming are just so much bunk to him. Generally, he couldn't embalm a rabbit. Often, he is not an embalmer at all."

As Lawrence Jordan walked into the storefront quarters of the Universal Undertaking Company, Jamal rose up from his desk to greet him.

"Salaam, Brother," said Jamal.

"Salaam," Jordan replied. Why did he do that?

Abdullah was a tan man with a fierce mustache and goatee. His arms bulged with muscles, and Jordan supposed that Jamal worked out evenings at some gym. The man was at least a foot taller than Jordan, and as he looked down on his visitor, he bared a mouth of perfect white teeth. Jordan thought about his own teeth; at least the gap was filled now.

Jordan introduced himself.

"Lawrence X. You a Muslim, man?"

"Naw."

Jordan explained that he had come to see the new company. Abdullah laughed. "You're lookin' at it, baby," he said.

198

"I see."

"What do you see, Bro'?"

"You're a . . . broker."

"Riiiiiight. What's wrong with that."

"Nothing, man. Think you can make it this way, more power to you."

"I'm gonna make it, baby. Know why?"

"Unh-unh."

" 'Cause people gonna wake up—gonna be woke up—'n' see what Lovingood and all the resta these niggas been doin', baby, that's why. Lovingood was the Devil, man. Lovingood was Satan."

And Abdullah went on about how all his funerals went for one hundred and forty-five dollars—embalming, casketing and burial. Tatum, he explained, leased him his facilities for the embalming. Then he took the body to a church or straight to the graveyard. "Low overhead, baby."

"Guess they don't have much of a service," Jordan probed.

"Much as anyone else," Jamal responded. " 'Course I don't pay no preacher to say some words over 'em. Hell, that's the trouble with us now: too many jack-legged preachers holdin' us down. Preachers 'n' undertakers. Shit. They're all the same, all workin' for the devils. You know that, Brother."

"Not necessarily."

"What do you mean? Hell, you was workin' for the worst of the lot. Where do you think old man Lovingood got his bread? From the ghetto? Hell, no; he was in with the devils. They backed him. Everyone can tell you that bread Lovingood was spendin' was Teuffel money. And Valentino money. The Mafia! That's where Lovingood's money came from. 'N' Fannie Fears 'n' all the rest of 'em."

"I don't know anything about that."

"Well, you'd best be findin' out before you run back here tryin' to get into something. Really, might as well forget about settin' up in this town. I got their number, all of 'em. When the people find out, baby, what's goin' on, Jamal will be on top."

"Had any business yet?"

"Had lotsa business."

"Haven't read anything in the paper about it."

"Hell, I don't advertise in no jive-time newspaper. 'Specially that phony-ass *Afro-Citizen*. Phony niggas! This town is full of 'em."

"Why are you here then? Why don't you go back to Cincinnati?"

"Already got a Brother in Cincinnati. We're spreading out, Jordan. I mean the Brotherhood. The jive-time, blue-eyed devil Judeo-Christian world is on its last legs, man. Better come on over to us, while there's still time. Listen: You seem like a shrewd dude, Jordan. Dig: When you get out of school, come on back here and help me. Can't pay you too much. *Yet.* But I've got to fight their shitty little phony Funeral Directors Association. And I need help. I bet you know plenty about ole Lovingood, man, plenty."

"Maybe. I know he was a good man. He was putting me through school."

"Aw, man, damn! Don't you see what he was doing? You think it was because he dug you? Because he wanted to help you? Man, you're a chump. It was because he was trying to perpetuate the system. I know; I've heard about you. Lennie Valentine told me all about you. Man, Lovingood took a look at you, saw you had some potential, some guts, and sent you to school to throw you off the track. The same old Cardboard Murphy game. But you can still make it, Jordan. Forget about trynna be a socialite, man, and do something for the People."

Jamal was holding Jordan's arm in a vise grip. Jordan backed away. "We'll see," he said. "Stay cool. Got to leave, Jamal. Due back at school on Monday."

"Say hello to that devil Eason for me."

"Yeah. Sure."

As he left, Jamal came and stood in the door. There were flies coming in. Outside, it was hot and stuffy. Why hadn't Jamal moved up on the Row with the others? If he really wanted to fight. Why was he down here? Jordan thought about the psychology of grief. One of the elements of that psychology, especially in this city, was location. That's how Lovingood became Number One. He put his place on the Boulevard, where the people aspired to be. Jamal was making a mistake, the mistake of his life.

Jordan hurried down Fifteenth Street to his car. He looked

back at the Universal Undertaking Company. Abdullah Jamal was still standing in the doorway, looking at him. Jamal's brow was wrinkled. There was an ominous look on his face.

The phone woke him up. He had been having the Dream again. This time the place was Jamal's storefront and Jordan's name was a blue neon in the window. It was hot, and the flies were crawling all over the door. Clare came and said she had the money. Jordan told her he was afraid to open the door. Then Southwall Lovingood came, in top hat and tails, and asked Jordan if he liked the funeral. And Clare screamed and said the flies were getting on Southwall, and Lovingood begged Jordan to come out and get them off.

Jordan sighed into the phone: "Hello. . . ."

"This is Wayne, ah, Lovingood. The funeral *director*."

"Yes?"

"I thought you might want to know my father mentioned you in his will."

Jordan was speechless.

"He left you some money. A thousand dollars."

"Well. . . ."

"I'll mail it to you at school."

"Gee, Wayne. . . ."

"Oh, yes. And about school. Or rather, *after* school."

"Yes?"

"Hope you find something."

"How do you mean?"

"I mean there's nothing, no opening, for you here now. We've just hired a new associate funeral director. I believe you know him. Mister Jerome Montague, *T.* Jerome Montague."

20

Half his inheritance went for tuition. The other half he hoarded against the day he would graduate and have to find a job. Maybe it wasn't too late to try the art thing. He could get a job as a day laborer somewhere, perhaps in New York, and study by night.

He got a desperate note from Clare, halfway through the mortuary administration quarter:

> Don't give up. We're going to make it, I know we are. Maybe Mrs. Lewis or Tatum will give you something. Know they're not the biggest, but it could tide you over. Also, there's that new place. Universal. The man, I hear, is a little militant, but he's been getting a lot of attention lately and I hear he's looking for help. None of the other undertakers in town will work with him. Why don't you write him?

Jordan crumpled the letter.

In his plush office at school, Sam Eason gave Jordan a paternal look and commiserated: "Sure sorry about ole Southwall. But don't let that turn you around. We often get requests for graduates—not too many from your people, of course—but something might turn up. Meanwhile, you're smart to stay in school and get the degree. As a funeral director and embalmer, you can command three or four times as much as your mere backroom man. I can't stress too much. . . ."

And Eb Minifee, looking forward to joining the family business in Carolina, mused: "Damn. Sure wish there was something we could do for you, man. But you know how it is. . . ."

But Marcella Ransom said, "I think you ought to talk to my

father. I really do. I've told him all about you and he is very interested."

Jordan had a month to go at Gresham. He began packing his textbooks in boxes. Mrs. Simpson demanded the rest of the rent—in advance. He paid her. Eb Minifee moved back with his uncle and aunt.

Marcella persisted: "Listen. I've told my father we're coming up this weekend. No, I've already told him. He's expecting us. Don't disappoint him. It's only a half hour drive."

En route they stopped at a drive-in. Marcella's earrings danced in her hair as she wiped pizza from the corners of her mouth. "Something good's going to happen to you today, Lawrence. I can feel it."

They came to a military base. "We get a lot of cases from the Army," Marcella said. "Most of them from car accidents and brawls." She turned off the expressway, drove through an industrial area of smokestacks and wire fences, rounded a corner by a group of restaurants where soldiers and young men in caps loitered. One of the soldiers whistled after Marcella. "This is Lake Boulevard," she said. "We're half a mile down the road." They passed ramshackle houses. The houses gave way to a stretch of two-story buildings. The bottom sections of the buildings were bars and pool halls. More young men—none of them in uniform—lounged around the buildings. "Not too many soldiers come down here," Marcella said. "They get into terrible fights with these men." Jordan wondered if Marcella had ever had an affair with a soldier.

On one corner was a café with dingy windows. Marcella turned past the café and drove up an alley behind it. Long rickety wooden steps led down to the alley from the apartments above the café. There was a long porch stretching across the top of the building. Marcella continued past the building and pulled into a glass-littered parking lot next to it. On the lot was a gray Buick hearse. Set back from the alley, narrower than the apartment building, was a single-story brick structure with a single back door. The screen had been removed from the door.

"Well," said Marcella, "this is it. Ransom and Picou."

They went into the back door. The large room beyond it was darkened. Marcella opened a door, then closed it again. She checked another door; it was locked.

"Nobody home," she said. "Maybe they're over at the house."

She opened the front door. A tawny balding man was sweeping down the sidewalk. "Come on," she told Jordan. The man was tall and thin and wore black suspenders. He had on a gray silk tie and light gray suit pants. It was Achilles Ransom. He didn't look like Marcella. Although he was light-skinned, he was light in a different way, and his bone structure was different. Ransom was a bony man, almost delicate. He wore spectacles, big square-shaped glasses with wire frames. He was very formal.

Marcella kissed him on the cheek. He gave her a little hug, put down his broom, and walked up the steps with her. Jordan put out his hand. Ransom shook it but did not smile.

"Daddy, this is Lawrence Jordan," Marcella said. Then to Jordan: "I'll be right back, Lawrence. You men probably have a lot to talk about. I'll run over and say hello to Mother."

Ransom nodded at her gravely. He cleared his throat. "Perhaps I should show you around," he said, watching Jordan closely.

Ransom went to his office, got out a green sweater, and turned on the light in the long, narrow outer room. Apart from a single catafalque, two potted palms and a floor lamp, it was bare. "We put chairs up in here if we use the chapel," Ransom said. The carpet was wine-colored. It was also old and stained and worn in several places. Behind the partially open venetian blinds at the front of the room, Jordan could see gold lettering, "Ransom & Picou/Funeral Directors," on the broad window. Ransom turned out the light and opened the padlock on a door across the room from his office. "This is the ah, *preparation* room," he said, licking his lips. His voice was like his attire: immaculate. Ransom flicked a switch just inside the door.

They descended precariously steep stairs into the basement. The steps were bare wood, unpainted, gray with age. It was dank in the narrow basement. A single naked light bulb illuminated the room, although Jordon saw the customary fluorescent light over the aluminum embalming table.

Above him, he heard cars rolling. The basement extended out under the street.

It was windowless. Around the walls, Ransom had stacked equipment: stretcher, body positioners, two velvety church trucks folded but still on their wheels, boxes of rubber sheets and tubing.

Ransom disappeared into the darkness at the back of the basement. Presently, a second light bulb came on there. Ransom cleared his throat—a signal that Jordan should join him there. There was a deep alcove in the back. In the little half room was a second embalming table. There was a body on the table, under a sheet. "This serves as a storage room," Ransom said, and turned off the light. It was very cold in the back of the basement.

Back at the top of the steps, Ransom turned off the light below and motioned Jordan to his office. Ransom buttoned his sweater around him fastidiously.

In the office, Ransom dusted off a hard-backed chair for Jordan with his hand and took his seat behind an uncluttered desk. On the wall opposite Jordan's chair was Ransom's funeral director's and embalmer's licenses. That was all. There were no pictures, no mortuary school plaque.

Ransom lit a pipe and folded his skeletal hands as if to pray. He looked down at his desk. "Marcella, ah, has told me something about you," he said. "Perhaps we can begin by your telling me more."

Jordan told him about Lovingood, school, the recent tragedy.

"I'm quite sorry about Mister Lovingood's, ah, demise," Ransom said, studying his fingers. "I knew him, you know. We met years ago. At a convention in Chicago." Ransom watched his fingers fold one over the other. He took the pipe out of his mouth, an incredible orifice, little more than a line in his face. "Ah, Marcella tells me you are quite a fair restorative artist?"

"Well, sir. . . ."

"Really gifted work, I hear. *Inspired.*"

"Oh, no. . . ."

"But then of course you would be modest." Ransom leaned forward and turned his head slowly toward Jordan. He looked at Jordan vacantly, as a French poodle might. "May I ask you something, Mister, ah, Jor*dain?*"

"Jordan."

"I see. Mister Jord*an*. What has motivated you to pursue mortuary, ah, work?"

"I'm not sure. I guess I need the money."

And Jordan told him about his sculpting, his study back home, and about Wayne Lovingood's peremptory action. Ransom listened and nodded with the air of a psychiatrist. When Jordan finished, the undertaker resumed his scrutiny of his fingers for a long time. Jordan studied the licenses on the wall. He remembered how you could see the prep table from the steps leading down to the basement. He missed Lovingood's.

Finally, Ransom stood up. "Well, sir," he said. "I can hardly use a sculptor around here."

Jordan flexed his jaws.

"But I do need an embalmer who can do dermasurgery and help direct funerals."

Jordan started to speak. But Ransom held up a yellow hand.

"Of course, I can't pay you much. We average only two cases a week. That includes the fall, when there's a high infant rate and several drownings in the lake. In winter, we're lucky to get one a week. Our people here have little money, too, even up here. And there's always, ah, my daughter, who'll be working with us, though frankly I expect her to marry soon."

"Well, I'm not sure—"

"So all I can offer you is seventy-five a week. Plus room and board at our place. We have a small apartment on the second floor. In the back. It has a screened-in porch. Very pleasant in summer."

"Well, I appreciate your offer. But I'll have to think about it."

"Yes. I understand. When you've made a decision, you can tell Marcella. She keeps me informed. Would you like to, ah, see the hearse?"

Achilles Ransom took great pride in his hearse. It was seven years old and, after the body compartment, left little room for the driver and a passenger. The car's surface and its chrome appointment, however, were immaculate. "We wash it once a week," Ransom said. "We do have a family car, a newer vehicle, which we keep at home. It's a Sedan DeVille. My wife drives it."

"Gray?"

"Yes. I'm a firm believer in putting color in funerals. For example, I never wear black clothes for a service. Browns, grays, even pastel blues. I think one can be colorful without being tawdry, don't you? Actually, a man is well dressed if you don't notice him."

"I prefer black myself."

"Black, in funeral service, carries outdated connotations. It was part of the whole syndrome which ascribed mystery and secrecy to the work of the, ah, mortician, as though he were a high priest or a sorcerer, the keeper of some esoteric tradition."

Jordan glared at Ransom. "But in a sense, he is. It is the people who create the undertaker. And the people want black. It is part of the psychology of grief that people expect something mystic, sacred, private, in the last rites. Funerals are for the living, not the dead. There's a morbid projection by the mourner. He imagines himself in there, in the box. This frightens him. But he likes it. People don't come to the undertaker to get brightness, color. They have enough of that in everyday life. They come to the embalmer, I mean to the *funeral* director, for darkness. They pay him for the sense of mystery and shadow he casts over death. And they pay him well. I can do more with a little shadow, Mr. Ransom, than you can do with a hundred colors. And shadow costs nothing."

Ransom mulled over all this. He cast a sidewise glance at Jordan as he closed the back doors of the hearse.

"Perhaps you will change your mind," he said, "if you, ah, join us here."

21

They were in the basement prep room at Ransom's, operating. Marcella, white-smocked, gloved, was closing an incision along the collarbone of a young man, Jordan was daubing up. Marcella's eyes were lowered; she seemed to be studying the suture, a worm stitch, as she worked the needle, a number 42, zigzagedly through the flesh.

Jordan turned to clamp more cotton in his forceps. As he did, he was startled to feel Marcella's glove on his arm, a gentle pressure. Marcella's eyes were still on the body. She had left the needle sticking halfway through the lips of the incision.

Still showing him her profile, still looking down at the incision, Marcella spoke softly, matter-of-factly. "Lawrence Jordan, I love you. Will you marry me?"

Then she went back to her suturing. The catgut made a moist squeaking sound when she drew it taut.

Upstairs, Achilles Ransom buttoned a red sweater around his bony torso and relaxed elegantly at his desk, observing the fold of his fingers.

"How long have you been with us now, Lawrence?"

"Six months."

"How does your apartment suit you?"

"Fine."

"Plenty of room?"

"Yes, sir."

"Does Marcella ever come up there?"

"Sometimes. Not often."

"Was she up there last night?"

"No, sir."

"Has she ever spent the night up there?"

"Once. We didn't do anything. Just talked."

Ransom pursed his lips. He made a little tepee with his fingers. "You've been here six months now?"

"Yes, sir."

"You like it here."

"Yes, sir."

"And you want to marry my daughter."

"Yes."

"Why?"

"I don't know. Because I love her."

"She's a very pretty girl, isn't she?"

"Yes, she is."

"She'll be a great asset to any upcoming young mortician."

"Yes, sir. She will."

"And you do love her?"

"Yes, I do."

"And you do understand her?"

"I didn't say *that,* Mister Ransom."

Ransom threw his head back and laughed. It was the first time Jordan had seen him do that. The laugh came up out of Ransom's delicate anatomy and gurgled in his throat. Jordan wriggled in his chair. He hoped that Marcella, still working below, couldn't hear the laughing. Ransom laughed until tears formed in the corners of his eyes. He wiped at the tears, then got serious again. He looked straight at Jordan.

"She's not really my daughter, you know."

"She isn't?"

"That's right. Her real name, before we changed it, was Marcella Picou."

"Your old partner?"

"Exactly. Marcella's mother was his wife. That was a long time ago. She was his wife for some years after Marcella was born although Mrs. Ransom and I were already, ah, together when Marcella came along. It was very complicated. But I'll tell you about that aspect of it some other time. Not that there's anything to hide. They were—the Picous were—quite happily married until he had his first, ah, breakdown. An unfortunate thing. Vertis really wasn't cut out for this business. It became too much for him. He got too, ah, *involved* with his work, if you perceive my meaning."

"Was he brown-eyed like Marcella?"

"No, but very fair. Very fair. He was shorter than I am. But immaculate, considerate in every thing he did. The way he dressed, the way he spoke. He was very fond of straw hats. I, ah, admired him greatly. His taste. He was thin like I was, and light-haired, too. People used to say we looked like brothers. *Broth*ers."

Ransom turned and studied his fingers. He seemed to have forgotten momentarily that Jordan was present.

"Does Marcella—"

"Not all of it," Ransom whispered. "She knows most of it. She knows about his, ah, misfortune. She knows about her mother and me, about his taking it to heart, about his moving to California, about his tragic death out there. She doesn't know—she thinks I keep his name up on the window out of respect for his memory. She thinks I am her father."

"I see. But why did you tell me? Of course I won't tell her, but—"

"Because I hope it will help you understand her better, understand *us* better. I wanted you to know what you're getting yourself into."

"Then you mean?"

"Of course. My blessings. Ah, *son*."

Clare brought six suitcases with her. She changed clothes three times a day. She moved in the little apartment with Jordan, but spent most of her time downstairs talking to Camille Ransom: "I mean Lawrence's daddy didn't give a damn about us, honey. . . . Lawrence basically is a good boy. . . . If it hadn't been for *South*wall *Loving*ood. . . . Your daughter's such a darling child. . . ."

Clare Jordan seemed pleased by the impending event. Privately, however, she told Jordan, "I just hope to God you know what you're doing. Hell, these people don't have nothin'. It's too small, this town. Everybody'll know your business. Marcella is *pretty*, but I don't trust her, never have trusted light people. . . ."

Jordan was ashamed of her; why did she have to bring up things like that? Clare was getting beside herself. And she was losing her beauty. Funny that he hadn't noticed it before now. But next to Camille Ransom, Marcella's mother, Clare looked shallow, painted. Camille Ransom was older. But she wore no makeup and, like Marcella, had pierced ears. Camille kept her weight down and had a natural easiness, an inherent grace. Clare was getting dumpy. And raspy. One of the suitcases she brought was filled with hats, cheap spangled ones with odd shapes.

What he hated most of all was the way Clare baited him. "I guess you'll be happy up here," she said, sprawling on the little divan in his apartment. "Maybe a *small* town is right for you. After all, back home there's all that competition. And Wayne Lovingood is certainly moving ahead. Yes, sir; he's quite a man. . . ."

The wedding was held in the Catholic church four blocks from the Ransom house. Jordan had decided against converting, but he agreed to raise any children they might have in the church. And he took religious instructions at night for a month while the bans were publicized in church. Marcella dragged him to mass each Sunday. Achilles Ransom, himself a non-Catholic, sympathized with Jordan. After all, Ransom had undergone similar trials.

It was a simple affair, although it did cause some stir in the town. Jordan didn't know most of the people who attended the ceremony. They were friends and neighbors of the Ransoms, and most of them were fair-skinned people. Marcella's maid of honor was an Italian girl named Farentino, someone she had gone to high school and college with, her best friend in the town. For his best man, Jordan called up Ed Minifee, his old roommate, who was still at Gresham. Also from the big city came members of the mortuary elite, including an indifferent, dark-eyed Tommie Roddenberry, somewhat effeminate like Eb, certainly no threat to Jordan.

It was over before he knew it, and his nervousness seemed unnecessary when it was done. Jordan remembered little of the actual ceremony: Marcella, radiant in white with a formidable veil opaquing her beauty, her presence diminishing the darker beauty of her bridesmaids. A solemn Achilles Ransom in patent-leather shoes and pearl-gray tails. Gold glittering on the white vestments of the priest as he consecrated the host, murmured Latin, a polished chalice, vows, congratulations. In the vestibule a kiss, a cake, a ring. Clare at the reception bragging about how Jordan had taken care of her.

They had no honeymoon, just a few days to themselves in the house while the Ransoms took Clare on a tour of Chicago.

They slept late and ate enormous lunches, never taking off their pajamas. On the wedding night, Marcella had slipped into his bedroom in full-length, bodiced gown while he lay smoking a cigarette, getting up his nerve. She came and stood by where he lay, still wearing her earrings, and he probed her mouth with his tongue and put his head up under the gown and pulled at the curly fur there with his mouth. He got on her and exerted himself again and again until she begged for mercy. Marcella wasn't as good to him as Herece or even Thessalonica Wingate Montague. She couldn't respond with the abandon of the other women. But Jordan liked Marcella's action well enough. In the morning Marcella told him he had made her sore, and Jordan laughed and apologized. He smelled her hair, and reaching deep within himself, summoning his source of extra energy, feeling a resurging need, Jordan climbed back on his wife.

The next Monday they were back in the basement of the funeral home, laying open flesh under the fluorescents. The Jordans settled into a narrow routine dictated by the town, the mores of Marcella's parents, and the family's grim profession.

22

Kewaunee, Illinois, was a suburban mosaic of humanity: Polish taverns facing Armenian churches, Jewish clothing stores near Italian restaurants, Puerto Rican groceries flanking soul food cafés. From Milwaukee to the north rolled endless barrels of German draft beer. And with the beer came good spirits. On the West Side on Saturday night, at the Wolzywoski Inn, one minute they were watching *Dick Sinclair's Polka Parade* on the television above the bar; the next they were frugging to the wailing of James Brown, imprisoned in the jukebox. On the South Side, at the Down Home Café, the menu included Polish sausage and chicken cacciatore—alongside hog maws, greens, and cracklin' bread.

On the surface, Kewaunee was the realization of an American dream. But the little township of fifty thousand people was as deeply divided socially and ethnically as its soil was gutted by primordial ravines that ran down to the lakeshore.

Kewaunee was a study in contrasts. In winter the blizzards were so intense that school was canceled for weeks at a time and some families waited to be dug out of their houses. The lake boiled up then, hurling arrows of icy wind through the pea coats of sailors and the leggings of little girls. In summer the lack of trees and flatness of terrain made the city a furnace at midday; sunfire was bright orange on the panes of westward windows and breathing air was thick. Wavy lines danced over the steaming waters of the lake.

Between them, the warring equinoxes cracked Kewaunee like a cold dish in an oven. Gradually the cracks widened, and the land got bent and veined.

Germans founded the town in the late nineteenth century.

Their legacies were the stern First Lutheran Church, the shadowy, wood-paneled decor of the New Heidelberg Restaurant near the North Side, and the stately Friedland Colonial Funeral Home.

Next came the Armenians, fleeing the wrathful Turks. Across the burgeoning thoroughfare called Grosstrasse (later Main Street) the carpet dealers—Valerian, I. Nestorian and Gertmenian—had humble beginnings.

More Germans came after World War I: disaffection with the Kaiser. Between the wars, Italians began sifting up from Chicago, menaced by gangland warfare.

World War II brought the greatest single wave, and that was black. From the South, from Dixie, and from Chicago came inscrutable faces of ebony and bronze, descendants of the proud Ashanti, the stubborn Dinka and the slant-eyed Benin of Africa. And of the amorous French plantation owners of Louisiana Territory—these last with hazel eyes and auburn hair: Marcella's people. With the Afro-Americans came to the Down Home Café; Sally Sally's and R. B.'s, favored bars; the tailor shops, beauticians', barbers'; wailing churches; peeling pool halls.

After the war came Jews, more blacks, and finally Puerto Rican, Hispanic spin-off from New York.

All came; few mingled.

The South Side was Lawrence Jordan's concern. The lifeline of the South Side was Lake Street, itself a microcosmic Grosstrasse in the ghetto's life. In another sense, Lake Street was like the twenty-foot ravine that isolated the South Side from Kewaunee's well-kept downtown. Lake Street was the dividing line between the older ghetto families and the new.

East of Lake Street, the blocks tumbled row on row into the lake itself. Where the flat, open Illinois land met the inland sea the shoreline was a bluff. East of Lake Street, the houses deteriorated the nearer they were to the lake. From older, two-story wooden frame hostels with rotten roofing, the dwellings plunged down to the single-story tar-paper shacks of Front Street.

Jordan ventured down to Front Street only when Ransom accepted business there. A thick, greasy kind of people inhabited the place: scowling men and women with shaggy hair and scars on their faces, beer and wine smells in their mouths.

Their parents had come north from Alabama and Georgia and Tennessee for a better life. Finding only a worse existence in the dismal tenements and housing projects and alleys of Chicago, they had come still farther up the lake to Kewaunee, where it was rumored that black men had big two-story homes with barbecue pits in their backyards.

Achilles Ransom *did* have a barbecue pit. And trees. And fenced yard, like most of the elite on Elm Avenue, which was to the area west of Lake Street what Front Street was to the Bluff. Elm Avenue was the Promised Land, the Sugar Hill, of South Side Kewaunee. On Elm Avenue lived the well-to-do of the tiny ghetto enclave, the barbers and rodent exterminators and café owners and postal workers. Some of them traced their roots in Kewaunee back three generations, like electrician Bill Waymon, a tan-skinned man who ran unsuccessfully every two years for the Board of Aldermen and who headed the nearly defunct Kewaunee NAACP.

Waymon lived three doors from Achilles Ransom, and the electrician's modest brick home was considered a showplace.

Across Elm Street from Ransom lived Ricardo Bartholome, the West Indian realtor and building contractor who reportedly owned half the tiny houses on the Bluff. Bartholome's home was no showplace, but it was considered a toss-up among the townsfolk who was richer, he or Achilles Ransom, who had divided the town up funerally with Kurt Friedland and Joe Farentino, the "Catholic" undertaker.

The mortician kept to himself. The Ransom home was a nine-room frame dwelling. Ransom had converted the front porch into a tenth room, and Jordan spent many of his summer evenings there, listening to symphonies with his wife. The Ransom living room stretched across the front of the house and boasted an enormous stone fireplace. Its French Provincial appointments, like those in the formal dining room, were solid mahogany. In the wide kitchen and in the sewing room behind, the walls were knotty pine. Upstairs were the bedchambers, simple rooms, and Jordan's two-room apartment and porch.

Oddly, his parents-in-law spent most of their summer evenings on his porch while he and Marcella relaxed on theirs. Jordan's porch looked down on marigolds and violets and roses by the back fence. The flowers and a large air-conditioned house trailer were Ransom's only real luxuries. He chided Jordan for not having a green thumb. "Flowers," Ransom said, "are the only real innocents of this world."

Once a month in summer, Ransom would hitch the trailer to the funeral coach and spend a few days in Wisconsin by a lake. Since someone had to be on call, Jordan usually stayed behind. During these weekends he would sculpt anatomical figures of men and women in a new medium—dermatine wax. Often, Marcella stayed behind with him, and they made love on either porch and ate ice cream, which Jordan brought in from a little café down on Lake Street.

Achilles Ransom was sixty-three; he didn't look it. Jordan told him so. "Well, after all," Ransom quipped, "I am in the business of preservation."

Ransom had started in undertaking as a boy and was apprenticed for five years. As a young man, he had come north to seek his fortune and met Vertis and Camille Picou, also Creoles, in the big city. Together, they had launched the partnership. The states in those days had no uniform licensing laws. Ransom stayed abreast of developments in his field by visiting Gresham College. When the state did begin administering state board examinations, Ransom had no trouble passing. After that, it was merely a matter of renewing his license.

Achilles was a quiet man who seemed content with merely living. Jordan wondered why such an articulate man could be so content in a little town like Kewaunee. He tried to imagine what Ransom must have been like in the city, in the early days. All Ransom would say about it was: "We had some fine funerals then. My partner and I used to wear white Palm Beach suits in the summer. We had a whole fleet of Buick cars. One time, we buried the mother of the singer Sweet Lettie Ross. So many people came we had to hold it in a park by the lake. That was our finest hour."

Ransom wore expensive suits. He got them from Chicago, and they fit him perfectly. He was never without his suspenders or a tie. Even when he relaxed around the house, he wore a silk tie. He kept his collars buttoned and his ties in taut Windsor knots. This seemed to be a point of pride with him.

Twice a week Jordan and his father-in-law ate at the Down Home Café. As he was with most of the townfolk, Ransom was cool but cordial to the woman who ran the restaurant. He always ordered greens and ham hocks and black coffee. Going to the café was a ritual with Jordan and Ransom.

On Lake Street, Achilles Ransom was known as a stiff man who made it his business to speak politely with everyone without becoming embroiled in serious conversation. Jordan's impression was that the Lake Street toughs resented Ransom's imperious manner and his retiring ways but respected him out of fear of what he represented. And Ransom took leisurely walks up Lake Street, looking in shopwindows, nodding at the young men outside the pool halls. Looking grim and elegant all at once, Ransom would float by some pool shark or petty hustler and remark, "Good morning, Mister Pretty William. How is your health?" or "Take it easy on those cigarettes, Mister Bad Boy Junior. We may be seeing more of you."

He called everyone Mister or Miss. At one time or another, he had buried a relative of nearly every soul around. Yet only a handful had ever been to his house; even his neighbors called him *Mister* Ransom.

Ransom was miserly, a tendency which manifested itself not by denying his family but by refusing to make improvements in his business. Ransom constantly complained of high overhead, a subject on which he was eloquent.

"It's a pity that we aren't able to do more for our infant dead," Ransom would remark during the baby season, peering down at a tiny coffin. "It would be appropriate and quite befitting to offer some manner of special consideration for the little ones we see so much of. Perhaps a Babyland Slumber Room where we could display several of the little tykes simultaneously in a little cluster as in a maternity ward. But alas, this increasingly exorbitant overhead, coupled with the positively shameful irreverence displayed for even incipient human beings, prohibits us from doing more for our little charges."

Translated, this meant that people weren't willing to give babies expensive funerals—and Ransom was hardly going to give them a suture more than they paid for.

Tucking in the silks around one of his infant clients, Ransom would turn to Jordan, sweeping the worn and ragged carpet with the ancient broom.

"We can hardly afford provisions for our adult dead," Ransom would say, throwing up his bony hands. "While Social Security and veterans' benefits remain nearly constant, inflation robs us of our due. And the death rate is down. The costs of fluids, surgical equipment, embalming devices, cosmetics, automotive accessories, the rolling stock itself, even the floral tributes are up, way up. Caskets are sky-high. Vaults are out of sight. Concrete linings, *positively required by state law,* cost a minimum of eighty-five dollars. Body positioner and burial garment manufacturers have priced themselves right out of the market.

"People have to eat. Food is up. Clothing is up. Housing is up. Transportation is way up. Gas and lighting and furnishings.

"Every week, in the arrangements conference, people come to me and say, 'Mister Ransom, I can't afford to give Willie a decent burial. We don't even have enough to eat.' Of course, they exaggerate. But they ask me to help them, give them some kind of cut rate, some kind of discount. They seem to think the undertaker is in business for his health, that he can change his prices around like a meat market.

"What can I do?"

There were several things Ransom could do. And he did every one of them.

First, he kept the overhead to a minimum: kept the lights off, the heat off, the fans off; forwent business cards, matchbooks, calendars, uniforms for softball teams and other promotional gimmicks; skimped on the prep room; made few telephone calls; paid Marcella and Jordan a hundred and fifteen dollars a week (a joint salary only one and a half times what they would make separately); used Camille Ransom as a beautician and funeral assistant; refused to give preachers an honorarium— which was laudable—charged rental of "space" taken up by bodies whose survivors could not come to terms; retained his old hearse year to year and used it to make pickups, as well as dispositions.

Next, he colluded with Friedland and Farentino to have all South Side cases referred back to him.

Finally, he kept his prices competitive with the downtown undertakers' without making the outlays they did for drapery, building space, carpeting, rolling stock and advertising. He set his own minimum prices for adult and infant cases. Anyone over three was considered an adult. Jordan estimated that Ransom's average outlay on each of the fifty adult cases he handled a year was two hundred and fifty dollars; for the twenty-five infant cases, one hundred and fifty dollars. He charged a minimum of six hundred and fifty dollars for adult funerals and two hundred and fifty dollars for infant and veterans. Adjusting for costs of caskets and vaults (infants were buried "piggyback" in unmarked sections of the cemeteries and didn't need vaults), Jordan figured that Ransom made at least fifteen thousand dollars a year from his business and probably more likely twenty thousand dollars. And Ransom had long since paid for both his house and his funeral home. In addition, he owned the building next to the home, whose tenants included a laundry, pool hall, and the Down Home Café, as well as five families up above. In the early days Ransom had often taken a trust deed on one of the sordid one-bedroom houses on the bluff and fifty dollars as payment for a funeral. Over the years he had acquired title to scores of houses, and every month Camille Ransom spent two whole days collecting the rent. If Rick Bartholome owned half the bluff, Ransom owned the other. And with the sale of his property in the big city before he moved to Kewaunee, Ransom had bought parcels of land stretching all the way into Wisconsin. The land had never been developed. Ransom liked to look at it slipping by as they drove up to Zion in the hearse on funerals.

With the price of cosmetic fluid soaring the way it was, Ransom calculated development of the land would be impractical. Besides, then he would have to pay taxes on it.

Jordan was one of the few people in whom Ransom confided. Jordan supposed that Marcella's stepfather also confided in her mother, but he had no way of knowing for sure.

Camille Ransom, who looked like an older version of Marcella, was in direct contrast with Achilles. She was short, stocky and outgoing. Indeed, she was so talkative and friendly (though not toward her tenants below Lake Street) that she talked to the dead, though in a way different from Southwall Lovingood's. Jordan discovered this after his second month with Ransom, when he was working on a body and Camille came in to do the hair. Mrs. Ransom brought her own equipment, a traveling case containing curlers, oils, permanent, and makeup.

"How do you do, Mister Jordan?" Camille cooed. Then to the body: "Good afternoon, Miss Lucy. It has been awhile, hasn't it? I hope T. R. isn't taking this too hard."

And she went on gossiping with the corpse as she worked.

Achilles Ransom was not romantic about his work; he preferred pruning roses to draining blood. Southwall Lovingood approached their calling as an art. Ransom saw it as a trade. Southwall loved the spectacle; Achilles abhorred panegyrics and tears. His emphasis on color in funerals actually was an attempt to minimize the tragedy of death.

Lovingood had measured his success by the bodies he had shown; Ransom by the money he made.

But Ransom did not hurry through the embalming procedure, as Southwall would. But then Lovingood had more business than Ransom. And the bodies were buried sooner.

Ransom was niggardly in everything else, but he did not economize on embalming fluid. "It's better to overembalm," Ransom told Jordan and Marcella.

Jordan underembalmed his first case.

Ransom was furious. "The mortician's first responsibility is to disinfect the body," he roared. "That comes before restorative art, fancy display, anything."

Jordan went to his textbooks. He read up on causes of embalming failure. He checked his dilution indices. Then he went downstairs to Marcella, who was watching television.

"I can't understand it," Jordan said. "I did everything according to the book. Why did he say I hadn't set it up right?"

"The textbook is wrong."

She was still engrossed in the TV set. Jordan took her hand. Marcella grinned at him and tossed her hair. "What should I do?" he asked.

"Try ligaturing the artery," she replied.

He did, and it worked. Jordan's cases began turning out better, and Jordan found a new respect for Marcella. And a new sense of threat: Marcella was a better embalmer than he would ever be. She was a better embalmer than anyone needed to be.

23

Lawrence,

April showers. Nothing much to report this week. Oh, yes! You remember that Abdullah Jamal who came here last year and opened the Universal Undertaking Co.? Well, he and Wayne Lovingood are into it. Jamal has been printing literature saying that the other undertakers charge too much money, hundreds of dollars, for services they don't perform. Last week he had an article in the *Afro* about the other undertakers making payoffs to the Mafia (clipping enclosed). Jamal specifically named Southwall as one who had been financed by them. Psyche says Wayne was infuriated. This Jamal is causing lots of trouble. He has become a sort of hero to the young men on the street, and he and Lennie Valentine are getting a lot of poor folks riled up about the way Lovingood and all of them are acting. You remember Lennie.

Wayne has been elected head of the Funeral Directors Association. Just like his father before him (we all miss Southwall so). Wayne has sworn that they will run Jamal out of business. Nothing but a whole fucking mess going on. In a way, I'm glad you had the sense not to get involved in all this hankypanky by staying up there in Illinois. It may be dull, but I guess that's what's for you. You never were really *committed* —like Wayne. Guess Kansas City's just too much for you.

Nothing more going on. Except that Herece and her husband are fighting. He turned out to be a good-for-nothing kind of man. Drinking all the time and beats her. Hope all is well with you. Love to Marcella and family.

Mother

P.S.—Do you know if Southwall *did* have anything to do with those people down on the North End?

Clarisse Jordan reread her letter to her son. Yes, that was it; she had said all she wanted to. Clare had not given up. She was more determined than ever to have things her way. She had achieved what she had set out to do with Jordan: She had put him in position. Now all that remained was to reap the benefits. But Clare needed her son where she could control him. Not off in the sticks somewhere. Her mission now was to get him back to Kansas City. She would use any means she could to accomplish that return.

Clare reread the most important lines: *You never were really committed—like Wayne. Guess Kansas City's just too much for you.* That was the key. Something like that in every letter, prettied up on fluffy pink paper perfumed. Love, Mother. Enclose the funeral notices, report some goings-on. Issue a veiled challenge. Clare realized now that she had failed in raising her son. She had tried to control his intelligence, and that could not be done. He was a stranger to her with that piercing look of his. She knew she couldn't keep Jordan bound to her forever any more than she could his father. There was too much else in them driving them. This thing called art. But this Clare knew about her son: He could not resist a challenge. That was his greatest weakness and that was what she counted on. Jordan ignored all those around him who gave in to him and worshiped him. He paid marvelous attention to those who challenged him.

The best way to get attention from Lawrence Jordan was to challenge his manhood on every level. Thus Clare made a point of mentioning something about Herece or Thessalonica in every letter. These were the only women he had lost; someday he would be driven to regain them.

Lost in thought, Clare sniffed the pink pages of her missive and inserted them neatly in an envelope. She wondered how long it would take him to return. Could Fannie Fears help hasten the event?

LAWRENCE,
Sweltering in this heat. Herece and her hubby have separated. She's living with Psyche again. Sometimes I just don't understand this town. Folks killing each other left and right,

222

you know how that is. Last week, the Mafia was at it again. There was a bombing over in Little Italy. The Valentino Funeral Home. Nobody was hurt, but there's a lot of tension on the North End. One of the Valentino brothers—the one named Joseph—said they'll get the ones who did it. The Valentinos and Teuffel, that old German undertaker, were squabbling. Psyche told me that Wayne thinks Jamal is mixed up in all this. Sure wish they'd let each other alone. It just divides the community.

Jamal's still raising Cain but nobody pays much attention to him anymore. The Funeral Directors Association was successful in getting most of the major suppliers to refuse orders from Universal. Jamal's talking about going back to Cincinnati. His friend Lennie Valentine's back in jail again. Ho hum. That child spends half his life in jail. Extortion this time. Lennie and some more fellows tried to start a protection racket, but the shop owners got together and told the police.

Congratulations on your raise. Two hundred dollars doesn't sound like much back here, but I guess in a small town it goes a long way. Too bad you don't have something like Lovingood's. They're really running 'em through down there (see clippings). Wayne's really turned into a fine man. Do you ever hear from him? He and T. J. Montague (Thess is as pregnant as a jaybird) really have a lot on the ball. They just got some new Cadillacs. Sharp.

Love to all. Take care. Hope to get up that way maybe next summer. More later.

MOTHER

"I'm going to California."
Psyche Lovingood was shocked at her daughter's words. "Why, Herece?"
"I'm just weary, Mamma. I'm just so tired of Kansas City, everything. I've got to get away. And think."
The church had failed her when she prayed to save her marriage. Herece had not let herself believe that until the very end. Without the church, without a man, her life was empty.
She had miscalculated. Lawrence Jordan *was* the man. Now where was he? Married and living elsewhere and not even thinking about her.
All right then. Herece would be gone, too. There were bad

223

vibrations in Kansas City, very bad. They started when Lawrence left.

Herece called her cousins in Los Angeles and told them she was coming. She hated to leave her mother alone, but Psyche had been oblivious to everything since Southwall died. Psyche would survive.

"Who knows, Mamma?" Herece said at the station. "Things may be better in California. I may meet someone there."

They cried in each other's arms at the station, Psyche and Herece, but the crying was not for them alone. They grieved for all the women without men who ever lived, all the lonely betrayed women of the world.

LAWRENCE,

Thought I'd better tell you right away about the Jamal slaying. The clippings tell most of it. They found him in the back seat of his car. The police said on TV today that someone tried to make it look like a suicide.

They're shipping the body back to Cincinnati. The Funeral Directors Association, as much trouble as he gave them, are paying for it. They said it was the least they could do. Lennie Valentine is still in jail, so they can't accuse him of doing *this*.

Glad you're not here now. Just awful the way people are carrying on these days. Hate to think about it. Tell all I said hello. Oh yes—ran into old Mrs. Samuels today. You know, the woman who goes to all those funerals. She told me to be sure to tell you hi. It's getting chilly here; time for hot toddy and fur coats. Love.

MOTHER

Lynford Valentine was dressed entirely in black. He had on a black silk tie and a black dress shirt, a black narrow-brimmed hat with shiny black band, black trousers held up by black suspenders, black gloves, black socks, black shoes and an expensive black leather trench coat. Lennie had lost some weight in jail; his dark attire made him look even thinner than he was. The black of his trench coat contrasted nicely with his teakwood skin.

To top it all off, Lennie was wearing sunglasses—at night. All the young men around him were wearing sunglasses. That was their trademark.

They bivouacked on a parking lot next to the crumbling storefront that had housed the Universal Undertaking Company. Peeling gilded letters on the window of the storefront still proclaimed it to be that company. Lennie liked that. It gave a little irony to his operation.

Two men in dark glasses and black suits flanked the doorway of the building. They frisked several young men who came to the door, then nodded permission for the visitors to enter. Periodically, the men on the door looked nervously at the parking lot, then up and down the street. Another man, similarly attired, surveyed the situation from the roof. He had a rifle with him with a telescopic sight.

The men on the door disappeared inside, and there was a period of long silence. Then from the roof came the signal. Lennie's followers gathered closely around him, covering him from all sides. They looked in all directions and started walking. They went in the back way.

Inside, Lennie lifted a revolver from his black shoulder holster and handed it to the man guarding the door there. The man gave Lennie a gold-toothed smile.

There was much noise up front. The room was buzzing with conversation; the place was packed. Lennie adjusted his suspenders and took a series of deep breaths. Behind his glasses, in his mind, a street scene flashed: the Turk. Turk's look of fear and Lennie's grinning. Silence. Then three shots. That's all there was to it. Really, Lennie liked the Turk. So he sent him on to heaven. Lennie would send a lot of friends to heaven before it was finished. That was his destiny.

Valentine heard himself announced. Black curtains on the doorway parted, and Lennie stepped into the room. He received a standing ovation. Ignoring it, he went directly to the lectern. He did not take off his coat or hat. Behind him, covering the wall from floor to ceiling, was a giant photo of Lord Abdullah, Lennie's predecessor. Lennie bowed before the picture and raised a clenched fist in salute.

"Jamal!" he cried.

"Jamal!" the others echoed.

"*Jamalu'allah!*"

"*Jamalu'allah, Jamalu'allah Salaam!*"

He turned and surveyed the lean and hungry faces of his au-

dience. Some were dark, and some were light. Some were fearful; some were bold. But all were lean and hungry.

"Who killed Jamal?" Lennie shouted.

"The Mafia!" came the answer.

"Who killed the Mafia?"

"Our Black Brotherhood."

"Who brought forth the Brotherhood?"

"Jamal! Jamal!"

"Jamal lives on. Jamal lives in his Brotherhood, and I am his
follower."

"All right."

"Right on."

Clenched fist salutes.

"Listen," Lennie said, warming to his subject. "Lotta niggas
talkin' 'bout power, talkin' 'bout control. They gonna bring
Power to the People and don't even control the turf."

"Right on."

"Shut up. Just listen. The root of our problem ain't the poli-
ticians or big business or the fuckin' cops. Dig here: Who controls the government, the cops, the business? Who controls the
ghetto? Who controls the turf? The goddamn Mafia!"

"Jamal!"

"The Mafia controls the turf because they have their thing
together. Each member is subordinate to the group. Can you
dig it? Each member is expendable. Now there ain't that many
Mafia cats; there ain't that many. They got thirty million
niggas scared of 'em, and there ain't that many. Why else would
they have to bring a dude in from Chicago to make a hit?
'Cause they don't want nobody to know who done it? Bullshit!
'Cause there ain't that many of 'em.

"We done peeped their whole card. The Brotherhood is with
it, baby. We're already operating in Chicago, Detroit, Newark,
Nassau, Philadelphia and New York. And here in Kansas City.
Kansas City is the home ground; Jamal is the founder. If you
didn't dig Jamal, you wouldn't be here. I am just his servant.

"You didn't come to hear about no Cosa Nostra. We all
know what they're puttin' down. You came to hear about the
Brotherhood. 'N' we came to tell you 'bout it. But we can't tell
you as a group 'cause some of you are spies. We ain't scared of
spies; we'll get you later. But we want to talk to true Brothers.

226

We need you. Jamal needs you. So when I leave here, I want the true Brothers—the cats that ain't afraid, the cats that don't believe all these ugly rumors they're spreadin' 'bout Lennie and the Brotherhood—we want all the Purebred Brothers to talk to our lieutenants. They'll make an appointment for you to talk to us in private, 'n' we'll tell you more about it.

"Membership in Our Thing isn't all that easy. It ain't no Cardboard Murphy game. You have to prove yourself before Jamal. We have three circles leading to the Inner Ring. Before you get there, we may ask you to do it to your own mother. A man must pass through all three, and until he's in, he's on his own. But when you're finally in, when you're with us, when you're in the Brotherhood, not even God can bring you down. Jamal!"

"Jamal!"

"*Jamalu'allah.*"

Wrapping his leather coat around him, Lennie hurried to the limousine they kept running for him. His lieutenants would conduct the remainder of the meeting. They protected him. Lennie permitted himself a secret grin. He had really got his thing together in the jailhouse; every angle was thought out. When word reached him that Jamal had been rubbed out— that his bad-mouthing the Mafia had finally got him wiped out by the Mafia itself—he knew just what steps to follow. Blame it on Lovingood, even try to connect *Wayne* with the Mafia (not impossible in Kansas City, where strange alliances were an everyday occurrence). Then follow the natural progression, Abdullah's role as martyr, Lennie's as avenging angel, and ride Jamal all the way to Fat City.

Lynford Valentine slid into the back seat of his bulletproof limousine and fanned himself with his black hat. It was all so very natural and easy.

Why then was he sweating?

24

Adultery was the number one pastime in Kewaunee, Illinois. Rick Bartholome was known to be going openly with the wife of Bill Waymon, the electrician. The husbands of beauticians were seeing the wives of barbers. Even cousins were going together. On the street, Jordan heard one boy remark to another, "My mother's boyfriend came and parked outside the house yesterday, but my father chased him off. . . ." The second year of his marriage, Jordan had fears he would come home or to the funeral home and catch his own wife in a compromising situation. He wondered if the Ransoms—Achilles and more especially Camille—had outside interests. Mrs. Ransom invariably went shopping on Thursdays and often didn't return until late at night. Achilles Ransom went off on long forages into the country, supposedly to check on his land.

There was something dead about Kewaunee. It wasn't only the lack of recreation or entertainment. It wasn't only the dulling monotony of the neighborhoods and the beer halls. It was in the people, in the air. It was in Marcella. At first, Jordan had been too busy perfecting his techniques and learning funeral direction to notice Marcella's shortcomings. The situation had settled down to a system whereby Marcella did the main embalming while Jordan did the cosmetic work and arranged the services. Achilles Ransom took more time off and puttered around his gardens or went off to Wisconsin with his wife. On funeral days, the whole family sometimes pitched in, handling everything themselves. They ate their biggest meals on those days, then retired early.

It was one of those times that Jordan had felt particularly affectionate, passionate, and wanted a response from Marcella.

He had directed a flawless performance, a big funeral at one of the small churches, and Achilles Ransom had complimented him.

Lawrence Jordan crawled in the bed beside his wife and rubbed her backside.

"Lawrence," she said, "wasn't that a fine service today?"

"Mmmm-humm." He kept rubbing her.

"You did a good job on the body. The face looked just like she had never suffered."

"Mmmm. Roll over."

"Oh, Lawrence, do we have to? I just want to lay here and savor it—today, the service. I've never been happier in my life. I think the cemetery in Zion is beautiful, don't you?"

Silence.

"Lawrence, what's wrong with you?"

He had the Dream again, woke up sweating, and found Marcella gone. She had gone back to the funeral home, down in the basement, to savor the events of the day. The next day was Thanksgiving, and she helped her mother make turkey and dressing.

Jordan didn't mean to get involved with Tina Clay. But she pressed herself on him in the graveyard. He took Tina to defy Marcella.

He had stayed behind to make sure the gravedigger pushed dirt on the casket and the flowers. Otherwise, the man might take the flowers and sell them back to the florist. Jordan watched as the little tractor pushed a mound of dirt into the depths. Then he trotted back to the hearse. It was gray and chilly.

Tina Clay pulled up next to him. He had seen her at several funerals, watching him. She hung out at the Elks Club. Her husband was a truck driver who wore a process.

"Oh, sir?" Tina called through her window.

He got out and went to her.

"Yes, ma'am?"

"How you feelin'?"

Jordan blushed. "Okay."

"Just wondered. You work *aw*ful hard."

"What can I do for you?"

"I don't know. Maybe a lot."

Tina was leaning out her window. She opened the car door and swung her legs around so they faced Jordan. She placed one of her feet in the door of the car, on the little ledge. Her coat was open; she crossed her legs. As she did this, she pulled at the lap of her dress with her long fingernails. She was showing him her thighs. They were coffee-colored.

"What are you doing this evening?" she asked. Her manner was nonchalant.

"Staying out of trouble," he said.

"With her?"

"Who?"

"Ransom's daughter."

"Uh-huh."

"She acts funny. Weird. I bet she's as cold as those dead bodies you all work on."

Tina pulled her dress up farther. Without knowing it, Jordan craned his neck and gaped. It was incredible under there.

"I've been watching you," Tina said. "I want you—"

"Oh?"

"To come over some time and see me."

"Well, I don't know."

"Like this evening."

"What about your husband?"

"On the road, won't be back for days."

"I have to go home and eat."

"You don't have to do that. Come on over my place. I'll give you something to eat. I'll give you lots of things to eat."

She swung around under the steering wheel, her dress still wrinkled on thighs Jordan knew he had to explore. "I'll wait for you behind the funeral home," Tina said. Across the road, the tractor nudged a few last crumbs over the fresh new grave.

"I'm sorry," Achilles Ransom said, studying his tawny fingers. "I understand your desire to further your education. I commend it. But I have to think of the business. It wouldn't be a month before we'd get a night call on some drowning or shooting. This is *that* season, you know."

"But it's only three nights a week," Jordan protested.

"I know." Ransom sighed. "But you can't expect the women to go out on calls."

"I've already signed up. They expect me at school next Monday."

"You should have thought of the business before you signed up. After all, it may be yours some day. Maybe then you'll understand what I mean. Can't you tell them you want to wait until summer?"

"Yes."

"Well, I'd better drive down there and withdraw before it's too late. Maybe I can still get the money back."

"Oh, Lawrence?"

"Sir?"

"I hope this little, ah, business with Miss Tina Clay is about to end. The whole town's talking about it, you know. Bad for our image."

"Who's Tina Clay?" Jordan asked.

Ransom made the tepee with his fingers and smiled at Jordan. It was a dark, imperative grimace.

Wayne Lovingood chuckled to himself. He knew he was a good-looking, well-heeled young man. Lovingood and T. Jerome Montague were dressed like identical twins. In their white Palm Beach suits, they were the talk of the Midwestern Morticians Convention.

Montague was at the bar, with Marcella. He seemed to be taking quite an interest in Marcella. They were laughing and gesturing. Lawrence Jordan looked over his shoulder at them.

"Two fifty," Wayne Lovingood said.

"No," Jordan said. "How is Herece?"

"As well as to be expected," Lovingood replied. "She gets her final degree in a month. Two seventy-five. Positively my last offer."

"Glad to hear that," Jordan said. "I mean about Herece."

They went in to the bar. Montague was telling Marcella, "Then we started using Bondal. . . . Oh, hello, chaps."

"This young man of yours just won't consider any of my offers," Lovingood told Marcella, seating himself next to her. Jordan sat next to Lovingood and struck up a conversation with a cemetery lot salesman from Omaha.

231

Wayne tapped Jordan's shoulder. "Now see here. Three hundred. That's absolutely as high as I can go."

"Uh-huh," Jordan said. He ordered a martini.

What had possessed them to come to the convention? In previous years, it was held too far away: Minneapolis, Cleveland. But this time it had been held in Chicago. Achilles Ransom had been under the weather; he asked them to go. It was just a half hour drive from Kewaunee.

Somehow Jordan had never expected to run into Lovingood and Montague here. Or Fannie Fears and the others. But of course, they took an active interest in the running of things. The morticians from his hometown were political people.

Lovingood's offers had intrigued him. Now it was three hundred dollars! What if Jordan took the job for only a year? Then he could come back to Illinois and go to the Art Institute while still keeping his hand in things at Ransom's. And he would have saved up the money to do it. Ransom could be made to understand. The old man had gotten a new tolerance for him in other matters ever since he had broken up with Tina Clay. Ransom had come to see that art was a lesser vice than women too close to home.

But, no, Jordan would never forget the way Wayne had treated him after Southwall had died. That could have ruined Jordan's life. He hated Wayne for it. What was to keep the young Lovingood from pulling something like that again?

A contract.

"It seems a bit overly formal to me," Lovingood said in his hotel suite. Jordan turned to go. "But if that will reassure you, Lawrence, I'll be happy to have one drawn up and send it to you. Really, I *can* understand. And I must apologize for the abrupt manner in which I approached you when my father passed. But there was so much on my mind then. . . ."

Fannie Lartarska Fears lay back on the pink chaise longue in her overdecorated suite. She was wearing emerald silk brocade, a floor-length housecoat with subtle dragons on it. "I would consider Wayne's offer seriously," Fannie said, appraising Jordan with her eyes. At the corners, the eyes were made up to look slanted. "Wayne has come a long way in three short years. He's done an excellent job with the Directors Association. Better than Southwall, really. Of course, he's nothing near the craftsman his father was. Southwall was an undertaker's undertaker."

"I just don't trust Wayne," Jordan said.

"Don't worry about it." Fannie yawned. "You'll have the contract . . . if things don't suit you over there, you can come in with me. Like all of us, I was very much impressed with the paper you read on cosmetic surgery. Personally, I can't see the reason for *total* restoration, but I admire your concern. You must be quite a restorer. . . ."

"Thanks, Fannie," Jordan said. "Can I be sure I can count on you?"

"You may bank on it, baby," Fannie said.

Marcella said, "Whatever you want to do, dear. Daddy will take it hard I'm sure. But if you explain that it's just for a year. . . ."

Achilles Ransom brushed dust from the slick church truck in his chapel with a withered hand. "The tragedy of it all," he said, "is that the government won't do anything about it. Inflation threatens us all, and they concern themselves with the high cost of dying. Why doesn't the Senate investigate the high cost of living instead sometime? Here I am unable to afford even a decent church truck; my daughter and son-in-law, the finest and most trustworthy, ah, associates I ever had, are leaving me; I'll have to hire some adolescent fresh out of embalming school and pay him a fortune while he underembalms cases for a year. You're sure it's just for a year?"

"Yes, sir."

Ransom adjusted his tie, which was already adjusted. He wrenched his leonine hands and grimaced at Jordan.

"Give my regards to your, ah, mother." Ransom sighed.

25

Clare had bought the house she wanted, a modest six-room bungalow on a quiet street a mile south of Lovingood's. When Jordan had left Kansas City, Lovingood's customers had all been to the north; now they were moving farther and farther south of the funeral home, and Jordan foresaw that the boulevard where Lovingood's was would someday become the new Undertakers Row. The old boundaries were breaking up; the old residents in the south of town were selling their homes to make way for the younger, darker newcomers. On either side of Clare's house there were "for sale" signs in the yards.

Jordan lived with Clare. He looked forward to the day he would go back to Illinois; he was anxious to get back to sculpting. He had regarded his stay with his mother as only temporary, until he could find a place for Marcella and himself. He looked at kitchenettes, but they reminded him too much of the tiny apartment they had in Illinois. He wanted space. He looked at houses near Lovingood's, but most of them were for sale. The few he found for lease were too expensive.

Clare told him, "Don't worry about it. You can stay here. I got plenty of room, Lawrence."

He had left Marcella in Illinois. She was helping her father until the new apprentice arrived.

Clare's *was* convenient to Lovingood's. In the warm months, he had walked to the funeral home. Clare had left the dental office a year ago, soon after Jamal's death, and now was receptionist at the Fannie Fears' Funeral Home. "We're a mortuary *family* now," Clare said. In the summer, she drove Jordan's old Buick, sans purple drapes, to Fears; in winter he dropped her off, then drove to Lovingood's.

Clare seemed to have found herself. She still wore heavy makeup, but it was applied more tastefully. She had got rid of the false eyelashes she'd worn when she had come to Illinois for Jordan's wedding; though she had aged, she had lost weight, controlled her dumpiness. Jordan supposed that was Fannie's doing. Fannie knew how to paint and doctor herself from years of applying cosmetics to the dead. Clare's penchant for clothes had got stronger, really, and the clothes were more expensive. That, no doubt about it, was Psyche Lovingood's influence. With Herece in Los Angeles, going to school there, Wayne had purchased a home for his stepmother not far from Clare's. Clare and Psyche had become best friends. They partied together, shopped together, and went to church together. Most of their activities still centered around Les Dames, to which Thess Montague now belonged. Later Thess sponsored Marcella for membership in the club.

In Jordan's childhood, Clare had been bossy and restrictive, like the time with Herece. Now she seemed freer, liberalized. She even encouraged Jordan to go out and have a good time. Before Marcella arrived, he did that. He went out with Bates and got drunk; they did the town with a couple of women Bates knew and afterward Jordan had thrown up, he was so drunk and so ashamed. He sensed Clare knew this, but she kept her distance.

The relationship between Wayne Lovingood and T. Jerome Montague was curious. They began as drinking buddies at embalming school, a common pairing at Gresham; the elegant Montague was Wayne Lovingood's first real friend, and Wayne couldn't bear to lose him after they graduated. Plying Montague with booze—and money—Lovingood convinced Montague to settle in Kansas City, and he assured Montague of a job before he had checked with his father. With little to look forward to in his own hometown, Montague found the offer irresistible. They hadn't counted on Lawrence Jordan.

When Southwall informed Wayne that he already had an apprentice, Wayne had been afraid to tell Montague that he could not guarantee him a position. Instead, hearing from his mother that Thess Wingate's father was looking for an embalmer, Wayne had written to her on Monty's behalf. Thess approached her father, who wrote to Montague, mentioning that

Wayne had recommended him highly. Wayne was elated, Wingate pleased, and Thess, for different reasons, was excited. Ultimately, it worked out to the advantage of everyone except Lawrence Jordan. When Southwall Lovingood died, it was natural that Wayne would replace Jordan with Montague.

Montague had begun with Lovingood's as coequal to Major Bates. But during the years Jordan was in Illinois, Montague had risen almost to independent status. Now he was listed on the masthead below Wayne as an "associate funeral director." Actually, Montague frequently took in his own cases, embalmed them, directed their dispositions, and paid Wayne rent on use of equipment and chapel. In reality, he was as much a funeral broker as Abdullah Jamal had been. The difference was that Montague had ingratiated himself with Wayne Lovingood and Jamal had not.

And Montague had a toehold in the business. His marriage to Thessalonica Wingate, now one of the city's leading party givers, had allied him with Thess' father. Indeed, Jordan's favorite funeral establishment still carried the name LaCour, Wingate & *Montague*. It was the understanding between Monty and Wayne Lovingood that Montague could continue to work with his father-in-law as a "consultant" because of the unusual association. In actuality, Montague flitted between Lovingood's and his father-in-law's in his black Mercedes sports car, raking in the dollars. His income was almost as large as Wayne's.

But Wayne found their association profitable in more ways than one. Montague brought more business to Lovingood's. Monty's specialty was women, living and otherwise. His love affairs were notorious. References to him ("That prominent playboy-mortician . . .") appeared in Ponchita Perez's weekly *Afro-Citizen* column constantly, and Monty was even reputed to be having a running affair with the columnist herself. Ponchita's references to Montague gave him valuable publicity. As his reputation in the boudoir grew, so did his business in the preparation room. The women were said to give him their bodies while they were alive and promise them to him again when they were dead. But there was something odd about Montague's attraction: He drew far more elderly matrons, widows, and spinsters than vivacious young swingers. His business was

236

heavy with the bodies of aging clubwomen. The Young Things, however, came to their aunts' funerals to look at Montague.

Monty was an excellent hairdresser, and this further determined his specialty. In his home state, his mother had been inspector of cosmetology; in this position, Helen Taliaferro Montague headed the board which granted licenses to hairdressers. She also had the power to revoke licenses. Bates told Jordan that Helen Montague made a small fortune taking bribes, and that was how she put her son through a series of exclusive private schools, then Gresham. Whatever else she did for him, Taliaferro Jerome Montague's mother assured his success: She taught him to do hair. Monty liked to recall how he thrilled to the clink, clink, clink of his mother curling hair in the basement of their home and how by the time he was eleven he was doing it himself. Before he attended Gresham, he went to a famous cosmetology school in New York. He had considered opening a salon in the East, but decided to go on to embalming school because it had always been his desire to do something for the "whole woman."

Montague spent more time on his coiffures than he did on his embalming. He was often approached by Thessalonica's friends to do their hair and always refused. Since he graduated from Gresham, Montague had practiced his art only on the dead—and his wife. He also was a fair dermatologist, though he was no match for Lawrence Jordan. Jordan suspected that Montague had taken credit for some of Jordan's own restorative work since Jordan had returned to Lovingood's. While Montague as a funeral director was familiar to the public, Jordan was virtually unknown. On the masthead under Major Bates, Jordan was listed merely as "L. Jordan, Embalmer." With his special clientele and his connection with two leading mortuaries, Montague was content to let Jordan embalm and restore most of his cases at Lovingood's. Afterward, Montague would come in, do the hair, apply the cosmetics, and dress and casket the corpse. He was very fussy about the folds in his cases' gowns and the positioning of their hands. He abhorred dust in any form on a casket.

At funerals, surrounded by his women, Montague was diffident, gracious, oily. He would have made a great pimp.

At the mortuary, he was something else. He rarely dressed in suit and tie except for funerals. His customary attire was ascot and slacks; he also was fond of expensive cashmere sweaters. Since he had risen with Lovingood, Montague sported a large diamond ring on the little finger of his left hand and flashed the ring at every opportunity. Like Achilles Ransom, Monty advocated color in funerals. It was he who talked Wayne into the white Palm Beach suits. It was a good move; it attracted attention at funerals and set people talking about the Lovingood Mortuary.

Unlike Achilles Ransom, Montague was loud, boisterous, and frivolous. Jordan was shocked one day to find Montague dancing in the foyer over a corpse.

Montague had gone two months without getting a case he could call his own. Lovingood continued to do business. Every day Monty would drive in, asking with more bravura than usual if he had got any calls. It was almost Christmas and Monty had promised Thess a fur coat. Outside, the city was as white and cold as the palms of the bloodless dead. Snow flurries slanted through the street. Gathering his camel's hair coat about him, tucking his swagger stick under his arm, Montague started for the side door. Then he stopped, turned around, and said to Wayne Lovingood, "Look, baby. I'm broke. Can you let me have a couple hundred till next month?" The next day he came in and quietly helped Jordan embalm a case.

Then Montague got one.

He did it himself and called in Jordan to see it. It was a high-ranking member of the Eastern Star Lodge. She was being buried in full regalia—blue cape lined with red silk and blue serge tam, which Montague propped up pitifully in her stiff hands. He did not want to hide her hairdo.

"Looks fine, T. J.," Jordan said.

"I thought so, too—at first," Montague mumbled. "But there's something not quite right about it. Can't put my finger on it. . . ."

Jordan saw what it was. "It's the cape," Jordan said, reaching into the casket and pulling the rigid body toward him. He adjusted the cape so that part of it furled around over the woman's arm, revealing the red silk. Montague had placed the cape straight at the sides.

"That's it, baby!" Montague shouted. "That's the touch. You're a genius, baby."

Jordan grinned involuntarily. Monty could be quite likable at times.

Montague closed the lower lid of the casket over his case, a matron named Lettie B. Franklin, and wheeled her out to the foyer. That evening, the Eastern Star would perform its secret rites. Jordan began cleaning up the prep room, then remembered that he had to get his week's pay from Lovingood before Wayne went out drinking with Montague. Jordan left the preparation room and walked across the foyer.

There, against the south wall, he saw Sister Lettie Franklin asleep in her furled cape. Montague was standing over her, admiring his handiwork. He had given her a set of Shirley Temple curls.

"Mmmmm-mmmph, Lettie B!" Montague was saying. "You sho' look good tonight!"

Montague did not see Jordan cross the room and stare at him from the hallway. Except for the floor lamps flanking Lettie Franklin, the room was dark. Jordan was about to continue on when Montague rubbed his palms together over the casket, grabbed the creases of his trousers and broke out in a weird little frug. Monty danced around and around in little circles, holding his pants up around his ankles. He had on white socks. The elastic of the socks had worn out so that the socks drooped around Monty's ankles. As he danced, Montague paraphrased the words of an old soul song:

> Do, Re, Me, Fa, So, La, Ti
> Forget about the Re
> And bring the Dough to Me.

Jordan left Monty dancing in the foyer. When he returned, Monty had regained his composure. Montague was again standing over the casket with his hands folded—almost in mourning.

"Merry Christmas, Brother Jordan," Montague whispered.

"Merry Christmas, T. J.," Jordan said.

Montague's association also provided Wayne Lovingood with other opportunities. Not only did they share facilities, but they also shared Thess Montague. Thess was sleeping with Wayne while her husband ran after other game.

Thess was quite open about her affair with Wayne; in fact, she flaunted it in Jordan's face. He had first seen her again a week after he returned. She came in with her husband and Lovingood and was on Wayne's arm. Montague seemed oblivious to his wife's carryings-on; he went into the office to get some papers, leaving Thess in the hallway, hanging on Wayne's arm. Boldly she asked Jordan if he remembered her. He said indeed he did and looked significantly toward the chapel, then turned and walked away. After that, Thess had been cool toward him, which was the way he wanted her to be.

Major Bates was Jordan's only real friend at the mortuary. Major's hairline had receded back to the equator of his head, leaving only wisps in its wake. His mustache, which Jordan remembered fondly for its unerring twitch when they were about to get a case, was flecked with gray. He had a puffiness around his eyes. But Bates was as lively as ever, as afraid of the dead as ever, and pursued the dice and women with a fervor that had increased in direct proportion to his age. Bates and Jordan had one important thing in common—Southwall Lovingood—and that drew them together. Their favorite pastime was discussing how Wayne and Montague, for entirely different reasons, were disgraces to the funeral profession. Usually it was Jordan who pointed out such shortcomings as Wayne's inability to embalm and Montague's phony posturing at services. Then Major Bates would take over, sinking back into Southwall Lovingood's old chair, now relegated to a corner of the reception room, and recount the legendary feats of the late, great Founder. "*Southwall*," Bates was fond of declaring, "was an undertakin' man. He used to get 'em back there and set their butts on fire." To which Jordan would add a resonant "Amen!" When Montague and the younger Lovingood were around, they confined their observations to knowing nods.

437 South Elm Avenue
Kewaunee, Illinois
12 June

DARLING,
Better sit down when you read this. Get comfortable, have

240

your mom make you a double shot of something. Okay. Ready?

I'm pregnant!

That's right, two months gone. Just can't quite accept it, but that's what the man says. It kept getting worse and Daddy was afraid it was ulcers and Mother took me to the doctor. You know Dr. Garrett. We buried his mother last year. Cancer. Anyway, we can expect a little Jordan in late September, early October. I'm so excited. I've already got a name picked out for the baby, if it's a boy. I know you're going to like it.

Old man Bartholome died—heart attack—at his bar. I did him. A great service, our biggest in years. Daddy had to ask Weaver, Sergeant and Roddenberry for help, so Tommie came up. Know you'll be jealous, but don't be. I'm just sorry you couldn't be here; know you would have enjoyed it. That's probably my last funeral for a while. Daddy won't let me in the place. He insists that I rest. The new man hasn't got here yet, but don't you think I might as well come on down there? I want to be with you. And I'm no good any more up here.

Lawrence, I know this is going to mean changing your plans somewhat, but maybe you can ask Wayne for a raise or something. Forgive me for handing you another mouth to feed, but I just couldn't go on taking those pills. Against the church, you know. Luv to all. I miss you.

MARCEL

N.B.: I hope it has doe eyes just like you.

Clare was elated. "Of course you'll have to forget that silly business about going to the art school," she said.

"Not necessarily."

"What do you mean, 'Not necessarily'? Boy, you got responsibilities now."

"Don't call me 'boy.'"

"Well, I'm sorry, *Mister* Jordan. But you can't expect Marcella to carry the load while you run off to some damn school. She'll have to take care of your kid."

"Let's wait and find out what happens."

"I know what's gonna happen. You're gonna settle down, forget those childish ideas, and stick with Lovingood's. What do you want? You've got an education, a good job, a good wife, connections in your business."

"I want more than that."

"What do you mean more? You better hold onto what you've got. Hell, you couldn't even cope with Wayne when you were here before. How you gonna be an *art*ist?"

"It's very important to you to see me doing what I'm doing, isn't it? Honestly, Mother, sometimes I think I don't really know you at all. I sure as hell don't understand you."

"Don't curse me, boy. You ain't supposed to understand. Just get on with the business at hand."

Marcella arrived, and Clare adopted a fussy attitude toward her. Jordan was glad to see his mother engrossed in someone besides him. Nothing was too good for Marcella now: the best maternity clothes, the best food, the finest doctor's care. Clare paid for much of it out of her own pocket. On Saturdays when she shopped with Psyche, Clare began getting things for Marcella. She asked Jordan if Marcella would like this or that, if Marcella was comfortable.

Jordan decided reluctantly to stay at his mother's. Mainly, it was a way of saving money. And it was best for Marcella, who needed another woman to talk to. She was a stranger in Kansas City, and it would be months before she met anybody with whom she could be friends. He was glad to see Clare taking a maternal interest in both Marcella and the child she was carrying.

"Lord," Clare told Marcella. "I'm just so glad I held out and raised Lawrence the way I did. It was hard, but it was worth it. Just seeing this wonderful family in the making, knowing that the child will have security and a future, maybe his own funeral home, makes it all worth it, goddamn it!"

They had a boy. Marcella had named him Azrael after the Hebrew angel of death. He was given Jordan's middle name. The child did not have the Jordan look; he strongly resembled Clare, who grieved longer and deeper than anyone because Azrael Xavier Ransom Jordan was stillborn.

Azrael's death depressed Jordan, who saw his own image lessened by the tragedy. He couldn't bear to go through a funeral for the child, decreeing instead that the body should be disposed of at the hospital.

Clare began drinking heavily again and neglected her appearance. Around the house, she was strangely quiet, and often her eyes avoided Jordan's. It was as if she blamed the child's death on herself.

Marcella showed little outward concern over her failure to bring forth the firstborn. "I wouldn't have made a good mother anyway," she said at the hospital, trying to cheer Jordan up. But Jordan interpreted her remark as secret relief. He resented Marcella for it and from that day forward, neither he nor Clare ever mentioned the name Azrael again.

A month after her baby died, Marcella began to get restless. She was anxious to begin embalming again, a situation that to her seemed as natural as another woman's laundry chore. Jordan had asked Marcella to stay with Clare, who was still too wretched to go back to work, but one bright Thursday morning Marcella deserted Clare and slipped off to what she thought would be a job interview. Without telling her husband, Marcella had made a luncheon appointment with Wayne Lovingood.

Jordan finished and peeled off his gloves. He preferred the hidden sutures: worm stitch, continuous glover, double intradermal. Even over parts of the body that would not be exposed in the casket, Jordan took hidden sutures. It was better that way, consistent and exhaustive. Achilles Ransom had taught him well.

And for three years he had watched the flick, flick, flick of Marcella's needle as she closed her cases. That was the trick, that steady, precise flick. Like tying shoes.

Wayne Lovingood had never been able to fault Jordan's suturing or his restorative work. But he had faulted everything else in the past six months: Jordan's embalming technique, the way he dressed for funerals, the way he casketed a case. And Lovingood seemed insulted by Jordan's reminder that dark-skinned people ideally should be displayed under rose or amber lights.

"Just get your embalming together," Wayne Lovingood had snapped, "and let me worry about the lighting."

Lovingood had done nothing about the lighting. How did he expect Jordan's cosmetic work to be at its best? The lighting diminished its effect. It was the same lighting Southwall Lovingood had used.

Major Bates came in and cocked his head and looked at the body. "Pretty good job," he muttered.

"Thanks," Jordan said. "How was the funeral, Brother Bates?"

"Same as usual." Bates plucked a wilting carnation from his lapel and tossed it in the drainage bucket. "Everything on schedule."

"Good."

"Sure wish they'd let you work more funerals, though, Brother Jordan. Ain't no good being cooped up in here too much. These fumes get to you after while, man."

Jordan agreed. "Every now and then I take a break," he sighed. "I go out on the ramp and have a smoke."

"You really been pushin' 'em through," Bates said with an admiration Jordan appreciated. "Southwall would've been proud of you."

Jordan made a half-laughing sound. Then he got serious again. He took off his apron and got out a cigarette, opened the door and stepped out onto the ramp. Sunlight poured into the room. Jordan inhaled broadly. It was good to be out in fresh air. "Come on," he called to Bates.

Bates spread a sheet on the body and joined Jordan. "Let me bum one of those smokes, Bro' Jordan."

They sat on the edge of the ramp, dangling their legs.

"Hey, Jordan? Somethin's botherin' you, man."

Jordan flicked his cigarette into the driveway.

"You been actin' funny all day. Noticed it this morning. What's wrong?"

Jordan stood and kicked at the side of the building. "A whole lot of things," he said. "Where's Wayne?"

"Takin' the family home, I guess. Why?"

"Cause I'm'n kill that nigga when he gets back."

"What?"

"I'm gonna kill him, Bates."

"What for?"

"Messin' with my wife."

"Marcella? You sure?"

"Sure I'm sure. She wouldn't lie about it."

244

"When did it happen, yesterday?"

"Right."

"I knew they were gone out to lunch, Brother Jordan. But I saw you in the back 'n' figured you knew about it and everything was okay."

"It was. I mean I thought it was."

"Well, what happened?"

"He asked her to . . . sleep with him. At lunch. She told me about it when I came home. Damn!"

"Wait a minute, Brother Jordan. Wait one minute. Calm down now, calm on down. Why did they go to lunch in the first place?"

Jordan hit the wall with his fist. The thud reverberated in the preparation room, rattling a surgical cabinet.

"You know how headstrong Marcella is. Well, she got the idea that if she came down here and talked to Wayne herself, spoke to him directly, maybe he'd let her work a few days."

"Oh, no."

"Uh-huh. So she got all dressed up and went off half-cocked without tellin' anybody, without sayin' a damn thing about what she was up to 'n' came down here to talk to Wayne. Damn! I should have left her in Kewaunee."

"Aw, man. . . ."

"Montague and I were in the chapel getting ready to take the body on out to the car. I thought I heard Marcella's voice up front. You know the kind of husky voice she has? Well, just on an impulse, I went up there. She was sittin' in Wayne's office, talking to that damn fool. Wayne seemed amused by all this. And he knew her coming down here caught me by surprise. He must have thought she was on the make or something.

"Before I could say anything, Wayne's telling me that they're going out to lunch and discuss a little proposition. Made me so damn mad I almost got him right there. But I figured I'd wait until I got home and bawl Marcella out about it. Shit, I came home and my mother said, 'Something's wrong with Marcel.' I went in our room, and there she is on the bed cryin'. Man, I'm gonna hurt Lovingood. Baad."

Bates shuffled nervously on the ramp, then moved between Lawrence Jordan and the door to the embalming room. "Beatin' on Wayne ain't gonna do any good," Bates said. "You know that. Man, Southwall give up on that boy long time ago. For a while there, though, we thought he had settled down."

"I oughta drag him over to the house and make him apologize."

"Hush now!"

"Don't tell me to hush!"

"Let me handle this, Brother Jordan. Let me handle this. Go on home. . . ."

"I'm not goin' anywhere. I just want Wayne. I'm gonna wait right here for him. I'm gonna finish this case, probably my *last* case. No! Lovingood's gonna be my last."

Jordan waited an hour for Lovingood. He aspirated his case with Bates assisting him, part of his attention firmly fixed on the foyer outside.

He and Bates were finishing up when they heard Wayne come in.

"Lovingood!" Jordan shouted. "I want . . . to talk . . . to you!"

"No, Bro' Jordan," Bates whispered in the prep room. "Forget it."

Jordan brushed Bates aside and strode into the foyer. Lovingood was irritated. "There's a cigarette butt in the driveway," Wayne said. "Who put it there?"

"I did," Jordan said. He was almost up to Lovingood.

Behind them, Montague came in the side door. "Let's hit the streets, baby," Montague said cheerfully to Wayne. Wayne motioned him to be silent.

"You threw that cigarette in the driveway? You know better than that."

Jordan leaped at Lovingood like a cat and felled him with one terrible blow. Jordan's fist throbbed; his hands were attuned to sculpting.

"You know better than to mess with my wife, too," Jordan said, standing over Wayne. Jordan was about to kick his teeth out. Wayne struggled to get up. There was a dazed look on his face.

As Jordan lunged at Lovingood, Montague grabbed his arm. "Now look here, my good man—" Montague was saying.

Jordan dropped Montague, too. Monty fell across Wayne's legs.

Wayne got up, holding his mouth. It was bleeding.

"You're fired!" he told Jordan.

"I quit!" Jordan said.

Jordan walked to the door, then turned and whirled on Lovingood again. "Next time I'll kill you. I swear it!" Wayne rolled his eyes ominously but said nothing.

Montague still sprawled on the floor, out cold. Major Bates looked at Monty and shook his head. Wayne glared at Bates. "What're *you* looking at?" he said to Bates through his fingers. Jordan walked through the door, leaving it wide open.

Bates tipped his fedora jauntily onto his head. "You had that coming, boy," he told Wayne. Then to the open door: "Wait for me, Brother Jordan. I'm leaving, too."

26

The next edition of the *Afro-Citizen News* carried a full-page advertisement announcing a new mortuary: Jordan & Bates, Limited.

Peering down from opposite corners of the ad were the images of the new funeral directors, dark-suited and appropriately grim. Bates had wanted to use the pictures of them smiling, but Jordan insisted on using the soberest photographs they had. The people wanted darkness, and Lawrence Jordan intended to oblige them.

Wayne Lovingood could have sworn there was a subtle smirk on Lawrence X. Jordan's face. Wayne read the body of the ad nervously: brief biographies of Jordan and Bates, mentions of Jordan's specialty in restorative art, Jordan's Illinois ties, Bates' longtime silent-partner association with one Southwall James Lovingood, dean of the Kansas City undertakers, now deceased.

For tax purposes, the new firm had been incorporated. Officers of the company were Lawrence and Marcella Jordan, Major T. Bates, and an unexpected partner, Clarisse Walker Jordan.

Chief embalmer was Marcella Ransom Jordan.

Wayne Lovingood balled up the newspaper and threw it at T. Jerome Montague, sitting with his feet upon his desk. The paper hit Montague's shoulder and bounced off onto the carpet.

"Dammit, T. J.," Lovingood said. "This is trouble, baby, real trouble."

Montague tediously brushed paper shavings from the sleeve of his iridescent worsted sports coat. He had just finished a case

248

—he was embalming again since Bates and Jordan left—and was in his magnanimous mood.

"Relax, Brother Wayne," Montague said finally. "You handled Jamal, didn't you? You can handle Jordan. Just blackball him from the Directors Association. Cut off his suppliers."

"I can't."

"Why not? What's to stop you?"

"My goddamned stepmother, that's what."

"What's dear old Psyche got to do with all this? She sleeping with Jordan?"

"No, idiot. But *his* mother, that *Clare,* is my stepmother's best friend."

Wayne put his head in his hands and ran his fingers through his close-cropped hair.

Montague took his feet off the desk, Southwall Lovingood's old desk. He loosened his ascot.

"Oh, yes, I see," Montague mused, "I see. . . ."

At her house, the new secretary of Jordan & Bates, Limited, lay across the bed on her stomach, trying to concentrate on the words in the ad. Outside the bedroom, they were partying. She could hear her son's voice above all the rest, challenging Major Bates to a drinking contest. Marcella was trying to get her husband to quiet down.

Clare read the ad over and over. Each time she came to her own name, she stopped. She looked at the name again and again.

Clarisse Walker Jordan
Secretary-Treasurer

It did look rather good.

Fannie Lartarska Gorham Fears stuck her head in the room. For this occasion, Fannie had abandoned her traditional Chinese attire for pink party pants. Fannie's hair was down, and she wore no makeup. She had a drink in her hand.

"Hey, Little Bit!" Fannie yelled. "Come on 'n' join the party. You can read the paper next week. At work."

She slapped Clare's behind.

Clare jumped. "Keep your mitts off my fanny, Fannie," she said.

Fannie Fears circled and sat on the bed. She looked down at the ad. "Isn't it wonderful?" Fannie asked. "It's just like when *South*wall, bless him, started out. Just think. I may have competition from you all someday!"

"I doubt *that*," Clare said, getting up. "Not with half the money in the place being yours. I sure hope you and Major know what you're doin'. Shit, puttin' an ad out before they've even got the equipment set up!"

"It's all right, honey," Fannie said, following Clare out. "Things're gonna work out fine. Besides, we're right there to keep an eye on things. . . ."

Achilles Ransom cabled reluctant congratulations from Illinois.

T. Jerome Montague slipped away from Wayne Lovingood and called his in.

Isadore Michaels came by the house.

And Fannie Fears, the Williams brothers, Lennie Valentine, the Right Reverend Richard D. Rideout, Thessalonica Wingate Montague, T. T. Fortune, Bob McGinnis, Psyche Lovingood, Sally Garrett and Eddie Lovelace (Clare's dentist) came, too.

Ponchita Perez came and wrote a column about the celebration in which she noted that "that well-known Spiritualist minister who used to sell real estate did a groovy bugaloo with that flamboyant lady undertaker at the Lawrence Jordans'!"

Sister Carrie Samuels followed Jordan around the house as he mixed drinks and accepted congratulations, telling him what a fine young man he was turning into and how tired she was of attending funerals at Lovingood's anyway.

Jordan hugged Sister Samuels to him and jokingly told her he'd give her the finest funeral the town had ever seen—after Southwall Lovingood's, of course.

Marcella was very proud of Jordan. She was anxious to be getting back into the work she felt she was called to.

Clare was the gloomiest one at the party. Jordan had thought the new move and the new publicity would please her. If it did, she seemed hesitant to show it.

"Party now," Clare told Jordan aside. "It'll be a long time before we're able to outdo Lovingood."

Jordan stopped short. He had been dancing with his wife.

"Mother, I don't care about Lovingood anymore. I've got my own thing."

Clare just looked at him. "You *better* care," she said. "They're probably over there right now, figuring out how they're gonna stop you."

Damn Clare. Why did she always have to spoil things?

Jordan & Bates, Limited, was located on Undertakers Row directly below the hill where the Fears Funeral Home was. From his front window, Jordan could see a corner of what he called the Pink Pagoda—Fannie's establishment.

He was midway between the nearly defunct Lewis Funeral Home and the fast-rising Williams Brothers Mortuary. Scattered around them were the other undertakers.

The neighborhood was decaying. In their great rush to the south of the city, the younger residents had left behind in the old neighborhood the aged, the indigent, the infirm.

Carrie Samuels herself lived only two blocks from Jordan's funeral home.

Their big ads in the *Afro-Citizen* belay the reality of the premises Jordan & Bates occupied. The funeral home was nothing more than a one-story storefront. In earlier days, the tiny brick building had housed successively a Masonic lodge, a community newspaper, a rummage seller and a fly-by-night church. In all, it comprised only fifteen hundred square feet. The footage originally had been one long room; the rummage dealer had partitioned off the back for sorting clothes and the church people had sectioned off the front of the building for offices for the pastor and assistant pastor. The offerings had been locked up there, and several times the offices had been broken into, with the result that the lock on one of the offices—formerly the pastor's—did not work.

The offices were really little boothlike cubicles on each side of the front door. There was just enough room in each cubicle for a desk and two chairs. Bates chose the office to the right of the door, Jordan took the one on the left, the one with the broken lock.

The place was filthy. The first order of business was to get it cleaned up and painted up. Jordan and Bates, assisted by Clare and Marcella and two dirty boys from the neighborhood, mopped the hardwood floors (only the offices were carpeted) and scrubbed down the walls. Afterward a workman was called in to fix Jordan's lock and whitewash the walls.

Beyond the cubicles lay a long but narrow room that had been the church sanctuary, meeting hall, Sunday school, everything. And the rummage seller's display room. The floor still had marks where the rummage stalls had stood. The room took up most of the building. Jordan had it carpeted and the windows, which were beyond cleaning, replaced. He left the makeshift wooden pulpit at the back of the room but had the long platform trimmed with fringe to make it suitable for funeral services. This would be the chapel.

Through a single door to the left of the pulpit was the tiny, windowless back room. It had a sink with rusty fixtures and a capped gas main. Jordan left the main capped, but scoured the sink and replaced its rusted handles with shiny new ones. When their new equipment arrived, he outfitted the back room with a stainless-steel preparation table, which he managed to tilt into the sink, a surgical cabinet containing instruments and fluids, cots and stretchers, a gleaming new pressure injector with glass percolator on rolling table, water-softening apparatus and, for emergencies, gravity equipment and stand. This was the embalming room.

The back room was so stuffy they would have to put a screen door over the back exit and keep the main door open during operations. To keep the fumes down and to protect the health of those working there, Marcella would have to use fluids with high odor suppressants and she would have to employ discontinuous injection on the bodies. This way, she could do part of the work, get out for air, then come back and finish—or let Bates or Jordan relieve her. Also, the door on the chapel side of the room was so narrow they would have to carry the bodies by hand into the chapel and casket them there. They could keep the coffins covered and stored at the front of the chapel until then.

In the back, Jordan allowed himself one convenience he had wanted for a long time: a large tilting drafting table for use in modeling replacements for disfigured corpses. He kept the table folded against one wall of the back room. He bought every kind of wax available and several bottles of liquid paraffin.

Now he was ready.

Clare walked down the hill and visited Jordan's new establishment. The only feature she found worth complimenting was the rug Jordan had chosen. It was plush maroon carpeting. It contrasted well with the pale walls.

"Not much, is it?" Clare observed.

"No," Jordan agreed. "But it's ours. Decor isn't everything. The business will be what we make it."

"Where are you going to have the services?"

"Right here if it's a small service. At some church if it's bigger."

"What will people sit on?"

"Folding chairs."

"Mmmmm." Clare turned up her nose. "You don't know what you're doing," she said. "Don't try to be so cheap. Spend some of the money."

"I am spending it. It's only fifteen thousand dollars."

"*Only* fifteen thousand?"

"Yeah. Some funeral homes are capitalized on hundreds of thousands of dollars. What do you want for nothing?"

"Look. Maybe Fannie and Major can afford it; I sure hope so. But I've given you every cent I have in this world."

"Don't worry about it. You'll get it back. And more."

"You don't even have lights in this place. Put some lights in the ceiling, boy."

"I've told you about calling me that. I don't plan to put any more lights in."

"How are they going to see?"

"Just by the floor lamps. People want darkness."

"Lawrence, you're *crazy*."

He showed her the hearse. It was a 1939 Packard. In the windows of the casket compartment, the curtains, violet velvet from another era, were moldering. The whole car had the odor of decay. It was heavy and boxy and leaned noticeably to the right side—the list of an ancient ship.

"Where did you find this rattletrap?" Clare asked.

"One of the dealers," Jordan replied, brushing dust from a fender. "Isn't it marvelous? Look at that grille."

"*Marvelous?*" Clare circled the thing. "It looks like . . . death itself."

Jordan nodded at the grille.

"Precisely," he said.

He had the Dream again that night. This time he was working out of a sunless prep room on the top floor of a five-story building. On the floors below, there were thousands of caskets on display and scores of bodies. He worked all the time. He was working with Southwall and Bates and Montague. They came in from a party, and Marcella met them at the top floor and said something terrible had happened and they had a body in there that had to be handled carefully. Clare came up on the elevator, and Jordan asked her if she had the insurance. She said yes.

"Give it to me. And go."

"No. I want to see what Southwall has."

"Please, Mother. You don't want to see it. It's got . . . things . . . on it you shouldn't see."

"You're scared of your own shadow. Where's Marcel? I'll go in there with her. I want your job."

"No; please."

"Are we going in or not?"

Major Bates stepped back and admired his handiwork. He had just put the wrought-iron "Jordan & Bates" signs in the hearse window.

"Looks good, don't it, Bro' Jordan?"

"Yes," Jordan said. Bates had insisted that the modern lettering would look better. It didn't. Jordan had wanted Gothic lettering.

"This old wagon sure looks nice."

"Thanks. It just needed polishing. And the seats changed, the drapes replaced. Look at that grille."

"Oh, yeah. Like the sun."

"Couldn't make it stop leaning, though. Just part of the car."

"That's all right, Brother Jordan. We'll have a new one 'fore too long. Then we can retire this one."

The next week they had their first funeral. Bates got it for them. An elderly man, and Bates knew his children. Bates heard about the death and went to the house to beg for the body. "That's the only way to do it." Bates told Jordan. "Folks don't know you're in a position to be helped unless you ask them. My mother used to say that."

Marcella did the embalming, with Jordan assisting. He had told her about the difference in the water, the speedier burials in his part of the country, but she needed practical experience really to understand. On this first case, she got it. It was good to watch the flicking of her needle again, to see her moving the fluid tubes here and there with all the grace of a ballerina. The family was whole again.

For their debut, Jordan and Bates chose black suits and black bow ties. They adopted an air of concerned formality. The funeral was held in a church, and afterward Jordan drove the body to the cemetery in his Packard hearse while Bates drove the immediate family in his own car. As they passed through the streets, children stopped playing and pointed to the procession. Jordan knew they were looking at his hearse. They had never seen anything like it before.

Sister Carrie Samuels attended the funeral. The next day she came into the funeral home and sat up with Lawrence Jordan. Bates was at home.

Jordan offered Sister Samuels some water from a thermos bottle he kept on his desk. She declined. She was wearing a scrawny black hat with a fake plastic flower hanging over it. The flower was supposed to be a daffodil. Her withered hands drummed on Jordan's desk.

"That was a mighty fine funeral you all had the other day, Brother Lovingood," she said. "Mighty fine."

"Jordan."

"Hmmmm? Oh, yes, yes. Brother *Jordan*. I'm sorry. Memory fails me so often now, you know."

"Yes, ma'am."

"He looked just like he was sleeping, Brother Jordan, just like—"

"Like he was at peace?"

"Yes. That's it exactly. You know that's the way I want to look when I go, which may be soon. Will you promise me that?"

"Ma'am?"

"Promise me you'll fix me up to look just like that. *Restful-like*."

"Well, if I . . . am called upon to arrange the services, I will, Miz Samuels."

"Oh, you'll be called upon to do it, all right. I don't have much money, but I'm going to insist that you embalm me. I want you to know that."

"Yes, ma'am."

"You tell all the others, too, you hear? Just promise me one thing."

"What's that, Miz Samuels?"

"Don't do it with all my clothes off. I mean, don't—well, I don't want no man—undertaker or otherwise—lookin' at me nekkid. You understand?"

"Yes, ma'am, I do. But remember you don't have to worry about that here, Miz Samuels. Marcella does all our embalming, and she's a woman."

Carrie Samuels pondered this. Clutching her purse to her, she got up and shook wrinkles from her polka-dot dress. Jordan surmised she had got the dress from the rummage store down the street.

"Well, Brother Jordan," she said, "guess that'll make it all right. Long's you menfolk don't come peekin' in now."

Jordan was amused by Carrie Samuels' unusual concern regarding her disposition. He remembered it at home and laughed. Then he told Clare about it. Clare did not think it was funny.

"You mean she actually promised you her body?" Clare asked.

"Yeah. On the condition that I didn't look at her 'nekkid.' "

"Well, you be sure 'n' honor that now."

"*Honor* it? Heck, I probably won't even get the body, Mother. Sister Samuels is livin' on Social Security. She doesn't have any relatives except a few nieces in Arkansas. So the church'll probably bury her, and you know how partial Rideout is to Lovingood's."

"Well, if she promised it to you, can't you tell them that and claim the body?"

"It doesn't work like that, Mother. I'd almost have to have it

256

in writing or something to prove it. Anyway, ole Carrie's just talkin'. She's just all bound up with funerals and funeral practice. She probably tells this to every undertaker she knows. And she knows them all. She used to tell Southwall the same thing."

"Maybe," Clare said. "But I wouldn't laugh at her if I was you. Cultivate Carrie, son, *cultivate* her. She might come in handy someday. You never know."

Jordan shook his head. Why did he have to mention it to Clare anyway? She was always getting the wrong idea.

Jordan & Bates, Limited, lasted two lean years. There was hardly enough work to keep the three of them busy, and Jordan finally had to begin doing work for other undertakers to keep them going. Bates talked continually of retirement. Carrie Samuels did come in handy. She got into the habit of visiting Lawrence Jordan at least twice a week. Always they would sit in his darkened office and talk. Jordan had an electric fan, and he suspected Carrie Samuels, who had none in her dingy apartment, came mainly to sit under the fan. He always obliged her.

Carrie Samuels knew a lot of people. She carried the word about Jordan to her friends. Even at other firm's funerals, Carrie was busy recruiting for Jordan & Bates. She would be in line, passing in front of the casket of some elderly member of New Jerusalem or some other wretch who'd passed away in the night and she would turn to one of the old women behind her and whisper: "Mmmm-mmmph. Don't she look awful? Sweet, sweet Je-Zus! Just *ter*rible. Shoulda gone to Brother Jordan. Now there's a undertaker. Makes 'em look just like they're sleepin'. Don't look at 'em nekkid, nither."

And occasionally that paid off.

Most of their business was elderly. They averaged one a week. Social Security paid the bills—plus whatever else Major Bates could dig out of the family. Bates was good with the elderly.

Among the embalmers, however, Jordan & Bates, Limited, was something of a joke. Wayne Lovingood, entering his fifth year as head of the Twin Cities Funeral Directors Association, forgot about his feud with Jordan and concentrated on business. And Wayne prospered.

Jordan was in the back, polishing his hearse on the glass-littered lot, when someone crept up behind him and stuck a gloved finger in his ribs.

Lennie Valentine.

Lennie had on a black and white pinstriped suit, elegantly tailored. He wore a jet black shirt and a white tie. He had on pointed patent-leather shoes, and around the little fingers of each hand, he wore matching diamond rings. He grinned at Jordan from behind his ever-present sunglasses.

He handed Jordan a card. It said:

UNIVERSAL UNDERTAKING CO.
L. VALENTINE, BOARD CHAIRMAN

"What's poppin'?" Lennie wanted to know.

"Nothin' much, Brother Lennie," Jordan said. "Got one tomorrow."

"Groovy."

"Well, it's *some*thing. Don't know why I let myself get hung up in all this though. Man, I'd much rather be off doin' some sculptin' or something."

"Not much dough, huh?"

"You got it all, baby."

Lennie laughed. On the streets, he was known as *Mister* Valentine. He got a kickback from every dice game on the streets. Also, Lennie finally had succeeded in getting the small merchants to pay him protection. Jordan & Bates was located in Valentine country, but Lennie had never approached Jordan for tribute.

Over his shoulder, Jordan saw Valentine's black limousine. There was someone in the back seat, smoking a cigarette, a woman with interesting legs. One of Lennie's henchmen, a dark burly fellow in khaki pants, was standing by the open rear door, waiting. This was the chauffeur-bodyguard who accompanied Lennie everywhere. When Jordan had his party, the bodyguard had parked himself on Clare's divan, following Lennie's every movement with his eyes. There was no doubt he carried a gun. Jordan saw little of Lennie around town. But they kept in touch. Sometimes they would recall the days when they were boys before each had gone his separate way.

"Man, you remind me a lot of another undertaker dude," Lennie said, cocking his head at Jordan.

Jordan kept on polishing. "Who?"

"Jamal."

A chill crept up Jordan's neck. "Why him?"

" 'Cause he was just like you. Tryin' to make it, baby, 'n' they wouldn't let him."

"You're making it."

"Yeah. But for how long? It's only a matter of time, Lawrence, before they get me, before I get my head whuppin'. You know that."

Jordan stopped rubbing the car. He looked at Lennie and studied his friend's face.

"None of us are makin' it," Lennie went on. "We never will until we control our own turf. Can you dig that? Jamal knew this and he tried to do something about it, and that's why they got him."

"But he was running an unethical business. He was a funeral broker."

"That's not why they got him. They got him because somebody found out he was in with us, baby, with the Brotherhood. Somebody ratted on Jamal."

"Who?"

Lennie smiled, making his gold tooth glint in the sun, and walked back to his car. The chauffeur grabbed the door. Lennie got in and barked to the girl inside, "Move over, bitch."

Jordan followed him across the scrubby lot. The chauffeur had closed the door and was moving around to the driver's side when Jordan reached the car. The chauffeur stopped and put his hand inside his coat, glaring at Jordan. Jordan ignored him and leaned in Valentine's window. "Who?" Jordan repeated. Valentine smiled again and nodded to the driver to get in and start the car.

"Lovin' good," Lennie said.

The car slipped smoothly away.

Jordan, gaunt and grim in his trench coat and black fedora, shuffled down Eighteenth Street in the rain. At intervals, he ducked in bars, secondhand stores, junkyards, a candy store, a

259

church with a corroded cross of lights in its window. It was Friday night, and he was making his rounds. This came under the heading of public relations. Whenever he saw a familiar face, he shook a hand, made conversation.

In a bar, he saw a man he knew. He had given the man one of the first cards he and Bates passed out in the neighborhood. Jordan ordered a beer and sat down next to the man.

"Hey, Brother Hasssskins!" Jordan said. "How's the family? What's happenin'?"

It was Southwall Lovingood's voice.

The old man shrugged. "Same's usual," he said, sipping a tumbler of wine. The man had dingy wino's teeth.

"Better take it easy on that Thunderbird," Jordan admonished, touching the old man's sleeve. "Don't want to see you down at the place yet." Jordan arched an eyebrow.

It was Achilles Ransom's warning.

Unconsciously, he had begun to mix the styles of the two embalmers who had favored him. Wherever he went, down the dark streets, under the bright lights, Lawrence Jordan mixed the singsong bluster of Lovingood with the grim humor of Ransom. And the people (Jordan called them "street people") loved it. It revolved around his style, his Friday night walks, his dreary establishment, his odd little hearse, and the aura of darkness with which he cloaked himself as well as his domain. Along the Row, Jordan was becoming well liked.

Lovingood and Ransom had combined in him. Out of the combination came a new concept. It was called the House of Jordan. Jordan did not remember when he first got the idea. But he told Clare and Marcella about it one night.

"It will be built around the idea of excellence," he told them. "This excellence will be my art and Marcella's embalming. We'll create the illusions people really want in funerals. And they'll pay plenty for it."

"But that's what everyone else is trying to do," Marcella protested.

"Yes, but they're busy trying to take the tragedy and darkness and sadness out of death. We're going to bring it back."

"With what?" Clare said.

"With the House, our services, everything. Our *style*."

"I think you've got something," Marcella said.

"He ain't got shit," Clare said. "Marcel, you ought to know by now Lawrence's always dreamin', talkin' big. Hell, you ain't got a pot to piss in, let alone a window to throw it out. How you gonna attract the kinda business you want in the first place?"

"Little by little, Mother. Right from where we are now. You know the people down there are already on our side. Heck, they know me wherever I go on the streets now. They think very highly of us."

"They think you're a clown, that's what they think."

"No, they don't. Even if they do, by serving these people, and by attracting some of the more respectable clientele, some of the younger families, eventually we can build up our trade. When we do, we'll be ready to move to better quarters—the House of Jordan."

"What kind of place would we get?" Marcella asked.

"I don't know. I've been thinking about a building something like LaCour's; I've always liked that. Something with more than one story, something that stands out. Or maybe even a house itself. I'm not sure."

"You're not sure about a lot of things," Clare said.

"Wait a minute, Mother," Marcella said. "Dear, this sounds *good*. It really does. But aren't we a little late? I mean the competition is too great. The others, Lovingood, Fears, Williams—even McGinnis and Fortune—have already got it pretty much sewn up."

"No, they haven't, Marcella; no, they haven't. They just think they do. Look. This town has always been known for its fine funerals, right? I mean there's noplace else in the country where people turn out for a good funeral like they do in Kansas City, right? 'N' these folks, even the poorest ones, save all their lives just so they can have a good sendoff. Right? It grows out of the old Southern philosophy: 'Well, I ain't had nothin' *durin'* my life; might as well have the best at the *end* of it!' "

"Okay. Yes."

"Well, all of us, Bates and I included, sit around and fight over pennies. We all fight for the same cases. You know that. But there's an untapped market out there in terms of *social* class. My proposal is to grab off a corner of the market, only a small corner."

"Who?"

"The rich."

"Ain't none of *us* rich," Clare said. "Not a one of us."

"Wrong," Jordan said. "Isadore Michaels is rich. Richard Rideout is rich. Psyche Lovingood is rich. A lot of your doctors and lawyers and dentists are rich. And your bankers and real-tors and insurance men. Hell, they've been draining the community for years and never puttin' nothin' back. Drivin' their big Cadillac cars and throwin' their fancy parties. Vacations every year to Europe and Canada and South America. And they have insurance, plenty of it. They may not be as rich as they'd like people to think, but they're rich enough to afford finer funerals than they're gettin' and if someone offers it to 'em, they'll go for it. A funeral, just like anything else that costs money, is status. If we can make them see this, if we can psych 'em out so much that they'll have guilt feelings about not having a House of Jordan burial, we'll corner the market. And not only the rich people. Eventually, we can have the whole market. And even beyond."

Marcella was staring at her husband in awe. "Beyond?" she asked in a whisper.

"Yes," Jordan said, gesturing broadly. "If we make the kind of dough I'm thinking about, we can move into cemeteries, monuments, fluids, waxes, caskets, garments—there's no limit. And don't forget horizontal expansion: other funeral homes, other cities."

"Then we could?"

"Exactly," Jordan told his wife. He knew what she was thinking.

Clare looked at them both and frowned. She got up and went to clear the dishes.

"Shit," she said as she left.

The only problem was capital. He had already borrowed five thousand from Fannie. Why hadn't he thought about it before he went in with Bates? Oh, well, Bates would be no problem. More and more now, Major was talking about getting out, going to California or somewhere and retiring. But it was a dilemma: If he could get the capital, he'd still have to buy Bates out, and that would reduce the money just enough to keep

262

them in the same predicament. On the other hand, he could make some kind of deal with Bates, maybe guarantee him a certain percentage of the profits for the rest of his life, which might not be that long. . . .

Jordan forgot his dream. Something had happened to the business. There had been a cresting of elderly deaths; now the curve turned downward. Jordan & Bates went a full month without a service. Was it Medicare? Better patent medicines? The competition?

"We got to do something, Brother Bates," Jordan said.

"What can we do? We can't go out and kill 'em."

"I've got one idea. Maybe it'll get us over the hump. At least it'll help us break even."

"What's that?"

"Farm our services out."

"How do you mean?"

"Well, all right. I do this work for Fannie every now and then, right? Well, why can't I do it for some of the others, too? I mean like Williams and McGinnis—even LaCour's. And the Kansas people? There's always a demand for good restorative work. Some of the others are hurting pretty badly in this area. And there's always Teuffel's and Newbody's and Applebaum and O'Reilly—all the firms. I mean at least for a while. In the meantime, maybe something'll turn up. You and Marcella can handle it while I keep us afloat."

Major Bates rubbed his mustache. "Sure wish my hand would get hard again," he mumbled.

Lawrence Jordan came in whistling. He kicked snow out of his galoshes on the small rug in the entrance. Bates and Marcella were talking in his office. "Hi," he said. "Any calls?"

"No," Marcella said, sighing. "How'd you do?"

"Great!" Jordan said, seating himself on his desk and unbuttoning his overcoat. "Ole Newbody's really satisfied with my work. Offered me a job outright today, but of course I turned it down. Man, I'm worn out! Best idea I ever had, eh, Bates? We can go on like this indefinitely."

"What's the take?" Bates asked.

"Three hundred." Jordan said, reaching for his wallet. "Not counting the hundred and fifty Orbach owes me. Had to charge him plenty for that case. Phew!"

He handed Bates his cut. Bates took it and shuffled back to his own office across the hall. It was good to be back in the money. Two weeks ago, Marcella had needed new shoes and they had to borrow the money from Clare. Jordan had wanted to wait, but Marcella cornered Jordan and showed him the soles of her shoes. Jordan got the money from Clare, but not without having to listen to a lecture on the responsibilities of a husband. Now he could pay Clare back; that was the first thing on the agenda. While he was at it, he might as well tell Clare they were moving out. At last he would have a place to himself. At last he and Marcella would be alone. Clare would still visit. But they had been married seven years now and were still living with in-laws. How the time flew!

At Jordan's desk, Marcella looked at him admiringly. She was still pretty, though she had never lost all the weight she put on carrying Azrael. Damn that name. Marcella tooled around in Jordan's chair. Her earrings jangled starrily.

"You really cleaned up this week, didn't you?" she said.

"Really. 'N' got another job to do tomorrow over at New-body's again. Just came in. A man crushed in a snowplow accident."

Getting out a cigarette, he found himself singing a little song:

> Do, Re, Me, Fa, So, La, Ti
> Forget about the Re,
> Bring the Dough to Me.

It was Montague's ditty. But Jordan at this moment was so elated he put Montague out of his mind.

"Lawrence," Marcella said, "you're cracking up."

The phone rang. "Let Bates get it," Jordan said.

Across the hall, Bates lifted the receiver. They heard him say, "Fannie? All right. What's happening with you? Sure is freezin' down here, girl. Can't turn on the heaters till we get somethin', you know. . . ."

Jordan turned back to his wife. "Got a surprise for you," he said.

"What is it?"

"Well, you'll find out at home. I want Mother to hear this, too. Been waiting for this for a long, long time."

"Brother Jordannn!"

Bates was calling him. Jordan liked to hear Bates call him that way. It reminded him of Southwall Lovingood.

"Yeah, Bro' Batessss?"

"Pick up the phone. It's Fannie."

Jordan picked up the phone. Marcella was getting her coat.

"Bro' Jordan?" Bates was saying. "He's on, Fannie. Tell him."

Fannie's husky voice vibrated in Jordan's ear. "Lawrence, honey? I thought you'd want to hear about this. . . ."

Marcella was bundled up and ready to go when he put down the receiver. Bates joined him in the room.

"What's wrong, fellows?" Marcella asked. "You both look like you've seen a ghost."

"We have," Jordan said. "Wayne Lovingood's calling a meeting of the Directors Association to stop me from working for the other embalmers."

Lennie Valentine arrived precisely at midnight. From his office window, Jordan saw the sleek black limousine slip down the street and around the corner. A minute later he heard Lennie's footsteps on the street. Jordan did not move. He kept staring through the window. The funeral home was in utter darkness, Jordan's face illuminated only by the glow of the garish blue Jordan & Bates neon in the window. It was the face of a skeleton.

The front door opened. A minute later, Jordan heard Lennie's voice in his ear.

"What's happening?"

"Lovingood's trying to ruin me," Jordan said without turning around.

"How?"

"The same way he did Jamal."

"Can I . . . be of service?"

"Talk to Wayne. Tell him to lay off."

"You mean you want me to *persuade* him?"

"No, no. Not that. Just talk to him. In words."

"Baby, words ain't gonna do no good. I tried that. Jamal asked me to do the same thing, Lawrence. Lovin'good needs a lesson."

"You don't have to hurt him. I mean he's not violent. He's just political. I thought maybe the *threat* of retaliation might make him lay off. I won't have anything to do with violence."

Valentine smirked. "Nothin' to do with violence?" Lennie asked. "What the fuck you think your business is all about? You make your money on violence even more than I do and I ain't no Sunday school teacher. Don't worry about Lovin'good. Just give the word. 'When the word is given,' baby. . . ."

"No. I don't want him hurt."

"Okay. There are other ways. Maybe his place catches on fire. . . ."

Jordan whirled on Valentine. He unveiled his eyes.

"Lennie—"

"Don't look at me like that, Jordan. Don't try to hypnotize me again."

"Hypnotize you?"

"I'm runnin' things now. Don't forget that."

"I'm just trying to convince you that I don't want any violence. Just the threat of it. If it has to come to the real thing, I'd rather just quit business. I'm finished."

"You may be finished anyway, Lawrence. Remember Jamal. It was Lovin'good, *Lovin'*good I tell you, who got Abdullah rubbed out. He'll do the same thing to you if you let him. We —you got to strike first. I mean it's not just for yourself, Jordan. It's for your mother, your wife, the people, Jamal!"

"I don't believe Wayne had anything—I don't believe he was the cause of Jamal's dying."

"You weren't here. I was."

"Even if he was, I'll just have to face that possibility."

"You gonna let them kill you?"

"I hope not."

"Then give the word, baby. Give the word."

"The word is talk, Lennie. *Talk*."

Valentine gritted his teeth. "Okay. But Lovin'good is mine. I'm gonna get him one of these days anyway, hear? I'm gonna get him. For Jamal."

"Will you talk to him for me?"

"Aw, man, damn! Yeah, sure. I'll talk to him. On one condition. . . ."

"What's that?"

"For a piece of the action. Can you dig it? Silent partners."

"Unh-unh."

"I don't mean any big thing."

"Unh-unh, Lennie. Not even a tiny little thing. This is my baby. You should know how I feel about this."

"You know this is my turf, don't you? I mean I can take what I want, nigga."

"Take it then. Try that and I'll close up shop first. I won't be hustled, Lennie."

Lennie chewed on a match. He put his face close to Jordan's, then sneered.

"Lovin'good's hustlin' you, mothafucka."

"I thought you were my friend, Lennie. A brother."

Lennie tore the match from his teeth. He stepped back in the darkness, then moved to the door. "So did the Turk," Lennie said.

"I'm sorry, Lennie," Jordan called out. "Lennie? Aw, man, I know you're my friend. It's just that I can't go for all this Brotherhood business, this Cosa Nostra stuff. You know what I mean?"

Lennie walked out the door. As he left, he said icily, "Take care of yourself, Lawrence."

Jordan watched the long limousine go back the way it had come, a panther in the snow. Snow began to blow on the window like soapflakes emptied from a high box. It was almost Christmas. He wanted to give Marcella a new dress, maybe even a coat. With a suede collar.

Jordan felt a chill. He reached in the darkness for his overcoat. As he slipped the coat on, he shuddered at how close he had come to signing Wayne Lovingood's death warrant. He couldn't do that, no matter what. He owed it to Southwall not to.

27

The explosion was a fist of fire smashing through the apartment. It shredded the ancient GE refrigerator next to the decrepit old divan in the tiny two-room flat. It tore the framed and faded photographs from the peeling wall. The whatnot case, with its odd little porcelain figurines and kewpie dolls, disintegrated, and fragments of whatnots melted in the fire. Shards of glass from the dusty front window peppered the rummage store across the street. Above the rickety, smelly backstairs with its bags of old garbage and stacks of yellow newspapers, the brittle back door blew out from its hinges.

Sirens wailed in the sunrise. The streets were full of people held at bay by firemen, who were pouring streams of water up at the flames. A dreary pall hung in the air, and echoes of the blast seemed to be sounding in the silence.

"It's Miz Samuels' house!" someone cried.

"Sure 'nuff!"

"She dead?"

"What happened?"

"I heard it all the way up the street."

"Sure is a mess. Je-Zus!"

Lawrence Jordan was arriving for work when he saw the crowds two blocks away. He left his car in front of the funeral home and ran toward the smoke. He fought his way through elbows and shoulders until he saw Seldom Seen, one of the neighborhood wineheads.

"What happened, Seldom?" he asked, grabbing the man's elbow.

"There was an explosion," Seldom Seen said.

"Where?"

"Down up over the pawnshop. Miz Carrie Samuels' house."

"Was Carrie hurt?"

"Musta been," Seldom drawled, " 'cause she at the morgue now."

"Dead?"

"They don't take no livin' there, far's I know."

He called Clare from his office. She was not working that day. Clare took the news oddly. She had shown such kindness to Carrie Samuels beginning with Southwall's funeral; sometimes Carrie Samuels came to visit her. Yet Clare kept her wits. She had fortitude, Jordan's mother. There was a moment of silence on Clare's end; then she started pushing.

"When did it happen?" Clare asked.

"Sometime this morning. Miz Samuels is dead, Mother. She's *dead*."

"I heard that. Where's her body?"

"Coroner's got it, I hear."

"Claim it."

"What?"

"Claim it. She promised it to you, didn't she?"

"Yes, but that don't mean shit. She promised it to everybody."

"Not in writing."

"She didn't promise it to me in writing, Mother."

"Oh, yes, she did. I've got the papers right here. Right here."

"Huh?"

"I said I've got the papers here. She came up to Fannie's one day last month and asked me to type them out for her. Said she wanted you to have them. I forgot to give them to you."

"I don't believe that, Mother. It sounds—"

"Never mind how it sounds. You better believe it. You better be glad she did it. Don't ask questions! Just get down there and make that claim. Go on, boy, don't be so damn scared."

"Mother, it wouldn't be legal."

"It's legal all right. She signed it. Lovingood can't get this one from us. Fannie'll back you. I already asked her."

"But how did you—"

"Somebody else told me about it just before you called. A fellow, a man I know. Don't worry about that now. Get down there."

Clare hung up.

A minute later Marcella called. "It's on the level, Lawrence," she said. "Your mother's telling the truth. She does have the papers. The body's ours; it's ours!" Marcella was elated.

He had Bates stop by Clare's house on the way to get the papers. They studied them together.

"I'll be damned," Bates said, scratching his head. "Looks legal to me. Looks like we got a case on our hands. Let's go on down there, Brother Jordan."

As Jordan and Bates stood by, a deputy coroner lifted the bloody sheet from the remains. All that was left of Carrie Louise Samuels was a charred torso, burned beyond recognition. The limbs were missing. What remained of the head was little more than a scorched skull. It was the worst case Bates had seen, and it turned his stomach. Jordan was impassive; he had seen many like it.

"What killed her?" Jordan asked the deputy.

"Probably the shock wave," the deputy said, replacing the sheet. "Sure tore this old girl up."

"Do they know what caused the blast?" Bates asked.

"Naw. Probably a faulty heater. Or someone trying to get into the pawnshop. Fire Department's still investigating. You sure she ain't got no relatives, Mr. Jordan?"

"I'm sure. The church will confirm it. Reverend Rideout knows."

"Okay. She's all yours, what's left of her."

The deputy just stood there shaking his head.

Jordan paced the chapel. Now was a chance to test his theory of total restoration. He had to move swiftly; the future of the funeral home depended on it. They were almost bankrupt. In another week or a month, Wayne Lovingood would begin a smear campaign to force Jordan out, just as he had done Abdullah Jamal. Jordan would never use the same tactics against Wayne, but now he had a chance to stop Wayne his way, the artist's way. He could use his art to survive. It had to be good. He was going to sculpt Carrie Samuels, and it had to be believable, even to Carrie's own mother.

"Bates," Jordan barked suddenly. "Call the Fire Department. Find out if there were any photos of Carrie intact. If so, see if

270

we can get 'em. Call the church, too, her friends, anyone. We need as many photos of Carrie Samuels as we can get. As a girl, a young woman, front view, side view, anything. . . ."

He had a plan.

It had come to him instantly while he was pacing. He had to do it, he could not be stopped now; he knew he would succeed.

First, he called New Jerusalem Spiritualist Church and asked one of the women there to rush over a thick cotton slip, an A-cup bra, a long-sleeved church mother dress in Carrie Samuels' size, a pair of dark gloves, and the white cap the church matrons always wore.

Next, Jordan went out on the street and looked for Seldom Seen. He found Seldom at the filling station down the street, filling a wine bottle with water from a hose. "Want enough wine to keep you mellow for a month?" Jordan asked Seldom, taking the bottle of water away. "All right. Here's money. Go to the junkyards, the dress shops, the cleaner's, anywhere around here, but get me a roll of chicken wire about waist-high, bundles of newspapers, a dozen new coat hangers, some tar, a broomstick, some baling wire and a couple of clean burlap bags. What do you mean you can't remember all that? You want that wine, don't you? Move!"

He ran all the way back to the funeral home.

To Marcella he assigned preparing the head; to Bates the casket. "Make it black plastic, a sealer. Then get me false eyelashes, a bottle of peroxide, five handfuls of coarse human hair and a full-length wig. Make it the closest thing you can find to Sister Samuels' hair. Hurry!"

The Fire Department Investigation Bureau called and confirmed that a small photo album had been found in the rubble. The pictures were singed, but they were intact. The church also had some pictures in which Sister Samuels appeared. Jordan drove to the Fire Department and the church and got the photos. Together, there were fifteen photos of Carrie Samuels.

When he got back to the funeral home, he pasted photos everywhere in the preparation room: over the sink, over the prep table, around the walls, even on the ceiling. He wanted to surround himself with the memory of Carrie Samuels, with a panorama of her life. He pasted the photos around the room according to whether Carrie was profiled in them or facing the camera, whether she was looking to the right or to the left, whether she was young or old. The most recent photos of Carrie Samuels were on the ceiling.

Bates and Seldom Seen came in with their materials. Seldom had borrowed a junkman's wagon. He had remembered everything Jordan asked for, though Jordan was dissatisfied with the hangers. They were wooden. He sent Seldom back out for metal hangers.

"Slow down, Lawrence," Marcella urged him. "We've got plenty of time. That's all we have got."

He helped Bates carry the casket into the chapel. He returned to the back room and unloaded Seldom's wagon through the rear door. It was the chicken wire he wanted first.

The wire was perfect. He set the roll down on the floor and tightened it. Grasping the middle of the wire with his hands, he pushed inward. The wire became indented, pinched.

That would be the waist.

He snipped the coat hangers. He wanted the corners. With wire pliers, he fastened the ends of the hangers onto the chicken wire frame above the waist. He placed three corners of hangers over each other, touching at the points, and in his hands the pieces of the hangers became the breasts.

Jordan rolled the embalmed torso of Carrie Samuels to the prep room door. From there, Bates and Marcella lifted it into the waiting casket.

Jordan cut the chicken wire torso vertically in half, using the pliers to secure the loose edges of the half with the coat hangers on it. He placed the frame over the burned remains in the casket, noting its fit. He compressed the wire in places with his hands.

"Her shoulders would have come to right about here," he said, tracing an imaginary line in the casket with his hand. He rounded off the top of the wire frame at that line, bending the wire with his bare hands.

Bates and Marcella watched transfixed. Either Lawrence Jordan was a madman or he was a genius.

"Hand me the slip and the dress," Jordan mumbled.

Marcella got them for him.

He placed the slip on the frame and the dress over the slip. For the moment, he was only getting an idea of the way they looked over the frame.

The frame was too high; he would have to cut it down an inch in the back. The wire breasts were too pointed. Old women had sagging breasts. He would have to bend the coat hangers, round them off.

He lifted frame and clothing from the casket. "Leave the body just like it is."

Returning to the prep room, he cut more wire from the back of the frame. He bent the hangers till they were rounded and saggy. He worked on the frame for an hour. Then he heated the tar and tarred pieces of newspapers to the frame. When he had finished, he had the chest and torso of a female body.

He turned to the skull, already scrubbed and prepared with hot paraffin wax. This would be his base.

He passed a broomstick under the mold and placed the skull over the stick, noting its appearance. His eyes traveled constantly around the room in all directions, studying Carrie Samuels in the pictures. Finally, he had it. He marked the broomstick. He snipped off a small section of chicken wire and wound it around the broomstick, leaving just enough room for the stick to slide up and down. This would be the neck.

He halved the neck and bound it to the body mold. When he had coated it with tar paper, it blended into the frame.

Jordan slit both the slip and the dress and attached them, one over the other, to the frame. He discarded the backs of the garments. He left the arms of the dress and the length of the dress intact.

Back in the chapel, he found the casket closed. "Why did you close it?" he asked Marcella.

"People have started coming in, asking to see Mrs. Samuels," Marcella said.

"What did you tell them?"

"I told them she's . . . disfigured."

"Tell them I'm going to re-create her. Tell them *that*."

"Do you think you can do it?"

273

"You'll see."

He opened the casket while Bates kept more people behind the front door. He eased the dressed frame over the real body.

"Now," he said.

From the preparation room, he brought bound rolls of newspapers and a pair of gloves which he had stuffed with pieces of hangers, newspaper and cotton. He forced the rolls of paper up the sleeves of the dress and pinned the gloves to the sleeves. The papers were twisted and layered to give the appearance of arms. One of the arms fell across the midsection of the frame.

"Now," he said, "we close the box."

He closed the bottom half of the casket. In the box lay what looked like a headless, gloved body. Marcella gasped.

Jordan smiled. He knew he had it now.

People streamed into the funeral home. Bates and Marcella were busy the rest of the evening turning them away. As Jordan had instructed them, they told each visitor Carrie Samuels had been horribly burned. But Lawrence X. Jordan, a master of dermatology, was going to re-create her, they said. The people would see for themselves at New Jerusalem Spiritualist Church. There would be no wake.

Throughout the night, Jordan worked tirelessly on the most important facet of his re-creation, the face of Carrie Samuels.

He began by amassing a large ball of dermatine wax, which he flung onto his drafting table. He had barricaded the door so no one would see what he was doing.

Tilting the table toward him, he began working the wax with delicate fingers, reaching for the face of Carrie Louise Samuels. He was sculpting her back for the world.

Beneath him, the wax took first the form of youth. He was concentrating on the earliest pictures of Carrie Samuels, pasted haphazardly over the sink. As he proceeded, he turned to the pictures of Carrie as a young woman. The wax face altered accordingly.

In the night, the dermatine passed through the ages of man. Finally, it took the form of the face in three photos on the ceiling, yellowed by fire. The face became old and withered and tired. Lawrence Jordan tenderly closed its eyes.

Over an open flame, he baked it. Then he fitted it to the skull. It matched perfectly.

274

Then Jordan went into his office and went to sleep. It was morning.

While Jordan slept, Major Bates arranged the funeral in hushed tones with the Right Reverend Richard Daniel Rideout. Carrie Samuels had no money, but in gratitude for her years of service to the church, the church would bury her. Bates extracted as high a price as he could, reminding Rideout that the funeral would draw hundreds of the people who knew Carrie. The publicity from the case would draw many more who didn't. And Bates emphasized to Rideout the cost of Lawrence Jordan's unusual art. Rideout agreed to all their terms, decreeing that the funeral would be held that Sunday. Attendance was highest then, and the church could be prepared for a crowd.

Shrewdly, Bates told him, "You'll probably take in enough at the collection to more than pay for our services."

The community buzzed with excitement. Across town, Wayne Lovingood was phoning the other embalmers. "What does Jordan think he's doing?" Wayne asked them. "He can't restore a whole body. He's finally cracked up and thinks he's God."

Lovingood and Montague decided to attend the funeral. Wayne was sure Jordan would fail, and the result, if Jordan dared display it, would be disastrous. Then he'd have Jordan. He encouraged the others to be there, too. Then they could see for themselves that Lawrence Jordan was a charlatan, trying to take advantage of the oddity of the case.

The embalmers geared up to descend on New Jerusalem as they had not done since the death of Southwall Lovingood.

Back in his shadowy embalming room, Lawrence Jordan, awake and renewed from coffee and doughnuts brought in by his mother, worked on the final touches of his creation. He painted and powdered the face.

He had molded wax all around the skull. Only the face was smooth. He fitted the wig to the head and trimmed it accordingly. Bates had been unable to find coarse hair: Jordan would have to work with what they had. Intricately, hair by hair, he filled in the hairline around the face with a needle and fine tweezers. He put some of the loose hair on a strip of tape and transferred it to the humps above the eye bulges. These were eyebrows.

He was barricaded in the room all day. At dusk, he emerged and asked Bates and Marcella to leave the chapel and lock the front doors.

He had left just enough of an overhang of wax on the head to create the appearance of a neck. He now smoothed the wax over the wire neck form he had attached to the torso. Now it was almost complete.

Quickly, he positioned the contents of the casket. He tucked in the dress, firmly positioned the arms and tucked in the silks. Opening the lower lid of the casket, he pulled the dress down and anchored it with the burlap bags, filled with rocks. He switched off the lights and called Marcella and Bates into the room.

"I think we may have something," he whispered to them.

"Are you ready?"

"Can we see it?"

Jordan turned on the lights.

There, in the box, a woman slept. From every angle, every perspective, she was real, solid, dead. An hour ago, she could have been breathing.

It was Carrie Samuels.

Marcella stared, shaking her head incredulously.

Bates moaned and stepped back from the box.

"God," he said. "Oh, God."

Jordan called Clare down to see it. She walked down from Fannie Fears', anxiously. When Jordan unveiled it, she ran out screaming.

"I just can't believe it," Bates muttered.

Marcella was serene. "I can," she said. "I knew you could do it, Lawrence. That is why I've said you were *called*."

Jordan turned away from them and retreated into his office. He sat there for a long time, brooding in the dark. Would other people react as Clare had if they knew? The thought frightened him more than the reality of what he had just accomplished.

Who was he?

Morbid curiosity drew hundreds to the church. It was not as big or as colorful as Southwall Lovingood's funeral. But it had its effect. Dramatically, Jordan waited until the viewing to open the casket. There were gasps of astonishment throughout the church. The word of Jordan's accomplishment spread out into the street, touching the crowds waiting there. As a gesture to all the people outside, Jordan had the casket carried to the hearse open.

Lovingood stormed out of the church in confusion.

In his sermon, black-winged Richard Rideout made references to Jordan, "a man who cared," "a man inspired by God," "the only embalmer worthy of being a successor to that great churchman and undertaker who left us so recently. . . ."

In the crowd, Jordan saw people pointing to him, naming him.

"Is that him?" they asked.

"I heard she was burned up."

"She was."

"There's Lawrence Jordan. And Major Bates."

"That's his wife."

"Je-Zus."

As he made his way to the hearse, people touched him, thanked him. As he closed the casket over the illusion of Carrie Samuels, they crowded around him and pushed at him.

At the cemetery, Marcella told him, "You're coming into your own, dear. I'll follow you everywhere, even to the grave. . . ."

It was quite a day.

In a week, it was forgotten. But not within the mortuary fraternity. Lawrence Jordan became a new legend among the embalmers. His early association with Southwall Lovingood helped. In spite of protests from Wayne Lovingood, the others gave Jordan all the restorative work he could handle. The Funeral Directors Association voted unanimously against Lovingood to allow Jordan to do outside work.

Jordan & Bates, Limited, prospered. Marcella was exuberant about the new business. She talked continually of how contented she was, handling the cases they got. They began to average three a week.

There was talk started by Fannie Fears, of Jordan replacing Lovingood as head of the Twin Cities Funeral Directors Association.

Clare agitated incessantly for Jordan to campaign for the position. "We can do anything once we get it," she said. "We can strike against Wayne, too. Don't be scared. . . ."

Jordan ignored her. For the first time in two years, he and Marcella were solvent again. They informed Clare they were selling out to Major Bates, repaying Fannie Fears, and returning to Illinois, where Jordan finally would begin art school. Clare was hysterical. She threatened to commit suicide if they left her. Laughingly, they tried to calm her down. Then a telegram arrived from Illinois, announcing that Achilles Sampson Ransom had passed away.

28

They interred Achilles Ransom in Zion, Illinois, in an inexpensive little plot overlooking his real estate across the highway. There were no flowers. That was Ransom's way of getting back at the pilfering Zion gravediggers who had plagued him in life.

The rites were private. Apart from a priest, only members of the mortuary fraternity attended the graveside services. They were Camille Ransom, beguiling widow in black lace; the Jordans; Friedland and Farentino, Achilles' fellow collusionists, properly sober-faced; and the balding, paunchy, respective members of Weaver, Sergeant and Roddenberry, the prosperous funerarium in the great metropolis to the south. Friedland, at his late friend's request, had done the embalming.

Jordan joined the other men in bearing the closed casket from Ransom's aging gray hearse to the waiting ground. The casket was a cheap, vulgar, cloth-covered receptacle, angular and powder blue, and it was fuzzy to the touch. Inside, Friedland had confided, Achilles was quite comfortably stretched out in wine-colored sweater and matching tie, gray trousers and tan house slippers. To the end, Ransom had maintained his mania for color and informality in funerals.

The priest, a man from Camille Ransom's parish—Jordan thought it was the same priest who married him and Marcella —mumbled a few words over the box, flung holy water on it, and Achilles Ransom was quickly committed to the earth. In the parlance of the popular *Afro-Citizen* memoriams, Ransom was "gone, but not forgotten."

Indeed, it would be quite difficult for Achilles' loved ones

279

ever to forget him. Or be ungrateful to him. He left an estate valued, after taxes, at five hundred thousand dollars.

Camille Ransom got half the estate. The other half, including the Kewaunee funeral home, went to Marcella. For the Jordans, money was no longer a problem. Ransom's widow took his passing in stride. If Camille wept, none knew it. At the grave she bore her burden in much the manner Achilles would have wanted. She even said farewell to him as he was being lowered into the pit, as though he could hear her. It was a chatty, matter-of-fact good-bye with the same friendly tone Camille used in talking to the other dead. At dinner that day, she presided over the table with grace and dignity, leaving her husband's plate overturned and his chair empty facing her.

But Jordan speculated privately that Achilles would not have been totally pleased with the style of Camille's subsequent mourning. Actually, the penurious Ransom would be revolving in his grave. The day after the funeral, Camille bought a brand-new Cadillac Eldorado and hired a full-time maid. Two days after the funeral, vowing to continue her work at the funeral home later, she announced plans for an extended period of mourning . . . in the Bahamas.

Tommie Roddenberry, Jr., was left temporarily in charge of the funeral home. It was a duty he would discharge faithfully, since it turned out that Ransom owned a silent interest in Weaver, Sergeant and Roddenberry, as well as a modest piece of the cemetery in which he was buried. Ransom had acquired his interest in Weaver *et al.* by virtue of his having sold them his business in the big city for more than they could then afford. He had got a piece of the action from the cemetery by pointing as many bodies as he could toward Zion in the early days. Friedland and Farentino also shared in this latter enterprise.

"I'll back the House of Jordan with every cent we've got," Marcella said.

That, Jordan calculated, was considerably more than Wayne Lovingood would ever have.

Milton and Helena Goldman, Clare's old employers, were breaking up. Clare pointed it out to Jordan in the morning paper. "It's a disgrace," Clare said. "All that money and still no happiness. Guess she'll get everything now. Says he's selling their house."

Jordan didn't get the idea until noon. He was making his rounds along the Row when he crossed an intersection and looked up a side street at a big, crumbling house.

Then it struck him: The old Goldman mansion would be a perfect location for the new House of Jordan.

He could not reach the Goldmans. Later he learned from Mike Goldman, now a sociology professor at the University of Missouri, that the senior Goldmans had left town pending the final decree.

Jordan was pleased that Mike remembered him. Mike had grown into a spindly-legged, dumpy, absentminded creature. It gave Jordan a certain perverse pleasure to make his offer to the son of his mother's former masters.

"What?" Mike Goldman asked.

"I said I want to buy the place," Jordan replied as casually as he could. He waited to see the look of shock come over Mike Goldman's face.

But Mike seemed unimpressed. Jordan was disappointed at Mike's casualness, but delighted with his answer: "I'll have to contact my dad. . . ."

"Good. If he's interested, call me at this number. My office. If he's for it, I'll have the papers drawn up immediately."

"Okay," Mike said, turning to a stack of papers on a table behind his desk. He was quartered in a stuffy office big enough for only two people at a time.

Jordan looked at Goldman, who seemed to have forgotten he was even there.

"Say, let me ask you something, Mike."

Doctor Milford Goldman looked up through thick bifocals.

"With all your ah, *resources,* I mean your dad's money, why did you go into this? I mean teaching doesn't exactly pay a fortune and I hear you have to wait years to be a full professor or something. . . ."

Goldman smiled. It was the same easy smile Jordan remembered.

"Well, I've never cared much about material things," Mike

said. "Maybe it was because I grew up with them. I mean, we always had enough. I guess I'm just a lot more interested in people, helping them solve their problems."

"It's ironic, isn't it?"

"What is ironic?"

"That we should . . . in a sense, change places. You with the dreams. Me with the money. That's something, isn't it, Mike?"

"I dunno. Not really."

Mike Goldman excused himself. He had to prepare for a class. Jordan liked the art prints Mike had taped behind his office door. Matisse, Gauguin, Picasso, Modigliani.

Jordan and Bates dissolved their partnership. Jordan repaid Bates and Fannie Fears their investments plus a hundred percent interest. Each received ten thousand dollars. Clare elected to keep her five thousand in, though she resigned as receptionist at the Fears Funeral Home to become "hostess" with the new House of Jordan. "Finally," she sighed, "I'll be working someplace that has my name on it."

Major Bates was given the option of keeping the old business and all its equipment and having his own mortuary or joining the House of Jordan as associate director. He chose to remain with Jordan. Bates shrugged. "Never been worth a damn by myself anyway." Jordan guaranteed Bates an annual salary of twenty-five thousand dollars, and more if the new venture prospered.

Meanwhile, the Williams brothers had moved their operation onto the boulevard a mile east of Lovingood's. The big push was on. It was only a matter of perhaps five years, Jordan now figured, until the leafy boulevard became the new Undertakers Row. Jordan had maintained friendly relations with the Williamses, who built a modernistic funeral chapel on the boulevard. In no time, they had surpassed Fannie Fears' volume and were neck and neck with Lovingood. Behind the scenes, Jordan used his influence to promote the Williams' combine.

Jordan did not campaign for the presidency of the Directors Association. Instead, he backed Billy Williams for the position. Williams narrowly won out over Wayne Lovingood.

At first Lovingood vowed revenge on Jordan but thought

better of it when he discovered that the old Jordan & Bates storefront was boarded up. Also, he was too busy trying to stop the Williamses.

"Guess that's the last we'll see of Lawrence what's-his-name," Wayne smirked.

"Don't bet on it," T. J. Montague said.

Rumors circulated among the embalmers that Lawrence Jordan had gone bankrupt. Jordan allowed his competitors to believe this. He was offered several attractive positions, including one with LaCour, Wingate & Montague—by way of Thess Montague—but he calmly turned each offer down. The other morticians speculated on his reasons for rejecting them, finally concluding that Lawrence Jordan, the man who had restored an entire body, was too proud to accept. The only one who knew of the Jordans' good fortune was Fannie Lartarska Gorham Fears. And Jordan had sworn her to secrecy.

Reluctantly, the Goldmans agreed to sell their property to Jordan if he could raise fifty thousand dollars. They were dumbfounded when Jordan snapped at the deal. He put half the purchase price down and promised the Goldmans the other half within a year.

The old mansion, a twelve-room brick Tudor, was in serious disrepair. Their wealth dwindling, the Goldmans had maintained the façade of the house and the verdant five acres surrounding it. Within, however, the drapes moldered and the walls peeled. The old curving staircase, which Jordan had remembered fondly all those years as a symbol of affluence, was creaky and buckled. Without Clare to do the sweeping and dusting, Mrs. Goldman had closed off part of the house. The maid's room and dining room, the living room and recreation room had not been used for years. Spiders had spun ambitious webs in them. Furniture sat shrouded in the rooms, old dust settled in the folds of their coverings.

Only the bedchambers and bathrooms upstairs were acceptable. The breakfast room and kitchen below were satisfactory, but Jordan had no use for the kitchen. And he had different uses for the french-doored breakfast nook.

Jordan walked jubilantly among the trees of his estate. The place was smaller than he had imagined it over the years. And things—trees and bushes—were in locations other than he had

283

pictured them to be. But basically it was the same. The neighbors to the east had put in a brick wall running the length of the property. Good, that would give them privacy. By the patio he found the old chaise longue on which he had first flown with artistic ambitions. Now, in a way, those ambitions had been realized, though differently from the way he had imagined. The mind of man conceived, and it became reality. Only the reality was disaligned, out of focus, from the conception. Or was it the concept that was blurred, deficient?

The chaise longue was rusty now. The old, browning cushions were gone. Lawrence Jordan, master of the house, lord of all he surveyed, lay back on the rusty springs of the longue in the sun behind the house and exulted in what he had achieved. He couldn't believe it!

In the building, Clare and Marcella explored the big rooms, and Jordan knew his mother must be doing some private exulting of her own.

In a few days, the contractors and interior decorators were swarming through the house, transforming it into one of the finest funeral establishments in the world. It cost the Jordans twenty-five thousand dollars for the renovations alone. The appointments cost another twenty-five thousand.

Belowstairs, the walnut paneling of the recreation room was left intact. The floor was carpeted in royal blue. Powerful dehumidifiers were installed. The Goldman recreation room became the House of Jordan's casket display room. Jordan stocked only the finest receptacles: metallic full couches, cushioned bronze sealers. From Europe he imported several old-style coffins of hand-loomed brocades and satins with sculpted handles and crafted bodies. He also imported a focal point for the room: a marble sarcophagus featuring bas-relief reproductions of Michelangelo figures. This latter coffin he set in the center of the room on stone supports. From the steps leading down into the room, the display presented a panorama of elegance.

Beyond the doors in the west wall of the recreation room had been the immense basement. One corner of it had been sectioned off as a laundry room. Beyond the basement, next to stairs leading to the garage, was a small room that had been the chauffeur's. In memory of Achilles Ransom and as a gesture to

Marcella, Jordan had the entire basement transformed into a vast, totally equipped preparation room. This was the room that would not, could not be seen by outsiders. They could have economized on it, left it much the same as it was, added sparse equipment in the fashion of Marcella's father and still carried out their plans. But Marcella was a master embalmer and Jordan a master dermatologist. They would spend many hours here, perfecting their arts. In addition, it was Jordan's theory that the size and shape and appointments of the embalming room affected the deportment, the confidence, the very *style* of the mortician. He had worked in cramped rooms too long not to realize this. If the forbidden room was pleasing, then the rest of the house was in order.

Accordingly, they spent lavishly on the preparation room, which they came to call the laboratory.

On the first floor were the chapels. The sunken living room, which lay to the left of the stairway, became the East Chapel. Except for the church truck placed before the front window, the East Chapel was a plush formal showcase of mahogany, silver and brocade. Jordan expected it to become the more popular of the two chapels.

The dining room, just to the right of the entrance, became the West Chapel. It was furnished with movable oaken pews and a great oaken catafalque against the south wall of the room. Off the West Chapel to the south was the family alcove, dark and rich; to the west the organ room, created from the former maid's quarters.

In the hallway leading past the West Chapel to the slumber room was the powder room, restored to its elegance.

The breakfast room, with its paneled doors and french windows became a private, candlelit slumber room. The other half remained as the hallway through which the bodies would be wheeled.

The staircase was carpeted with the same claret red as the rest of the house. Jordan enhanced the stairs' upward curve with a set of discreetly positioned, glittering mirrors, dizzying to the climber.

Upstairs, the old Goldman bedroom became the offices of the firm. Moving their private library into the walnut bookcases, the Jordans and Major Bates presented a formidable trium-

285

virate among the French Provincial desks and settees. Jordan's own desk, larger than the others, occupied the farthest point in the room. The setting was important: It was here that matters of money would be decided. Jordan made sure the office in every aspect suggested wealth.

The series of closets and linen cabinets flanking the office hallway were removed and servant's quarters put in.

The other rooms were divided among the Jordans and became a private apartment. During working hours, the doors to these chambers would be closed. Clare was given Ruth's bedroom and bath as her own. Jordan and Marcella created four rooms of their own in the rest of the house by building an extension out over the garage and making a room from a large storage space the Goldmans never used. The Jordans had bedrooms, kitchen and formal dining room. They also used the screened-in porch off the East Chapel in summer. Since the East Chapel really was nothing more than a fancy living room, they also used it for parties and private gatherings.

Outside, Jordan had the four-car garage enlarged to accommodate six large automobiles. The driveway was lengthened and widened beyond the garage into a twelve-car parking lot. The grounds to the west, unfenced, were landscaped with high bushes.

Across the front of the property, Jordan placed a tall wrought-iron fence. On one of the brick columns flanking the long driveway, he placed a black plaque with gold lettering: "The House of Jordan."

He was almost ready. Now he made what he considered his most important purchase: Rolls-Royce rolling stock, sleek and classic and black. The hearse was specially made. Jordan decided that the simple elegance of the car should not be spoiled by nameplates in the casket windows. The House of Jordan would roll without announcing itself. The cars were advertisement enough.

There were three black family cars, the lead one featuring a wet bar for the relief of the immediate bereaved. This would be the car the chauffeur piloted.

Jordan bought the hearse but leased the limousines. He wanted to own all the stock outright, but the hearse alone had cost him fifty thousand dollars. It was a good investment; never again would he have to buy another one. Eventually he would buy the limousines to match it, but the hearse would do for starters.

Bates whistled at the new cars in the garage. "Man, we're really gonna ride high on the hog," he said.

"To many people," Jordan said, "your rolling stock is you. This is us."

"Don't look like shit to me," Clare said. "Fifty thousand dollars for that old box? Damn, boy!"

Clare rushed to ride in one of the cars, however, when the chauffeur was hired. They hired a quiet middle-aged woman as housekeeper. The chauffeur was Seldom Seen, who promised Lawrence Jordan (who did not take it seriously) that he would never touch T-Bird or Ripple again.

It had taken them five months to get ready. But the House was finally complete.

"Now," Jordan told the assembled staff, "we strike."

Lawrence Jordan strolled easily among his guests, clinking the ice in his brimming glass. They had all come—Fannie Fears and the others, the Right Reverend Rideout, Mike Goldman, Lennie Valentine, the mayor. The parked cars stretched four blocks away. His neighbors, curious about the strange dark people who quietly had moved in and boldly announced their intentions, came too. People Jordan had never seen before came and shook his hand.

He had hired a public relations and advertising firm, the best in the city, to make the announcement. Color supplements, showing the facilities and staff of the House of Jordan, had appeared in both the daily papers and the *Afro-Citizen News*.

In the supplement, Jordan published a letter to the community under the company's new letterhead:

THE HOUSE OF JORDAN

Mortuary

Greetings

I am Xavier Jordan, founder and director of the unique institution featured on these pages.

We have launched the House of Jordan at a cost exceeding $100,000. Every need, every contingency have been provided for. We trust you will be inclined to accept our services. No request, whatever its nature, is too great or too small for the House of Jordan.

The House, of course, was created for those who can afford the finest funeral service available. Because this does not include *everyone,* the House of Jordan is able to guarantee complete privacy, luxury and discretion for the fortunate few we intend to serve.

We are not a volume business institution. We do not expect to serve more than three families per week at our maximum. Thus, we shall give minute attention to every detail. I personally will supervise every operation, every movement.

We shall serve twenty-four hours a day, seven days a week. This is because we take such pride in our work that we actually reside on the premises. The House is really a "home." No other mortuary can honestly make this claim. No other mortuary can compare.

May I introduce you to the members of our family? My wife, Marcella. . . .

There followed brief biographies of Marcella, Clare and Major T. Bates, whom Jordan described as a "father." Southwall Lovingood was prominently mentioned as Jordan's early friend and mentor, "who graciously encouraged me in both the areas of art and mortuary science, disciplines which have come together to create the House of Jordan."

Finally, Jordan ended the letter with an invitation to the entire community to attend the Sunday open house. His daring signature, sans his first name and with the dots properly distant from the *i*, was reproduced at the close of the letter.

Most of the supplement was pictures. The Rolls-Royces, with a uniformed Seldom Seen holding open the door of the lead limousine, were displayed on the cover.

Ads also were run on radio and television, and Jordan made a guest appearance on a local talk show. The newspapers interviewed him, and film clips of the House of Jordan ran on the evening news of both television channels.

Most of those who came to the open house were middle-class. Ministers, lawyers, doctors, building contractors. And persons with pretensions of wealth.

That was precisely what Lawrence Jordan wanted. Who else

would spend the kind of money he wanted on a quarter's worth of metallic salts and a hundred cubic feet of dirt?

He made his way through the crowd in the house out onto the lawn, congratulating himself. Fannie Fears engaged him in light conversation for some minutes on the patio, but Jordan excused himself to get to a very special guest he had sighted near the garage.

Herece.

Herece, in a simple cotton dress, was standing by the bushes talking with Marcella. Marcella wore a white satin gown, elegantly fitted. Marcella's earrings, now glittering gold, were gracious counterpoints to the pale tanness of her shoulders.

But looking at them there, together for the first time, Jordan realized that Marcella, like her father, represented lightness and airiness, the antithesis of Jordan's ideal. There was more beauty and mystery in darkness, and Herece with her sable skin and smoldering eyes was the epitome of that beauty. Why couldn't it have been Herece who was greeting people with him today?

He took Herece's arm.

"Thought you were in Los Angeles," he said, playfully turning her around.

"Vacation," Herece said. "Mother finally got me back here in the sticks. Glad I came, though. Wouldn't have missed this for the world."

He became conscious of Marcella's eyes, watching him coldly. He took her arm, too.

"You've met my wife," he said to Herece.

Herece laughed, alabaster teeth on luscious ebony. "Yes," she said. "She's darling."

They made small talk about old times, undertakers as fathers, Herece's ex-husband, Wayne's prosperity. Jordan wondered: Did Marcella like Herece? Or did she hate her because she represented Lovingood?

One of the catering girls came up with sandwiches, and Seldom Seen, today dressed as a butler, refilled their glasses. The Right Reverend Rideout, his jowls smeared with mayonnaise from the hors d'oeuvres, came over and got his glass refilled. Then Rideout turned to Marcella. "Let me compliment you," Rideout was saying.

Jordan seized his opportunity. "Have you, ah, seen the rolling stock?" he asked Herece.

She shook her head.

They went into the garage. Outside, some couples from Rideout's church were oohing and aahing at the limousines. Jordan opened the rear door of the first family car, and they got in.

"Just like old times, eh?" he asked when they were seated. He lifted his glass and studied the gold water in it.

Herece's eyes remained downcast. "Yes, I guess so," she whispered.

He had to get a grip on himself. He was about to do something foolhardy any minute now. And that might blow the whole thing. He had too much riding on Marcella's goodwill to mess up now.

They sat silently in the car for minutes before Herece spoke. She stroked the dark velvet of the front seat as she talked.

"Lawrence?"

"Yes, darling?"

"Are you happy?"

He sat up. "Well, of course. I've got . . . well, everything now. Except you. Why do you ask?"

She smiled at him crookedly. "Oh, I just wondered, that's all." She rubbed against him as she turned to look out the back window. "Hey, we'd better get back out there," she grinned. "Before your wife thinks I'm trying to . . . *monopolize* you."

He seized her hand. She responded when he kissed her, then pulled away, shaking her head, fighting back tears.

"Herece, give me your address," he said. "I'd like to write to you."

"No, Lawrence," she said. "We can't go back."

Business rolled in. They evened out at two cases a week, giving Jordan enough time to sculpt on weekends. Marcella kept him abreast of the latest embalming advances, and Major Bates kept him full of good bourbon.

His policy was simple: Make at least a thousand dollars' profit on each case. They gave it to him and more, the affluent and the near affluent. He became adept at giving the people a show for their money. In no time, the House of Jordan became

290

legendary; people actually bragged that their loved ones had been ferried to the grave in a Rolls-Royce hearse.

Catering to the monied was hard work. People, Jordan found, took him seriously about no task's being "too great or too small" for the House.

For an eccentric real estate broker, he had to display the corpse of the man's wife sitting in a chair. He had a difficult time making the corpse look comfortable and at home.

Another family had their daughter, a pretty thing, buried clutching a doll.

For a family of five, horribly killed in an auto accident, he staged an open-casket funeral featuring a "bedroom" scene in which the victims, Mommy and Daddy in one huge casket and the three children in another, were made to look as if they had just turned in for the night.

It was all very private and very posh.

And it paid off. The first year they cleared one hundred and twenty-nine thousand dollars. And the Illinois property brought in something, too. Clare and Marcella were well pleased, and Major Bates got his raise.

Jordan's biggest thrill, however, was not the money. It was getting three of his sculpted pieces accepted by a small gallery on the Plaza. The *Afro-Citizen* did a story on it, and Jordan showed it to Clare and Marcella.

"That's nice, dear," Marcella said, returning to the floor plans she was considering for a new funeral home in Kewaunee.

"Shit" was all Clare said.

Why hadn't he made Herece give him that address? *She* would have been impressed.

29

Like a dowager queen, Clarisse Walker Jordan sat stiffly in a plush Provincial wing chair. Her wavy hair, streaked now with comely gray, was meticulously coiffered. Clare tucked the lap of her aqua blue shift neatly between her knees and thrust one of her gold-slippered feet forward in an imperious, high-handed gesture.

Lawrence X. Jordan stood behind his mother in a red paisley silk smoking jacket, resting a manicured hand on the back of her chair. Like Clare, his eyes were fixed on the doorway of the study. To Jordan's left, bright-eyed Marcella rested her elbows on her desk, her brassiere showing plainly under her lab coat, which was unbuttoned. Marcella's hair was tousled, and her fingernails were dirty. She sighed, turned back her coat sleeve, and looked at the expensive jeweled timepiece on her pale wrist. She was anxious to get back to the body she had left in the basement.

The door opened.

The new butler appeared, motioning a second man down the hallway toward the study. The visitor was tall and mustachioed and tan. He was elegantly dressed and strode into the study, smiling. He wore a summery candy-striped jacket, dark trousers and white silk tie over white shirt. It was T. Jerome Montague.

"You're late," Marcella observed. She had become quite touchy lately.

"I'm sorry," Montague said.

He kissed the hand Clare offered, then started to Marcella, who removed her hands from sight, signaling Montague that he was out of place.

"Punctuality," Marcella snapped, "is one of the marks of the House of Jordan. Remember that."

"Of course."

There was a minute of awkward silence. Then Jordan moved around to his desk and sat at it. The women turned to him, as did Montague. Jordan dismissed the butler with a wave of his hand and took a cigarette from a flashy gold box on his polished desk. He did not offer Montague a cigarette.

"Now then," Jordan said, "we may as well come straight to the point. We are—*I* am—prepared to offer you a position as associate director with the House of Jordan, Illinois operations, for twenty-five thousand dollars a year plus ten percent of the gross of the Illinois House."

Montague fumbled with the knot of his tie. He licked his lips. He searched Jordan's face, disbelieving what he had heard. Jordan kept his face stone. Montague looked away, first at Clare, who gave him an encouraging nod, then at Marcella, impatiently winding her watch. Clare smoothed her dress and shifted her feet. She arched an eyebrow at Montague and turned back to her son.

"Well?" Jordan demanded.

Montague tried to speak, but couldn't. He stifled a little gurgling in his throat. Plainly, he was at a loss for words—just as Jordan had planned.

Now Jordan stood up from his desk, took the gold box and walked around to Montague. He offered a cigarette to Monty, who reached for it greedily. The Jordans watched him intensely. Their eyes burned into his back and into his face. As Montague reached for the cigarettes, Jordan suddenly snatched the box back, placing his arm around Montague's shoulder.

"Of course," Jordan said, "you'll be on trial. The initial contract, therefore, will be for one year only. Let me say that it was my mother, Mrs. Clare Jordan, who suggested that we hire you. My wife has her doubts, and I remain open-minded. After one year, if we feel you have served us with energy and dedication, if we feel you are worthy of the House of Jordan, we may be inclined to extend the contract for, say, five years. With a little bonus thrown in now and then for particularly dedicated service."

Jordan thrust the cigarettes back at Montague. Montague grabbed one, lit it jumpily, took a long drag on it and blew a tongue of smoke into the room. He was sweating.

Breathing heavily, Monty grasped Jordan's hand and stammered, "Say no more, Lawren—I mean Mister Jordan, *sir*. I accept it. I'll take it. Thank you, thank you very much. Mister Jordan, I promise, despite our little differences of the past, that I will—"

"Very good, Montague," Jordan said, freeing his hand from Monty's grasp. "I say this calls for a drink, eh, Montague? Ladies, what is your pleasure?" Jordan pressed a single button on his desk.

The butler reappeared with a large tray containing glasses and bottles. They drank to the success of the new branch of the House of Jordan, showed Montague copies of the plans for the new building now rising on the outskirts of Kewanee, and instructed Montague to tender his resignation to Lovingood.

Then, led by the balding butler, Montague backed out of the room, scraping and bowing, blessing the Jordans, promising hard work and dedication in Illinois, and protesting that although it would be very hard indeed to leave his friend and longtime associate Wayne Lovingood, he would somehow find a way to break the news to dear old Wayne.

"Give my regards to Thessalonica," Jordan chirped. He felt Marcella's eyes boring into his then.

There had been tension in the study before Montague arrived and after he left. And he was not the cause of the tension. It came from the three residents of the long brick mansion that called itself the House of Jordan.

Marcella sat her drink down unfinished and frowned at Lawrence Jordan. "I hope you know what you're doing," she said.

"I do," Jordan replied, trying to maintain an air of casual confidence. "Monty is a tiresome fop, I'll grant you, but he's a good embalmer. And he's great with women. I mean with their hair. And their makeup."

"If he'll turn on Wayne, he'll turn on us," Marcella said, her eyes hazel ice on Jordan's face.

"If he doesn't work out," Jordan said wearily, "then we don't renew his contract. If he really screws up, we tear up his contract. But don't worry. He knows a good thing when he sees it. Did you see his face? God, I thought he was going to break out in that silly little dance of his right here in front of us all!"

Clare got out of her chair and mixed herself another drink, a double shot. "Didn't I tell you?" Clare asked them. "Montague would sell his own wife up the river for a fuckin' dollar."

"I know it!" Marcella said. "But what's to stop him from selling *us* up the river?"

Lawrence Jordan knew what was going to stop Montague, but he couldn't tell them. What a fool Montague was! Jordan no more intended to keep Montague on in Illinois past a year than he intended to let Clare continue acting as if she, and not he, were the master of the House. No; he would let Montague get a taste of what real money was like, what real luxury was like, and then he would cut Montague off with a vengeance. Vengeance was the key word here: Without Montague, Wayne Lovingood would be ruined, his business would fail, and the whole community would see how incompetent Wayne really was. That would leave Jordan alone as clear successor to the late, great go-getter Southwall Lovingood. Damn Southwall! Why did he haunt Jordan so? Bates, Clare, Fannie Fears, even Marcella—they kept Southwall before him, kept the man *alive* as a paragon of mortuary science. Hadn't Jordan shown by now that he, not Southwall Lovingood, was the man? Hadn't he?

He had to get Wayne, had to. Wayne had to pay for all the insults, all the sneers, all the trouble he had caused Jordan. As long as there was a Lovingood's, the House of Jordan was in danger. Only a month ago, Wayne—with Montague's formidable assistance—had stolen a body right out from under them— Reverend Richard Rideout! Jordan had secured permission from the family, was ready to roll, but he forgot about the wife. Rideout's widow was in the county jail. She had caught Rideout and one of the shapely young New Jerusalemites, a choir member, in bed at Rideout's cattle ranch in the Ozarks. And with the preacher's own shotgun, she had ended it all for the Right Reverend Richard Daniel Rideout. It had been a perfect House of Jordan case: wealthy, prominent, sensational, and requiring extensive restoration of the features. And Jordan had let Wayne Lovingood, a third-rate undertaker, steal it away. As soon as he heard about the slayings, Jordan had called Rideout's mother and got the body promised to him. But Wayne and Montague, bluffing their way into the jailhouse, had talked to the wife and got her to assign the body to them—in writing. It was the funeral of the year, and Jordan had let it slip by. And Clare, curse her, had reminded him: "*South*wall never would have let *that* one get by him, boy, no, sirree, Bob!"

Well, Wayne was about to get his. And after him, Montague. In another year, Jordan would be so well entrenched that he would be able to blackball both Wayne and Montague from the funeral business anywhere within five hundred miles. Of course he wouldn't do that; he would have a milder vengeance: Wayne and Monty would never again work in a funeral home large enough to compete with the House.

Jordan wondered if Montague really would sell his wife. Perhaps. The thought intrigued him. Maybe during the year, Jordan could find out. Thess Montague's promiscuity was notorious anyway. After she broke up with Wayne, there had been talk about her and one of the Kansas morticians.

"*I've* got work to do," Marcella said.

Jordan ignored her. The tension between them was building to a boil. It had begun when he and Herece got in the car at the open house. Marcella hadn't seen them but found out about it anyway. Jordan had shrugged it off. But Marcella had been on guard ever since, and once Marcella even hinted at economic reprisals if she ever caught him with another woman. Of course, he had his affairs. Lawrence Jordan without an affair was like Marcella without a case to embalm. But he had to curtail most of his activities. And he had all but given up other women when he realized finally that in all his other liaisons he had been seeking the one woman who could hold him and satisfy him and keep him: Herece Lovingood.

Marcella stormed out for the preparation room, where Bates was minding the shop. Clare watched her go down the hall.

"What's the trouble now?" she asked Jordan. "Can't you kids stop fussin' and fightin'? Get a hold on yourself before you do something rash."

"Don't tell me what to do!" Jordan yelled. "This is my house. You live here at my mercy and don't ever forget it! I'll deal with my wife as I want to. It's none of your business. Go out and get soused. That's the only thing you do well anyway."

Clare cried. She just couldn't understand what got into Jordan, she said. Here she was trying to help him, guide him, and he shouted at her and said unkind things to her, his own mother.

"Aw, I'm sorry," he said, escorting Clare to the door. Immediately he hated himself for giving in to her. All his life he had been giving in to Clare, saying what she wanted him to say, doing what she wanted him to do. He had assumed she would be pacified after they started the House. She would see that he was better than she gave him credit for. She would become dependent on him, stop nagging him, would go back to clothes and parties and being the socialite she always wanted to be, and he would take care of her and be rid of her.

But he had been forced to reevaluate Clare.

Clare Jordan had a flamboyance, a style, all her own. He had lived with his mother nearly half his life and had never really known her until now.

It was Clare who figured out how to break Lovingood. Psyche Lovingood had told Clare about Montague's mounting gambling debts. Monty had overextended himself, assuming that Lovingood's would continue to do a heavy business. Then the Williams Brothers, with Jordan's backing, pulled ahead. Montague's income dipped. Monty borrowed money from his father-in-law to pay his debts. But it was not enough to satisfy his creditors, North End gentlemen with a reputation for settling bad debts swiftly. Lennie Valentine had offered to lend Montague the money—at exorbitant interest. Montague turned him down but offered to pay Lennie for protection. Lennie, in turn, turned Montague down. Valentine was already in trouble with Monty's creditors and wasn't ready to confront them yet.

Clare suggested that Montague now might see the wisdom of accepting a Jordan offer. It would give him the kind of money he needed to pay off his debts, and it would get him out of range of the enforcers until he did. In addition, Clare told her son, it would leave Wayne Lovingood defenseless and in no position to compete with Jordan. Montague was Lovingood's drawing card, and without him, Wayne was lost.

"Great God, you're right!" Jordan admitted to his mother when he heard her idea.

"I don't like it," Marcella protested. "I wouldn't trust Montague with my dog."

Clare had only walked away. She knew Jordan would see it her way. And though Jordan and Marcella were feuding, Marcella still usually went along with what her husband decided in matters of business.

Why was Clare after Wayne Lovingood? Jordan pondered this for days but found no plausible answer. True, he and Marcella had reasons for wanting to stop Wayne, and perhaps they had somehow communicated their desires to Clare. But in the end, it was Clare, Psyche Lovingood's best friend, who set things in motion.

Clare followed up her initial mention of the idea with little quips to Jordan around the House: "Montague is Lovingood's strength . . . Monty's desperate for money, you know . . . Time is running out for Montague—and us, too."

In the end, Jordan had argued Marcella down and called Montague. Clare insisted on being present when Montague came. She had increasingly butted into Jordan's business, and he half expected her to try to conduct the interview. But she already had been drinking that day, and it was all she could do to sit there and look dignified.

Clare's drinking was getting worse. It was a source of embarrassment to both Jordan and Marcella, and it reflected badly on the House. Jordan wouldn't have minded it so much if Clare had kept it private. But she hadn't.

Fannie Fears, a notorious alcoholic, was a bad influence on his mother. It never occurred to Jordan that Clare's association with Fannie would lead to their carousing together. About the time Jordan purchased the House, Clare took up with Fannie. She seemed to be competing with her to see who was the wildest, the fanciest, the drinkingest.

Jordan was pleased to see his mother having fun. She had waited and worked years, and now that they had money, Jordan saw no reason for her to stay home knitting. But Clare got beyond herself.

She and Fannie Fears rode around town, usually chauffeured in one of Jordan's family cars, boozing and flirting. Jordan accepted his mother's appetites; after all, that no doubt was where he got *his*. And Clare was doing nothing that Camille

Ransom wasn't back in Illinois. The difference was that Camille did hers with discretion. And with older, responsible men. Clare, it turned out, retained her penchant for young men, men Jordan's age or younger. Again, Clare seemed to be competing with Fannie, whose interest in men young enough to be her grandbabies was well known to Jordan.

Jordan hated Clare, however, for an indiscretion he considered inexcusable. Reported Ponchita Perez in one especially juicy *Afro-Citizen* column:

> *The Odd Couple:* That handsome young Eighteenth Street gangster and that well-heeled socialite mother of a terribly exclusive young undertaker, seen sharing the back seat of her Rolls-Royce together. The thug is one of the best friends of the mortician, but what the mortician doesn't know is that his mother is even *better* friends with the mobster, whose initials are L.V. . . .

Clare confirmed it. But she claimed that she and Fannie were waiting for a light on Twelfth Street, and Lennie Valentine's limousine pulled up next to them, and before they knew it, Lennie had got in their car. "He said he hadn't seen you for a long time and just wondered how you were," Clare told her son. "So I told him. We all went out and had a drink, just one drink together, and Lennie left. Said he couldn't be seen out in public too long because somebody was after him and he had to go. There was another man with him all the time, a real mean-looking character, and they left us in the joint we were in. That's all that happened, and I don't know why that old hussy at the paper tried to make something of it. . . ."

Jordan believed her when, a few days later, someone took a shot at Lennie from a rooftop down on the Row and Valentine went into hiding. A contract reportedly was out for Valentine's head. A carload of Valentine people invaded Little Italy and beat up a Mafia lieutenant's nephew, and reprisals were expected. There was tension building up on both the North and the East Sides for days; then nothing further happened. But Valentine remained in hiding.

At Jordan's urging, Clare had taken a vacation to the West Coast, where she visited Herece in Los Angeles and lost bundles of money in Las Vegas.

When she returned, she startled Jordan by asking if he could help her get a funeral director's license.

"Why?" he asked. "You don't need it. You make more money than most directors—without putting in the hours they do. Better leave that stuff to us."

"No," Clare said. "I want a director's license. Something could happen to you or Marcella, Bates, any of us. I just want to make sure we're prepared for emergencies."

He was dissatisfied with Clare's reasons. It struck him: Clare, who was afraid of bodies and death, again was trying to compete with Fannie Fears.

"Forget it," he told her. "We've got too many directors as it is who don't understand the other aspects. Like Wayne Lovingood."

Clare didn't forget it. She began pushing in other ways. She insisted on assuming more duties at the funeral home. She argued that her job as hostess called for her to meet the public oftener than she did. Jordan had Clare greeting visitors to the House, escorting bereaved families through the rooms to the caskets of their loved ones. On funeral days, Clare helped them control the flow of traffic through the funeral home or church. She comforted the grieving, administering smelling salts to the women who collapsed in the aisles. She wrote funeral notices for the papers, and she answered the business phones. For this, Jordan paid her a small fortune. In addition, since her life savings were still invested in her son's enterprise, Clare shared in the profits of the business.

Clare begged to accompany the chauffeur in the first family car in funerals. In this way, she argued, she would be better able to comfort immediate survivors. Her work would end not at the service, but at the grave. Jordan realized that Clare's desire to go all the way with a funeral grew out of a certain inherent morbidity; she had always been fascinated with death and things connected with death. This, Jordan reasoned, was because Clare feared death more than even he did. She dwelt on it, dreamed of it, and her exuberance in carousing and enjoying sensual pleasures was a desperate attempt to negate it.

Jordan permitted Clare to ride in the family car. Patrons of the mortuary were impressed with the extra attention, and it gave Jordan hope that the increased responsibility would make

Clare settle down. She continued to drink, however, and several times got high before funerals. Tipsy, her breath smelling of gin, she would clumsily descend the winding staircase to greet the bereaved.

Once Clare and Seldom Seen got soused together and scandalized an entire funeral. Jordan had to apologize to a family, so unbecoming was Clare's conduct. Seldom was so drunk he couldn't drive in the funeral, and the service was delayed while Jordan frantically dug up a replacement. Clare and Seldom stayed behind while Jordan and others went to the cemetery. When they got back, there was Clare in the servant's quarters, partying with Seldom Seen.

Jordan thought it odd, therefore, that Clare demanded Seldom's dismissal the next day for insolence. She said Seldom had tried to seduce her. Jordan liked Seldom. But he disliked the old man's drinking on the job and his temerity in doing it with Clare. Seldom Seen, like Jordan's old 1939 Packard, was a good-luck charm around the House and Jordan could not bring himself to fire him. He compromised by reducing Seldom to mere chauffeur's status and gave his room to the new butler, a sober, quiet man. Seldom got a room in town, though many nights he slept in the garage on a cot in the back compartment of the old hearse. Those were the nights Clare kept him up till three or four in the morning and it was impractical for him to go home.

Ironically, Clare's antics put her in the limelight. As head of the exclusive Les Dames, Clare had become something of a social arbiter, eclipsing even Psyche Lovingood, who had arthritis and didn't get around much, and Thess Wingate. She was invited to numerous parties and charitable events and, despite her drinking, was one of the most sought-after status people in town. This position was enchanced when *Ebony* selected her one of the best dressed women of the year. Clare's name began to appear in the *Afro-Citizen* more often than Jordan's or Isadore Michaels'.

Clare's attitude toward Jordan and Marcella changed accordingly. To Jordan she was domineering, bitchy; to Marcella, patronizing and critical. She found faults with Marcella she never noticed before: Marcella didn't take care of herself, didn't know how to dress, how to make friends, how to socialize.

301

Jordan warned Clare that Marcella was still the power behind the House. But Clare sneered: "Yeah, but you've got *her* fooled. She'll do anything you tell her to."

Publicly, Clare began to assert that she was one of the "founders" of the House of Jordan and that it was she and Southwall Lovingood together who encouraged Jordan in embalming and art. And after Southwall died, she said, it was she alone who supported Jordan and Marcella during the lean years.

She referred to herself as a funeral director, an undertaker, and to the public she was. Her previous association with Fannie Fears and now her lucrative position with her son's mortuary gave her all the appearance of a mortician to laymen. Yet Clare was afraid to go downstairs after dark unless Jordan escorted her. "The bodies," she said, "I don't like the bodies." She never rode in the hearse.

Clare's good fortune had gone to her head. Several times, Jordan reminded himself that he and Clare inevitably would clash. He found himself plotting strategies for stopping Clare, such as his attack on her in the study. But he had reasons not to antagonize Clare too soon. One was her tears, the way she had of making him feel guilty for saying anything to her. Another was her indiscretion. He was afraid he would anger Clare so much that in a moment of drunken vengeance she would reveal things about the house he didn't want the public to know. Such as where he got his money. Or the trouble he and Marcella were having.

Finally, there was the well-being of the House itself. Clare somehow had become as much a symbol of the House of Jordan as Jordan himself. Her social standing, her notoriety, her acceptance by Fannie Lartarska Gorham Fears—all appealed to the people Jordan served. They dreamed of it themselves, strove for it, and when they saw someone like themselves who achieved it, they rewarded them. They rewarded Clare by giving their business to the House of Jordan. Clare herself attracted a sizable clientele. She earned her keep, and she knew it.

Still, he would have to stop her and do it soon. What was at stake was not merely the integrity of the House, but the House itself. No doubt he could expect Marcella's allegiance in a showdown with Clare. Marcella long ago had become fed up with his mother's conduct and his indulgence of it. And Marcella held the purse strings—something Clare had forgotten.

The Fears Funeral Home announced plans for a sumptuous Spanish-styled mortuary, pink and red tile, on the boulevard west of Lovingood's and Williams Brothers. The enclosed patio of the building would have a fountain eight feet tall. Mrs. Fears was buying new rolling stock but promised the new cars, Chrysler Imperials, would be as bright and distinctive as the old ones. Of course, they would be pink.

Predictably, Wayne Lovingood's business dropped off sharply after Montague left for Illinois. Forced to do his own embalming until he could find more help, Wayne produced a series of botched corpses, and the public, particularly the church folk, were quick to notice. Wayne found himself defending his work to preachers and matrons all over town. And for the first time he missed a meeting of the Funeral Directors Association. In the funeral column of the *Afro-Citizen,* the notices of Lovingood Mortuary cases dwindled to one or two a week. Some weeks even the scrawny Tatum's Funeral Parlor outdid Lovingood's—the ultimate disgrace. Fannie Fears became the leader in numbers of bodies per week.

Jordan had expected nasty phone calls from Wayne the minute Montague walked out. Instead, there was silence.

The House of Jordan celebrated, and Jordan, accompanied by Major Bates, did a little carousing of his own.

"Well, Brother Jordan," Bates said laughing, "I don't know what we can do for encores. I'd give anything to see Brother Wayne's face before I leave."

Leave?

"I been at it a long time, m'boy," Bates said. "Kinda tired now. I guess I mainly just stayed on to see this day."

Jordan tried everything: more money, more position, increased benefits, bonuses, outright gifts. But Bates was adamant. "Wanna do a little fishin'," the old man said, "maybe a little travelin'; you know, just kinda take it easy. Enjoy some of this money I been puttin' aside. You sure been good to me, Brother Jordan. . . ."

They spent two full days on the town, drinking, chasing women and recalling the old days. Jordan tried to pretend Bates wasn't leaving. "Your name will always be on the masthead," Jordan told the old embalmer. "You've been just like a father to me." And Lawrence Jordan cried: "The only father I ever had. . . ."

In the back seat of their limousine, Bates put his arms around Jordan and held him for a long, long time.

30

Lawrence X. Jordan jerked violently in his sleep, jostling Marcella. She nudged him with a sharp elbow in return, and Jordan recoiled, his hand shooting out, knocking over the ornate marble lamp next to the bed. "Major, Major," he moaned, "don't leave me, Brother Major. I'm scared, too!"

"Lawrence, hush."

"Major—"

"Lawrence, for God's sake, wake up."

"Wake—"

"Yes. You were having it again. The Dream."

Jordan sighed, struggled out of bed and into the black satin robe with "X.J." on the breast pocket. Jordan wrapped the robe tightly around him; he was drenched with cooling sweat.

"I'll be in the study," he told Marcella as he picked up the fallen lamp.

She did not reply and was snoring before he was out of the room.

Pouring himself a bourbon, Jordan scanned a copy of the new *Afro-Citizen* placed on his desk by the butler: Isadore Michaels passed away in his sleep and would be buried by the Fears outfit on Tuesday, a major coup for Fannie; Clarisse Walker Jordan selected "Mother of the Year" by a downtown civic group; Thomas T. Fortune returns to LaCour & Wingate; the late Right Reverend R. D. Rideout's widow released on bail; a new Community Action Council, headed by a young lawyer, formed to fight the war on poverty; Ponchita Perez's mother visiting her from Alabama; Lennie Valentine, supreme commander of the mysterious Brotherhood, still in hiding; Major Bates retires.

Jordan threw the paper aside and swiveled in his leather chair.

Bates' departure had jolted him in a way he had not foreseen. Even since Major had left, Jordan hadn't known a full night's sleep. Instead, he retreated into his study in the darkness, seeking to blot out the Dream with his art, attempting to sculpt away the ugliness which pervaded his whole existence. He approached the work with all the courage he could muster, barricading himself in the study with his drafting table, a mirror, his slugs of wax, and three fifths of bourbon. And after three days and nights, Jordan gazed upon his masterpiece, and what he saw chilled him more than all his fear.

He had fashioned his own face.

It was a death mask. The smooth tan flesh had shriveled to an ashen countenance, furrowed by the fumes of unnatural fluids. Faint grooves had formed around the corners of a mouth no longer sensuous, but drooping in despairing acquiescence; the pale lips were indifferent, immobile.

But worst of all, Lawrence Jordan's eyes looked dead. His grim work had sucked out their luster: His fear had turned to fascination and finally weariness with death, and the light had gone out in his eyes. All the innocence had been wrenched out of them while the hands, encased in rubber, fashioned death masks.

What had happened to his life? His consciousness turned inward, and he flew back in time to Kansas, his grandmother's steady faith, his drawing of the angels, his move to Kansas City, Lovingood, and Clare. And as his attention turned inward, he found his former spirit and realized he still had his old power deep within. That power *was* the spirit. It transcended fear of death.

His soul found rest and he fell into a deep, nondreaming sleep.

When he awakened, Lawrence Jordan looked in the mirror. There was new fire in his eyes.

The words of Lennie Valentine echoed in his inner ear: *None of us are makin' it. We never will until we control our turf.* Lennie meant that in a different sense, but Jordan realized the truth in Lennie's words. Most of his life, Jordan had tried to make something of his life without first controlling his own turf—the inner reaches of his mind. With his attention and desires locked on material things, Jordan had been subject to their changes, their deaths. Because he lived in them, he died in them; he died their myriad deaths.

In seeking life, he had attached himself to death. Yet the old fear persisted. Whenever something he loved dearly went away, as in the case of Major Bates, he dreamed the Dream again and had another death.

You're scared of your own shadow, Clare maintained. And Herece asked: *Are you happy?* Happiness was all he wanted, and what was happiness but the absence of fear?

Lawrence looked down at the newspaper on his desk. Clare, Montague, Fannie, Lovingood—all lived life through that paper. They let the paper chart their lives. Each time it chronicled another step for them through life toward a single point— and that point was well known to Lawrence Jordan. Indeed, it had been his constant companion and provider for a decade. And his greatest fear.

In seeking to immerse his consciousness in death, Lawrence Jordan had become the food of vulturesses—Marcella, Fannie, Clare. And Thess and Tina Clay. They too sought life in death with him, death's pretty child.

He thought about Marcella, victim, victimizer. He'd found her coldness, her aloofness desirable. Unconsciously, he looked to her to save him from himself. Now he found her only repugnant, chilling. Perhaps she really had the grim calling she professed to have: Her long hours in the various preparation rooms, the fondness with which she recalled playing in the caskets, her glorying in his work—all confirmed that calling. Marcella had come into the world with the chill of death in her, and subtly, indirectly, she transferred it to everything she touched. Being married to Marcella was a living death, though like Achilles Ransom, she had succeeded in disguising what was better left in darkness. As far as Jordan was concerned, the entire mortuary business was better left in darkness—or destroyed. He had felt that way when he first passed under the shadow, and he had begun to feel that way again.

Finally, at the age of twenty-nine, Jordan no longer feared the darkness life had placed around him. He feared far more that lack of light he found inside himself. His reinvigorated mind began working to dispel that greater darkness, and without his realizing it, nature began to support him in his desires. Fate was about to spur him to action.

31

Marcella's voice crackled over the intercom: "Brother Jordan?" She was copying Bates; she had been doing that since Major left.

Jordan slowly rose from his rattan divan and walked to the speaker mounted in the brick wall. He pressed the voice button.

"What is it?"

"I know you're busy, but—"

"Never mind that. What do you want? If it's not important, save it. There's something very important I want to tell *you*."

"This is pretty important, Lawrence. Fannie called. Somebody just bombed Lovingood's. Ugly rumors are out. A special meeting of the association has been called. You'd better get up here."

Jordan was horrified. Here he had hurt Wayne, was planning to hurt Montague, and this had to happen. Was the world coming apart? He and Marcella hurried to the Williams Brothers Mortuary for the meeting. As they passed Lovingood's, Jordan had the car stopped so they could see the damage. The outside of the funeral home was unscratched, but on the left side, Jordan could see the glass was out of all the windows.

The blast had been minor. It damaged the reception room badly, but Wayne Lovingood, who had been out on a call, was unhurt. Jordan found Wayne waiting for him at the meeting. All the embalmers were gathered in the Williams Brothers chapel when the Jordans came in. They did not have as far to come as Jordan. The crowd buzzed as he escorted Marcella to a seat near the front. Fannie Fears waved at him and pointed anxiously to the lectern. Wayne was at the microphone. Marcella slid into the pew, and as Jordan waited to be seated, Lovingood pointed to Jordan and shouted, "Look at him! He comes up in his big fancy car, with his big wealthy wife, and takes his seat among us like nothing at all has happened. Look at him!"

Jordan glared at Lovingood. Had Wayne gone insane? What was this all about? The room buzzed. Jordan remained standing.

"What are you talking about?" Jordan asked Lovingood.

"You know what I'm talking about," Wayne screamed, pointing straight at Jordan. "Getting Montague wasn't enough, was it? No, you had to finish the job. So you got somebody to do it for you. You'd be too scared to do it yourself."

Jordan couldn't believe it. Wayne actually was accusing him of bombing the funeral home. Jordan walked to the lectern. He tussled with Wayne for the mike. Billy Williams broke them up. Aretha Vinson, the Kansas embalmer, shrieked, "Stop them, stop them. They'll kill us all!"

Lovingood still had the mike. He backed away from Jordan holding the microphone to his mouth. "Now is the time to do something," Lovingood said. "Now. Before he bombs somebody else."

"Are you out of your mind?" Jordan bellowed, struggling against Bill Williams' grasp.

"No, it's you who're crazy," Lovingood said into the mike. "First you killed that old lady. Now you're trying to get me. Who will it be next?"

"What old lady?"

"You know who I mean. I don't remember her name. But you do. The one you . . . fixed up."

"He means Carrie Samuels!" someone shouted.

"What are you all talking about?" Jordan asked, perspiring.

Billy Williams restored order. Jordan and Lovingood were enjoined from further argument pending investigation of the bombing. Williams pointed out that there had been a more serious crime, the slaying of Abdullah Jamal, some years ago when Jordan was not even residing in the city. He cautioned Lovingood against making accusations without proof to back them. "Mr. Xavier Jordan is one of our most prominent citizens. . . ."

309

"Hear, hear," Fannie Fears agreed.

"Wayne is just trying to make us look bad," Marcella protested. "He's nothing but a sneak. Ask him why my husband quit working with him!"

It was like a nightmare. Most of the embalmers backed Jordan in the fight—while still voting to seek police protection of their own establishments.

Jordan was at the police station all night. It was Saturday morning before he was released.

The police confirmed that Carrie Louise Samuels died as a result of a massive explosion set off by unknown assailants.

"Why wasn't I notified?" Jordan demanded.

"It took us a long time to figure it out," an investigator told him. "But it *was* incendiary. Ingenious little device. Don't you read the papers? Planted in the wall heater to make it look like an accident. We never would have known if the liquor store man hadn't found the fragments."

"When was that?"

"About six months after the incident."

Jordan understood then. That was about the time Achilles Ransom had passed. He would have been in Illinois then. When he returned, the others were reluctant to bring it up again. Or afraid. Jordan had been so engrossed in remodeling the House he hadn't heard later.

"Who would do something like that?" Jordan asked.

The investigator puffed on his pipe. He grinned at Jordan. He was a red-faced man. His face wrinkled when he grinned. "We don't know," the investigator said. "But we do expect to find that the parties who killed that old woman and the person or persons who bombed that funeral home are one and the same."

"But who—"

"We thought you might be able to answer that, Mister Jordan."

"But how would I know anything about this?"

"How much do you know about Lennie Valentine?"

32

Clare was not home. She told Marcella she was going to town and wouldn't be back until late. Jordan was determined to find her. Frantically, he and Marcella telephoned Fannie Fears, Bates, Psyche Lovingood, taverns, and bars. Clare was nowhere to be found.

"What's the hurry?" Marcella wondered.

"I'll tell you later," Jordan said, "after I get *her.*"

They drove around looking for Clare. Some of the street people had seen her earlier in the day but didn't know where she was going.

Jordan's stomach boiled. Points of pain grew in his midsection. It was the worst pain Jordan had ever experienced. He was sick, nauseated. He kept thinking about Carrie Samuels, Abdullah Jamal, Wayne Lovingood. Was there a connection? Marcella drove home while Jordan doubled up in the seat next to her, gasping for breath. At the House, Jordan took antacids.

The sun sat, leaving the House of Jordan rectangles of yellow light in the black air. Jordan couldn't sleep. Carrie Samuels, Jamal, Lovingood, Valentine and Clare went around and around in his head. He turned on all the lights in his study and sat behind his desk waiting for Clare. Why did Clare just happen to have those papers on Carrie Samuels?

Clare came in at 4 A.M. Jordan heard her struggling up the stairway. She was drunk. She was humming a church song as she climbed. He met her at the top stairs, in front of her room.

"What the hell you doin' up so late?" Clare demanded.

"Waiting for you, Mother. I've got to talk to you."

"Well, go to bed. I don't feel like talkin' now."

"Where've you been?"

"Out. Around. None of your damn business. Since when are you my keeper?"

"I've been at the police station, Mother. I was there all night."

"I know that."

"They think Carrie Samuels was murdered, Mother. They think the same person who did it bombed Lovingood's."

"So what? You didn't do it."

"No. But I know who did."

Clare straightened up then. She looked at her son's face, steadying herself on the banister. "Who?" she asked.

"You," Jordan said.

"Are you crazy, boy?"

Jordan knocked Clare against the wall. He struck her again, knocking her down onto the landing. He stood over her, fists clenched, ready to strike again. She raised herself up on the step.

"Oh, God!" Clare screamed. "He's trying to kill me!"

From her quarters, Marcella called worriedly. There was no one else in the house.

"I will kill you," Jordan said, "if you don't tell me the truth. You've been with Lennie tonight, haven't you?"

Clare whimpered on the step. "Why are you doing this to me?" she cried.

"Answer me!" Jordan demanded. "Speak up or so help me, you'll envy the way Carrie Samuels got it. I want the truth."

Marcella ran out and grabbed Jordan. "Stop it!" Marcella screamed. "What happened?" Jordan pulled away from her and started at Clare again.

Clare hid her face in her arms, cringing. "All right!" she said. "Yes, yes, yes, I was with Lennie."

"And he killed Carrie Samuels, didn't he?"

"Yes," Clare sobbed. "I think so."

Marcella almost fainted. Jordan steadied her.

"I told him about the papers," Clare went on. "I told him that silly old woman had signed her body over to us and that I sure wished she'd die or something so you could get the business. But it was just talk, I thought. After she got killed, I was afraid to tell you about Lennie."

"What's your connection with him now?" Jordan demanded. "Why do you still see him?"

"We—I give him money," Clare said. "He's my silent partner."

Now it was clear. Lennie had tried to tie in with Jordan, but Jordan was too smart. So Lennie got in anyway, through Clare. Jordan looked down at his mother, shaking his head violently. "You damn fool," he said.

Clare looked up. "Who's a fool? Who're *you* callin' a fool?"

"You," Jordan said. "You had to go and let Lennie get us. Everything was all right, I thought. Finally, I had conceived something, something great, and I made it a reality and you had to ruin it. Why?"

He started at Clare again, but Marcella restrained him.

Clare stood up, wiping her eyes. She glared at Jordan and spat at him. "You never made a reality out of *anything*," she screeched. "You weren't smart enough to. I was the one who kept you alive. I was the one who went to Southwall way back when and got him to help you and you ruined it by antagonizing that dumb-ass kid of his!"

"Mother, I'm sick and tired of hearing you go on about how *you* and *South*wall did everything for me. It was Mister Lovingood and not you who encouraged me. You haven't done a damn thing."

"The hell I haven't! You think Southwall did it out of the goodness of his heart. Well, think again, boy. Shit, I was sleepin' with him!"

Jordan struck her again. Marcella tried to stop him, but he pushed her aside. "Shut up," he said. "You're lyin'! Southwall never could do anything like that."

Clare wiped her mouth. Blood was trickling there. "Okay," she said. "I'm lyin'. But you know better."

"Lennie got Lovingood's, too."

"I didn't say that."

"But it's true, isn't it? Isn't it?"

Clare looked old and tired. "I suppose." She sighed. "I mentioned that we were going to get Montague and that we had almost broken Wayne off good and I guess Lennie got it in his head to finish Wayne off. But I didn't tell him to. He said something about wanting to get Wayne for a long time. For you and that other man. . . ."

"Jamal," Marcella said.

"Yes, that's it. Jamal."

Marcella gathered the throat of her housecoat around her neck. Her eyes were glassy. "What'll we do?" she asked Jordan.

Jordan ran back up the steps, leaving Clare on the landing. "You're going back to Illinois," he told Marcella, "where you should have stayed in the first place."

"But—"

"No 'buts!' It's all over. You know that. Pack your bags. You can file for divorce when you get there."

"What about the House of Jordan?"

"There isn't any House of Jordan. There never was. It was all an illusion. You, me, Mother, all of us in this business, we're all illusions. We're dead! Get packing!"

Marcella ran out sobbing. In the window, dawn appeared. Wearily, Jordan turned to his mother, who was sitting on the stairway, shoes off, holding her head between her hands.

"You!" he yelled. "Get out of my house. Go on; I'll send your clothes to you later. Get out."

Without looking at him, Clare got her shoes and stumbled down the stairs. At the front of the steps, she looked up at him, frowning from the darkness.

"You're scared," she said. "Scared of your own damn shadow." Then, flashing anger: "I'll show you. I helped build this house, and I'm not going to let you take it away from me. I'll be back."

"Get out."

"Please, Lawrence . . . don't make me . . . do what I have to do. . . ."

"Out!"

"Listen to reason. . . ."

"That's what's been wrong all this time. I've listened to you all my life, let you run my life. You and Lovingood."

"Lawrence! I'm scared. The bodies. . . ."

"They won't hurt you, Mother. It's the living you have to watch out for. Like Lennie. . . ."

"I'll tell Lennie what you're doing!"

"Fiiine, Mother. You do that."

"You bastard!"

Clare was gone. In the silence, something flashed in Jordan's mind: a body, a coffin, a kiss.

He hurried into the apartment. He had to get Marcella out of there; he was sure of that. It was only a matter of time until Lennie Valentine arrived. Clare had gone too far to let go now.

33

The body of an elderly barbecuepit owner reposed in the West Chapel in a hand-loomed silk casket. Jordan sat Marcella's luggage down on the front pew and closed the rose-patterned lid of the open coffin. With great effort, he maneuvered the body off the catafalque onto a waiting church truck and placed the bags on top of the casket. He rolled the casket through the rear chambers of the house to the elevator. Jordan pushed a button, and the rear wall of the elevator opened on the garage side. Marcella was waiting for him there, veiled, dressed in black. She said nothing. Under the veil, she was weeping mechanically.

"Grab these bags," Jordan commanded. "Put them in the car. Not the limousine. The Buick."

She took the bags to his old car. Jordan rolled the casket into the corner nearest the elevator. He tapped the lid of the box. "He'll be all right till I get back," he said aloud to himself.

He and Marcella backed the Rolls limousines out of the garage one by one and parked them in line across the street from the Jordan estate. Finally, Jordan drove the great hearse out and parked it in front of the family cars. The cars were his one concession to the world he had known so long: Marcella would need them in Illinois.

He drove Marcella past the gates for the last time in the old Buick. He stopped the car across the street from the majestic limousines. Marcella looked at them through her window.

"They'll be all right," Jordan consoled her, "until you can send for them."

Then he took her to the airport.

He did not wait with her for her flight. He left her standing by an observation window in the terminal. "Good-bye, Lawrence Jordan," she said. Marcella's words were nearly muffled by the scream of jet engines, revving up. He waved a farewell.

Jordan hurried down the corridor to a phone booth he had seen when they came in. Nervously, he dialed a familiar old number. Lovingood's.

Wayne Lovingood hadn't expected Jordan's call. After Jordan answered, there was a gap of silence on Wayne's end.

"Listen," Jordan said, "I haven't time to waste. I know who hit your place. And it wasn't me. Can you be at my place in half an hour? I promise you you won't be bothered with me again."

"Who was it?" Lovingood demanded.

"I'll tell you when you get here. And bring your first-call car. I've got a case I want to turn over to you."

He hung up.

Jordan knew what he had to do. His pulse jerked in his neck. As he drove back, he went over the steps in his mind.

He parked in front of the gates. Down the winding road, there was no sign of Lovingood's black paneled pickup truck. Jordan tried the radio in his old car. It worked. Soul music, loud, lively, blared from the speaker. Jordan shut it off abruptly.

Lovingood was coming. As the car neared Jordan's, Jordan could see Wayne at the wheel. There was another man with him.

Lovingood followed Jordan's car to the garage. Jordan motioned Wayne to back in, but Wayne turned the wheel over to the other man and scrambled out to meet Jordan.

"Who did it?" Wayne demanded. He looked at Jordan obliquely, as his father would have.

"Valentine," Jordan said, "Lennie Valentine."

Wayne was awestruck. "Why?" he asked.

"He thinks you put the finger on Jamal."

"But I didn't, Lawrence. Honestly I didn't. I thought Valentine did."

"It doesn't matter now. Look, Wayne. I haven't got much time. I'm . . . closing up, going out of business. I want you to take this case off my hands. Take it to your place. The family will contact you later today. You can make arrangements with them for the burial. It's a good case."

317

Wayne was genuinely concerned. "What are you going to do?"

"I'm going away. To California. Maybe I'll look up Herece."

"Where's Marcella?"

"Gone. Home. It's all over between us."

Wayne's face brightened. He shook his head knowingly, then sought Jordan's confirmation of something he long had suspected. "It was Marcella who had all the money, wasn't it?"

Jordan was not angry. "Yes," he said. Jordan moved around the panel truck to the casket. "Come on, Brother Wayne. I'll give you a hand. He's heavy."

"It's a he?"

They loaded the body into the van, and Wayne shook hands with Jordan. "Good luck . . . *Brother* Jordan," Wayne said.

"Thanks, oh, and I think you'll be hearing from Jerry Montague soon. Don't be too hard on him, okay? And do me just one favor."

"What?"

"Call over to the university for me some time when you get a chance. No hurry. Ask for Mister—Doctor—Milford Goldman in sociology. Tell him I said I'm sorry for what I had to do, but I think he'll understand. Okay? Now get out of here. *Fast.*"

Jordan knew what he had to do. He got a long chain and a padlock from the garage workbench. He took them to his car, turned around in the parking lot and drove to the gates. He parked in the driveway a few feet from the gates, locked them with the chain and jogged back to the garage.

For one last time, he sat in his Packard hearse, running his fingers over the velvet seats, opening and closing the door, turning the steering wheel. Things might have been different if he'd stayed with this humpbacked old carriage. . . .

But he had no time to reminisce. He got buckets and a Coke bottle from under the workbench and carried them across to the gas pump. He filled the receptacles to brimming. He tore off a piece of his shirt and stuffed it in the bottle. That would be the wick.

He made several trips to the gas pump. Gasoline sloshed in the buckets as he carried them into the House, their contents spilling onto the carpets.

He poured gasoline on the caskets in the display room down

below, leaving the marble sarcophagus dry. He did not go into the preparation room: that would be taken care of from above. He left a trail of gasoline from the display room up the wooden steps to the entrance hall. He doused the doorway to the display room with gas. He soaked the sumptuous draperies in both chapels. He spattered the polished pews in the West Chapel with gas and the couches and chairs in the East Chapel. He poured more gas over the slumber room floor and let it trail him back to the garage.

With the pump, he bathed the Old Packard hearse. He left the pump running pools of high-octane gasoline over the garage floor.

From the gates came screams. It was Clare and Valentine. Jordan ran around the building. Clare and Valentine were clawing at the iron gates, trying to get in.

"Lawrence, you open this gate right now!" Clare screamed. "Open it!"

"Come on, man," Lennie yelled.

There were two men with Valentine. They began trying to scale the brick gate columns.

"Lawrence, what are you doing?" Clare screamed.

He ignored them, running as fast as he could to the front door of the House. He had the gas-filled bottle in his hand.

At the door, he stood looking at the hallway. The carpeting looked moist. Excellent; he had done a good job. He lit a cigarette. For the first time in his life he felt really free, in charge, his own master. He was about to become a man.

"Lennie, do something!" Clare screamed. "He's going to ruin us all. Oh, Jezus. Jeeeezus!"

Jordan blew smoke to the east. He really had to stop smoking; it was a barbarian practice. He touched the orange tip of the cigarette to the wick. It took flame. He raised the bottle slowly, casually, and flung it at the door of the display room stairs, under the great curving stairway Clare had loved to descend for funerals.

Livid fire spewed in shards from the display room door. Flames sprang up from the carpet like cypresses. In no time, the hall was heat.

Flames licked at the brick exterior of the entrance. Ominous black puffs squeezed under the window of the West Chapel.

Jordan's face was warm. He heard crackling. Something was falling in the basement.

He stepped back. Upstairs, curtains billowing out over the West Chapel caught flame from the doorway inferno. The curtains seemed to be trying to shake the orangeness from their tails.

At the gates, Valentine had one of the men by the pants seat, trying to boost him up the wall. The man tumbled back down onto Lennie's shoulders. Jordan observed that the man had garters on his socks.

Jordan walked toward them. Clare, on her knees, was reaching through the gates as though she could grasp the flames and halt them. The upstairs of the House was now on fire.

Now they were all reaching for him, through the gates. They screamed unintelligible things. Jordan threw back his head and laughed at them. "Take it, take it." He laughed. "It's all yours now."

Behind him the garage exploded. The fire had reached the pumps. The heat was intense; it seared the back of Jordan's neck. Sirens wailed in the distance, to the north. Jordan had a sudden whiff of burning pine cones. One of the trees near the house had caught fire. As the garage explosion mushroomed at them, Valentine and the others shielded their faces from the heat. Jordan turned around in it, the tears on his face indistinguishable from the sweat. He looked into the face of the ruining edifice. It was the sun.

"Good-bye, Southwall," he whispered.

Leaving Valentine and Clare cringing from the heat, Jordan quickly undid the padlock on the gate and ran for his car. One of Valentine's men, crouching, fumbled with the lock and chain. Clare was still draped in the gates. Valentine wrenched her out and began pulling the gates open. As he did, Jordan pressed his accelerator.

The black Buick roared through, smashing against the gates, throwing the men to either side. Lennie Valentine tripped over Clare, who was sobbing quietly in the grass. The sirens, now to the east, grew louder.

Once he was on the street, Jordan headed west for the Kansas Turnpike.

He never looked back.